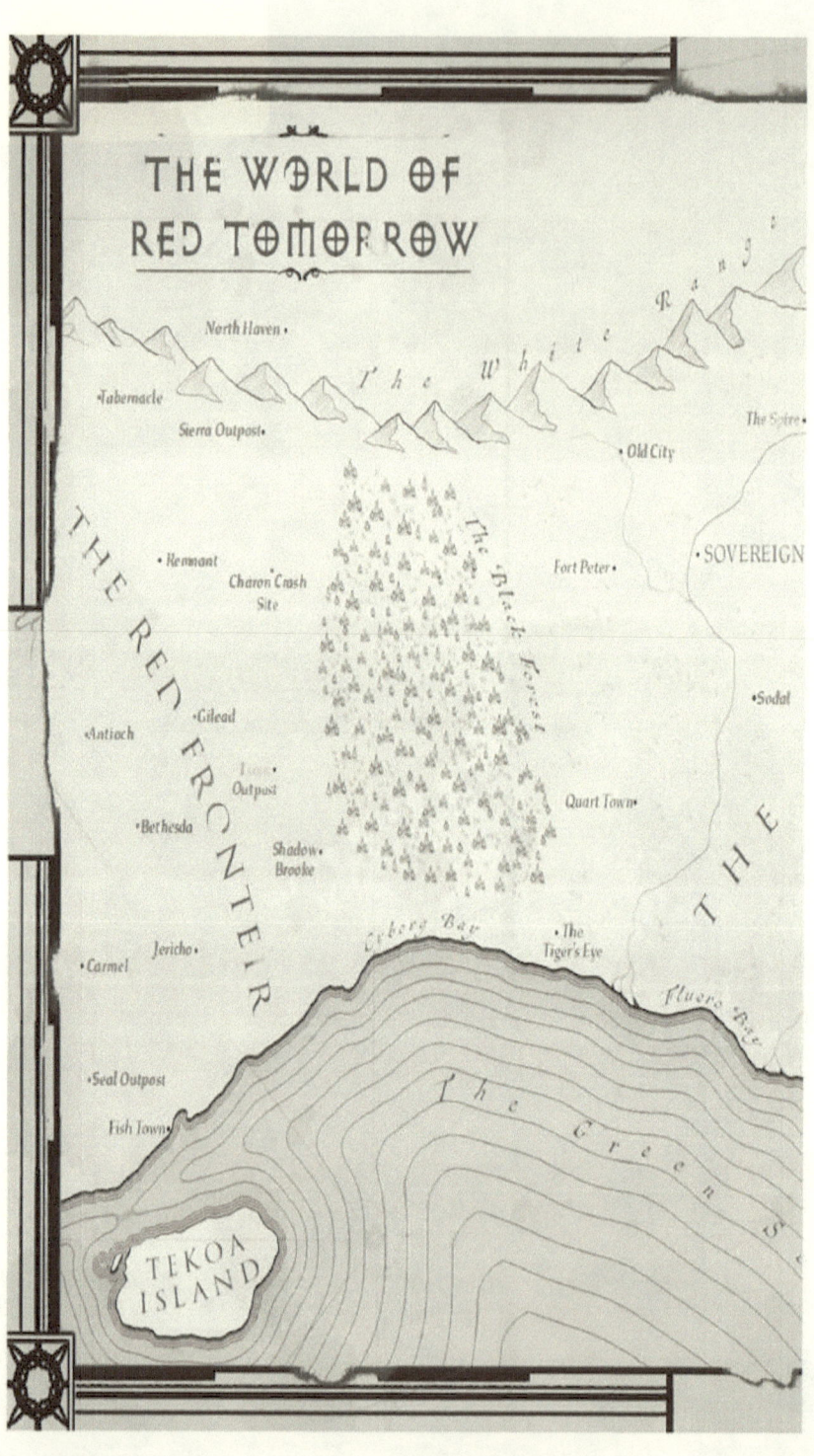

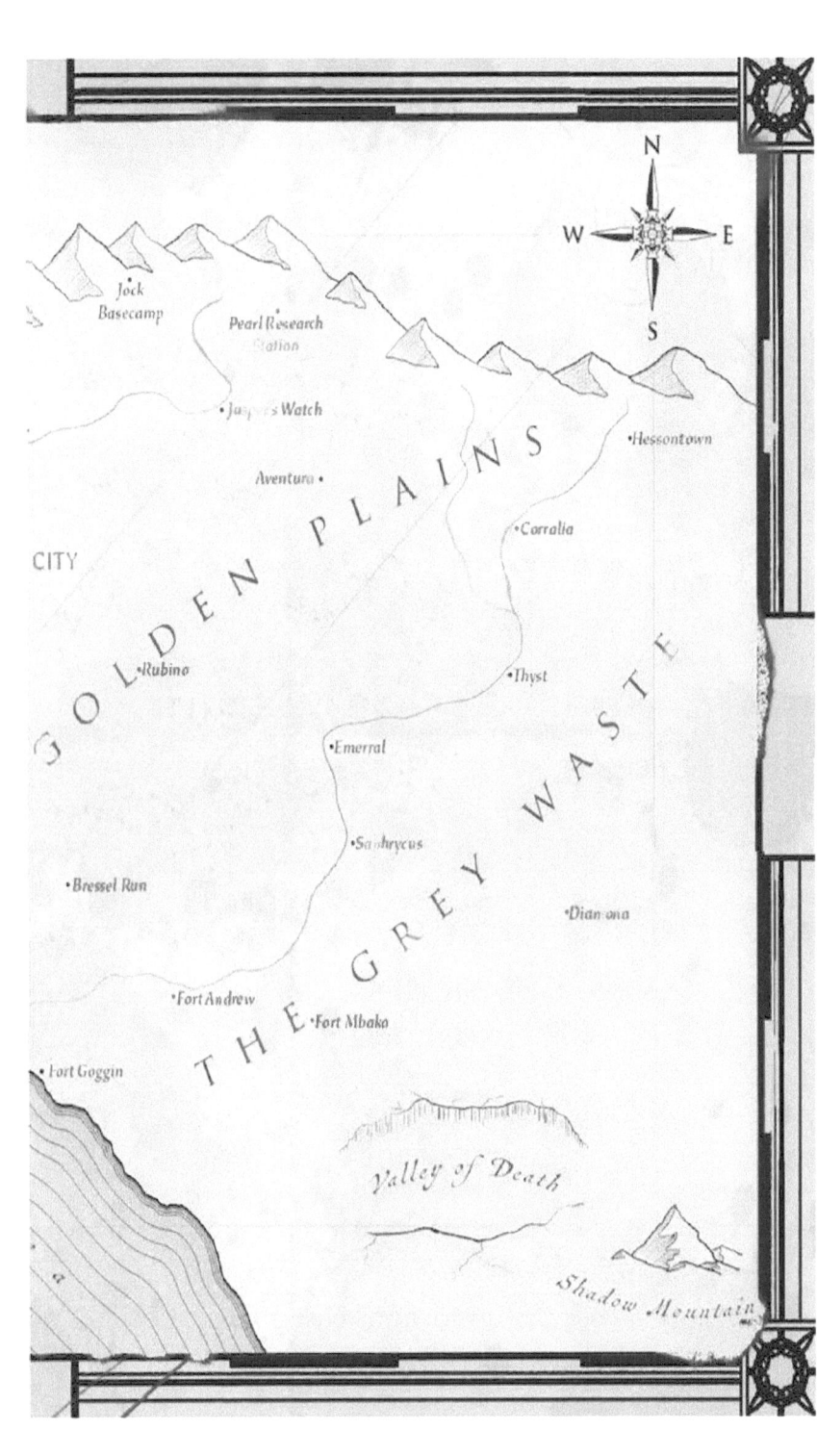

This is a work of fiction. Similarities to real people, places, or events are entirely coincidental.

THE RED FRONTIER: BOOK 1 OF THE RED TOMORROW SERIES

First edition. November 17, 2023.
Copyright © 2023 Joseph Cruz.
Written by Joseph Cruz.
Editor: N. L. Carter
Cover Artwork by Stephen Youll.
Cover Design by Jamie Warren.

THE RED FRONTIER:

BOOK 1 OF THE RED TOMORROW SERIES

JOSEPH CRUZ

TABLE OF CONTENTS

PROLOGUE

Raymond Redmin had Stage IV cancer, and he was running out of time. He and his wife, Eva—both doctors—understood the situation: no matter what treatments they explored, this cancer would eventually win. With only months left to live, he was given an unexpected twist of fate when a government science agency presented him with an extraordinary alternative.

DOCTOR WITH TERMINAL ILLNESS TO BE FROZEN ALIVE.

The news went global. Raymond was chosen to be the first person put into full stasis with hopes of waking up in a future with potential cures for his disease. He became a famous figure across the world—media appearances, interviews, press conferences...it nearly exhausted him. Yet, in the end, it made him feel less alone. He had been given a death sentence, but all of humanity seemed to be by his side.

The world's sympathy for Raymond's situation was nothing compared to the unwavering support from his wife, Eva. Her love shone through even in his darkest hour, and he clung to it as an anchor while he faced the uncertain journey ahead. His little boy Jack, just two years old, became a heartbreaking victim of the circumstances. Raymond could not comprehend how he would be taken away from his son, never watching him grow.

Whenever he spent time with Jack, he held him close. He often wept in private out of anguish at the thought of missing his son's life. No matter how much he wished it, Raymond had no control over this cruel fate.

On the day of the procedure, he felt a sense of fear, yet eagerness to take steps toward a cure.

"Don't let me sleep in too late," Raymond said, kissing Eva on the forehead.

Eva hugged him tight, soaking his hospital gown. She wore scrubs not unlike the ones they would wear to work as doctors. Now he wore the hospital gown as the patient. Raymond hugged his wife and never wanted to let go, unsure whether this would be their last time.

Raymond stepped onto the platform with a feeling of anticipation in his stomach. The room was bright, modern and clinical, with white walls and chrome fixtures. Doctors and technicians bustled around, heads bent as they studied the digital tablets in their hands. The atmosphere hummed with energy and purpose. Above them was a gallery full of spectators, with his wife Eva seated in front. He gave her a smile, and she returned one with tears welling up in her eyes.

He laid down on the gurney; it was soft, and his pillow was comfortable. This operation would be the first of its kind—the world was watching intently.

Nurses connected his IV, and as it pierced Dr. Brown gave him some reassuring words; they repeated the process until Raymond was ready. A nod from the doctor signaled to the nurse, who began to inject sedatives into Raymond's arm. He turned his head towards the gallery—Eva silently mouthed, "I love you," and put a hand up against the glass wall. Raymond attempted to return her sentiment but felt sleep taking over before he could do so.

The cryostasis trial had several phases. This first phase would be a sustained sedation state for five days. This was essentially a data-gathering trial to determine whether Raymond's body would even tolerate prolonged sedation.

He awoke five days later, as scheduled. His awareness returned in chopped bursts of confusion. He was somewhat aware while the endotracheal tube was still in his mouth. A nurse was speaking to him, telling him they were about to wake him up. He could barely move and struggled to open his eyes. His next memory was of the tube being pulled from his mouth and a nurse quickly suctioning the mucus from his pharynx.

"Dr. Redmin, welcome back," the nurse said.

After a few hours, Raymond was fully awake, sitting up in bed. He felt fine. He joked that he had gotten a full five days' rest. Eva came to see him, and they were even allowed to bring his son Jack. Raymond cried when Jack came into the room and crawled around the bed. Raymond swore he had gotten bigger in the past five days.

Raymond spent the three weeks at home, spending quality time with Eva and Jack. Although every day, it seemed he was called back in for diagnostic testing at the lab. For the next trial, Raymond would be intubated and sedated for an entire month. When he left the house, Jack was playing with blocks in his playpen. Raymond kneeled and kissed his forehead. The next time he would see him, he would be another month older.

Again, he stepped onto the platform, surrounded by doctors and scientists. Eva sat at the gallery, and they gave each other another farewell, unknowing whether he would ever wake up. But sure enough, his next memory was the tube being pulled from his mouth.

He coughed and asked with a hoarse voice, "Did it work?"

"Yes, Dr. Redmin," the nurse said. "You were asleep for 28 days, but you did great."

The medical team took precise care of his body during the month.

"The endotracheal tube pressures were monitored to avoid any laryngeal damage or erosion, but the tube had to be replaced three times," the Pulmonologist later explained.

Raymond was still groggy from the procedure. "Any lung complications?"

"We took care not to cause barotrauma. Your lungs demonstrate no damage."

"Other than the metastatic cancer," Raymond said.

"Unfortunately," the doctor replied, "but we enacted the protocol to provide electrical stimulation to your muscles, preventing any atrophy. During your sedation, you underwent passive aquatic therapy to prevent skin breakdown and venous thrombosis."

"You guys took me swimming." Raymond smiled.

All in all, Raymond again awoke feeling refreshed. The cancer was still there, however. None of this was intended to treat his terminal illness. The ultimate goal was to successfully keep him in stasis until medicine and technology could hopefully one day provide a cure.

He walked somewhat unsteady out of the transport vehicle with the hospital staff accompanying him. He felt normal, but his body seemed to struggle getting used to functioning normal again.

"God," Raymond said, walking through his front door, "he's gotten so big."

Little Jack saw his father step through the front door and immediately ran to him.

"Daddy!" Jack said, hugging his leg.

Eva hugged Raymond's arm, putting her head on his shoulder. She soaked his shirt with tears. Raymond sobbed for an eternity, and he could not decide whether they were tears of sadness or joy. The three held each other tight like they were frozen in that moment.

Raymond knew every minute was now time borrowed. The next trial would be drastically different. Now the periods of sedation would involve cryostasis. Instead of just under chemical sleep, Raymond would actually be frozen alive.

The news programs and podcasts clamored for interviews. Raymond reluctantly accepted most of the offers, the first one being a popular cable TV news program.

"How will this next trial be different?" asked the morning news host.

Raymond eventually got used to the publicity. He just hoped that public awareness would continue to spur continued funding and research for the project.

"Well," Raymond said to the interviewer. "They'll begin the sedation as usual. But then transition me from cooling to total stasis."

"Are there any risks to cooling?"

"Arrhythmias, muscle and nerve damage, and thromboembolism, to name a few of the complications," Raymond said. "We know these risks from standard cooling. For example, patients after a cardiac arrest. We cool them to reduce brain oxygen requirement and thus limit brain damage."

"Interesting," the interviewer said, eyes glazed over.

"But no one has ever actually undergone full cryostasis," Raymond said. "At least not successfully. Every cell in my body would be frozen in time."

After months of preparation, the cryostasis trial began. After all the preparation and publicity tour, Raymond was brimming with anticipation. He wanted to get the procedure over and done.

Raymond again stepped onto the gurney. Again, the induction agent put him to sleep. Again, Eva in the gallery was the last image he saw.

Two weeks later, Raymond awoke. For some reason, he had expected to wake up cold and freezing like in the movies. Instead, he woke up groggy but dry in a warm hospital bed. There was no tube to remove. Over the past two weeks, they had frozen his body, thawed him, and here he was, awake two weeks later like nothing happened. The diagnostics were perfect. He had not remembered a thing. Raymond felt like a time traveler. He was the first successful cryostasis patient in history.

The news broke worldwide. Thousands clamored to have the trials started for those with terminal illnesses. Some survivalists and adventurers even offered to go under the procedure electively. People wanted to go to sleep and wake up in the future. The possibilities were exciting. But to Raymond and Eva, they just wanted him to live long enough for a cure.

The next few trials grew longer and longer. First, it was several weeks, then several months. The time between trials grew shorter. The cryostasis had been halting the progression of his cancer while he was frozen. However, the cancer gradually began to manifest during his "awake" periods.

In one particular incident, Jack was 4 years old. Raymond had missed a large part of ages 2 and 3 while in and out of stasis. They were at a park, and Jack was playing on the swing sets with Eva. Ray was sitting on the bench, blissfully watching them. He coughed, and red blood spurted onto his hands.

"Eva," Raymond said, wiping the blood from his hand.

She looked at him, wide-eyed and terrified.

"Don't tell Jack," Raymond said.

"Jack," Eva said to their little boy calmly. "It's time to go back home now."

Within hours, Raymond was back at the hospital.

The diagnostics showed that the cancer was now progressing rapidly. Some advised against putting him under in this condition, but others argued that it would only get worse. Ultimately, Raymond and Eva decided to go through with the process. This time, he went under for ten whole months.

From then on, life became a series of short episodes for Raymond. After he woke up, he was able to spend a few weeks with his wife and now 5-year-old son. They had made some breakthroughs in cancer treatment over the past year. They gave him treatment to try and halt the cancer when he woke.

It soon became a yearly process. Raymond went under, then would wake up to see his family for a few weeks while he received cancer treatment. Eventually, they scheduled the "awake" periods to coincide with the holiday season. Raymond would wake up around the end of November and go back under at the beginning of January.

His family handled it surprisingly well. Eva was his rock. She was there every time he went under and every time he woke and never once complained.

The media appearances continued. Raymond Redmin became a household name. Every classroom in the world awaited his awakening each year like an international holiday.

"It is fascinating what they have been able to accomplish," a Congressman said to Raymond.

Raymond was a special guest at the White House, speaking casually to the President and other VIPs.

"You know, in addition to all of these great doctors and scientists," Raymond said. "It's my wife Eva who is keeping me alive. She has saved my life every day since the moment we met."

At times, he felt so unworthy to be considered a worldwide celebrity. He felt guilt for the time spent when he was frozen asleep, and then the time while awake being taken up by interviews and medical testing. As Jack got older, Raymond made it a special priority to spend time with his son, reviewing all the events of the past year he missed. It brought him great joy, but also great pain, to hear about all the things he had to catch up on.

Jack was a good kid. He never complained and never made Raymond feel bad about the situation. The four to six weeks every year to spend with his family. Raymond was a dead man offered eternal life. He felt like the most cursed and most fortunate person in human history.

At times, however, Raymond felt like a visitor to his own life. The transition between stasis and awake periods increasingly made life feel dream-like. His life became a montage of memories, mostly watching his son grow up before his very eyes. One moment, he was watching his son in his 1st-grade play; the next, his son was showing him his 2nd-grade art project.

Jack grew quickly. Raymond tried picking up him at 9-years-old, realizing he had grown much since he was 8. To Raymond, that was only yesterday. At 10, Jack hurt his arm playing soccer. He was already in a sling when Raymond woke up. He wanted to be there for his son when he had gotten hurt. The thought of Jack crying from the broken wrist while he lay frozen in a lab somewhere pained him. And before Raymond knew it, the sling and splint disappeared from Jack's arm. He was a whole year older and bigger.

Adolescence came quicker than Raymond was ready for. After all, to Raymond, he was only holding baby Jack in his arms just a few months ago. Now Jack was 12-year-old with a girlfriend he had not told his mother about. By 13, that girl was long gone, perhaps by some episodic teen drama that unfolded over the past year that Raymond missed out on. Of course, Jack filled his father in on the whole story when he woke up.

Raymond's favorite memory was taking 14-year-old Jack camping one weekend. By now, there was some progress with Raymond's cancer treatments, and they allowed him to safely go out for the trip. He and Jack barely slept that weekend. They talked and talked. Jack was bursting at the seams, excited to tell his dad everything that had unfolded. High school was a thrilling series of social victories and emotional defeats.

He took Jack for a camping trip in the woods. It was a cold winter night, but the fire they made was perfectly assembled.

"Jack, I wish I could have been there for you through all that," Raymond said.

"Dad," Jack said at one point, as they roasted marshmallows over the fire, "I don't want you to be sad. I miss you when you're asleep...but whenever I don't know what to do...just do whatever I think you would do."

At 15, Jack was already a star quarterback for his high school team. Raymond was honored at the first game he was able to attend. He stepped out onto the field and was given a standing ovation. Robotic drones buzzed about the field, filming the event for the worldwide media. At 16, Raymond and Eva teared as Jack dressed up for his fall winter-semi-formal dance. Jack and his new girlfriend Erin, his likely high-school sweetheart, stood at the base of the stairs, smiling for pictures, as Raymond wondered where the time had gone.

Jack, you've grown up so fast.

Raymond was proud of his son. Jack had become a well-liked and athletic teenager. He was offered several scholarships to colleges, and he chose West Point Military. He wanted a leadership role in the government but also wanted to challenge himself with military education and training.

For Jack's high school graduation ceremonies, Raymond was offered special VIP seating in the front. The entire world knew him as the first Frozen Man. By now, Raymond was wheelchair-bound. The cancer had spread, and he was mostly debilitated. They wheeled him into the graduation arena, and thousands of people stood to give him applause.

Raymond didn't feel right that day. The oxygen on his nasal cannula was usually adequate. But today, he felt tired. His breathing was more labored than usual. He ignored it. His son Jack would be called up for his diploma soon. He saw him in line. Jack gave him a wave.

I'm so proud of you, son.

As Jack went to take his diploma and shake hands, Raymond involuntarily let out a huge cough. Blood gushed from his mouth. He tried to suck air back in, but the blood only clogged his airway. He fell out of his wheelchair, gasping for breath. Eva was next to him, yelling for help.

Upside down, Raymond saw Jack jump down from the stage.

"Dad!"

The world turned black. Raymond was so embarrassed. *Did this have to happen in front of thousands of people? In front of Eva? In front of Jack?*

"Dad!"

"Ray, wake up!"

Raymond awoke in bed, staring at a moving ceiling. He felt sluggish. Jack and Eva were wheeling his bed down a hallway.

"I'm sorry, guys. I didn't mean to mess up your graduation," Raymond said.

Jack gave him a sympathetic look. "Dad, that was two years ago."

Two years ago?

"We're going to be alright, honey," Eva said. "I'm sorry we had to wake you up. But we're all going to be okay. The government said they would protect us. I'm gonna have to freeze you again; you just have to trust me. I love you."

Raymond looked at them curiously. Now, Jack was wearing military fatigues. So was Eva. An explosion was heard outside. Raymond tried to pick his head up and watched soldiers run down the hallway in the opposite direction. The action of picking up his head made him lightheaded. His eyes closed involuntarily, and he fell back to sleep.

His next memories were a rapid-fire sequence of confusion. There were voices he could not identify. People yelled. Explosions boomed. *And was that...gunfire?*

He had no concept of the passage of time. He felt jostled about. There were several memories of him going under and being frozen again.

"Dad," he heard Jack's voice. "Listen, we need to get you to safety. I... Hey, lock down the doors!"

The jarring sounds and confusing imagery passed over his consciousness like a dream. The sounds of abrupt gunfire shook Raymond awake. Now he was lying down in a glass chamber. He panicked and began to scream and tried to push open the glass.

"Dad!" Jack yelled.

Jack was standing over the chamber. He was holding a large automatic rifle. To Raymond, he looked somewhat older. Jack looked to be in his early, perhaps even late 20's. He was a dashing young man wearing a military jumpsuit.

"Dad, it's me. It's alright. Listen, we need to put you under again; it isn't safe here. Don't worry; I'll take care of Mom. I'll see you when you wake up."

Before Raymond could say anything, Jack hit a button, and the glass chamber filled with smoke. The muffled sounds of gunfire were heard outside the glass. He saw Jack running toward the commotion, firing his automatic rifle. Raymond breathed in the gas, and his eyelids felt heavy. He banged his fist against the glass. He wanted to stay awake, to make sure Jack was safe.

Jack, what is happening?

Raymond felt himself pulled into a deep slumber, wondering if he would ever wake again.

ONE

Raymond smacked his head against glass, shaking him from slumber. He brought his hands up to his face but could see little through the thick mist. He pressed his hands against the cold, fogged glass. Beyond it, he noticed flashing lights and the sound of muffled alarms outside the glass casket. The air in the chamber was thick with the faint, sour smell of chemicals and electricity, and a metallic, slightly bitter taste lingered on his tongue.

He was disoriented and confused but could only worry about whether Jack and Eva were safe. He needed to get out to find them.

Before he could scream for help, he was suddenly thrown about the glass chamber onto his head. Raymond could not tell if he was upside down, whether the chamber was moving, or where in god's name he was. He struggled to reorient himself and felt the panic of claustrophobia as he remained overturned.

A loud rumble led to a violent quake, jostling Raymond about the chamber. He felt the urge to vomit, pass out, and cry all at once. Suddenly, the glass door hissed open. He rolled out of the casing onto the floor, only now realizing he was naked. He squinted at the brightness of the room and held his ears as he was bombarded with an onslaught of sensory overload.

And my god, it's freezing.

He slowly crawled across the cold metal floor, shivering with every movement. He was in some kind of lab. Several other glass containment units lined two walls, facing each other. There were other people inside, frozen in cryostasis. Only Raymond's glass containment unit had opened. Something must have gone wrong.

Where am I? Where's Jack? Where's Eva? I need to find them; they're in danger.

Another tremor seemed to make the world tilt on its side, and he rolled across the floor, hitting his side against the wall. He felt a sense of frustration, confusion, and anger all at once.

Is this an earthquake?

He reached up against the wall, feeling the pant leg of a white jumpsuit hanging on the wall above him. Raymond groaned, pulling down the much-needed clothing. In equal parts frustration and desperation, he squirmed about the floor, jamming his legs and arms into the jumpsuit. It was thankfully soft and padded underneath, giving him a comforting warmth after he had crawled across the unforgiving cold floor.

Raymond struggled to his feet. He felt stronger than previous times he had awoken. Perhaps they had refined the waking process. He had no IV lines or tubing connected. He could breathe and move with relative ease after a few minutes. He stood against the wall, taking several deep breaths. They were full breaths, smooth and effortless. Healthy.

I can breathe normally again... Did they cure my cancer? Did it work? But then...how long have I been asleep?

He paused to enjoy this newfound comfortable breathing. He had not felt this in a long time. However, just as he was about to take another long breath, the room rumbled again, bringing him to his knees. He summoned the determination to stumble to the nearest door. He fumbled for a doorknob, a switch, a button, anything to get it open. Nothing. He began to bang on the door, yelling. His voice surprised him. It was crisp and clear, a far improvement over the hoarse cancer-ridden vocal cord paralysis he used to have.

"Hello?" he yelled. "Help me! I'm in here! Anyone? Eva? Jack?"

After a few minutes of screaming for help, he gave up and looked around the room. Emergency lights flickered, and the alarms continued to blare. The two exits were closed, with no obvious way to open the doors. He resolved to be resourceful. He searched the room for something to pry the doors open with or even an object to ram it open if he had to.

As he stepped away, the door behind him hissed open.

"There's one awake in here," said a young woman in a white jumpsuit. Her name tag read Lieutenant Jacqueline Barnes.

"Where am I?" Raymond asked, with his hands up in defense. "What's going on?"

"He's the only one," Barnes said, holding a hand over her ear.

Raymond suspected he must be on some military base. "Listen, I was in that thing, and then..." Another quake shook them both to the ground. "And then that happened. Seriously, what is going on?"

"Sir, we'll need to get you to the emergency vessels now." She grabbed his arm and hauled him up.

Raymond had little time to formulate a response. That was enough of an explanation for now. He followed the young officer down several hallways, where light fixtures flickered and sparked. They were thrown into the walls by the occasional seismic shake.

"Are we being attacked?" Raymond yelled over the sirens. He was desperately trying to keep up with her as she bounded down the halls at breakneck speed. "My name is Raymond Redmin. Are my wife and son here? Are they safe?"

Barnes suddenly stopped in place. Raymond stumbled into her and nearly knocked her over.

"You're..." She turned, staring at him wide-eyed.

"What? I'm Raymond Redmin," he said, "My wife and son, Eva and Jack, are they here?"

She shook her head, looking at the ground. Her silence filled him with a sense of dread.

A male voice yelled from far down the hallway, "Barnes! You've gotta move it; we're running out of time."

"Let's go!" Barnes grabbed Raymond by the arm again, pulling him along.

They bounded down endless hallways. Raymond had little time to orient himself. The shaking was increasing in frequency and magnitude. Pipes began to explode out of the floors and walls. Circuitry was exploding around them. An open wire sparked near Raymond's face. He yelped, falling to the ground, startled.

"Come on." Barnes returned to pick him up. "We have to..."

Raymond did not hear her finish that sentence. Instead, she dropped to the floor next to him with a thud. Her face fell next to his, as a thick line of fresh blood ran down from the side of her head across her shocked open eyes. A metal beam, broken off the ceiling, had struck her in the head.

Shit.

He jumped to his feet, examining her head wound. He ran his hands through her hair, identifying the large laceration over her right temporal scalp. Raymond could already feel the cranial bone indentation. He checked the back of her head, ran his fingers down her cervical spine, and quickly glanced down at her body. No other injuries, but the head injury was severe.

There was a jacket on the floor near him. He laid the arm of the jacket on the floor under her head. He carefully rolled her onto her back, then wrapped the jacket arm over the wound. He hastily knotted it, knowing this would do very little to help the bleeding.

He pulled her eyelids open to check her pupils. He slid down, dropping his ear to her chest. Her heart sounded fast and clear. She was breathing. Raymond put his hand on her chin, notching it open to make sure her airway was clear. He looked up and down the hallway. They had not passed any other people. He was lost and alone with a critically injured stranger.

"Dr. Redmin," an older male in a jumpsuit called over, while running from the far end of the hallway.

"Hey!" Raymond said, looking up at nothing in particular, "I need help; she's badly hurt. She's..."

"Dr. Redmin," the man said, "Listen to me. You need to leave her. You need to go now."

"I'm not doing that. Where's the nearest medical supply? I'm a doctor."

"Dr. Redmin," the man said impatiently, "We don't have time for this. My name is Captain Adam Eckhart. You are on board the UNSS Charon."

Raymond's mind began to swirl.

"A spaceship, Dr. Raymond. A spaceship that's about to make a crash landing on Mars. You need to leave the Lieutenant, doctor. We're going to hit the atmosphere in less than five minutes. We need you to survive this, sir."

Mars? Raymond was already struggling to make sense of the situation but hearing that they were crashing to another planet made him dizzy with confusion. *And wait, Mars doesn't even have an atmosphere...*

Raymond looked down at the young officer. The jacket arm was doing little to abate the bleeding from her crushed temporal bone. She was already pooling blood below her head.

"I can't leave her!"

Silence.

Raymond grabbed her under her armpits and began to pull. The lights had all but turned off. He was going nowhere in particular. He came across a closed door, trying to kick it down. A massive explosion threw him into the opposite wall. He rolled onto his back. He covered his face as sparks and dust flew into it. He felt a sudden tug of his clothing. Captain Eckhart was pulling him. Raymond fought and struggled.

"Come on," Eckhart said, "You go, I'll get her."

"But the girl..."

"Trust me, just go!"

Raymond looked down at the bleeding young woman. He felt a pang of guilt as the overwhelming logic of futility took over. There was likely nothing he could do. He had no idea where he was and had no means to help her. He felt useless and vulnerable. Raymond began backing away, with his conscience torn in two. She was a stranger, but then again, Raymond's entire life was dedicated to helping strangers.

Captain Eckhart grabbed Raymond by the shirt and pulled him to his face. "Run down this hall, and don't stop. For anything."

Raymond looked down at the girl. He looked down the dark hall and back at the captain, inches away from his face.

"Now!" the captain said, pushing him along.

Raymond hobbled into a run. He went straight ahead, arms out in front of him, lest he run straight into a wall in the pitch dark. After a familiar sound of a door hissing open, he saw a sliver of bright light growing at the end of the hallway. He ran headlong into it. As he continued to struggle with leaving the injured stranger behind, he also began to process what Captain Eckhart said.

Wait a minute. I'm on a spaceship? Mars?

Human silhouettes pulled him into the light. He was blinded by the sudden change in brightness. He was jolted about and thrown into a seat. Again, he fought against the mystery arms all around him.

"Stop! Just stop!" a female voice said. "We're strapping you in."

Raymond relaxed for a moment, surrendering himself as he heard clicks and zips. They were roughly handling him, locking in his limbs and head to a seat. His eyes began to adjust. He was in cramped quarters, sitting across from other people wearing sleek white jumpsuits. Many were bruised and injured. Some appeared to be crewmen of the ship; others seemed to be civilians wearing Raymond's similar look of confusion. His overwhelming sense of fear was only slightly relieved, knowing there were others alongside him who appeared just as frightened.

"He's in, come on, come on," the female crewman said.

The crew who had secured him frantically buckled themselves in next to Raymond. Captain Eckhart stumbled in, carrying Barnes over his shoulder. The blood was dripping freely from her head. Raymond meant to criticize his technique but thought against it. The captain laid her into another seat, strapping her in.

Raymond turned to his right, where the male crewman he just buckled himself in.

"What is happening?" Raymond asked.

The crewman turned to him, perturbed. "We're crashing. We're freakin' crashing onto Mars. We're gonna die."

The captain, running by, snapped at him, "Hey! Stop it. We're gonna make it, okay?"

The crewman nodded, unconvinced. Listening to his dialogue made Raymond start to panic.

"What about the Ark?" the captain asked.

"The Ark is secure," someone else yelled.

"Alright, everyone, you have your orders. When you hit the ground, we rendezvous at the Ark. Under no circumstances do we let anyone take that. The Ark is the priority; am I clear?"

"Yes sir!" was heard throughout the room.

Who are these people? Raymond thought.

"Listen to me; this is very important, Dr. Redmin." Captain Eckhart again positioned his face inches away from Raymond's. "When you hit the ground, just stay close to the others. I promise we'll explain everything."

Things were too chaotic for Raymond to muster a reasonable response. The ceiling above them sparked and flashed with electrical shortages. Emergency sirens blared incessantly in the background.

"We need you, Dr. Redmin," the captain said. "Good luck."

"Need me for what? Wait!"

The captain ran into the next room, yelling commands at people, "I'm gonna bring the ship down myself. Get strapped in now! Eject at 20,000 feet!"

Handlebars descended on Raymond's shoulders. He was reminded of a rollercoaster's safety bar, except this was much more uncomfortable. It squeezed in against the sides of his head until he could not move his neck in any direction. Another pad descended on the top of his head and kept pressing down. Raymond screamed, feeling like he was about to be crushed. The machine stopped just as he felt his lower back buckle from the pressure. He felt like he had been placed into a pretzel machine.

The rumbles evolved into a persistent violent vibration. The sounds escalated and drove Raymond into madness. He looked across at the person sitting across from him. The ceiling had collapsed onto him. A metal pipe had lodged firmly into the unfortunate passenger's neck, squirting blood everywhere. Raymond felt his own head swell. They were upside down now. The room began to spin, and free-floating objects were thrown everywhere. The squirting blood from his injured neighbor began to coat all the passengers. Their screams were drowned out by the deafening sounds of chaos and thunderous creaks of ripping metal. Raymond felt like he had been thrown into a washing machine set on blood rinse.

Suddenly, he was thrown back. He remained in his seat but had been violently pulled out of that little room of terrors. He screamed, realizing he had fallen out of the spaceship. A rush of wind pounded his face shut, and he felt like he couldn't breathe. Fully expecting the vacuum of space to kill him immediately, he was bewildered by the brightness of a blue sky. Absolute horror and fear turned into sudden awe.

A blue sky? Mars?

He watched himself break away from the massive spaceship. The other passengers sitting next to him were also being ejected from the ship as well. Raymond had no control over his fall, however. After a brief moment of relief, he began to spin in a frenzy, locked into his seat. He struggled to move his arms and legs, but all he could do was scream. The world became a mess of colors and nausea.

He felt the sound of a loud zip and then a pop. His cyclone descent had stopped. His eyes darted around, seeing the blue skies and horizon below him. He struggled against the tight cushion locking his head into place. Raymond managed to discern his situation. He was suspended in the air by a parachute. It was large and loomed wide.

He noticed other escapees falling through the air deploying their own parachutes. The escape seats had deployed puffy balloon structures around the bottom and sides of the seats as well. Raymond suspected he would hit the ground like a marshmallow at this rate. He took in a sigh of relief that exhaled as broken weeping.

Where am I...

Raymond watched as the spaceship flew past them. He read the side of the hull, where UNSS Charon had been painted on the side. The ship struggled to make a landing onto the red desert that Raymond could only assume was Martian soil. He was immediately cognizant of his breathing.

If I'm on Mars, why am I able to breathe... And are those...trees?

The spaceship began to make a landing just outside of a large forest. Raymond squinted and could swear all the trees in the forest were black. He looked to the horizon. Beyond the forest was a mountain range, in the other direction, an ocean. Raymond deduced that this could not possibly be Mars. He must have heard them incorrectly.

The UNSS Charon hit the ground with a thunderous boom. It buried itself into the entrance of the forest, sending dust and shockwaves across the black foliage. The shockwave hit Raymond mid-air, and his escape seat was thrown about. He began to spin, tethered to his parachute. The world again turned into an LSD trip of colors and churned his insides.

This time, Raymond gave in. The ride had been too chaotic, the sequence of events too confusing for his mind to handle. He closed his eyes, surrendering to the impending blackout as he floated to the ground.

Before fully losing consciousness, he could swear he heard a motorcycle below.

CHAPTER

TWO

The Red Frontier of Mars was a vast wasteland, stippled with small colonies of humans scraping to survive. It was a harsh existence, but for Kira Skyler, it was home.

At the far edge of town, Kira sat atop the roof of the town tavern. She took a deep breath and looked out across the red desert. The badlands stretched as first as the eye could see and in all directions. The town of Remnant was half a day's ride to the nearest frontier settlement. Isolated to their own, their community had learned the value of self-reliance and simple living.

Their town motto: *In defiance, we remain.*

"So, tell me what you learned from Mr. Strauss," Kira said.

She turned to look at her younger brother Owen. He was thin and sickly at 11 years of age. He was recently stricken with Crimson Fever, mostly confined to bed rest. He begged Kira to take him to the roof that morning, and she obliged.

"I mean, I'm basically an expert now," Owen said.

This week, the wandering historian Jethrow Strauss came through the town. On his visits, he would recite his scribbled findings and musings to the townspeople. Knowledge and historical records were scarce out in the Frontier. Instead, many townspeople settled for vague religious dogmas and prophetical omens. Luckily, Kira's young brother took a particular interest in discovering factual history.

Kira smiled. "Well then, history expert, tell me what I missed."

"Well," Owen earnestly said. "The earliest we know about our people on Mars was about 200 years ago when the first settlers arrived to relocate the population from Earth."

"Earth," Kira said musingly. "Don't you mean the blue god?"

"Ugh, I hate how they call it that. It's a planet!"

"Just like this one, huh?"

"Just like Mars!" Owen said. "Fun fact, Mars used to have no atmosphere. You couldn't even breathe here! The Earth's government re-created the environment to support human life so we could live here. We came from Earth!"

"And then they just left us here," Kira muttered.

"Well, yeah," Owen said. "The Silence. Just one day, we stopped hearing anything from Earth. Just poof. Suddenly, not a single radio transmission or anything from them...and no one knows why. And they never sent any more ships back here, either. When the old Mars government sent all those expeditions into space to investigate, none of them ever returned. We kept trying and trying, and..."

Kira finished his sentence, "Then we just gave up."

"Yeah," Owen said. "So that was The Silence. And I guess after that is when all the wars started."

"Right, the AI Wars."

"Well, no," Owen said. "Actually, first it was the Mars Riots, then the Republic Civil War, then the Dominion Wars, and *then* the first, second, and third AI Wars."

"That sure is a lot of fighting to keep track of."

"I know about every battle during each one!"

"Maybe we need to tell Mr. Strauss to stop telling the kids all the war stories. There are so many people who do great things without having to kill and hurt other people. No more of those... Zeltan stories."

"But the Zeltan stories are the best!" Owen said. "Us natural borns don't do anything cool."

Kira snapped, "Hey, don't call us that. We're people. The Zeltans aren't any better than us."

"But..." Owen said. "They technically are, right? Genetically perfect?"

"No, not perfect," Kira said. "No one is perfect. Nat... ugh, I mean, people out here on the Frontier, we can do great things too. There are great people who have done great things without the Zeltan Kingdom's help."

"Oh yeah, like who?"

"How about, like Dad?" Kira asked.

Kira's father, Quentin Skyler, had been a well-respected leader and engineer in their community. A poor town of traders, Remnant struggled to remain relevant and viable. Quentin elevated their town to modest prosperity with his useful robotic inventions. That was until Crimson Fever claimed the lives of a third of their populace, Quentin among them.

Kira had sat with her father in his dying days. She remembered seeing him reduced to a wasted, gaunt version of his robust former self on his deathbed, burning from fever and hacking horrific gobs of bloody sputum onto his bed sheets. Kira could not recount when exactly her father died. When she thought he had passed, his eyes would open with terror, gasping for breath. For days, she watched her beloved father suffocate, drowning in his bodily fluids. When it was finally over, she never cried again. In a way, she was relieved his suffering was over.

Owen was silent. He usually withdrew himself at the very mention of their father. Even more so now that Owen himself was afflicted with the very illness that claimed the life of their father so recently.

"I'm sorry," Kira said. "I didn't mean to bring up Dad."

"No, it's alright," Owen said. "But are *you* okay?"

Kira didn't even realize her eyes were welling up at the mere mention of her father.

"I'm fine," Kira said. "We're gonna be okay, you know that right? I won't let anything happen to you. We're all we got left."

"I know." Owen gave a weak smile.

Kira hugged him. While he usually would groan, roll his eyes, or push away, he let the hug sink in for about a minute. She heard him sniff back his emotions as he stood up.

"I'm actually gonna head inside," he said. "Mr. Strauss gave us some drawings. He got a look at some really cool Zeltan weapons and armor when he passed through Cyborg Bay."

"Do you need help getting down the stairs?"

"Nah, I can do it," he said, waving her off.

Owen walked away, pretending his walking cane was a sword. He made playful swinging sounds, portraying himself as a Zeltan warrior, as he often liked to do. But as he walked down the stairs, she could hear his faint coughing.

Kira cycled through various stages of grief as she sat high on the rooftop. Currently, she seethed with anger. Kira could bet that the Zeltan Kingdom, in all their riches and splendor, would have been able to cure her father and all her other friends and family afflicted with Crimson Fever. At least, they could have eased their suffering. Instead, the Zeltans sat in their utopian Kingdom to the east, past the Black Forest, sitting on the Golden Plains, while the lowly Natural Borns were left to scrounge the dust of the arid Frontier.

"I'll find a way to save the town," Kira said. "I promise, Dad. You'll be proud of me. I'll find a way...somehow."

It was midday, and the sun's warmth weighed heavy above Kira. Most of the townsfolk wore flat-brimmed hats. A familiar hum brushed along her leg. A mechanical fox held her hat in his clenched teeth, offering it to Kira.

"Thanks, Swift," Kira said, taking the hat and petting the robot fox's head.

Swift had sworn himself to Kira's family since her grandfather rescued him during the AI Wars so many years ago. Several years ago, android journeymen stopped by the town in their travels. The fascinating visitors offered Swift refuge in their fabled city North Haven in the White Range. Out of loyalty to the Skyler family, Swift chose to stay with his human friends in Remnant. He was Kira's protector and closest friend. Every night since she was an infant, he lay at the foot of her bed, ready to shield her from the dangers of the world.

She had heard stories of Swift's artificially programmed brutality. After all, he was initially created for war, a deadly anti-personnel weapon proven on the battlefield. Swift sat dutifully on the dirt road, loyal to her now. His master Quentin, her father, was dead. Kira was all he had.

Swift cocked his head to the side and hummed. She managed a smile, adjusting her brimmed hat to her head. Her mother was long dead, she watched her father die of Crimson Fever, and her little brother Owen was progressing through the same stages of the illness. She was losing everyone she cared about.

She recalled the prophecy that the town preacher echoed that morning in the sermon. It was a prophecy passed down for generations amongst the scattered settlers of the Red Frontier. They foretold that the struggling desert towns like Remnant would find salvation one day. Kira couldn't help but hold onto that hope for her town, friends, and family.

In the days before the end, the blue god will break his vow of silence, having pity upon his forgotten people. He will send a sign of flames from the sky. From the East will arrive four angels of deliverance. They will bring healing, wisdom, power, and courage to the people of the Frontier. Under a mighty sword, they will deliver the people from evil. And the people should rejoice. It will be a sign of the one who is to come. The hero, the one who will save us all. Enemies will tremble, and armies will fall at his feet. He will lead our people to salvation. Eagerly, we await his coming. The silent savior from the shadows.

"You're really going out there, aren't you," said a voice climbing up the ladder beside her.

It was Benny Fong, the trader's son. He was 19, a year younger than Kira, and they had grown up together. She considered him a close friend, although she suspected he thought of her as more. Nevertheless, his obvious feelings of unrequited affection never made her feel uncomfortable.

"I have to," Kira said. "If I don't find that healer, someone else is gonna die... Because Owen..."

"I know," Benny said. "I get it. But we don't even know if this healer is real."

Months ago, travelers from the East told stories of a healer named Guaritore in the Black Forest. He apparently studied the medicinal arts of the Old Earth and stockpiled relics of technology in his hidden refuge. According to the stories, he was revered as a prophet by the savages of the Black Forest. Out of cruel irony, the only way to reach the miracle worker was to risk certain death by journeying deep into the dark forest to find him.

"We've been through this," Kira said. "We don't have any other choice. We're dying. Our town is dying. Otto? Margie? Nicholas? My dad? How many more before we decide to do something about it?"

Benny looked down at his feet.

Kira gave him a soft punch on the shoulder. "The answer is *no more*. I'm going."

Benny gave a conceding sigh. He kneeled to pet Swift, who nuzzled him in the face. Swift was hesitant around most people, even other townsfolk he had known for decades, but he trusted Benny like family.

"I'll have Swift," Kira said. "He'll protect me."

Benny looked up at Kira and gave a sad nod with a sigh. "The bike's in the garage."

They climbed down the outer stairwell of the tavern and walked down the road, past the trading post and newsman podium. Townsfolk gave them courteous tips of the hat, many offering condolences for Kira's father. They knew what she intended to do. Most knew Kira well enough that she would not be talked out of her radical plan to save the town. Or perhaps they believed in her chance to succeed. Even so, no one offered to join her quest. The tales of cannibal savages in the Black Forest scared the townsfolk to their core, even the gallant Red Riders.

"Condolences for your dad, m'lady," said a familiar voice behind them.

It was Casey Jarrett dismounting from his horse. With his high boots, wide-brimmed hat, and scruffy features, Casey was a spitting image of the prototypical cowboy of Old Earth. He wore a duster-style coat with tassels hanging off the chest and arms, with two gun holsters strapped to both sides of his waist. He was strong and rugged, but all that machismo irritated Kira.

He was a Red Rider, a loosely organized group of mercenaries-for-hire on horseback. They charged each town a fee to protect them from raiders, cyborg pirates, and savages. They knighted themselves as the self-appointed heroes of the Red Frontier.

Casey stepped in front of Benny, ignoring him. He took his hat off and put it to his chest.

"Thanks, Casey," Kira said, looking straight ahead, uninterested in conversation. After a moment, she continued walking.

"Hey, hey," Casey said, stepping in front of her. "Where you off to so quickly?"

Kira was silent, defiantly staring straight through him.

"Whoa, wait a minute." Casey broke into a grin. "Are you doing what I think you're doing? Tell me those rumors aren't true. You ain't seriously going out there to the Black Forest?"

Her annoyed silence gave it away.

"Wow, okay," Casey said. "Well, number one, you're gonna get yourself killed. Do you have any idea what's out there? Did you hear about those two Riders ambushed a few weeks ago? They were *Riders*. Fully grown men who could take care of themselves in a gunfight were dragged into the forest by those Hairies. Probably eaten alive. It's a damn death trap. Even *I* wouldn't go near that place. Right, boys?"

Casey was flanked by his two lackeys, Toby and Pete. They nodded in agreement.

"I can take care of myself," Kira said.

Casey chuckled with condescension. "No offense, little lady, but you're gonna have to excuse me if I find that hard to believe. What are you gonna protect yourself with?"

"She's going with Swift," Benny said. "He's gonna protect her."

"Ain't nobody talking to you, Fong." Casey glared at him, then turned back to Kira. "Seriously, what's your plan? You're just gonna waltz into the Black Forest and ask nicely? That guara-whatever healer guy probably isn't even real."

"He is," Kira said defiantly, stepping forward in anger. "And he's the only chance we have left. More people are going to die. I'm not going to let that happen."

"Alright, alright," Casey said, with his hands up. "I get it. But at least let us go with you. My bet is that you'll turn around once you see the edge of the forest. That's what most townies do. The Hairies might damn well come out of the forest and chase you down, even if you decided to turn back. You're gonna need protection. Y'know, more than this, uh...thing." He gestured dismissively at Swift.

Swift hummed menacingly, baring his metal teeth. He began to pace toward Casey and his goons.

Casey's hand moved to the gun on his hip, but he stopped short of placing his hand on it. Tobey and Pete stepped back, wide-eyed. Swift could tear out their throats before any of them could unholster their guns.

"Swift"—Kira placed her hand on his back—"it's okay."

"It's alright, Swift," Benny echoed.

Casey laughed nervously. "Y'know, those things are technically outlawed. Can't trust an AI."

Swift hummed, seeming to warn Casey.

"Y'know what?" Casey said, shaking his head. "Forget it. You wanna go out there and get killed, go right ahead. We're better off not getting ourselves killed too. Just don't say I never warned you. Let's go, boys."

Casey placed his hat back on his head. Tobey and Pete followed him, keeping a worried eye on Swift.

"Good boy," Kira said, patting Swift on the head.

Benny had offered to join her, but she saw the fear in his eyes. He had a good heart. He was by no means an adventurer, much less able to stand his own in a fight. He was, however, a prodigious engineer, even at 19. His father owned the trading post, and Benny liked to forage through the junk, particularly old robotic relics. Her late father, Quentin, the great inventor, took Benny under his tutelage, and together they created several inventions to salvage their struggling town.

Kira ducked under the garage door roof as Benny hauled it up. The walls were lined with robotic prototypes, tools, and various mechanical parts. Kira couldn't even fathom their function. She felt a sudden pang of grief, knowing her father worked on most of these inventions with Benny. At least, back when he was healthy... when he was alive. Benny had vowed to Kira that he would continue her father's work.

"He'd be proud of you, Kira." Benny looked at the ground. "He always has been. Just saying."

Kira smiled. "Thanks."

Their eyes met for a moment. Benny turned away awkwardly. He fumbled at the tarp next to him.

"Uhm..." He clumsily pulled the tarp off the motorcycle. "Yeah, so, here it is. Fully loaded and tank's full."

The motorcycle looked like a piece of junk. They had salvaged old Earth footage of gas and oil-powered motorbikes. Kira's father and Benny used those designs of inspiration and took years to build the motorcycle from scrap. Three years ago, Kira dared Benny to take it for a ride. When he declined, she took it out herself in the middle of the night. Those were perhaps the best few hours of her life. She rode it across the Red Frontier with Swift blissfully striding alongside her.

When she inevitably crashed the bike into an embankment, she lay there, injured and miles away from town, expecting her father and Benny to be angry. Instead, they were just glad that she was alive. The bike was eventually rebuilt, and they allowed her to ride out with it every now and then.

"Take this with you." Benny picked up the circular rotor at the back of the bike. "Y'know, if you need help."

It was Benny's remote aerial drone. He was afraid of riding on the motorcycle, so whenever she would ride out, he would follow her and Swift with the drone. He had fashioned unwieldy goggles to transmit a live camera feed from the drone while he controlled it with a joystick salvaged from a deconstructed exo-mech.

"Just yell if I'm about to crash the bike into a ditch again."

Benny was unamused.

"I'm kidding," Kira said. "I'll be fine. But I'll take it with me. I might need someone to talk to. No offense, Swift."

Swift gave a playful hum.

"One of these days, Swift," Kira said, "you're gonna let Benny install something to let you talk. I can't imagine all the things you'd want to say."

Swift gave her a soft nudge with his nose.

Kira was already on the bike, pushing it out into the street. She turned the ignition switch and kicked the motorcycle's engine to life. The townspeople stopped to marvel at the strange machine. The children ran out onto the street with joy. The engine was loud enough to drown out the sounds around her. She saw people mouthing words of encouragement, and she gave a polite wave.

The dust began to pick up. She strapped her goggles and looked at Benny, standing timidly in the garage doorway.

"I'm coming back," she said, muted over the loud engine.

"You'd better," he mouthed back.

Kira playfully shooed away the children that had congregated around the bike. She took a deep breath and stepped off the clutch. The bike roared to life, and she bounded down the dusty street of Remnant. The bike picked up speed fast, and within seconds she was well out into the Red Frontier, headed east toward the Black Forest.

Kira rode for hours. Swift bounded at breakneck speed to her right, with Benny's remote drone flying overhead to her left. She appreciated the company. The bleak, dry wasteland of the Frontier added little to reflect on. Kira remained focused on her mission. Through hell or high water, she would find this healer, Guaritore. She would bring back a cure for her town. She was their only hope.

On the horizon, she saw black dotted lines. They were trees. Apparently, an unexpected side effect of terraforming, the forest's foliage grew pitch black. This only reinforced its menacing reputation. Thousands of savage Aggros made their home there. Even the great Zeltan super-humans dared not conquest the dark forest. At least not after the disastrous attempt to conquer the forest earlier that century.

"What am I doing..." Kira said to herself.

Swift turned his head as if he heard her. He strode beside the motorcycle, but she figured he needed a break. Swift needed sleep and rest just as humans did, to an extent.

She brought her motorcycle to a stop. The Black Forest was completely visible now. Behind her was the setting sun. Its light only shone briefly into the forest before being swallowed into darkness.

Kira took a deep breath. She looked up. The blue dot in the evening sky was there. Earth, the home of their ancestors. Some prayed to it as a god. Kira was not beyond praying for miracles at this point. She studied the blue dot with new interest. She had seen it before, but this time, it was different. There was another dot next to it.

The second dot glowed red. It grew quickly. Kira and Swift stood, bewildered. Soon, it revealed itself to her. It was a flame, a fireball hurled from the heavens. *Were the stories true? The blue god was a heavenly entity casting down damnation on the red planet?*

When Kira thought to react, the ground rumbled, and the black trees shook in reverence. The fireball was crashing to the ground. If Kira didn't know any better, she could swear it was aimed directly at her.

The frenzied hums of Swift roused her to action.

"We have to go!" Kira yelled, mounting the motorcycle.

She turned back west. The Black Forest must have called on celestial intervention to keep her out. Her motorcycle blared at full speed. She looked over her shoulder. The fireball was certainly falling from the sky and coming straight for her. If she did not leave the area, she would surely be engulfed in flames.

"Swift!" Kira yelled over the engine roar and the grand arrival of the falling star. "Get word back to town; we have to…"

A blinding light and then a deafening thunderclap consumed her senses. She felt her body tossed into the air, weightless.

She sensed her body thud against something, but she felt no pain. She felt nothing. Kira concluded that she was dead.

What a strange way to die, she thought.

THREE

C aptain Darien of the 1st Ranger Division of the Zeltan Kingdom grinned as he stared at himself in the mirror. His cape looked silly. Magnificently blue and flowing down to his calves, it attached to golden clasps on his shoulders and draped over sturdy grey battle armor. *A bright blue cape for battle, how beautifully impractical.*

"Just another adjustment," said Cole Tailor.

All the Zeltans only had one name, with the secondary name signifying their pre-determined "placement" occupation. Through a rigorous algorithm of their inherent genetic makeup, as well as their performance through their first 13 years of life, the Kingdom carefully designated individuals to specific vocations. For someone as detail-oriented to minutiae as Cole, he was certainly appropriate for a humble living as the royal tailor.

"Very well," Darien said.

He was in no rush to attend the ceremonies. Darien considered these pleasantries to be a nuisance.

"No, no, no!" growled the young Lieutenant Tristan from across the room. He had been berating his poor tailor servant. "The folds are all wrong!"

Darien held little regard for the lieutenant. Tristan descended from the original Ruling line, a descendant of the first King Adam himself. Two hundred years of careful hierarchical selection ensured him a prestigious seat in the Council of Princes. When he turned 30, Tristan would have been eligible to compete for the ultimate prize of Kingship at the annual Placement Games.

He had publicly challenged and humiliated the sitting King Gareth. Instead of being eventually eligible to compete for the honor of presiding as king of the great Zeltan Kingdom for their customary one year of rule, he was now merely a cautionary example of wasted potential. A bright future, thrown aside for hubris.

"I'll do it myself!" Tristan yelled. He stamped his feet like a child, although a grown man of 21.

What a damned fool. This boy of a man, Tristan Prince, would now be second-in-command of Darien's Ranger squad. No exo-mech swordplay could salvage this insufferable whiner.

"Is he...always like this?" whispered Cole Tailor.

"Yes, unfortunately," Darien said. "The Lieutenant has always been a rare prodigy, even at a very young age. He excels in all academic disciplines and has set records in the combat trials. As you know, he is virtually undefeated in exo-mech dueling at the yearly Placement Games."

"Of course, sir," the tailor said. "I didn't mean any offense."

"Nothing to apologize for. The Lieutenant is, despite all his accomplishments, just a spoiled boy who refuses to learn things the hard way."

"You're all useless!" Tristan yelled, storming out of the room.

Outside the window, Darien looked down at an exo-mech standing valiantly in the courtyard below. Exo-mechs were massive humanoid robotic suits of armor, towering about 4 times taller than the average Zeltan human. For display, they stood decorated and fitted with an impractical titanium sword and shield. *Ridiculous.*

"Aren't they magnificent, sir?" Cole Tailor said.

"Truly," Darien said. "But I've seen them in wartime. They are tools for death."

During his time on the Eastern Front, on the battlefield, they truly reigned as demonic beasts, wielding colossal machine guns and other monstrous tools of death. In the Kingdom, meanwhile, they wastefully stood as ceremonial symbols of valor, and, even worse, used as sport for the aristocratic class. Exo-mech dueling was the most popular event at the Placement Games. Each contender piloted an exo-mech, which was fitted with a blunted sword and shield. They would hack and parry at their opponent until the eruption of metal parts and sparks left one champion standing.

A perversion of warfare. Darien looked down at the ceremonious exo-mech with disdain. They would never know the real horrors of war, the physical and mental exhaustion of battle.

A sudden flashback pulled Darien's mind away. In his vision, he remembered seeing hordes of man and machine laid at his feet, as far as the eye could see. The smoke was rising into the red sky, along with the smell of burnt flesh and the sounds of his brothers screaming in agony. There was soot in his eyes. He fired his rifle desperately and blindly as the enemy closed on him.

"Captain?"

Darien shook out of his hellish reverie. "Um...yes, yes. Very well."

"What?" Tristan cocked his head to the side. "I mean, sir. I said, how do I look?"

Both Lieutenant Tristan and Cole Tailor stared at Darien with concern.

"You'll look... well, for the crowds, Lieutenant." Darien put his hand on Tristan's shoulder. "But your attention should be focused on our mission. This is the Black Forest we are being sent to, not a sport arena. When the first bullet flies past your head, those wrinkles in your cape will be the least of your worries."

Tristan froze momentarily with his mouth open but immediately recovered with feigned confidence, "Well then, sir, I'll make sure the enemy is never able to fire the first shot."

Darien entertained him with a nod. *We're going to die, and it will be because of this fool.*

Darien walked toward the doorway with Tristan following behind him.

"Wait, what wrinkles?" Tristan muttered.

Darien walked down the Military Command Hall. Long windows made a spectacle of the bright blue sky and happy crowds waiting for them in the courtyards below. Trumpeters stirred the people to excitement. Meanwhile, scores of soldiers lined the hall, standing at attention and bidding Captain Darien and Lieutenant Tristan goodwill.

They approached a well-dressed man with a golden half-cape over his left shoulder. It was the distinguished Colonel Nathan, commander of all the Infantry Combat Divisions. A dignified member of the Zeltan High Command, he was often found in deep thought and reflection. He stood gallantly at a window, staring out into the crowd as if he were studying a painting from Old Earth.

"The human spirit finds joy in battles fought elsewhere," Colonel Nathan said. "They cheer not just for you but for the idea of a noble cause, confronting our enemies with confidence. Lest you forget, Captain, you are more than their idea of a brave soldier." He turned to look at them. "There is no greater honor than to fulfill your duty—"

"And my duty is my purpose," Darien continued the statement.

Nathan, Darien, and Tristan recited together, "Now until eternity."

Colonel Nathan smiled. "Lieutenant, I trust you will serve us proud."

"Yes, sir," Tristan said, standing up straight. "We'll find that traitor Julian, and we'll bring him back, and we'll—"

Darien interrupted, lest Tristan make an even bigger fool of himself, "We will do what needs to be done, Colonel. As always. The mission will be completed to the satisfaction of the Crown and people."

"Captain Darien," Nathan said, putting a gentle hand on his shoulder, "I have the utmost confidence that you will succeed. Words cannot express how proud I am of you. Now and always."

Darien's heart swelled with pride, but he quickly fought not to show it. Colonel Nathan had become somewhat of a father figure to him. After all, Darien's former commanding officer Julian was the traitor they were being sent to apprehend. In the wake of Julian's treason, Colonel Nathan helped to keep Darien focused and motivated. Eventually, Darien rose to succeed Julian's former position as Captain. Darien felt that he owed much of his success to the wise Colonel.

"Forget your training," Colonel Nathan said. "Simply be the leader, the soldier you already are. You are ready."

"Thank you, Colonel," Tristan said as if the words were meant for him.

Colonel Nathan's eyes moved to Tristan with a calm finesse. "It's okay to be afraid, Lieutenant."

"What?" Tristan asked, caught off guard. "Me? I'm not afraid. I—"

"It's okay," Nathan said. "It waits for you there, in the dark forest. But just as I have seen you so elegantly defeat all your opponents in the arena, you will find and defeat your fear. Victory is yours to retrieve, Lieutenant Tristan. You simply need to go get it."

"Well, yes, sir!" Tristan said proudly.

Colonel Nathan stepped back, his half cape flapping beside him. "You must be on your way, good Rangers. You have already made me proud."

The gallant Colonel strode away with his beautiful secretary following close behind him. Tristan gave her a wink, but she scoffed in return. Valerie was tall, slim, but held a perpetual expression of solemnity. Her glasses were constantly brimming with head-up display data being fed to the miniature computer system within it. There was not any activity within the Kingdom that she and the Colonel were not immediately aware of. It was suspected that Colonel Nathan's intricate spy network permeated every facet of the Kingdom and beyond.

"If you would kindly put aside your theatrics and libido, it would be much appreciated," Captain Darien said, shaking his head as he walked down the grand hall.

The roar of the crowds swelled as they made their way into the staging area. Darien mounted his Foxhound bi-quad, the Ranger's signature one-manned vehicle that would transform between two-wheeled and four-wheeled modes in an instant. This allowed speedy transport and all-terrain versatility for their ranging in unpredictable Martian environments.

He slowly rode through the large doorway, past the legion of mechanics wishing him words of encouragement. Darien gave each of them polite acknowledgment. Twelve Rangers were already lined up outside, sitting side-by-side on their bi-quads. They turned to the captain. He smiled and signaled that saluting would not be necessary. He pulled up next to the bulky, gray-armored soldier in the front.

"Serge

"Captain." The giant nodded, hidden behind his helmet and visor.

In Darien's opinion, Sergeant Marcus was the prime example of the ultimate soldier. Descended from the Vanguard line and standing at a towering 8 feet tall, Marcus was truly a beast of a warrior. The Kingdom bred the Vanguard to function as their frontline blitz weapons of war. Marcus and other Vanguards possessed unbelievable strength and speed. Darien witnessed firsthand their prowess on the battlefield. A single Vanguard could decimate an entire enemy battalion himself.

Again, Darien snapped back to his moment of hopelessness years ago, when hundreds of AI enemies surrounded him and his comrades. He remembered the single Vanguard bursting from beneath a mound of bodies and machines. Darien would later identify him as Marcus, the silent killing behemoth. In a lightning strike of machine gun fire and explosions, the armored soldier had torn through the enemy line in the blink of an eye. He could appear to be everywhere at once, quicker than a Ranger and as powerful as an exo-mech. He was a silent specter, standing atop the mountain of blood and flesh he had created, framed against the hellish war-torn background.

Marcus's kill count from that battle was a four-figure estimate.

The trumpets blared, and the crowd roared into a frenzy, shaking Darien from his reverie. He was motioned to move forward into the Royal courtyard. He led the file of Rangers into the bright morning light. The people of the Zeltan Kingdom lined the streets and city windows, throwing confetti and waving handheld flags. Darien's bi-quad bobbed slowly as his tires made their way over the uneven cobblestones of the old-fashioned town square.

Tristan assumed his position as second in command. To Darien's dismay, Tristan had to be at his side. The Lieutenant waved proudly to the masses, flashing his perfect teeth, with his golden blond hair blowing in the wind.

"Yes! To victory!" Tristan repeated the chanting of the crowd.

Darien looked up at the King's balcony as they rode past Castle Zeltan. There, the newly crowned King Gareth nodded approvingly of the Ranger caravan. He was a large and powerful man, an obvious champion of this year's Placement Games. Behind him stood the 10 Queens, selected among the female Royal line. Gareth had the grand prize of daily fornication with each (or all) of these 10 beautiful Queens for the remainder of the year, with their expected progeny planned for the next generation of Royal offspring.

The king would sit at the throne for one year (one half cycle around the sun for Mars, but years were named with reverence to the 365 days of Old Earth). During peacetime, they had little responsibility except to contribute to the royal genetic lineage.

Darien glanced at the Queens. Young, perfect, and intoxicating, it was no wonder that the Royal Princes fought so desperately each year for the Kingship.

As for the Soldier class, particularly Darien's Ranger line, he had been paired with several females descended from warrior ancestry. He remembered his first assigned pairing. Her name was Tara. She was a shy but rugged girl eventually placed into the weapons crafting line.

After their mandatory encounter, Darien never saw Tara again. The Kingdom ensured a strict separation of selected procreation and romantic relationships. Before his confirmation into the Ranger Corps, he had several other assigned encounters. As instructed, he never allowed himself to dedicate romantic feelings to these partners, or even lust, for that matter. He was a soldier. His progeny would be, too, though he would never meet them either.

He scanned the cheering crowd. There were children accompanied by their assigned Governesses. *My children could be out here, and I would never recognize them. They would never know me as their father.*

"Ha-ha! For the Kingdom!" shouted Tristan. He waved his fist in the air to the joy of the children. He pulled himself up to stand on his bi-quad seat, balancing himself, and it trudged along slowly. With his stunt came a thunder of applause. *He's the city's damned hero, and he hasn't yet fought in one real battle,* Darien thought.

From the castle balcony, King Gareth maintained his composure, but the entire Kingdom felt his jaw clenching. After all, Tristan was their popular young champion. However, in the throes of glory, no one would ever forget that Tristan's actions had undermined the structure of the 200-year establishment.

Darien was sitting in the crowd about 10 months ago at the Placement Games when it happened. Tristan, who had defeated all competitors in his age group once again, publicly challenged the new King himself to a duel. King Gareth, 10 years senior to Tristan, was forced to accept the challenge or appear weak in front of the entire kingdom. The public exo-mech between king and popular champion was one for the ages and unprecedented in disrespect for the crown.

Tristan was not eligible to compete for Kingship until he turned 30. But in his hubris, he ignored the 200-year-old traditions for his own glory. The brief exo-mech duel was halted shortly before Tristan would have landed a winning blow to the king. Gareth should have had Tristan killed, but in the interest of wisely retaining his people's approval, he instead punished Tristan with re-placement from the Royal class into the Soldier class. In Gareth's wisdom, this essentially prevented Tristan from securing a place in the Prince's Council and would certainly preclude him from ever competing for the yearly kingship.

Furthermore, Tristan was re-assigned not only to the infantry, but to the Ranger Corps, the only regiment of the Kingdom's military that regularly saw combat and high mortality, even in peacetime. The King just so happened to plan a daring Ranger incursion into the deadly Black Forest, a savage no man's land where entire platoons of Kingdom soldiers would disappear, likely eaten alive by the cannibal Aggro tribesmen or mutant wildlife of the Black Forest that could only be conjured up in the worst of nightmares.

Darien now looked upon the new second-in-command with scorn. *Because of your ridiculous stunt and the King's damaged ego, 13 fine soldiers are being sent to die*, Darien thought.

Just then, Tristan smiled proudly up at the King, waving mockingly. "He thinks we're going to fail," Tristan tried to yell over the crowd's deafening noise, "but we're not! We're going to catch that traitor. We're going to bring him back, and we'll be heroes!"

Darien was seething with anger. He thought about stopping his bi-quad and shooting Tristan in the head for all the crowd to see. Before he had the chance to fulfill his wonderful fantasy, Sergeant Marcus spoke up behind them.

"Sirs," the armored giant said, "they are ready."

The 14 Rangers were lined up two-by-two. The main city street was sectioned off for their grand exit. As rehearsed, Darien signaled to the event organizer. Behind their caravan, King Gareth's voice boomed over the loudspeakers.

"Citizens of Zeltan," the king's voice reverberated, "join me in wishing the very best for our 14 brave Rangers of the Royal Kingdom."

Lies, but applause nonetheless.

"They will venture far out to the Black Forest and apprehend the traitorous Julian. They will return him here to stand trial before the Royal Court, and I shall pass my judgment for his crimes against our beloved Kingdom."

Julian, the former Ranger Captain, now lived as a murderous recluse in the Black Forest. Dozens had already died trying to capture him.

"Go forth, Rangers. Return with the traitor. Bring us victory!"

On cue, Darien switched his bi-quad into two-wheeled mode. He revved the engine and held tight to the handles. For show, the Rangers sped down the main street of the Kingdom. The main gate quickly approached, with hundreds of adoring townspeople in full acclaim. He could hear Tristan hooting in joy behind him. As they zoomed out the city gates, fireworks shot into the sky.

Quite a fanciful funeral procession.

Darien and his 13 Rangers spread out into a V formation as their bi-quads cruised west across the countryside. The Zeltan Kingdom lay centered in the terraformed area of Mars called the Golden Plains. Through an unpredictable effect of terraforming, most of the grass in the Plains was yellow. Over 200 years, this "golden" grass proved as reasonably healthy as the standard green grass on Old Earth. It was believed that the black trees and foliage of the Black Forest occurred because of similar unpredictable consequences of terraforming the Martian soil.

They had a few hours of riding at full speed to arrive at the Black Forest. Darien would have been content to spend the entire trip in silence. After all, an isolated squad of Rangers would be tempting pickings for a band of outlaws to ambush. They needed to focus.

"Can someone say anything?" Tristan said over their comlink earpiece. "Anything?"

"Lieutenant," Darien said, "this isn't a social excursion."

"I get it," Tristan said. "With all due respect, sir. We've been training for weeks. I'm second in command, and no one's barely said a word to me."

"Consider it a professional courtesy," said a voice over the comlink. Darien recognized it as Barrett, Fireteam Bravo's heavy machine gunner.

They settled down at Fort Peter, located about halfway between the Kingdom and the Black Forest. The brief stop was jarring for the novice Tristan. He had barely settled himself down to eat his meal before they were ready to leave again. As they readied their bi-quads for the remainder of the journey, the captain studied Tristan.

Tristan's vexing pride was fading as they rode further from the haven of the Zeltan. Darien saw it in his eyes. There was a telling fear that he had seen consume other young men. It was a hollow void that rookie soldiers stared into, a sudden realization that you were about to kill or be killed.

Darien could see Tristan's hands shaking as he stared into the far west, where the outline of black trees began to dot the horizon. He dared not to interrupt the young Lieutenant's revelation. He could reassure him later. For now, Darien trusted the looming terror of the famed Black Forest to strike humility in Tristan's heart.

Fear is a bitter taste you'd best get acquainted with, before you are forced to swallow it whole.

The forest began as a dream in the distance. As they rode closer and closer, it became a terrifying nightmare. The trees towered as tall as Castle Zeltan. The sun set behind the blackness, taunting the Rangers with a chilling sense of dread.

Darien was not impressed. He knew death came both in the darkness and the light of day. Fools would fear danger lurking in the dark recesses of a ghastly forest, but Darien knew better. You were just as apt to have your head explode from a sniper bullet while enjoying a midday walk. It was all a matter of preparation and acceptance.

From the Royal Ranger Creed: "Always, I am prepared to face the dangers unknown and to accept the task at hand."

However, just as they approached the Black Forest, the evening sky appeared to tear open. First, it started as a curiously appearing red dot in the sky. Then, it grew into a fireball that Darien could only assume was artillery fire. Its trajectory was toward the west edge of the forest.

"Hold!" Darien yelled.

The 14 Rangers came to a halting stop. Tristan damn near flew off his handlebars. They watched in bewilderment as the sky lit up in a hail of flames. Darien studied the main fireball.

It's a ship... It's a damn spaceship.

Since the Silence event 200 years ago, no spaceships had ever returned to Mars. *Were they finally receiving word back from the fabled Earth government? Why did they abandon us so many generations ago? Why were they returning now?*

Darien watched as the flaming ship shook their world as it attempted a crash landing. Its trajectory would be on the far side of the Black Forest; curse his luck. As it crashed, the sonic boom pulsed out of the forest, shooting entire trees and branches at them.

Instinctively, most of the Rangers ducked behind their bi-quads. Marcus leaped up, tackling Tristan to the ground. His mammoth body and armor curled around Tristan, clutching him like a baby.

"Hey." Tristan squirmed. "I command you to let go!"

A large tree branch crashed against Marcus's back, but he barely reacted with a flinch. He had saved the young Lieutenant from an unceremonious arboreal death.

When the debris settled, Darien looked up. The Black Forest was still there in its defiance. In the far distance, the evening sky was alive with fire and smoke.

"Let's go," Darien said, readying his gear. "Fireteam Alpha, scout right, incursion maneuvers 638, fall back on protocol 4-1, communications ready willing. Fireteam Bravo, forward hold, incursion 638, fall back protocol command imprompt, communications earshot. Hoo."

"Rah!" all the Rangers said in unison.

"Wait." Tristan struggled to catch up. "We're going in there? What was that? We should go back and get help; we should—"

"We need to find out what happened and then get word back to Sovereign Command," Darien said, grabbing Tristan firmly by the shoulder. "This is what we do. We're Rangers. You're a Ranger, right?"

"Well, I uhh—"

"Look at it this way, we're going to be the first people to encounter a spaceship in 200 years," Darien said. "You realize what this means? We might solve the mystery of the Silence. A find like this would be legendary."

"Legendary," Tristan repeated in a daze.

That got his attention.

FOUR

Raymond Redmin awoke in bed, nestled comfortably among the warmth of soft blankets and pillows. He rested his cheek with repose as his head swirled. He dared not open his eyes, though. The world felt like it was spinning. He thought perhaps he was drinking the night before. Perhaps it was a bad sleeping position. *Where is Eva?*

He tried to shift his arms, but they were constricted. He tried kicking his legs, and they remained frozen. Raymond opened his eyes in a panic. He stared at red dirt inches away from his face. He was trapped amongst inflated brown padding. The situation rushed back to his consciousness like a tidal wave. He was upside down, trapped with just barely enough space to breathe.

He began to scream, but it echoed within the small air pocket between his face and the dirt. His neck veins swelled as he yelled and struggled to free himself. The panic accelerated, and he almost passed out again.

I just fell out of a crashing spaceship. I'm on Mars. I'm trapped in an escape balloon. I'm going to suffocate. And I want to throw up. Don't throw up. Don't throw up.

Raymond heard muffled voices, and his padded encasing began to move. He screamed for help. He heard tearing and ripping. It sounded like stabbing. He felt a hand grab his ankle. They were pulling at his leg, but they only pulled him against the harness attached firmly to his thighs and groin.

"Hey, hey," he screamed. "I'm stuck; be careful!"

The voices grew louder. The language was foreign, spoken in grunts. He felt them roughly cut him out from his harness attachment. They continued to pull at him, and he was gradually pulled out by his legs. Raymond squinted at the bright light of day as several figures stood over him, speaking an indistinguishable language.

Oh god. Are these Martians? Aliens?

Overwhelming fear superseded his confusion and disorientation. He rolled over to scramble and run away, but they flipped him on his back, and the unmistakable barrel of a gun was pointed directly in his face. Raymond cowered and braced for a fatal gunshot to his face. It never came. He slowly opened his eyes and brought his arms down.

Long-haired, shirtless human brutes stood over him. They frowned, one with a rifle still pointed. They were human, thank god, but Raymond noticed distinguishable cranial bossing and exaggerated physical features. They resembled football players on steroid regimens gone wrong, who had also forgotten to cut their hair or shave in years. Raymond noted that they were multi-ethnic as well. Between the four of them, two were light-skinned, the other two darker, with no identifying racial traits. They all wore dirty long hair and frightening tattoos over their torsos and arms.

Raymond struggled to make sense of this situation. He had never seen people that looked like this before. As usual, his innate curiosity of the scientific unknown started to override his multitude of emotions.

They grunted at him, seemingly trying to communicate. Raymond put his hands up.

"Wait, wait," Raymond said. "English. Do you speak English?"

More grunting.

"My name is Ray." He put his hand on his chest.

The savage holding the rifle opened his eyes wide and moved in close, threatening Raymond.

"Whoa, whoa, wait," Raymond said.

Raymond looked around. They were standing in the middle of a barren, red landscape. It certainly looked like Mars. *Jesus, this is Mars. I'm on Mars.* The weather was temperate. The sun and blue sky above were identical to Earth. The question still lingered in Raymond's head. *Why am I able to breathe on Mars? More importantly, who are these guys? Martians?*

The strange savages certainly resembled and acted human, but their language was more akin to caveman talk than any language Raymond could identify. They motioned for him to walk. After he hesitated, they grew impatient and shoved him. After escaping a crashing spaceship and spinning down to the ground like an unhinged roller coaster, he was relieved to be walking in a straight line, despite at gunpoint. He walked around the deflated escape chair/parachute and then noticed movement just behind.

"Holy shit, holy shit!" Raymond yelled.

He fell backward to the ground as a giant brown rat appeared from behind the escape chute. It was enormous, its body the length of an adult human with a grotesque tail doubling its size. With frightening speed, it crept toward Raymond, sniffing and baring its teeth.

He had never seen something like this creature before. It was big and grotesque, and Raymond wanted to be anywhere else. His fear jolted his heart so quickly that he worried the organ may explode.

One of the savages let out a grunt. The rat looked up and obediently backed away.

Raymond slowly crawled backward, pressing himself pitifully up against the leg of one of the strange brutes. Never looking away from the monstrous rat creature, he sought safety, trying to put the barbarian between him and the creature. The savage, annoyed, kicked Raymond off and gave him an additional kick to the stomach.

"Oof," Raymond blurted.

By now, he had felt a broad variety of nausea and abdominal discomfort. He didn't mind the physical suffering. He just wanted answers.

"Just stay down," a female voice said next to him. "Don't make any sudden movements."

"Huh?" Raymond looked up.

A young woman was kneeling next to him. She wore a dirty duster coat, and her brown-red hair was unkempt. She had dirt and dried blood over her face, but underneath were kind eyes. She was bound at the wrist by crude twine. He deduced that she was their prisoner too.

"Who are you?" Raymond asked, pushing himself up to a sitting position.

"My name is Kira," she said. "I'm from Remnant."

"Rem…what?"

One of the savages picked Raymond up by the back of his jumpsuit. He roughly grabbed Raymond's wrists and tied them together with a vine. The vine had soil and rough black leaves on it. It scratched Raymond's skin and left a painful abrasion. He couldn't help but study the vine and leaves themselves. The leaves were jet black. *Fascinating*. He was pushed forward and motioned to start walking.

To Raymond's amazement and fear, there were four total monster rats. Each savage mounted them like a horse. The vine around Raymond's wrists suddenly pulled him forward. He was tied to one savage and this girl, Kira, to another. They stumbled forward together. He wondered how he ended up as a prisoner, and what had happened to the others from the falling spaceship.

"What the hell is going on?" Raymond asked.

Judging by her attire, she did not look like she had fallen out of the spaceship with him. Then again, nothing was following any logic so far.

"Aggros," Kira said.

The girl stumbled. The rats moved at a slow but unpredictable pace. Raymond and Kira struggled to remain close enough together to talk.

"What are you saying?" Raymond asked. "Where are we? Who are these guys?"

Kira gave him a perplexed look. "They're Aggros from the Black Forest? I've never seen them before, but all the stories are true. Even the aggrats. They're real."

"You mean those giant rat things?"

"Yeah," Kira said. "The aggrats. They're even bigger than I thought. They say that the Aggros capture people from the Frontier and the Plains and feed them to the aggrats."

Raymond gave her a blank stare.

Kira studied his face. "You don't know what I'm saying, do you? Wait, are you… are you from that thing that came out of the sky?"

"Yeah. The ship. Where is it? I mean, I woke up on this ship, and they said we were crashing on Mars…and I'm supposed to get to an Ark…and then I wake up down here…and then those barbarians and their giant aggsters…"

"Aggrats."

"Right," Raymond said. "Kira, right? Kira, what the hell is going on, and where am I?"

"We're just west of the Black Forest," Kira said. "The Red Frontier… On Mars—"

"Stop right there," Raymond said. There was too much information for him to handle at once. "We're talking about the planet Mars, right?"

"Well, yeah," Kira said.

"Okay, because as far as I know…" Raymond replied, becoming frustrated. "On the Mars that I know, people can't breathe on it. There are no black forests or people living on it. And there are definitely no giant rats on it. So, tell me, what the hell is going on? How long have I been asleep? What year is it!"

The Aggros holding Raymond's vine gave him a harsh tug for causing a commotion. Raymond fell to the ground, but he picked himself up after being dragged along. Kira tried to help him up.

"I'm good, I'm good," Raymond said. "Just please. What year is it?"

"It's been 198 years since the Silence," Kira said.

"Since the what?"

Kira gave him a concerned look as she was dragged along. "Who are you?"

"My name is Raymond Redmin," he said. "I'm from Earth. I was put into cryostasis in 2037. I…I had cancer. They put me to sleep. Then something happened. I don't know how long I've been asleep."

Her eyes opened wide. "Oh my god; you're from Earth?"

"You're not?"

"Well, no," she said. "I was born here, on the Frontier."

"What's the Frontier? And what's this Silence? Please tell me I haven't been asleep for 200 years." He laughed uncomfortably.

"People from Earth settled here over 200 hundred years ago. We're descendants of the first settlers."

Raymond's heart sank. He stared into nothingness as he marched. Humanity had long settled onto another planet, and he slept right through it. His wife, his son, all his friends and family... they were all gone. For the next few moments, all the people he had ever known, all the places he had ever been, his entire life, flashed before his eyes. He had lost everything and everyone all at once. In that moment, he felt the despair of losing a loved one, infinite times over.

"I'm sorry," Kira said.

Raymond took a few minutes to respond. He trembled with grief, but also sought to make some sense of this surreal situation he was in. The experiments were intended to extend his life so that he could spend more time with his family. Instead, he had lived far beyond any of their lifetimes, even apparently Earth itself.

"Just...just tell me everything. You said 200 years since this... *silence*?"

Kira took a deep breath. "After the first settlers came, something happened. One day, we just suddenly lost all contact with Earth. They stopped sending communications. They didn't respond to ours. Ships stopped coming here. We sent ships out into space to find out what happened. None of them ever came back. Until today, no ship has ever come from space. They just...left us."

Raymond suddenly shared her feeling of abandonment. "And that was 200 years ago?"

Kira nodded. "We called it the Silence. We waited and waited, but after a while, we realized we were alone. People panicked, and our government collapsed. War after war almost tore the planet apart. The Republic, the Order, the Dominion, the Omega Mind...I wish my little brother were here to explain it all to you. No matter, though; the Zeltans have been in charge now."

"Zeltans?"

"Oh, right," Kira said. "This must be so strange for you. The Zeltans, they were this...human augmentation project that the first settlers started; genetic engineering. They're supposed to be stronger, faster, and smarter than us. And I guess because they're so much *better* than us, that means everyone thinks that they deserve to be the ones in charge."

"These guys?" Raymond motioned at the brutes on rat-back. "They're Zeltans?"

"No," Kira said. "When they tried to replicate the original Zeltan program, they were unsuccessful. As with everything that isn't 'perfect', they see these people as abominations. The Zeltans cast them off into the Black Forest, where they created their own tribe culture. We refer to them as Aggromen."

"And the Zeltans," Raymond said, "where are they?"

"They sit in high castles and control the Spire in the middle of the Golden Plains. The Spire is the reason we can breathe and live here. You can see it beyond the Black Forest up there." Kira pointed ahead.

Far past the forest, Raymond could just barely see a large black needle-shaped object piercing into the sky. It was impressive, perhaps larger than any skyscrapers he had known on Earth. It seemed like it was hundreds of miles away, yet he could see it reached far up into the stratosphere, maybe into space.

"The Spire," Raymond said. "Are we going there?"

Kira laughed while shaking her head with sadness. "No. That's at the center of the Golden Plains. That's way beyond the Black Forest. The Zeltan Kingdom. The Zeltans don't go out here to the Frontier. Us natural borns, we're not allowed there."

"I know I'm asking a lot of questions, but natural born?"

"I'm a descendant of the first settlers," Kira said. "I wasn't created in a lab. I was born. I knew my mother and father. They raised me. I have the freedom to live my own life. But the Zeltans' society is designed. They were created by the first settlers. They call themselves perfected humans. Anyone who doesn't fit their grand design is cast off into the Black Forest, the Red Frontier, or the Green Sea."

"That's called eugenics."

"Whatever it's called"—Kira looked down—"I think they just wished the rest of us would have died of starvation or all killed each other by now. But out here on the Frontier, we made a life for ourselves without them. We have towns. Peaceful towns. We're surviving; well, we were until the Fever."

"Tell me about that."

"The fever," Kira said. "It comes, and you start coughing. Then you stop eating. Then the blood...my father...the others...people have died. I came out here to go into the Black Forest and find a healer there. He's supposed to have medicines from Old Earth. It's stupid, but I had to do something. I just..."

"Kira, tell me," Raymond said. "I'm a doctor."

"Wh-what?" Kira said, wide-eyed.

"I'm a doctor, Kira. Before I, y'know, went to sleep on Earth, I was a physician. If I can see what this healer has, maybe I can help."

Kira stared at him for a few moments. "You're...you're from the prophecies."

"Uh, no, probably not, I—"

"No, no," Kira said. "I didn't believe them either. But the priests. They pray to the blue god—uh, Earth. They always talk about how the blue god would send angels down to save the Frontier. The angels of deliverance."

"Okay," Raymond said uncomfortably. "Well, I know I'm definitely *not* that."

"No, wait," Kira said, "I'm serious. In the prophecies, the four angels of deliverance are supposed to come to the Frontier as a heavenly host. They're supposed to each bring healing, guidance, hope, and salvation. They're supposed to fight for us and save us. One of them is supposed to have a sword—"

"Whoa, whoa," Raymond said. "Listen, again, I was a doctor from Earth. For some reason, I woke up 200 years later and on another planet. I just want to find out what happened to my family. I just want to find out what happened to me."

"But you can help us."

"I mean, I can try," Raymond said. "I don't have any tools or technology that I had. Without that, I can't do much."

"But if we find Guaritore, the healer?"

"Well, yeah," Raymond said, "sure, I guess. Is that where we're going?"

"Yes and no," Kira said. "The Aggros are taking us into the Black Forest, but I don't know where in it."

Raymond looked ahead to the towering, terrifying black trees and the deathly darkness they guarded. "What's in there?"

"I don't know," Kira said. "There is no way this is a coincidence. I came out here to find a cure for my town, and you just fall out of the sky. The first ship to come from space in 200 years. We were meant to be here."

"Don't get me started on that determinism stuff." He clenched his jaw. What meaning could there possibly be for him to lose everything and end up in this damned strange future.

"This was meant to happen," Kira said. "We'll figure a way out of this. We should be focused on how to get ourselves out of this situation before these guys feed us to the aggrats. Then we need to find the others that were on your ship. We need to find the rest of the angels."

"Well, I hope those angels can fly," Raymond said.

He looked to his side; miles away was the smoking wreckage of the ship. The nose of the ship had dragged across the ground, creating a massive ditch and crater. It had come to a stop at the outer edge of the forest, knocking down a few trees. He could not imagine anyone that did not eject from that ship could have survived.

"The Aggros are probably bringing the survivors to where they're taking us," Kira said. "We'll break ourselves out, and then we'll find Guaritore and get back to Remnant."

Raymond shook his head. "Alright, well, any ideas on how to go about that?"

"Swift is out there somewhere," she said. "He'll find us."

Raymond's brain could no longer contain the new terms and names. "Okay, who the hell is Swift?"

FIVE

C olonel Nathan walked into the Council Chambers late enough to make a grand entrance. The golden half-cape was draped across his left shoulder while his right hand rested on the hilt of the saber on his belt. As he entered, the circular chamber with its high ceilings was abuzz with conversation.

"Colonel Nathan," King Gareth announced over the ambient discussion, "good of you to join us. We were just about to begin."

King Gareth was a large man with arresting yellow-brown eyes and a commanding presence. His beard was thick, brown, and wild, half-curling around his neck and face like a lion's mane. His voice boomed like a low rumble of thunder.

"Your excellence"—Nathan put his hand over his chest and gave a bow—"it would be my honor."

King Gareth responded with a glowing smile. Nathan quickly studied his face. The King was not yet immune to pleasantries. Every year with each new king was always the ripe time for manipulation via the colonel's practiced tools of flattery and ingratiation.

"Sir," said his assistant Valerie.

Valerie held out the chair for Nathan, and he slid into the seat with perfect grace and elegance. He touched her hand with his white glove, and she blushed.

Valerie was a statuesque figure, her dark brown hair pulled back in a sleek, neat style. Her glasses featured a head-up display that kept her informed of everything happening within the Kingdom, and she made sure to keep Colonel Nathan well-informed as well. He had created an extensive network of spies that gave him more knowledge than anyone else on the planet.

"Thank you, Val," he said. "Please inform the gardener of my plans."

"Yes, sir," she whispered, looking around to see if anyone was listening.

As Valerie stepped out of the Council Chambers, the doors shut, signaling all into a silence. The room was fantastically decorated with tapestries hanging from the high ceilings. Sitting atop the Royal Tower, the circular chamber was usually bathed in sunlight shining through the glass ceiling in all directions. Tonight, however, the Council met under the moon and starlight, providing a beautiful backdrop to the crucial meeting.

Every seat in the circular gallery was filled. The entire Council of Princes, the military officer brass, and the collection of town governors all sat about in concerned discussion.

"And we can confirm that this is indeed a spaceship?" asked Prince Silas. "From Earth?"

"Yes, yes," General Samuel, Commander of the Zeltan Army, said. "We've been through this. Captain Darien and his Rangers witnessed it firsthand, and our reconnaissance confirms this was a ship originating from space."

"And based on the designs," General Leonard of the Aero Corps said, "it appears consistent with manufacturing from the pre-Silence period. I'm afraid that's all we know so far."

"We *would* know more," General Samuel said, "if you would send a damn squadron to fly over the Black Forest so we could see for ourselves. The natural borns, the androids, pirates, or even the savages...gods, the savages. Any of them could have their grubby hands on that ship right now."

"Well, General," Leonard said, "as we discussed, the Airborne Accords with the Haven Alliance..."

General Samuel slammed his palm on the table and sat back. "Damn those androids to hell! Our predecessors fought to quell Artificial Intelligence in the Kingdom, and we bow to peace treaties with these...machines."

"But to keep the peace—" Prince Bartholomew said.

"Peace?" General Samuel replied. "What threat do these androids pose? They are disarmed, de-militarized, and monitored. They sit idle in the mountains to the north. I say the skies should have been ours years ago. This is our Kingdom, and we go where we please! Especially when we have goddamn spacecraft falling from the sky!"

The room broke into an uproar. Colonel Nathan observed calmly. The dozens of princes sat scattered amongst the circular theater. King Gareth sat at the center, observing his new subjects, most older and more experienced than he. Chamberlain Dean stood at the parapet, calming the crowd. Nathan sat in the sectioned area for the high military officers; Chief Commander Arthur and the Generals of the Army, Navy, and Aero Corps argued amongst themselves.

"It's our heritage," General Samuel said. "And this is the third meeting tonight, and we have accomplished nothing."

"We need to find out what's in that ship," Prince Silas said. "It could be a threat to the kingdom."

"Send the air cavalry!" said a voice in the crowd.

"Send Halo Troopers!" said another.

"Just get the mechanized infantry to plow through that forest!"

"A show of force might draw us into another war!"

"Our forces are already engaged with the rebels to the East and the Corsairs to the South! We can't afford to divert a full invasion force into the Black Forest!"

The bickering continued. Colonel Nathan listened intently to all conversations at once, gathering mental notes. These would be important for any future moves to be made. He mastered the art of drawing out personal bias during confrontations and arguments. Tonight, he planned to use the spaceship's unexpected arrival for his own benefit.

"Enough!" Colonel Nathan stood up. "My friends, hold your tongues for a moment!"

The room fell into a hushed silence as Colonel Nathan made his presence known. His mannerisms were usually quite reserved, but it was rare that he spoke in such a loud, commanding tone of voice. Everyone was captivated by what he had to say, and the lingering sense of fear kept them from speaking out.

"King Gareth," Colonel Nathan continued, now in his usual calm demeanor, "I ask, what are your thoughts?"

The King was caught unexpectedly and stammered, "I…uh…"

"Apologies, your excellence." Nathan gave a brief bow. "What I meant to say was how fortuitous that you had sent the Ranger expedition into the Black Forest. In your wisdom, you provided an elite force able to personally investigate this matter for us. My friends, King Gareth truly has placed us into quite an advantageous position, am I correct?"

The princes and generals muttered to each other. None could argue that, at least not in the king's presence. After all, the expedition into the forest was known to have been a ruse to lead Prince Tristan to his sure death.

"Well, I, uh…" King Gareth said, uncomfortably adjusting his royal garments. "Well, of course! And Colonel Nathan, how are our Rangers doing?"

"From our last transmission," Colonel Nathan said, "they have set up a position within the Black Forest."

"Colonel Nathan," Chief Commander Arthur said, "every faction on the planet will be descending upon the wreckage. I trust the capabilities of the good Captain Darien and our Rangers, but you certainly don't mean to suggest we send them alone?"

"Of course, General," Colonel Nathan said with a bow. "The Rangers were created as a small, rapidly deployable force for reconnaissance and quick missions. Before we deluge our Kingdom headlong, it would be wisest to observe the situation surreptitiously while proceeding with a clear purpose. I say we go about this with grace."

"Grace?" King Gareth asked.

"Yes, your excellence," Colonel Nathan said. "On my word and my faith, Captain Darien will provide us good intelligence on the matter. I also have my informants placed amongst the Red Frontier and the Green Sea to keep us updated. Once we know what we are dealing with, then we will send the appropriate forces needed."

The council members began to nod in agreement.

"And what if the savages are rummaging through the wreckage as we speak?" General Samuel asked.

"General," Nathan said, "I assure you, their simple minds are not to be feared."

"No, I mean," the General stammered. "I don't fear them; I'm just saying—"

"We take what is ours when the time is right," Colonel Nathan said. "We are the dominant species. We are the better. Isn't that right, your excellence?"

"Well, yes, yes, of course." King Gareth nodded approvingly.

"With your approval, my king," Colonel Nathan said, "I suggest calling a large enough combined force of mechanized and foot infantry, with warship and carrier naval support, to march past Cyborg Bay. They wouldn't dare risk open conflict with us when they see the might of our entire military at their doorstep."

"And of the Aero Corps?" General Leonard asked.

"General," Colonel Nathan said, "certainly, you have the most important part to play. Since we would be calling our forces back from the east, we will need your aerial forces to maintain our south and east borders. And Chief Commander Arthur, perhaps we could have General Samuel amass his Army and General Chester his Navy, and we could call our banners together in a grand force once again. The grand military force under Commander Arthur would certainly be a sight to behold for those cyborg pirates who have increasingly shown us disrespect these past few years."

"Yes, yes." Chief Commander Arthur tussled his white beard in deep thought. "Those pirates have certainly grown bold...too bold. This is good. King Gareth, the Colonel's plan may serve us ten-fold. We have no greater opportunity than now."

King Gareth nodded approvingly. "So be it. Very well, Chief Commander. And Colonel, any further suggestions?"

Colonel Nathan addressed everyone with authority, "My king, let us show this planet who we are. I will ensure that our path is laid safely before us. At this very moment, I am coordinating my intelligence agents to ensure a smooth march toward the Frontier. We can have our forces fully assembled in two days. With the might of our full military, we can simultaneously quell the pirate nuisance, establish a new trade route with the Red Frontier, and extend our kingdom's presence westward, which should have been done decades ago. And, of course, we will take what is ours by destiny. From the wreckage of the crash, we may discover the answers we have been seeking since The Silence. The time is now, my friends. By the grace of His Excellence, King Gareth, we are the Kingdom!"

Thunderous applause erupted. King Gareth himself nearly stood up and clapped but then composed himself.

Colonel Nathan held up a hand and signaled toward the King in feigned humility. His plan was falling into place one piece at a time. He scanned the crowd. All seemed to be in agreement. He did not allow himself a false sense of security. There were snakes here. But he was the deadliest serpent.

The meeting continued for about another hour. They decided on Colonel Nathan's plan to rely on the Ranger squad to provide actionable intelligence while the Kingdom amassed their full military force. After all, the Black Forest had been shooting down Kingdom air vessels for decades using inexplicable anti-air weaponry. Lest they rush into this, Colonel Nathan had warned, they may make a fool of themselves in front of the whole kingdom.

Hours passed, discussing the monotonous details of the upcoming military campaign. When they had revised the minutiae enough, they resolved to resume talks in the morning. Nathan took this time to walk out to the royal gardens on this quiet, clear night. A canopy of pale stars lit up the sky and a cool breeze rippled through the trees. His shoes padded across the soft, thick grass as he walked slowly down the gentle slopes until he reached the rows of flowers that stretched out in front of him like piano keys on a magnificent instrument.

The moons of Deimos and Phobos shone full on the brick paths that meandered through the roses and perennials of the royal gardens. The gardens were Nathan's favorite place to take long walks in silent reflection, but after a few steps, he stopped for a moment to look up into the clear night sky. It was calm tonight, with only crickets and tree frogs in his ears. He stood there a long time before walking slowly down one of the paths, hands clasped behind his back. He was escorted by two royal guardsmen, adorned in golden cloaks, carrying automatic submachine guns. They knew to stop and leave the Colonel to himself once they reached his garden. It was his personal grotto that was closed off to all, including the royal guardsmen.

"I informed the gardener," Valerie said, appearing behind him from behind a hedge. "He requests an audience, sir."

Nathan took a deep breath of the cool night air. "Thank you, Valerie."

The Colonel followed Valerie down a maze of high bush hedges. They reached a staircase hidden behind vines. Valerie gently moved them aside, ushering Colonel Nathan down the unlit pathway. Nathan raised his monocle to his eye, allowing him to navigate in the pitch dark. After a short maze of underground hallways, they finally reached a flat video screen on the wall. The security system identified Nathan and Valerie via retinal scans and voice activation. The screen then flashed to life.

"Hello, my friend," Colonel Nathan said to the shadowy figure.

On the screen, he appeared as a black shadow with two glowing red eyes.

"Julian, I had forgotten how menacing those cybernetic implants looked," Nathan said. "Terrifying, but a pleasure to see you again, of course."

"Thank you, sir," Julian said. "So, what do we do about this... spaceship?"

"We proceed as planned. The Kingdom has agreed to march our full forces, leaving in two days. Arthur will lead them south through Cyborg Bay and then west to the Frontier."

"Pawns, all of them." Julian shook his head. "And what of the Forest? Are you sending any more trouble my way?"

"Yes," Nathan said. "We will be sending an entire platoon of 4 more Ranger squads, also leaving in two days. Major Hayter will be leading that mission. They will be seeking to support Captain Darien's squad. And what of the captain right now?"

"Knee deep in Aggro territory. I imagine they'll need some time and space to fight their way through. Maybe we'll offer them a nudge. They are close to where we need them to be.

Nathan nodded approvingly. "Has Guaritore made any progress?"

"He has the Aggros pulling tech from the ship," Julian said. "We could stockpile most of it underground, but since you're sending all of these Ranger squads to come kill me, it might get a little complicated."

"No, no," Nathan said. "This is fortuitous. Keep drawing Captain Darien and the Rangers in as planned. Have Guaritore funnel the tech through our usual channels. Whether the Kingdom intercepts it by force or through the Bay black market, they will get it secondhand after we have already processed it. Meanwhile, we will continue to gather the data from the wreckage. The entire world will be descending upon it soon."

"This is gonna stir up quite the conflict," Julian said. "Shall we tally victors now?"

"The board is finally becoming clearer," Nathan said, "but there is much more story to tell."

"And the Captain? You said you were considering bringing him into the fold."

"Captain Darien," Colonel Nathan said, pausing. "He is an important piece in all this, whether he realizes it or not. But for now, I'd prefer to keep him ignorant to our plans. His devotion to the crown and the Ranger Corps is incorruptible. That being said, he could be useful to us in his predictability. You trained him well."

"Too well."

Nathan nodded. "Do try and keep him alive. As I said, he may be useful to us in the future."

"I'll play nice," Julian said, a smile appearing in low light under the stars.

"Excellent," Colonel Nathan said. "Best we have control of the pieces on the board before the other players arrive."

CHAPTER
SIX

Benny Fong stood up in his pew. The townspeople of Remnant continued to bicker loudly. Benny looked up at Mayor Rolfe, who settled down the crowd from his place up at the parapet. He assembled the townspeople into the cramped church. It might have usually housed less than 100 churchgoers during a Blueday service, but tonight the place of worship was lined to the walls with concerned and terrified residents.

While the people were worried about the implications of the unknown flaming sign from the sky, Benny was more concerned about Kira.

The air was thick with uncertainty. The walls were close, pressing in on the people as they jostled to make room. The people's voices swelled and crescendoed like waves crashing against the church walls. Rolfe's deep baritone rose above the din, an authoritative presence as he implored his constituents to listen.

"Now, now." Mayor Rolfe motioned with his hands. "Let's settle down. Now, whatever that was that fell from the sky, we all saw it."

Mayor Rolfe was an obese man with thinning hair combed over a receding hairline. His jowls bounced when he moved and talked. He was an excellent politician but probably cared very little about his townspeople. Despite his hearty physique, he did not appear healthy. His flabby skin looked pale and sickly compared to his dark shirt and black slacks.

"A sign from the blue god!" preacher Ezekiel exclaimed. "Judgement is upon us!"

"It was the Zeltans," yelled the farmhand Tom Garlund from the back. "They're coming to kill us! We need to leave now!"

The crowd again roared into a panic of nonsense.

Benny tried to open his mouth to speak, but his words were drowned out by the confusion.

Mayor Rolfe lost his patience and slammed his fist down on the parapet. "That's enough! You hear me? Enough!"

The crowd settled down.

"Alright." Rolfe sighed. "As I was saying. We all saw it, but Benny Fong saw it up close with his...uh—"

"The drone," Benny said. "The drone's video feed."

"Yes, yes," Rolfe said. "With his gadget. Benny can tell us what happened. Go ahead, young man."

Benny's heart took a surge of adrenaline as the congregation turned to look at him. Stares of fear, anger, and impatience assaulted him. He opened his mouth to speak again, but only a quivering breath left his mouth.

Benny's father, Harold Fong, gave him a soft nudge on the leg. "It's alright, son; tell them what you saw."

"Right." Benny took a breath. "Well, I was following Kira with the drone. She was almost at the Black Forest. We saw it. And then the spaceship came out of the sky."

"Spaceship?"

"Impossible!"

"It's a sign from the gods!"

Grumbles among the crowd were immediately silenced by the Mayor. "Enough! Benny, are you sure you saw this? This wasn't a falling meteor or something of that sort?"

"Well," Benny said. "It was definitely a spaceship. You could see writing on the side and everything. It looked like it was trying to land, but then it crashed. Right outside the Black Forest. It crashed and...Kira—"

"What happened, Fong?" Casey Jarrett asked impatiently.

Casey and his lackeys were leaning against the wall behind the mayor. He was smoking a pipe of harsh with his face hidden underneath the brim of his hat. No one dared tell him not to smoke inside the church. The burning harsh gave off an acrid, yet sweet, smell of smoke, intensified by the cramped space of the church. It was a heady smell of the harsh plant that grew defiantly from the Red Frontier desert soil. It permeated the air and created an atmosphere of intimidation. The pipe's smoke curled around the brim of Casey Jarrett's hat, creating a cloud that seemed to menace all who looked upon it.

"Fong!"

"She—" Benny said sadly. "She got caught up in the blast. But she's out there. She's alive. I couldn't get the drone to fly, but the video feed stayed on. I saw them...there were Aggros."

"Aggros?" Mayor Rolfe asked wide-eyed. "The savages. Are you sure?"

"It was a little while after the crash," Benny said. "They came out of the forest and started opening up the ship, but Mayor Rolfe, Kira might be hurt. She could be in trouble. Those Aggros might have her. We need to do something."

Mayor Rolfe hesitated to respond, so Casey stepped forward instead. He handed his pipe to his lackey and pulled up his belt.

"You're damn right we're gonna do something, Fong," Casey said. "Whatever that thing is out there, we need to find out what it is and what it wants. We could be in danger, and we gotta protect ourselves." He patted the revolver at his hip. "And if they're in league with the Hairies, we need to be prepared."

"Yes, I do agree," Mayor Rolfe said, "but what chance do we stand to defend our town? Sheriff Bellick has the fever, and we only have 60, maybe 70, able-bodied men to fight."

The crowd again broke into panic.

"Here's the plan," Casey said. "I take my boys out there on horseback. We find out what it is we're dealing with. Meanwhile, everybody else here, get the women and children ready to move north to Tabernacle."

Benny hated how Casey naturally drew a following. Nevertheless, the crowd was all in agreement.

"But..." Benny said. "What about Kira?"

"Relax, Fong," Casey said. "I'll get her back. All of you, lock up your windows and doors. Grab a weapon and get ready. Me and the boys are riding out now. We'll be back by tomorrow."

Casey and his two lackeys marched down the aisle. Benny half-expected the congregation to break out into applause. Old lady Betty touched Casey's arm and wished him a "the light god bless you," to which the gallant cowboy gave her a tip of his hat.

Spare me the theatrics, Benny thought. *Kira's in real danger.*

"I'm coming with you," Benny said.

Some townspeople chuckled.

Casey stopped in place with a grin. "You wanna come *with us*? You can't even ride a horse."

"No, I mean," Benny said. "I mean, I can follow you with a drone. I have an extra one in the garage. I can watch you guys from above and get a better view of the wreckage. It'll be easier to find Ki—"

"Stop," Casey said with his hand up. "Just stop. You think I want one of those loud toys of yours giving us away to the Hairies? They'll see us coming from ten miles away. No. You stay here. That goes for all of you." He looked around the church. "Stay here and wait for us to get back."

After Casey and his toadies walked out the door, the congregation began to file out quickly. Fear reduced the volume level to a minimum. Mayor Rolfe even walked briskly out of the church before formally dismissing them.

"Son," Harold Fong said, "we need to get packed. Let's go."

Benny had no intention of packing tonight. He didn't care what Casey, his goons, the townspeople, or what anyone said. He was going out there. He was going to find Kira.

CHAPTER
SEVEN

It was only hours until daylight, but Captain Darien would not have known otherwise. They were deep into the Black Forest, where the canopy cast a heavy shade over the ground, completely blocking out the sky. Darien's 14 Rangers moved slowly through the eerie darkness with resolve.

Darien spent the past few weeks creating hundreds of pre-planned maneuvers for his squad. As standard for all Zeltan soldiers, especially Rangers, they spent weeks or even months dedicated to memorizing every detail of every formation. During drills, Darien would give one of the 800+ pre-programmed code phrases, and the squad was required to act upon it. He ensured his team had complete knowledge of every other soldier's movements just in case a teammate became injured or incapacitated.

For military-line Zeltans, this was merely routine. They were bred and raised specifically for this mental and battle-ready capacity. But to Darien's surprise, Lieutenant Tristan, despite being from the royal line, absorbed the maneuver catalog with exceptional competency. They designed most formations to surround Tristan and leave him at the center where he would cause the least disruption. This would also give him the most likely chance of survival, lest Darien would have to deal with the nuisance of carrying away Tristan's dead body.

"Obstruction spotted ahead," Tristan whispered over their comlink. "Be aware at clock 2, Fireteam Bravo. Suggest reformat maneuver 236."

"Bravo team leader confirms obstruction. Agree with reformat maneuver 236, awaiting captain."

Darien smiled. "All teams, reformat maneuver 236. Recon, mark new clock 12."

The prince may make a fine Ranger officer after all.

Darien's Ranger squad consisted of 14 men, broken into four fireteams: Alpha, Bravo, Charlie, and Delta. In most squad formations, Charlie was designated left-facing, Bravo forward, Delta right, and Alpha at center. Even after only weeks of training, the squad fireteams moved in coordination like a living, breathing entity.

Fireteam Charlie was designed to apply a constant barrage of pressure from their left, drawing enemies to the front and center. This prevented any enemy flank or pincer enclosures. They were led by First Sergeant Roland, Charlie Team Leader, a no non-sense veteran who had Darien's full faith and trust. Private Carl was Charlie Team Gunner, a large-bodied and historically aggressive soldier carrying a massive belt-fed machine gun. Private David was Alpha Team Support, a diligent and hard-working soldier carrying the brunt of ammunition and supplies for the fireteam. Finally, Specialist Jason was Alpha Team Grenadier, a genius geometrician and strategist, carrying an assortment of lethal explosives and ordinance.

Bravo Team was re-designed by Darien to be their destructive forward attack. Sergeant Marcus, the Vanguard, was hand-selected by Darien and placed into the squad as a tool to break enemy lines and morale with his sheer lethality and blitzing speed. Marcus, in fact, was not originally designated to the Ranger regiment, as per Zeltan tradition and laws. As a child, he was placed into the Vanguard regiment, a completely different branch of the Zeltan army infantry. However, after Marcus saved him in the field of battle years ago, Darien insisted that Marcus be placed into his Ranger squad roster. This drew criticism from command until they saw the genius in Darien's maneuver designs involving the Vanguard death machine.

Filling out the rest of the Bravo fireteam was Staff Sergeant Scott, Bravo Team Leader, newly promoted but demonstrating promise in training. Corporal Ryan was the Team Medic, an exceptionally quick and nimble soldier, able to travel between fireteams to provide immediate care amid a battle. Finally, Specialist Nicholas was Bravo Team Recon, an extraordinarily gifted Zeltan with superhuman sight and hearing, able to identify the exact locations of multiple enemies during a fight by merely listening to the sounds of their gunfire.

Delta Team generally covered their right flank. They were led by Master Sergeant Barrett, the team's drill sergeant, who developed a reputation for his disciplinarian personality and obsession with military order. Specialist Vincent was Delta Designated Marksman, an uncomfortably quiet sharpshooter with the spatial awareness and skill to shoot a spoon out of your hand while you were running at full speed. Their fireteam centered around Private Zachary, Delta Team Heavy, a jovial adrenaline junkie, bearing the weight of a metal suit, more often seen on a vanguard soldier, and wielding a massive belt-fed chain gun. The Heavy would draw fire while the rest of the team neutralized the exposed targets. Finally, Private Ethan was Delta Team Assist, providing real-time maintenance and support for the Heavy.

Alpha Team only consisted of Captain Darien and Lieutenant Tristan. While the Captain oversaw the overall squad maneuvers, Tristan would remain at his side, watching his rear flank and ensuring he was always protected. Darien and Major West had serious reservations about placing the untested Prince at Darien's side in battle. However, over the past few weeks, he showed competence and, to Darien's surprise, even showed flashes of brilliance.

"Captain," Tristan said, "recon is detecting purposeful movement in the trees."

"Wildlife?" Darien asked.

"Probably," Tristan said, "but I see it too. They're all scurrying away but avoiding direction clock eleven."

The sounds of anguished wildlife cries could be heard.

"Fireteams, go dark," Darien said over the comlink. "Recon, channel is yours alone."

Specialist Nicholas replied, "Infrared is a mess. Too much interference. Bugs, birds, trees. Give me a second."

Darien readjusted his visor to an intermediate setting between night and infrared. The forest was alive with mutated insect life, much to the failed genetic experiments of the Zeltans and others during the Domination Wars. He held out his hand. It took a moment for him to realize it, but it was a white, stringy substance adhered to his gloves.

"What's this crap?" Tristan whispered.

The entire squad seemed to notice it at once. It had neither a sticky nor slimy consistency but seemed to come from every direction.

"Spiders, captain!" Nicholas screamed. "Every direction, up above! God damn spiders!"

Darien looked up. Millions of legs moved about. The low visibility of the dark forest at night hid them well. He could not tell which were tree branches and which belonged to the fabled gargantuan arachnids of the Black Forest. A previous Ranger expedition into the forest encountered giant spider ambushes and barely survived to talk about it. He drew in a breath of momentary terror but let it out with focused resolve. The team needed their leader to remain calm.

"Alpha Center," Darien yelled, "formation nine-two. Recon mark clock twelve. Grenadier fire flares quarter clock. Gunner cover overheard perimeter. Heavy, track a way for Marcus."

In an instant, the 14 men shuffled into formation without a hint of confusion. Grenadier Jason fired four flares up into four quadrants to light their perimeter. The team quickly shut off their visor aids. In an instant, the light from the flares illuminated their portion of the forest. The terrifying figures of the giant spiders loomed overhead. There were hundreds of them, some twice as large as a human. The illumination revealed their predicament. The Rangers were surrounded, ready to be devoured.

"Charlie clock nine, Delta, clock three," Darien said. "Bravo and Alpha provide overhead. All fireteams, engage!"

The cacophony of gunfire exploded like fireworks. Darien and Tristan remained at the center, watching the movement overhead. The bodies of the spiders fell from the trees onto them. One, partially alive, fell next to Tristan, but Vanguard Marcus turned around to casually crush the mutant arachnid with his boot.

"Pair up," Darien said, realizing the falling spiders could break their ranks. "Prepare for close combat."

The squad continued their endless volley of gunfire while the infinite spider horde continued. Grenadier Jason set the surrounding trees ablaze with explosive shelling, which provided effective shielding against the smaller spider nuisance. However, the larger arachnids only charged at them with bodies of nightmarish flaming demons.

Darien had to think quickly. If he didn't make a quick assessment of the situation, their fighting space might collapse around them. He identified an escape route for them, untouched by the fire. He nodded at Heavy Zachary and Vanguard Marcus.

"Vanguard rush," Darien said. "Private Zachary, clear the way for him."

"Here ya go, ya freaks!" Zachary laughed. He whirled up his chain gun and blazed the entire way forward. Trees, spiders, branches, and dirt exploded like a god was tearing creation apart into a million pieces of paper.

Marcus knelt to a sprinting position, ready to charge forward. Darien clenched in tense anticipation. He had all the faith in Marcus and the team, but even after all their training, even one miscalculation could spell disaster, and it would be all on his responsibility.

Heavy Zachary caused the most ruckus and drew the attention of the spiders, who began to descend on him from above. Some managed to land on him and began to lash and bite at him. In his metal suit, he laughed and fought them off with his wrist blades. One giant spider on his back raised a deformed claw, intending to decapitate the Heavy.

In that instant, Marcus arrived, tearing the arm off that spider, stabbing the claw into the spider's head, then throwing the claw into the face of another spider in front of him. Marcus kicked into a tree, deftly shooting the rest of the spiders off Zachary while doing a sideways somersault through the air.

"Ha-ha!" Zachary exclaimed. "Woo! Look at that Vanguard go!"

Darien's team momentarily stopped to witness Marcus, the star Vanguard in action. The armored-clad giant hopped up the trees with ease, never hesitating to stop, while firing his machine gun at spiders in all directions. He began to pick up momentum and began to run across the tree branches, ablaze with fire. Marcus began encircling the squad from above, knocking spiders to the ground.

To Darien, this was not a surprising sight. He had seen Marcus in his full fighting capacity amidst the battlefield. While the others awed at the extraordinary, armored soldier's deft agility, Darien felt only pride. Marcus was truly the perfect soldier, and it was an honor to have him in his squad.

"Divide pairs," Darien exclaimed. "Dextro, provide ground fire. Levo, provide close security."

As rehearsed numerous times in training, the squad split up into groups of two. One dropped their primary weapon and brandished their sidearms or melee weapons, while the other continued to fire into the forest at ground level. In an increasingly exhilarating whirlwind, Marcus was still leaping across the treetops, easily dealing with the spiders.

Darien continued to fire his assault rifle, but Tristan brandished his saber. Darien initially considered the ornamental saber useless for this forest ranging, but he could see a glint of excitement in the former prince's eye. Perhaps this was just the weapon they needed. This was a better time than any to use his swordplay to their advantage.

Oh hell, if it makes sense, then I'll allow it. But just this once.

"Lieutenant," Darien said, "can you cut a path to clock twelve?"

Without responding, Tristan charged ahead. He nudged past Heavy Zachary, who was startled by Tristan's agility and speed.

"All teams," Darien said, "provide cover for the Lieutenant. His trajectory is forward clock twelve. Marcus, watch his overhead."

Darien turned around and watched his squad fluidly transform into an effective mobile entity, leaving behind the fiery battleground behind them. He looked ahead, now with night vision aid. Darien's visor flooded with transparent display data, indicating where his teammates were and the enemy and other hazards. Every atom of his essence worked toward maintaining absolute focus. They were doing their job, and he resolved to do his to the best of his ability.

Tristan was tearing through the spider horde with ease and grace, perhaps as impressively as Marcus had done in the treetops above. Speaking of which, Darien looked up as Marcus continued to jump from tree top to tree top. He and Tristan had improvised a system by which Marcus would shoot the spiders or destabilize their positions to allow them to fall in front of Tristan so he could finish them off with his saber. Tristan was lavishing in tearing the spiders apart, all their innards and goo splattering in all directions. In fact, he seemed to be having the time of his life.

"Captain," Tristan called out while he hacked away. "You never told me it would be this fun!"

The squad encompassed Darien, providing effective cover on all sides. He took note. None of their squad had been injured. They survived overwhelming odds with ease. Darien was proud of them. The planning and training were working. He was proud of himself. The spider horde began to dissipate, and Darien could feel their collective relief.

We might all survive this after all.

"Man down, man down!" someone yelled.

It was Corporal Ryan, the team medic. Something had torn through his chest. At first glance, Darien couldn't tell if it was a spider-inflicted injury or a friendly fire bullet. Terror pulled his heart up to his throat.

"Casualty maneuvers!" Darien yelled.

The team huddled with their back to Corporal Ryan, guns facing in all directions.

"It's a bullet," said Bravo Team Leader Scott. "He was hit by a bullet!"

Instinctively, the team shot off smoke grenades in all directions except forward. Marcus jumped down, picked up the Corporal, and began running.

Darien took off after them, with the team organically following behind like a human shield. He shook off his feelings of uncertainty and fear. He could feel his heart racing, unusual considering their training. Zeltan soldiers were conditioned to control their heart rates even amid extreme physical stress. With his heart beating, he could literally feel his self-doubt start to encroach on his focus.

"Recon," Darien said, running at full pace, "we need shelter!"

"Up ahead," Specialist Nicholas said. "Cave indwelling. Clock 10, approaching half minute."

The team ran full speed toward the cave, with Heavy Zachary and Gunner Carl providing rear cover. Unusually, there was no return fire.

"Are you sure it was a bullet?" Darien said.

"Yeah," Bravo Leader Scott said. "Clean through."

"Man down, another man down!" someone said.

Recon Specialist Nicholas was on the ground. He clutched his wounded leg, crimson blood seeping through his uniform.

There's a sniper out here.

Without hesitation, Charlie Support David dragged Nicholas into the cave as the rest of the squad provided more smoke cover, and the machine gunners shot blindly into the smoke.

Darien shuffled the team into the cave, peering out beyond the smoke to see who their assailants might be. He took deep breaths, also focused on accounting for all his team members. The very last thing he would allow is for any of his teammates to be left behind.

"Ugh!" said Private Zachary, the Heavy.

An audible ping of metal-on-metal resounded through the air. The sound made Darien flinch and then clench in frustration. Zachary stumbled backward into the cave, where the rest of the squad caught him before he fell. He was hit square in the chest. Luckily for him, he wore a giant metal suit that could deflect most bullets.

Darien scurried into the cave with the rest of the team. He made sure to be the last one in. There would be none left out there. He helped them haul Zachary's large, heavily armored body into the cave to safety.

"You alright?" Private Ethan, Delta Assist, said. "It dented you."

"What, seriously?" Zachary looked down.

A bullet had hit dead center of his chest plate, causing a dent in the Ranger insignia.

"That was from a sniper's bullet," Ethan said. "Captain, there is definitely a sniper out there."

Captain Darien nodded. He looked at the injured. Their Medic lay sputtering blood as the rest of the team listened to him giving them medical instructions. Their Recon lay on the ground, gritting his teeth as they provided a tourniquet to stop the bleeding from the bullet wound in his thigh. As a squad leader, this was a scene straight out of his nightmares.

"Send me out there, Captain," Specialist Vincent said. "I'll find your sniper."

Vincent rarely spoke. His voice was always a raspy, haunting whisper. It had an eerie quality, as if something dark and ancient whispered through his lips.

"No," Darien said. "There's something not right about this. Aggros don't shoot like this. They don't just take out your Medic and your Recon. He's sending a message."

"Who?" Tristan asked. "Who's sending a message? You mean—"

"We have to be prepared for the possibility that..." Darien said, "Julian is out there right now."

The name sent shivers down the spines of the collective squad. Even the cool-headed Marksman Vincent seemed now hesitant. Darien made sure to tell the team exactly what he thought they were up against. They needed to be ready.

"If it is him," Darien said, "or someone trained by him, he's waiting for us. He's a former Ranger; he knows how we operate. He's trying to slow us down."

"Well, isn't this who we came out here to get?" Tristan asked, sword in hand. "Let's go get him!"

Marcus put his giant hand on Tristan's shoulder to calm him down.

Julian, Darien thought, looking out into the smoke covering the entrance to the cave. *I don't know what made you betray the Kingdom, but we're ready for you. We're ready. I'm ready.*

CHAPTER

EIGHT

Raymond and Kira drudged along through the pitch-dark forest. They were walking for hours. They were allowed a few breaks, and the Aggromen savages tossed them crude twines of meat and skins of water. At first, Raymond hesitated to take their food and drink. After all, he wondered if his stomach would even tolerate their Martian food. But a man had to eat. With hesitation, he ate the meat... whatever strange creature it may have come from.

"I'm beginning to think that no one's coming to rescue us," Raymond said.

"I told you," Kira whispered in Raymond's ear. "He's following us; we'll be okay."

Raymond looked around in frustration. They were being led into a nightmarish forest, mostly populated by mutated wildlife waiting to devour them. Their path was illuminated only by the primitive torchlight of the brute savages on the backs of monster rats.

"Excuse me if I find that hard to believe," he whispered. "I don't know what your robot fox is waiting for."

"He's here; I know it," Kira said, looking around in the darkness.

Up ahead, Raymond finally saw some illumination of the forest. The sounds of drums grew louder and closer. As their destination finally came into view, Raymond could make out a large grotto surrounded by torch fire. Crudely built wooden walls and guard towers marked the entrance to this strange manmade gathering in the center of the black forest.

The torches lit the area in an orange haze, and beyond the light, he could see the silhouettes of savages dancing and jumping in a rhythm of some kind of tribal ceremony. The guards on the outside swayed back and forth, holding primitive lanterns as they patrolled. The torches lit up the darkness in a small clearing. Their flames danced along the wall, flickering in and out of the slits cut into the wood. The wall was adorned by hideous, dancing masks of bone and skulls, placed in a circle around the entrance to the grotto.

"What is this place?"

"I don't know," Kira said. "This might be where the Aggros live. But no one's ever been this deep inside the forest to see this."

No one who has made it out alive, probably, Raymond thought.

As they were led through the wooden gates, Raymond finally let go of any hope of salvation. The realization was numbing. He thought about whether they would torture him, keep him as a prisoner, eat him, or feed him to the rats. At this point, he was giving up any hope of surviving this nightmare. There were skulls hanging from wooden pikes as decoration. He entertained the idea of running into one and impaling himself to end it all right then and there.

"There's other people," Kira said. "Look!"

A large wooden cage was placed suspiciously close to the main fire at the center of the camp. Dozens of people stood wide-eyed in fear. The savage leading Raymond took him roughly by the arm and shoved him toward the cage. He brought out a large knife, and Raymond winced. The knife cut the vine from Raymond's wrists, which were bloodied and raw from the trip.

After some grunting, the Aggroman brute threw Raymond into the cage with the rest of the prisoners. Raymond hit the ground hard. The earthy smell of the forest has been replaced by the smell of sweat, body odor, and other human scents. The torches spur the smell of burning wood into the air. Someone picked him up by the armpit.

"Are you a sleeper?" a man asked.

"What?" Raymond asked, wiping dirt off his jumpsuit.

"You're definitely a sleeper," the man said. "Oh my god, we didn't think any of you survived the crash." The rest of the prisoners came to Raymond, helping him get up.

Kira came tumbling into the cage afterward, and the wooden door shut hard. An Aggro tied the door tight with a thick vine as a pack of mutant aggrats hissed at them from outside.

"And the girl?" the man asked. "Where are you from?"

"Um..." Kira said, confused. "From Remnant, on the Frontier."

The prisoners looked at each other. They quickly turned their attention away from her and back to Raymond.

Kira picked herself up from the ground. "Wow, okay. Thanks for the help."

"Listen to me," the man said in Raymond's face. "My name is Lieutenant Grimes. We came with you on the ship, the Charon."

A wave of relief rushed over Raymond. He had reunited with at least some people from the ship. Perhaps they could explain to him what the hell was going on.

"Are you from Earth?" Raymond asked. "My family. My name is Raymond Redmin. Was my family on board?"

"Raymond Redmin?" Grimes let go of Raymond and stepped back wide-eyed. "You're Raymond Redmin?"

"Yeah," Raymond said, looking around. The other prisoners stared at him. "Why does everyone keep looking at me like that? Tell me what's going on. What am I doing here?"

"Dr. Redmin," Grimes said. "You've been asleep—"

"I know, I know," Raymond said, frustrated. "I get it. I've been asleep for hundreds of years. I'm in the future. I'm in space. We're surrounded by rat monsters, and nothing makes goddamn sense. Now please, just tell me why I'm here and where my family is."

"I'm sorry, Dr. Redmin," Grimes said, looking at the floor. "You weren't supposed to wake up. We were delivering you and the other sleepers...and then—"

"And then what?" Kira asked.

"Something went wrong," Lieutenant Grimes said. "We're not supposed to be here. Not here, not now."

Grimes turned toward the main bonfire at the center of the camp. The Aggros were chanting and playing their drums louder. They sounded tribal and menacing. Some kind of chieftain or priest was singing cryptic incantations as others performed odd rituals around the fire.

Something about the intonations of the chanting and the ominous drumbeats sent a feeling of dread through Raymond's soul.

"Oh my god," said one of the female prisoners. "It's happening again."

An Aggroman hastily opened the gate, and the prisoners jumped back in fear. He breathed heavily, staring down each of the prisoners. Raymond looked down at the ground. He deduced that his best chance of survival, at least temporarily, would be to avoid eye contact.

"Raymond!"

Raymond looked up as the Aggroman grabbed Kira's arm.

"No!" Raymond yelled, trying to pull her back.

The Aggroman effortlessly shoved him aside. Raymond stumbled backward, watching Kira kicking and screaming as the brute dragged her out of the cage by the hair. He had only just met her, but he felt a duty to protect her. She was just a young woman, annoyingly idealistic, but good at heart. He could not just let her just get taken away by these savages.

"Kira!" Raymond shouted.

The other prisoners held him back, despite his struggling.

"Dr. Redmin," Grimes said, holding him back, "I'm sorry, there's nothing you can do for that girl."

"What's going to happen to her?" Raymond asked as he watched in horror.

"Some kind of sacrifice," Grimes said. "They've already taken away a few of us and..." He trailed off.

The savages dragged Kira up the stairs of their temple structure. A large Aggroman with tattoos and multiple piercings and jewelry stood at the opening of the temple. Raymond deduced he was some kind of priest. The strange Aggro priest walked out to the platform hanging over the fire. There was a wooden pole at the end, and Raymond identified the clear appearance of fresh red blood dripping from the wood. The priest held his hand over his heart, bowed his head toward it, and then turned back to face Kira.

"We need to do something," Raymond said.

"I'm sorry, doctor," Grimes said. "She's the third one tonight. These people... I think they're sacrificing us for some kind of ritual."

"Raymond, help!" Kira screamed.

An Aggroman tied her hands behind the pole as she cried and struggled. The priest's incantations grew louder, and the other Aggromen in the camp chanted in unison. The priest brandished a large knife and raised it in the air.

"Haatah! Haatah! Haatah!" the Aggromen chanted, raising their rifles in the air.

Raymond wanted to look away, knowing this poor girl's fate. She gave him some semblance of normalcy during their long walk. Although Raymond had grown annoyed by her optimism, it only made her pitiful cries now even more tragic. From up on the platform, she looked wide-eyed and tearful down at Raymond, who was pressed helplessly against the wooden cage.

After struggling against the wooden structure keeping them captive, Raymond's stomach churned in powerlessness. He could only mouth, "I'm sorry," as the priest walked toward her with the knife. Kira pleaded for her life, but her cries were drowned by the chants of doom.

At that moment, Raymond missed his wife. He remembered looking up at Eva's face in the gallery each time he was put to sleep. He remembered her glassy eyes, the tear-filled windows to a soul hurt with the possibility of never seeing a loved one again. She was gone, and here he was in this strange place. Raymond decided he would probably die here. Perhaps that would mean he could see his wife and son again soon. Once again, he felt vulnerable and unable to do anything to change his fate. He broke down at his powerlessness.

As the priest readied the knife to perform whatever savage act they had planned for Kira, gunshots and screams were heard outside the camp. The drumming stopped, and the priest looked around in confusion.

"What the hell?" Grimes asked.

The prisoners pointed toward a corner guard tower. The large, meaty body of a guard fell from the tower. Blood spurted from his neck, and his head seemed only attached to his vertebral column. More screams were heard from outside. The Aggromen rushed to open the gate and assess the commotion. Sporadic episodes of gunfire, screaming, and then silence followed.

Raymond, in his own confusion, looked up at Kira; she was still tied to the pillar but was mouthing something to him. *What is she saying?*

The priest was distracted, looking over the platform, trying to see what was happening beyond the walls.

Gunfire. Screams. Then silence.

"Doc, come on," Grimes whispered.

Raymond had not even realized that the prisoners were making their escape. They managed to undo the crude knot of vine holding their door closed. The two dozen or so prisoners were using the confusion to sneak out of the cage. Raymond looked up at Kira; she was trying to tell him they were escaping.

"Kaa-lah!" an Aggro yelled.

They were discovered. Grimes kicked the door open, and all the prisoners ran frantically in all directions. A few male prisoners overpowered an Aggro, wrestling a rifle away from him, using it to shoot a hole in his chest. The muscular brute shrugged it off and smashed his fist into one of the prisoners' faces. Another rifle shot to the Aggro's chest finally brought him down.

Raymond fought the urge to try and help the injured prisoners. The group was moving, and he was forced to step over those who had been hurt and killed. It took every ounce of his willpower not to kneel and see if he could help them, and he struggled with his inherent struggle of self-preservation and altruism.

It was mass chaos as the prisoners either tried to flee or fight. Raymond was following Grimes, who seemed to be leading him to a low part of the wall that they could climb over.

"Come on, I'll give you a boost," Grimes said.

"No, wait," Raymond said, looking up at Kira, still tied to the pole high above the fire. "We have to get her."

"What?" Grimes said. "No, no. Forget about that girl, Dr. Redmin. We must get out of here. You have to survive this; you don't understand."

Suddenly, Grimes was knocked aside. An aggrat pounced on him, digging its teeth into his shoulder.

Grimes yelled, and Raymond froze. The aggrats still drove a paralyzing fear through him. He looked around for a weapon. There was a pointed wooden stake nearby. He grabbed it, wrestling it from the ground. Meanwhile, he could hear Grimes' blood-gurgling screams. By the time Raymond had the long stake ready, Grimes was already torn to a bloody mess.

I was too late because I hesitated. He died because I didn't act quickly.

The aggrat, dripping with Grimes' blood from its teeth, turned and hissed at Raymond. He gripped the long stake tightly. He stepped backward slowly, and his hands were shaking. The aggrat crept toward him with hungry malice. He threatened the aggrat with the sharp end of the pole, but the aggrat simply grabbed the wood by the teeth, pulling it out of Raymond's hands and snapping it in its mouth. And at that moment, Raymond decided that his death by a mutant rat attack was all but certain.

Suddenly, something fell onto the aggrat. Some kind of metal object. But it was moving with ferocity and speed. Raymond stood frozen as the aggrat seemed to burst into bloody pieces. He could see it now. It was some kind of amalgamation of metal and fur ripping the mutant rat into pieces within seconds. It was the shape of… a fox.

"Swift!" Kira could finally be heard in the commotion.

Raymond stepped back in fear as the metal fox emerged from the blood-drenched rat remains. The fox was robotic but moved with the vitality of a real animal. In an instant, it leaped forward, tearing through Aggromen and aggrats with ease. Within a few seconds, it had forged a way up to Kira. Raymond figured this route was as safe as any and shadowed the little robot fox's bloody trail.

His heart was beating so loud that he had trouble thinking. His senses were awash with adrenaline as the camp was ablaze in the madness of the prisoners uprising against the Aggromen captors. He felt exhaustion and stimulation simultaneously. His legs carried him unconsciously through the pandemonium.

Raymond ran up the stairs, looking down at the chaos. Many prisoners were either shooting at the Aggromen or vainly fighting off aggrats. Torches had fallen over, and the fire was beginning to spread throughout the camp. By the time Raymond reached the top of the platform, the robot fox was undoing the vine tie from Kira's wrists.

The priest had picked up a rifle, aiming it at Kira and the robot fox. With an instinctive drive to protect her, Raymond ran full force into the priest, knocking him down as the rifle shot into the sky. The burly priest pushed him away. Raymond nearly rolled off the ledge into the fire. He took a moment to recount what he had just done, surprising himself with that act of brave stupidity.

As he tried to figure out what he could do next to combat this savage nearly twice his size, he looked up as the priest snuck up on the robot fox in a bear hug.

"Swift!" Kira yelled.

The priest struggled to contain the feral robot thrashing and biting at him. Kira grabbed the ceremonial knife intended for her and stabbed the priest in the back. He winced, throwing Swift to the side. The robot fox gave a pained hum as it rolled on the ground. The priest turned around, glaring at Kira, trying to pull the knife from his own back.

He knew he had to do something, so without much thought, Raymond leaped up, pulling the knife from the priest's back. Raymond yelled out, and in the rage of adrenaline, he stabbed the priest numerous times again in the neck. Blood sloshed and squirted.

He had never killed anyone before, and especially not with his bare hands. Although horrified at the action of doing this up-close, he was also shocked to see that the Aggroman priest turned to look Raymond in the eye. He fumed with anger as blood continued to spurt from his neck and flow down his chest. Raymond could do nothing but step back in fear.

"Raymond, get down!" Kira yelled.

Raymond jumped aside. She had picked up the rifle on the ground and shot the priest in the stomach. He grabbed his bleeding neck and abdomen simultaneously as he stumbled backward. After a few more steps backward, the priest's eyes rolled up and he went limp, falling off the ledge into the fire below.

Raymond dropped the knife he had, looking down at his blood drenched hands. He was trembling. He had contributed to killing a man, if these could be considered men. But nonetheless, he had a sense of satisfaction and relief. This feeling disturbed him. Despite the chaos below, they had narrowly escaped an up-close encounter with certain doom.

"Swift, are you alright?" Kira asked.

She came to the aid of the robot fox. Swift hummed energetically, hopping up. It briskly took off down the elevated path toward the temple entrance.

"Come on, Raymond," Kira said. "In here!" She pointed inside the temple.

Raymond looked down. The camp was ablaze with fire, and several Aggros and aggrats were bounding up the stairs to them. Panic set in, as he shuddered at the very sight of these monstrosities. He needed to be anywhere but here. Raymond picked up the knife and grabbed a torch as he followed Kira, and Swift ran into the dimly lit temple opening.

He heaved in exasperation, looking about the mysterious temple entrance. "What is this place?"

CHAPTER

NINE

B enny Fong mounted the horse and exhaled. *What are you doing, Benny?* he thought.

Casey and his Red Riders had left eastward toward the Black Forest a few hours ago. Meanwhile, some families rode northwest to Tabernacle. There they might avoid the Raider clans that would be arriving from the west. The remaining townspeople of Remnant garrisoned in their houses. Mayor Rolfe assured the townspeople that Casey would return before the Raiders came. The mayor also put out contract payments for additional Red Riders to defend the town.

Benny was not interested in the hypothetical Raider threat. Kira was in trouble, and he needed to go out there himself. He only wished he knew how to ride a horse properly.

"Okay," he whispered. "Let's go, Ella."

Ella had been Quentin Skyler's horse before he died. Quentin taught Kira how to properly ride on Ella. He even offered Benny lessons on horseback, but every time Benny declined. He was always too scared. Really, he only rode on a horse a handful of times in his life, and they were always long, slow journeys to other settlements with his family for trading.

"There you go, nice and easy," Benny said nervously as Ella trotted along in the dark.

Benny lied to his parents, ensuring them that he would follow the next caravan to Tabernacle. He said he would help the older townspeople with the trip in the morning and would then travel with them. He instead had his mind set on taking Ella out east to find Kira.

"Good, this is a good speed. We'll just stay like this and—" Benny nearly fell off the horse. "Whoa, whoa!"

Once Ella left the outer boundaries of town, she took off at full stride into the open frontier. Benny held on for dear life, clutching the reigns close and his head buried in Ella's mane. After a few minutes, he allowed himself to look up. They were riding fast, and the wind gushed past him. The clear night sky was illuminated by the moons and a billion stars.

"This is crazy," Benny said.

He laughed. The feeling was euphoric, and he allowed himself to enjoy the moment. He confidently sat up, still holding the reigns tight. He and Ella blazed across the beautiful landscape. Benny now realized why Kira always enjoyed late-night journeys to the frontier with Ella or the motorcycle.

This is freedom.

In his lonely, boring life in the settlement, Benny always thought that his only escape was daydreaming about the old world, reviving old technologies, and collecting relics of the heroes of the Dominion Wars and the AI Wars. He never imagined himself riding out into adventure himself. He was only just a natural born and, worse, a cowardly one. The world was dangerous, and he hid himself away from it for a reason.

That thought ended his moment of joy. Here he was, riding away from the protection of his town. He was by himself with no weapons. Just a horse and a bag of equipment in case he found his drone. Ella slowed to a brisk trot as Benny took time to reflect on his poorly planned adventure.

He fiddled through his bag, realizing he'd barely packed enough food and drink to last him one day. He hoped he would find Kira before then. In fact, he even preferred if Casey and the Riders found her first, then Benny would at least know she was safe and make it back in time for them all to escape to Tabernacle.

Benny found the multi-phase binoculars he had begged his dad to trade for. They were military grade, scavenged from a pirating raid, and somehow made their way through the trading route up to Remnant. They were broken, of course, but Benny tinkered with them for months, and it was in mostly working condition again.

He surveyed the dual moonlit horizon. Ella trotted along, making it difficult for him to focus on anything. He phased through night vision, infrared, and electric profile phases. Just as he was about to put the binoculars away, the infrared caught a small collection of dots on the far south horizon.

"Whoa, whoa, Ella," Benny said, trying to get her to slow down.

After many attempts, she finally came to a stop. He focused on that point in the horizon, zooming in as far as the digital binoculars would allow.

"What the hell..." he muttered.

It was a small caravan of vehicles and a tank, moving slowly. There were people sitting atop the tank, their legs hanging off the sides. Benny had seen these vehicles and designs before. His heart sank. They were Corsairs, natural borns who volunteered to help the human cause during the AI Wars decades ago. They agreed to crude cybernetic augmentation to enhance their abilities on the battlefield in a war fought between the superhuman Zeltan and the infinite terror of the Omegamind AI. Many of the natural-born volunteers were just wayward and poor teenagers. After the war, they were cast back out to the Frontier. In their rage over this betrayal, they turned to terrorizing the Green Sea as lawless pirates.

They're going to the crash site, Benny thought in horror.

He needed to get over there fast. Corsairs were always trouble. Even if the Aggros had not found Kira yet, she was going to be caught in the middle of a battle between them and the Cyborgs. Not to mention the Raider clans' inevitable arrival from the West.

For a moment, Benny considered turning around. Corsairs, Aggros, and Raiders. This was too dangerous. But Kira was still out there. He wouldn't leave her. She would do the same for him.

"Let's go," Benny said, goading the horse.

He had a new sense of urgency and determination.

"I'm coming, Kira," he said as they raced east across the Frontier.

CHAPTER

TEN

Captain Darien's boots sloshed through the wet mud as the Rangers crept further into the cave network. Backed into the cave by the unseen sniper, they discovered an underground pathway. Fireteam Charlie remained at the mouth of the cave while the rest of the squad went further to investigate.

"Captain," Lieutenant Tristan whispered, "you sure we should be going this deep in? What if the sniper collapsed the cave in? We'd all be stuck in here."

"I trust Specialist Nicholas," Darien said calmly.

As leader, he knew better than to ignore the concerns of his team members, but he also was conscious to maintain a semblance of control of the situation. He indeed trusted Nicholas' instincts, but constantly re-assessed the situation and their limited options. If he was wrong, he would take full responsibility, but he would never gamble with the lives of his soldiers.

Nicholas, their squad Recon, had a large bullet wound that tore through his thigh. He remained with Fireteam Charlie at the mouth of the cave. Even in his injured state, his heightened sense of hearing offered the cornered squad a way out. He claimed to hear running water somewhere deep in the cave. Sure enough, as

Fireteams Alpha, Bravo, and Delta went deeper into the cave, they too could hear some kind of underwater river. The water flowed downwards. They kept their lights off, relying on their night vision visors to lead their way.

"We sure could have used a Recon for this," Tristan said.

Nicholas would likely be okay, but by either bad luck or calculated manipulation, their Medic, Corporal Ryan, had perished. The bullet tore clear through his upper back and his heart. Every member of the squad was trained in advanced life support, but losing their medical specialist first was the cruelest irony. Worse yet, the bullet went through his backpack, damaging some of the resuscitative equipment they would have needed to save him.

Darien swallowed his failure. It was on him alone. He would provide Ryan the proper memorial and face the consequences. However, there was no time to wallow in self-pity. They needed to keep moving. They were being stalked.

"That couldn't have been an accident," Tristan said.

The fireteams moved in slow but purposeful movement through the pitch black. The footing was beginning to slope down and become slippery. Rocky crags and corners awaited every few feet, and Darien urged them to stay vigilant for enemies—human or wildlife.

"I don't think it was either," Darien said.

"So, you agree with me!" Tristan said.

"Dammit, keep your voice down," Darien whispered through gritted teeth. "But yes. I have a suspicion he targeted our Medic and Recon on purpose. Maybe even drove us into this cave."

"So then, why are we going deeper in?" Tristan asked. "This could be a trap."

"If it's Julian," Darien said, "stepping back out there would be worse. He could have killed you, me, and the officers. He's trying to slow down the squad. He wants to isolate us, one by one. Our best chance is to remain together."

"How can you be so sure?"

"I know him," Darien said. "He was my Commanding officer. I know how he thinks. He's testing me."

Darien was semi-confident in his assessment. He considered the possibility that he was wrong, but now was not the time to portray uncertainty to his team.

"I don't understand. Why would he be testing you? Doesn't he just want to kill us all?"

"He wants me to suffer because we left him. Because of what happened."

"Sir," Tristan said as they continued their slow descent. "I might be speaking out of place here, but what exactly happened between you two?"

Darien realized that he had held back much from the squad. During the past few weeks of training, they were only told that Julian was a former Zeltan Ranger who had gone rogue. In the past few years, he wreaked havoc on every Zeltan incursion into the Black Forest. Most squads returned to half their squad dead or seriously injured. The last Ranger squad's Captain was killed, and thus, military command appointed Darien as the ill-fated squad's new leader.

"It's a game," Darien said. "He's playing with us. I warned them. He wants me. He wants me to pay for what I did."

At this point, even the other Rangers appeared curious. They were all good soldiers. They would follow his orders to the very end. But no one had ever mentioned the obvious history between Darien and his former commanding officer, Julian. In their infinite wisdom, King Gareth and the military command thought it would be most poetic to have Darien bring Julian in for his due justice. In Darien's mind, they played right into Julian's trap.

Tristan broke the awkward silence, "Captain, what happened?"

Darien sighed. *He will never stop asking. I might as well tell them.*

"Seven years ago, Julian led our squad into the forest. He was a Captain; I was his Lieutenant. We were supposed to scout intel on the anti-air weaponry, possibly disable them to allow our air vessels to bombard the forests."

"But the Airspace Accords..." Tristan began.

"I know," Darien said. "The rumors are true. We're only holding up our end of the Accords because there are real anti-air capabilities here in the forest. Every vessel we send over is shot out of the sky from the forest."

"But I thought the Accords were just an agreement between us and the Haven androids," said Private Ethan.

"Why doesn't the Prince Council know about this?" Tristan asked.

"I guess, between us all here," Darien said, "we don't have as much control of this planet as we think we do. Someone has been shooting anti-air rockets at our ships from the forests for decades. The pirates and mercs are running rampant out on the Green Sea, and they have got our Navy chasing their tails. The rebels to the east are stretching our forces too thin. Even those rumors about the rogue AI beyond the Grey Waste might be true. Something's going on out there."

"Captain," Tristan said, "but what happened *here*, to you, to your squad seven years ago?"

Darien hesitated. He was specifically told by Zeltan High Command not to disclose the events of the failed Julian mission. After considering it for some time, especially after the ambush, he decided that he had owed more loyalty to his own squad than the military brass sitting safely miles away from here.

"When our squad first came out here," Darien began, "we were ambushed. It was the Aggros, there were hundreds of them. We fought through the forest, but we weren't prepared back then. We didn't have a plan. Julian took an explosion to his face, basically blinding him. We all were injured and tired. We lost hope. Julian wanted us to push further into the forest. He could swear we were getting closer. We were lost for days. The squad began to doubt his leadership. When he walked us into an ambush, and we lost three soldiers, the rest of the squad finally had it. It didn't happen right away, but sure enough… there was a vote of no confidence, and we acted on it."

"Mutiny?" Sergeant Barrett asked in disgust. "We didn't hear about this."

"Military Command swept it under the rug," Darien said. "If the world found out that the most elite and disciplined unit fell apart under duress, then one could make the case that even genetically perfected humans shouldn't be the ones leading this planet."

"That's...not possible," Tristan said. "What exactly happened?"

"To respect the dead," Darien said. "The long story short is that we turned on each other. We lost focus, and the squad fell apart. This forest ate us alive. I was the only one to come out with my life. I thought everyone was dead. I thought my Captain was dead. When we started hearing rumors that he was alive and murdering new Ranger squads, I knew he blamed us for leaving him here. He wants revenge on the Rangers. The Kingdom... Me."

"Captain," Marcus said. His rare participation in conversation was always a surprise. "If I may, our mission is here and now. You trained us well. We can defeat him in battle. Don't allow him to defeat you in your own thoughts."

The whole squad seemed to slow to a halt. What briefly seemed like uncharacteristic insubordination from Darien's handpicked star Vanguard was actually quite revelatory. Darien recognized it himself. The further he ventured into the forest, the surer he became that Julian was stalking them, the more distracted he became. He was afraid. The squad must have felt it. He led them down into the underground tunnels instead of devising a plan to confront Julian head-on.

"You're right, Marcus," Darien said calmly. "Thank you. I owe you all an apology."

"No apologies needed, sir," Sergeant Barrett said. "We're with you no matter what. Ain't that right, boys?"

"Hoo-ah," they all said in whispered unison.

Darien contemplated turning around. On introspection, his subconscious fear of Julian was clouding his judgement. This venture into the tunnels was foolhardy. Who knew what unnecessary dangers or even traps awaited them. He would reunite them with Fireteam Charlie at the mouth of the cave.

Dammit, he thought. *I put Fireteam Charlie in danger by leaving them there.*

"Captain?" Staff Sergeant Scott exclaimed, echoing through the cave. "What the hell is that?!"

Darien ran to the front of the squad to the end of the narrow tunnel. He stopped himself when he saw what Scott was seeing.

Tristan followed him. "What is it? What do you... What in the hell?"

Darien quickly switched off his night vision goggles. The sight before him was clear but inexplicable. The squad huddled together at the opening of the tunnel. It opened to a vast and large underground civilization.

"It's a village," Tristan said. "No, it's like a whole underground city."

The underground civilization stretched as far as the eye could see. There were mud huts and some crudely assembled stone buildings. The rocky ceiling high above them made Darien realize how far underground they had walked. Aggro savages bustled about, only illuminated by torchlight and hanging bowls of fire.

"This must be where they live," Staff Sergeant Scott said. "The Aggros live underground."

Darien was awestruck. He had heard stories of the Aggromen living within the Black Forest but had always assumed they lived a primitive lifestyle. After all, they only possessed the physical attributes of Zeltans, but were severely limited in intelligence. This vast underground city was surprising to Darien, but made sense, as the hostile forest life above would be nearly impossible for any degree of civilization to thrive.

The Aggro savages walking around seemed to have an organized system in place. They moved about in groups, trading goods and services with one another, and bartering with bits of metal and rare stones from the earth below. There was even a small market off in the corner that sold jewelry and trinkets made from natural materials found in the caves.

Darien heard gunfire in the distance, to the other side of the underground cavern. The Aggros began to grab their rifles and spears, running to the commotion.

"Fireteam Charlie," Darien said over the radio comlink. "We heard gunfire. Is that you?"

"No," First Sergeant Roland responded. "Not us. We're alright up here."

Then who is shooting? Darien wondered. "Fireteam Charlie. Meet us down here. We found something. Trap setting behind you, mark them. Proceed double column narrow corridors, watch corners."

"Acknowledged," Roland said over the comlink.

"Alright, squad," Darien said, "until rendezvous with Fireteam Charlie, stay in the shadows. Stealth procedures four-one."

The gunfire escalated in the distance.

"Someone up there is making the Aggros angry," Tristan said. "Let's hope they're on our side."

ELEVEN

Kira Skyler carefully moved through the darkness, sliding one foot after another along a narrow corridor that plunged even deeper into the depths. She held up a small torch that burned hot near her face, casting a bright light on the rough obsidian walls and glistening from glossy stalactites like beaded curtains. Water dripped from the ceiling above her head, and the path curved back toward the wall as if squeezed by some giant hand.

Her robotic fox companion scampered ahead in obscurity. Swift had night vision built into his machinery. Raymond lagged behind them, frequently losing his footing among the uneven rocks.

"Look at these engravings on the wall," Raymond said. "This must be some kind of temple."

She ran her hands along the stone pillar. Her fingers brushed over the crude carvings of human-like figures with exaggerated features and bodies. She stopped at a carving that had basic words using English etched next to them.

"They speak English?" Raymond asked.

"They spoke English once," Kira said. "Before they were cast out by the Zeltans. They used to live among them. The Zeltans decided they were too stupid and too dangerous. When a Zeltan named Joseph the Deliverer led them into this forest a hundred years ago, they proved the world wrong. They made their own culture here. When the Zeltans came into the forest to force them back into conscription as soldiers, the Aggros showed how strong they'd become and pushed them back out."

"They're huge. Of course, they pushed them back out."

"The Aggros are a little bigger than the Zeltans," Kira said. "And the Aggros adapted to this forest better. The Zeltans under King Magnus asked for volunteers from the Frontier to help root out the Aggros from the forest. My grandfather, Nathaniel Skyler, was selected for the excursion. The mission was a complete disaster, and the Zeltans never even paid the Frontier settlers for our troubles and losses."

"These Zeltans really do sound like a bunch of assholes," Raymond said.

"Even the Aggros would agree with us on that." Kira sighed.

They moved quickly through the mysterious temple, following Swift's purposeful prowl. Far behind them, they could hear the echoed grunts of Aggros. The temple was a giant maze of narrow hallways and dim-lit storerooms. They had not encountered any signs of life for quite some time.

Kira whispered, "Swift, did you find someth—"

Raymond bumped into her from behind, nearly setting her hair on fire with her torch.

"Hey!" Kira pushed him off.

"I'm sorry," Raymond said. "I... wait, what is this place?"

Swift looked back at them, humming and wagging his tail.

Kira lifted her torch, illuminating the large room. There was a small, crudely built rail track running across the center. One end came down from a dark hallway, and the other dipped down and disappeared into blackness. A small cart was at the center of the tracks, with a height of about shoulder length and wide enough to house the three of them. Swift hummed at the cart, motioning toward it.

Kira knew to trust Swift's instincts, but the room and its exit into the unknown were ominous. Perhaps with his night vision, Kira thought, Swift didn't comprehend the spookiness of the situation.

"I'm guessing he wants us to get in?" Raymond said.

"Yeah," Kira said, lighting some torches on the wall to better see the room, "but where does it go?"

They peered into the black void of the outgoing tunnel. Before they could explore the room further, they heard the grunting of Aggros and hisses of aggrats approaching from the entrance.

Flashbacks to moments before, when she was nearly sacrificed and killed, flooded through her head. They needed to get away from these savages by any means possible.

"We have to go," Kira said. "Swift, get in!"

The robotic fox leaped into the cart as gunshots erupted from the hallway behind them. Kira yelped in surprise as a bullet ricocheted past her. She scrambled behind to the other side of the cart as Raymond climbed in. She patted herself, checking whether she was hit. She trembled in relief when she realized she had escaped an untimely fate.

"Kira!" Raymond said. "Get in!"

Raymond leaned over the side of the cart, firing his rifle with a smooth succession of steady pings and booms, filling the room with its echoes.

Kira looked around. *We're dead in the water if we don't get this thing moving.*

She grabbed the edge of the cart and began pulling it sideways. It rolled along the tracks surprisingly well. As she built up the cart's momentum, Raymond continued to duck and shoot at the Aggros. Suddenly, a giant aggrat came around the side of the cart, snapping at her. She jumped away at the last minute.

Its monstrous face and teeth were something out of nightmares. She could only stumble backwards in fear, grabbing at anything around her to fight off this demonic beast baring its sharp teeth dripping with hungry saliva.

"Ray!" Kira yelled.

Raymond leaned over to her side and fired a well-placed bullet into the Aggrat's neck, stunning it for a moment. By now, the cart was rolling along, and Kira was exposed. Without the cover of the cart, she saw three Aggromen across the room, shooting at her from the hallway.

Without much thought, she stumbled toward the cart, which was nearly at the downslope of the exit track. She felt another bullet whiz by her, but just kept running. She saw Raymond continuing to shoot up ahead. He ran out of ammunition and reached out his hand.

In a desperate attempt, she lunged forward, grabbing his hand at the last moment as the cart dipped into the darkness. He pulled her close to the cart, and she grabbed onto the side for dear life, throwing a leg over the side. Her body hit the cart with a thud, but her adrenaline shielded her from any sensation of pain. She used every ounce of her energy to pull herself in.

The cart zigged and zagged, rumbling along the tracks. Kira was half in the cart, half out. A sudden jolt threw her up into the air, she felt her heart leap up into her throat. She could swear she had fallen off.

"We've got you, we've got you!" Raymond said.

Swift grabbed her pantleg with his teeth, and Raymond pulled her into the cart. She hit the bottom with a thud. Another hard turn threw them all against the side. There was just barely enough space to fit. They were speeding into a pitch-black void.

When she had a firm grasp of the sides, Kira peered her head out of the cart. She heaved in exasperation but remained hyperaware of the situation. They were approaching the end of the dark tunnel. The track began to level, but she wondered whether they would ultimately fall off the edge to their death.

"Hold on." She gritted her teeth, clutching the side of the cart tight.

The cart barreled through the end of the tunnel, opening to a vast underground cavern. Kira looked over the edge, first checking whether they were still even on a track. Indeed, the cart continued to rumble along, but she could not believe the view below her.

"What the hell?" Raymond said.

Kira looked over the edge. "What is this?"

A vast underground city of crudely built clay houses lay beneath them. Rough-walled, earthen homes with ragged roofs and irregular windows were scattered around a wide-open central clearing. Ladders of twisted vines and rough-hewn planks dotted the ceiling high above, their precarious strands giving way to gigantic rocks that jutted out like stalagmites. Their chipped edges looked sharp and threatening, glinting in the light of oil lamps as they swayed, illuminating the primitive civilization below. The track hugged the rocky wall in a wide spiral.

She breathed in air that was hot and moist. It smelled slightly metallic, and she wondered if there was some sort of smelting going on nearby. Her father had dabbled in smelting, and she had once found the metallic smell comforting. *What an odd moment to think about her father,* she thought. What an odd moment to feel relief while fear constricted her bones.

"This must be where they live," Kira said in wonder.

The sounds of automatic gunfire and explosions began to echo throughout the vast cavern. Kira and Raymond ducked instinctively. They stared at each other, heads on the floor of the cart, covered under their arms.

"Are they shooting at us?" Raymond asked. "I can't tell."

"I'll check," Kira said, pulling herself up to peek out.

"Wait, no!" Raymond said, pulling her back down.

She shoved him off. "Hold on... Raymond, look!"

He reluctantly looked over the side as the cart continued its long tour along the sides of the underground city. Below them, the Aggros were engaged in a heavy gunfight against a small group of caped soldiers wearing helmets and armor. From the cart's vantage point, Kira, Raymond, and Swift watched the entire battle unfold.

"Who are those guys?" Raymond asked.

Kira's gut filled with dread. "Zeltans, Raymond. Those are Zeltan soldiers."

Large and heavily equipped soldiers rapidly stormed through the Aggro town. Her eyes could barely keep up with their movements. There was no doubt about it. They looked and moved like the fabled super-soldiers she had grown to hate. They wore finely designed capes over their decorated armor. The Zeltans had big frames but were not grotesquely brutish like the Aggros.

She watched the unorganized Aggros step into their traps. The Zeltans would fire from behind cover, drawing the Aggros to the position. With flawless execution and lightning speed, other soldiers appeared from nowhere, taking down the Aggro targets, then disappearing into smoke within seconds. One part of the city was filled with smoke, then another with gunfire. It seemed like there were hundreds of Zeltans, but Kira surmised there were only a dozen or so. What began as a feeling of disgust turned into fascination. As much as she hated to admit it, the stories were true: They were *superhuman*.

Some of the Aggros began to retreat up a walkway out of the city. There were women and children, but most of the children were larger built than normal human adults. The women and children even carried weapons themselves, shooting at the soldiers as they were fleeing. She shook herself away from watching the battle when she felt the cart begin to turn away from the wall.

"We're coming to the end," Kira said.

The cart began to slow down as the track leveled out, leading them to the center of the underground town.

"It's leading us right to them," Raymond said. "Get your head down."

Kira, Raymond, and Swift lay flat on the floor of the cart as it chugged through the thick smoke created by the skirmish. The creaking of the old wood beneath them was almost drowned out by the roar of chaos all around. As the cart came to a stop, the smoke began to clear above them. The thick smoke from the skirmish choked their lungs, filling their nostrils with the pungent scent of burning oil and iron. They could hear the voices of the Zeltans nearby.

"Clear out, two one five," the voice yelled. "Thermo, four corner spread from Alpha position."

Kira held her breath, hearing her heart beating. She looked over at Raymond, who was breathing heavily. She put a finger to her lips and hoped the soldiers would pass. After a few minutes, she no longer heard the soldiers' voices or footsteps. She let out a quiet sigh of relief.

"You two in the cart," a voice yelled. "You have till the count of three until we toss a grenade in there!"

A wave of dread flooded into Kira's heart. She processed the situation as quickly as possible. The Zeltans were dismissive toward "normal" humans to a fault, but they would be better off exposing themselves than being mistaken for Aggros.

"Wait!" Kira yelled. "We're not Aggro! We're human, we're natural borns."

"What are you doing?" Raymond said.

Without answering, she lifted her hands, standing up in the cart.

"Sir," one of the soldiers said. "We've got NB's here. Step out of the cart. Slow. Real slow."

Kira began stepping out of the cart. She resigned to the gamble that that was the safest bet. For as cynical as she thought of the Zeltans, these seemed like trained soldiers. They would take them prisoner first, and she would have to figure out a plan of escape later. Raymond slowly followed her lead, as the soldiers had their guns trained on them. Kira kept her hands high in the air.

"Hey," one of the soldiers said. "Sir, two NB's confirmed and a bot. They're with a bot."

Swift was still in the cart, looking up at Kira. He hummed cautiously.

"The captain said to get them into one of these huts," one of the soldiers said. "There could still be Aggros lurking around."

Hands still in the air, Kira and Raymond were led into one of the clay houses. Swift followed closely behind, but Kira could see the wary looks that the soldiers were giving Swift. One had his gun specifically trained on the robotic fox, and Kira worried for his safety.

Once inside the house, the soldiers were tending to two of their wounded. A blue-caped soldier stood near the fire, examining the carvings on the clay wall. He turned and studied his new arrivals.

He was tall and handsome, with brown hair that framed his sharp jawline. His regal presence commanded the attention of everyone in the room. He wore a blue military uniform with padded armor and a cape draped over his shoulders, emblazoned with an emblem of allegiance. His pale, grey eyes seemed to pierce into the soul of whoever he looked at as if he could see deep into their minds. He had an air of wisdom about him but also carried himself like someone who had seen battle many times before. He nodded at Kira and Raymond before turning back towards the fire.

"So, what are two natural borns and a robot...fox doing so deep in the Black Forest?"

Kira remained silent. Raymond gulped. Swift was humming to signal danger.

The blue-caped commanding officer walked closer.

"Sir," a younger, blonde-haired soldier next to him said. He carried an ornate saber at his side. "Be careful. That bot looks dangerous."

"It's okay, Lieutenant," the blue-caped commander said. "I don't believe our new friends would be so foolish to attack us here. Not when we have so much to learn from each other." He walked closer to them, and Swift hummed menacingly.

"Swift," Kira said. "It's alright...not now, at least."

The blue-caped man's interest was piqued. "It's your pet?"

"No," Kira said with as much courage as she could summon. "His name is Swift."

"Okay then," the commander said. "Hello there, Swift. My name is Captain Darien."

TWELVE

Raymond Redmin wanted to feel apprehensive and distrusting of his new hosts, but there were injuries that required his attention. His focus narrowed and shifted to the use of his medical expertise. He knelt next to one of the wounded soldiers with a bullet wound through his inner right thigh. There was a tourniquet tied tight over it, but blood continued to saturate through.

"So, you're a doctor?" Captain Darien asked him.

"Yeah," Raymond said, not looking up. "I was. Do you guys have any supplies? Kira, you'd better get them up to date."

One of the soldiers handed Raymond one of the supply packs. Inside, there were bandages, surgical tools, and even an IV kit with bags of what he suspected was fresh plasma. He grabbed a tourniquet, wrapping it around the soldier's bicep as he prepared to place an IV.

"Hey," the blonde-haired Lieutenant said as he harshly grabbed Raymond's wrist.

"Lieutenant Tristan," Darien said calmly. "It's okay."

Raymond gave Tristan a harsh look and snapped his hand away. The wounded soldier was becoming pale. He was moaning, barely responsive to painful stimuli. His eyes were closed, and Raymond suspected he would be completely unconscious from the blood loss. He could barely feel a palpable pulse. Raymond placed the IV and held the bag of red fluid up.

"I'm assuming this is plasma?" Raymond asked the soldiers huddled in the room, all watching him cautiously.

"Factor Enhanced Concentrate," Darien said with a curious look.

"What the hell is that?" Raymond asked. "Whatever. If it's O neg blood, I'm hooking it up. This man is losing blood fast, and I'll need to hang this, then try to stop whatever is bleeding here."

Raymond had no problem assuming authority, even to strangers. He knew that in time-sensitive situations such as this, someone had to step up and take charge.

"Lieutenant," Darien said, "hold the bag for the doctor."

"Are you serious? I—" Tristan said.

"Until we find something to hang it on," Darien said. "And you, your name is Kira?"

"I have nothing to say to you," Kira replied.

Darien sighed. "Very well then."

"You NB's better show the captain some respect," Tristan said, holding up the bag of plasma.

"Kira," Raymond said, with a pair of clamps held between his teeth as he undid the tourniquet. "Just tell them what's going on. They might be able to help us get out of here."

"The doctor's right, Kira," Darien said, sitting on the stone-carved chair at the table. "This isn't an interrogation. I'm just curious how two natural borns and an android found themselves so deep inside the Black Forest."

"I'm from the Frontier," Kira said reluctantly. "Remnant. The scarlet fever's made it to the town. I came here to find Guaritore, the healer. We need medicine. We came looking for help because we sure weren't going to get it from you Zeltans."

Raymond looked back briefly. Darien was sitting back in the chair, nodding and studying Kira. Raymond sensed her boiling animosity and rage. She seemed to hold a contempt for the Zeltans that was palpable in her every action.

"I understand your frustration," Darien said.

"No, you don't," Kira said. "And I'm not frustrated. We're done being frustrated. We lived our whole lives out in the Frontier while you all live in your high castles. No, we're not frustrated. We're dying. And we've learned to expect nothing from you. Zeltans only care about themselves. We don't even consider you human beings anymore."

"Alright, that's enough," Tristan said through gritted teeth, squeezing the bag in his hand.

"Hey, hey," Raymond said. "Stop squeezing it like that. You're gonna blow the line."

"You better watch your mouth, NB." Tristan glowered down at Raymond. "Do you have any idea—"

Raymond defiantly stared back at the blonde soldier. He would not be talked down to like that.

"Tristan, please," Darien said, with a hand up.

Tristan scowled, looking away.

Darien turned back to Kira. "My only question would be, if you have an illness running through your town, then why would you need to travel into the Black Forest if you already have a doctor?"

As much as he tried paying attention to Darien and Kira's conversation, Raymond was busy sifting through the wounded soldier's muscles and fascia, seemingly as sturdy as steel. Eventually, he discovered the source of the bleeding. It was likely the descending branch of the medial circumflex artery. The femoral artery itself was luckily intact. Blood was everywhere, but he could see the vessels well. The soldier had long since lost consciousness and was not struggling. He could tie the artery off, and the leg would still have adequate collateral blood flow. He palpated the distal pedal pulses again to make sure he had an acceptable pulse.

It was medical emergencies like this that brought Raymond into somewhat of a subconscious flow state. He hadn't practiced in a long time since before his cancer diagnosis. There was something familiar and satisfying about it. His hands felt like they moved on their own, and his brain on autopilot, while he satisfyingly perused his prior knowledge to guide his actions. It was bliss.

"Well," Raymond said, wiping some of the blood that had spurted onto his face. "We're actually not together. Not sure if you saw, but I fell out of that spaceship that came out of the sky."

Darien, who had been calm and stoic this whole time, appeared caught off guard. His brow furrowed, and he sat forward in the chair.

Raymond looked at Darien directly. "I gotta tie off this man's medical circumflex artery right now, but the short story is that I was frozen on Earth a few hundred years ago, and now I'm here. I'm sure you have questions but let me get to this."

The room was palpably silent with shock. Raymond needed to focus, and he allowed them to stew with that information while he worked. He took a deep breath, clamping the vessel just proximal to the laceration. He took some sutures from the kit and began to tie off the artery.

"Is... this true?" Darien asked.

"It is. He fell out of the sky. I saw it happen," Kira said. "The Aggros picked him up and the others in the ship."

"There's more of them?" Tristan asked.

"Well, I'm not sure how many are still left," Kira said. "The Aggros took us to one of their camps. They were sacrificing people. We escaped, but I saw them kill a lot of the people from the ship. It's just Raymond, Swift, and me."

"And this android," Darien said. "From North Haven?"

"Uh...yeah," Kira said, her voice trailing off.

Although focused on his work, Raymond noticed that she was being purposefully avoidant regarding Swift. He remembered what Kira had told him earlier during the march to the Aggro camp. According to the North Haven Accords, all existing androids needed to be registered with the Zeltans, or they would be destroyed. Her grandfather discovered the android fox and confirmed he was not registered. They had been harboring Swift illegally for years. If the Zeltans ever found out, they would destroy him.

"Captain Darien, is it?" Raymond wanted to change the subject. "The real question is how we're gonna get out of here."

"Don't worry, doctor," Darien said. "We're scouting possible exits as we speak. I do expect the Aggros to return before then, though."

"Then we need to get out of here," Kira said.

"I'm aware," Darien said. "We need to make sure we have several options for an exit. It's not just the Aggros we have to worry about."

"Not just the Aggros?" Kira asked.

"Leave that to us," Darien said. "Please, doctor, just help my men, and I promise we will escort you out of the forest. I imagine the Kingdom would be very curious to meet a man out of time and far from home."

"Wait, no," Kira said. "He's coming back to Remnant. We need him to help my friends...my brother. They're all sick. We need him."

"There are more important things than worrying about Frontier NB's," Tristan said. "This one could be the key to connecting back to Earth. We need to get him back to the Sovereign Council."

"Did you even hear me?" Kira said, stepping forward defiantly. "I said we're dying. People will die. We need him."

Tristan scoffed. "Watch your tone with me, NB. I'm a prince. In fact, a ranger *and* a prince, and—"

"Enough," Darien said. "We'll figure this out later. Kira, find something to hang the plasma on, then help the doctor with what he needs. Lieutenant, check with Sergeant Marcus and sitrep the exit points."

By now, Raymond had successfully tied off the artery. He looked up at Tristan's saber hanging off his belt.

"Hey, wait," Raymond said. "Give me that sword."

"You must think I'm an idiot," Tristan said. "I would never give you my—"

"Lieutenant," Darien said, "give him your saber."

Tristan grumbled, reluctantly removing the sword and handing it to Raymond. He pulled out his ornately decorated pistol, aiming it at Raymond's head for good measure. "If you try anything."

Somehow, a pistol aimed at his head barely rattled Raymond now. His family was gone, everyone he ever knew and loved were gone, and he was living in a surreal nightmare. A swift exit from this madness would be blessing. In the meantime, he would continue trying to save this injured soldier.

"Relax," Raymond said, getting up. His legs had fallen asleep while he was kneeling. They were both numb and aching. His whole body ached. He took the sword, placing the end over the fire. Once it glowed hot and red, he brought it down sideways over his vessel repair. It singed the tissue and blood to a fragrant crisp. This would ensure hemostasis from any bleeding capillaries. When he was finished, he put the sword back on the floor.

"Wow," Kira said. "You fixed it."

The thigh was drenched in blood, swimming in a pool of congealed crimson, but the profuse bleeding had stopped. Raymond took the last pads from the kit and placed them over the repaired wound. The air was thick with the smell of singed flesh, like overly burnt steak on a hot grill. It stung Raymond's nostrils and brought back vivid memories of medical school, hours spent in the operating room. The smell was the same as it was all those years ago: antiseptic overtones with a hint of charred skin.

"Okay," he said. "Now I just need to sew the skin back up. It'll be rough. Someone will eventually have to open this up again for a formal repair, but it needs to be closed if we need to move him around."

"Well done, doctor," Darien said.

"Thank you," Raymond said, turning to Tristan. "Now would you mind getting that gun out of my face?"

THIRTEEN

Benny Fong looked around for something to tie the horse to. When he could not find anything, he placed a large Martian red rock onto the rope. He hoped Ella would stay put while he scouted the ship crash site. He paced around the rocky desert terrain, looking at the horizon in all directions. He was much further from home than he had ever been on his own.

After some time reconciling with his self-doubts, Benny climbed up a small hill and lay on his belly. He fiddled with the binoculars until he could find some decent imaging. It was just before dawn, and he identified cyborg Corsairs starting to explore the outside of the ship.

They had a unique electric profile. Most humans tended to show up on electric profile visualizers with bright concentrations in the brain, spine, and heart, with dendritic lines emanating to the extremities. The cyborgs' profiles were each wildly different. Some had bionic arms, others with complete overhauls of the cardiovascular system to artificial engines. He heard stories about how some were more machine than man but wondered what would drive any man to undergo such crude experimentation.

"Don't move or say a damn thing," a familiar voice said behind him.

Benny froze in place, and terror washed over him.

"Turn around, nice and easy, Fong."

When he finally summoned the courage, he placed the binoculars neatly on the ground and turned around with his hands in the air. It was Casey Jarrett and his lackeys Toby and Pete looking back at him and grinning. Casey had his signature revolver pistol aimed right at Benny's head.

"God damn, Fong," Casey said, shaking his head. "What in the hell are you doing out here?"

"I came to help." Benny's voice quivered with uncertainty.

Toby and Pete looked at each other and chuckled. Casey holstered his pistol and grabbed Benny's shirt.

"I told you," Casey said, with his face close to Benny's. "You're no good out here. You're just gonna get yourself killed."

Casey's breath smelled of lingering harsh pipe smoke. Burning harsh plants smelled sweet and pungent at the same time. Regardless, the smell always made Benny feel lightheaded.

"There's Corsairs," Benny said, pointing to the distance. "Cyborgs. I saw them."

Casey shoved him off, laughing. "You don't think we know that? Fong, we've been out here for hours watching them. Then you come strolling by like some goddamn tourist."

"But Kira could be out there," Benny said, brushing himself off.

"And what do you expect us to do about that?" Casey asked. "There's a whole army of Corsairs out there. We ain't shit against that. We need to send word to the other Red Riders, let 'em know what the deal is. We should ride back to town before the Raiders show up from the west."

"Wait," Benny said. "We can't leave without Kira."

"Listen, these ain't a small group of Aggie savages. Those cyborgs, they're organized. They have vehicles. Shit, they got tanks. The way I see it, we'd be safest relocating to Tabernacle. We'll let the Corsairs and the Raiders fight it out. This one ain't our fight. Come on, Fong, let's go. Before you make yourself look even more like an idiot."

As Casey and his lackeys started walking down the hill, Benny conceded defeat. He felt like crying, but he had embarrassed himself enough. He followed them, thinking about how stupid his plan was. He wondered what his friends and family would think of him putting his life in danger for no good reason. He hoped that when he arrived back at Remnant, Kira would be there, safe. He wondered if she would be glad that he came after her or if she would laugh at him like Casey and the others did. Regardless, this was inevitably going to be another embarrassing attempt in a lifetime of full of them.

This was a stupid idea. Benny thought, *What was I even thinking...*

As he amassed his brain full of paranoid and embarrassing thoughts, they went around to the corner where he left Ella.

"Hey," Benny said. "I thought I left the horse here."

"You lost your horse, Fong?" Toby asked mockingly.

"Heh, can't you do anything right?" Pete said.

"Shut up, shut up," Casey whispered. "No, Fong's right. The horse was here, and there's new foot markings." He went for his pistol.

"I wouldn't do that if I were you," said a voice behind them.

Benny turned, and his arms shot up immediately. Two men were standing there. One man had an arm stretched out, pointed at them. His entire arm was a gun barrel. It attached to the stump of his shoulder, horrifyingly affixed to several wires and tubes to his chest, neck, and arm. He had metal apertures and plating on his entire left side, from his face down to his leg. Only the right side of his head had hair, and it was long, dirty, and wavy, combed over metal domed scalp of the left side.

The other man was stroking Ella's mane. This man had two robotic monocles for eyes, and his hands were skeleton-like machinery. He was short and hunched like a conniving robotic pill bug.

"Now," the cyborg with the gun arm said, "before I turn you all into jam, why don't you play nice cowboys and put your little guns on the ground?"

Toby was the first to take his gun and put it on the ground. Reluctantly, Casey followed suit, gritting his teeth. Pete was shaking, his fingers touching the gun at his holster like he was in a duel. He stood, quivering hand at his hip, staring at the cyborg.

"Don't be stupid, boy..." the monocled cyborg said.

"Pete, don't," said Casey with his hands up in the air without looking away from the cybernetic mercenaries.

In the blink of an eye, Pete drew his gun at the cyborgs. Benny winced, shutting his eyes. He heard a large blast erupt from the cyborg's arm like cannon fire.

After a few moments, Benny opened his eyes. Pete was sprawled on the ground, many feet away from where he was previously standing. The cyborg arm cannon had blown a hole wide open through Pete's torso, nearly leaving the body in two separate pieces.

Casey remained standing, hands up, looking at the ground stoically. Toby stood wide-eyed in terror.

A deep sense of dread washed over Benny. The world seemed to pause at that moment. The horrifying image of Pete's gored body was burned into Benny's mind. He began to hyperventilate and panic.

"What about you, cowboy?" the cyborg asked Casey. "You gonna make some moves too?"

Casey picked his head up and gave the cyborg a menacing look.

"Go ahead, my friend," the other cyborg standing with the horse said. "Armory loves target practice."

"I sure do," Armory said with a grin.

Casey shook his head slowly, kicking his pistol forward slowly.

"That's good news, good news," said the other cyborg. "We got ourselves three prisoners and a horse. Blackheart's gonna be happy about that."

Benny's heart sank. *Blackheart.* That name was something you would only hear in travelers' stories.

Casey looked up. "Blackheart?" His voice surrendered a sense of vulnerability and fear.

"Oh yeah," Armory said. "Blackheart came himself to claim the ship. I guess you could say we're expanding the business to looting spaceships now."

Blackheart's reputation preceded him. He was the most notorious cyborg pirate on the Green Sea. Even the Zeltans feared him. He had the largest following of the Corsairs and was one of the staunchest leaders of the pirate movement following their split with the Zeltans after the AI Wars.

And now, Benny, Casey, and Toby were his prisoners.

FOURTEEN

Captain Darien watched curiously as Raymond and Kira hoisted Recon Specialist Nicholas closer to the fire where he would be warm. They attached the bag of plasma to a jagged edge in the clay wall. Nicholas was breathing but pale and resting in deep slumber at approximately the edge of death.

The small clay hut, lit by a fire of the hearth, was quiet and allowed Darien to think. The walls of the room were bare but for two hanging scrolls and a bladed club mounted on one wall. The soft light of the fire illuminated the dimly lit room where Darien sat quietly, his back against the far wall.

He had so many questions for the doctor. *What was Earth like? Did he have any idea why he was here? Did he know why they abandoned Mars two centuries ago?* Darien pushed these thoughts aside, remembering his primary responsibility to his squad. They needed his full attention to get out of this situation alive.

The squad was positioned all over this mysterious, small, underground village. He commissioned Fireteam Delta to provide rooftop watch. There were several entryways into the underground city. They were all openings high up on the rock walls, only accessible via crudely carved-out stairways. Darien suspected the

Aggros could come barging through one or more of those entryways at any moment, and they needed to be ready.

He had put his team into a precarious position. They were in an unknown place with no radio signal available for backup. It would not even arrive in time. His mind paced furiously, calculating the best possible solution to get his team out alive. The weight of leadership was maddeningly heavy, but he had to stay alert and ready.

Meanwhile, Fireteam Delta moved from house to house, making sure no Aggros lingered. So far, only dead Aggro warriors littered the ground. The women and children had fled. Despite Tristan's protests, Darien made the call not to attack them, although even the children had been firing weapons. Regardless, Darien wanted to maintain some semblance of honor. If they lost their lives here today, they would at least not lose their dignity.

Fireteam Bravo was depleted. Nicholas nearly bled to death from the bullet wound to his thigh. Corporal Ryan was dead, a sniper bullet tearing straight through his chest. Staff Sergeant Scott met an Aggro face-to-face during the village invasion. The Aggro had been lying on the ground injured but grabbed Scott's leg and wrestled him to the ground. Before Sergeant Marcus came over to blast the Aggro savage's head off, Sergeant Scott's face was already smashed in.

Two fatalities. That was unacceptable. The twelve remaining Zeltans had no time to grieve or process the losses. They were deep in enemy territory. Darien sent Marcus to investigate a peculiar rail system leading to a dark tunnel on the far side of the underground city. It differed from the primitive wood-based cargo rail that Raymond and Kira arrived in. This one was made of metal, polished, and smooth. There was a platform at the end, suggesting it was possibly a means of transportation. Marcus had ventured into the pitch-black tunnel where the railway led but remained in frequent radio contact.

"I'm so thirsty....and hungry," Kira muttered.

"I saw a basin of water over there," Raymond said. "But who knows what's in that. You'd better try to boil the water over the fire before we try to drink it." He slumped against the wall, sighing in exhaustion.

Darien pitied the natural borns. He remembered how often they were required to eat and drink. Zeltans could function at optimal performance for weeks without food. Their requirements for water were minimal. Sleep and fatigue were barely an issue. For decades, they had been at war with AI armies that required none altogether. To keep up with the enemy AI, the Zeltans felt obligated to push human capabilities to their maximum potential.

"Doctor," Darien said, pulling out a few meal bars from a pouch hanging from his belt. "Here, take these."

He watched as Raymond and Kira looked at the bars suspiciously. Kira took one, sniffing it. It felt like feeding animals in the wild. He felt a duty to care for these natural born creatures, but he felt that his compassion was misplaced. These were *people*, not animals.

"What are they?" Raymond asked.

"Relax, Doctor," Darien said. "It's food. I'm not trying to poison you. You can eat them."

Kira ravenously began to eat, sitting down on the ground contently. She proceeded to boil the water over the fire as she ate.

Darien smiled in brief amusement. He was internally so distraught after seeing his men injured and killed, that he barely allowed himself a moment of levity.

Raymond sat at the table with Darien and began to eat. "So why are you here?"

"Well, Doctor," Darien responded, "I believe I should be asking *you* that question."

Raymond gave a tired smile as he chomped through the chewy, protein-rich bar. "Well, I told you how I ended up here. I just woke up on that ship, and it crashed here. I really have no idea. One minute, I'm on Earth; the next, I'm on Mars in another time." Raymond shook his head. "But what I meant was, what are a bunch of soldiers doing here? Kira said you're all from a faraway Kingdom or something like that and that no one ever comes to this forest?"

"Well, technically," Darien said, leaning back against the wall, "this entire planet is claimed by the Zeltan Kingdom. We have just found certain areas too much of a risk to visit regularly."

"That's bullshit, you know that right?" Kira said with her mouth full.

Darien smiled sadly. "Bullshit indeed. In truth, Doctor, we don't have as much control over the areas outside the Golden Plains as we would like the rest of the world to believe. This forest, in particular, has defeated many previous Ranger Squads."

"Aren't you guys supposed to be superhumans or something?" Raymond asked, with a mouth full of chewy food. "No offense, but you all seem the same to me. You bleed red just like we do. I expected superpowers or something."

"Well," Darien said. "Everything is relative, isn't it?"

Darien's comlink blared.

"Captain!" Private David voice yelled through the device. "They're here. They're coming from all sides!"

Darien shot up in his chair. "Doctor, you and the girl stay here. Get Specialist Nicholas ready to move." He pressed his comlink to radio all members of his squad. "Contraction suppression to my position. Pair up and mark targets."

"What's going on?" Raymond said.

Darien had to be decisive. Every moment counted. He had rehearsed several plans of action, but the situation was likely to change by the moment. They needed to respond the threat quickly.

"Get ready to move out; stay close." Darien said to Raymond, "Your priority is Specialist Nicholas."

"We need weapons," Kira said, grabbing the injured Specialist Nicholas' automatic rifle and leaving him his pistol. Raymond picked up the deceased Sergeant Scott's automatic rifle and pistol.

"Oh... do you two know how to use firearms?" Darien asked reluctantly.

Kira pulled the clip out of the rifle, checking the ammo. She popped it back in, sighting the gun. She walked past Darien without answering.

"Very well then," Darien said.

Raymond grinned, slinging the rifle over his shoulders. He went to place Nicholas on a fur rug on the ground to slide him out of the house.

"Marcus," Darien said into the comlink. "Sitrep."

"Sir," Marcus said, radioing from his scouting of the mysterious new underground railroad. "Nothing so far. This tunnel goes straight for miles. No heat signatures or electric profiles."

That's it, that's our exit. We'll need to move the group toward there.

"Thank you, Sergeant," Darien said. "Return to rally point. Okay, squad, scout the weakest exit point. Mobile maneuvers two-two eight, with one full-in-cap and two escort modification."

"What's the plan, Darien?" Raymond asked as he and Kira began to drag Nicholas across the ground on the rug.

"There are only a few ways out," Darien said. "We're going toward the one of least resistance and apply maximum firepower. We're going to fight our way out of here."

CHAPTER

FIFTEEN

Raymond Redmin dragged the soldier named Nicholas across the floor. He used a fur rug to pull him from underneath. Kira tried to remove as much extraneous weight from the injured man as possible. The Zeltans were much larger than the average human. Raymond's thighs burned with lactic acid, just getting him to the doorway. A crescendo of gunfire erupted outside. His heart beat with both physical exertion and looming fear. He was never trained to save people in a warzone.

"What's the plan, Captain?" Raymond said, standing up from a squat, already exhausted.

Darien had his back to the wall, peeking out of the doorway, listening to chatter over his earpiece. He held up a finger. "Wait until I give you the signal. You both take Specialist Nicholas and follow me close. Stay close to me, alright?"

"I can help fight," Kira said, readying her rifle and stepping toward the doorway.

"No." Darien said, pointing at Nicholas. "You need to help the doctor get him out of here."

Kira narrowed her eyes, gritting her teeth.

"Hey," Darien leaned in. "Please."

Kira looked at the unconscious and injured Nicholas, then to Raymond, who nodded. She scoffed and threw the rifle over her shoulder, then grabbed the other corner of the rug.

"Okay," Darien said, tossing a pair of smoke grenades out of the doorway. "Ready... Now!"

Darien pivoted around the doorway, firing his assault rifle into the air. The gunfire spurted out a wild, high-pitched hiss of fire that bellowed into the air, followed by an earth-shaking boom that vibrated the walls of the room. Raymond yelped in response, muffling his ears with his hands as each deafening impact of gunfire threatened to burst his eardrums.

"Let's go!" Darien yelled, pulling Raymond's hands off his ears and placing them on the rug to pull. "Let's go, let's go!"

Raymond's heart jumpstarted with a bolus of adrenaline. He and Kira yanked the rug below Nicholas with all their might. He was backpedaling blindly through the smoke. He could hear Darien just behind him, continuously firing his weapon and yelling commands to his team.

"Watch your step, watch your step!" Darien yelled back.

Kira stumbled, but Darien picked her up immediately. Raymond looked around him. Gray smoke surrounded them, but flashes of gunfire and explosions were everywhere. He felt like he was caught in the dark cloud of a thunderstorm. He could do nothing except continue to backpedal and pull. Darien would occasionally appear from out of the maelstrom and grab him to redirect their course.

It felt like a living nightmare that he was trapped in. The dense gray smoke mixed with flashes of orange and red explosions, hot and bright against the cool palette of smoke. The smell of burning gunpowder filled Raymond's nostrils as he stumbled backward, and he could taste the acrid taste of ash from the explosions on his tongue. Everywhere, explosions were searing through the air, shaking the ground and vibrating through Raymond's body. Screams and shouts of orders, commands, and warnings floated through the smoke-filled air as they made their way through the perilous underground landscape.

This seemed to last for an eternity. In the chaos, Raymond was physically exhausted, but his body somehow continued to pull the several-hundred-pound injured superhuman through the miracle of sheer adrenaline. Kira looked like she was struggling more than he was. He had to pick her up after a nearby explosion rocked her to the ground.

"We're almost there, we're almost—" Darien yelled. "Dammit, stop. Turn around, turn around! Heavy enemy presence clock five, request cover ordinance!"

Darien pulled them behind a clay hut. The black smoke of cover began to dissipate. Raymond could finally see their situation. There were hundreds of Aggros spilling in from every orifice of the underground cavern's walls.

The cavern walls rose to an impressive height of hundreds of feet, almost as tall as skyscrapers. Holes in the jagged stone served as windows for Aggros, who peered out before they opened fire. Bursts of gunpowder illuminated the darkness with sparks.

"Oh my god," Raymond said.

Kira already pulled her rifle out and began shooting. They were pressed against the wall of a clay hut with some overhead cover and the cover of another wall to the left. They were exposed to their front and right. Darien continued to fire his automatic rifle forward while Kira was shooting around the corner. The bullets pelted close against the wall overhead.

A few strides in front of them was the metal railway. It did not seem like the Aggros built this one. The railway resembled a subway track that reminded Raymond of Earth. It led into a dark cave, but there was no train on its tracks. This must have been the exit Darien was suggesting.

"Sergeant Marcus," Darien yelled into his earpiece. "I need cover fire, strobe mark one four!"

Suddenly, a Zeltan soldier, much larger and bulkier than the others, burst out of the dark tunnel. He was completely covered in a gray metallic helmet and full body armor. He moved like a video put on fast-forward. Shooting a large machine gun while running, he began tearing through the Aggros that were beginning to swarm Darien's group.

"What?" Darien held his hand to his earpiece. "A train? Where?"

Raymond heard it too. There was a loud rumbling sound. Again, like a subway car. He peeked toward the dark tunnel that was getting brighter. Suddenly, a bullet flew by his head, and he dropped to the ground for cover. An explosion rocked the wall next to them. The explosion was deafening. It was accompanied by a deep rumble that shook the ground and made Raymond's whole body vibrate. The walls of the adjacent hut exploded, sending pieces of clay and mortar flying. Raymond was showered in dust and shrapnel as pieces of the wall rained around him.

A high-pitched ringing overwhelmed him, and the world began to move in silent slow motion. More bullets and explosions continued, but he struggled to wipe the soot from his eyes. A severed leg dropped to the ground in front of him. He feared that half of his own body had been blown off. He looked down. Both his legs were thankfully still attached and able to move from underneath the rubble. He looked down at his arms and patted his body. From what he could tell, he was at least not shot or dismembered. That was a good sign, considering the situation.

"Shit," Raymond muttered, but he was not able to hear his own voice.

The dismembered leg belonged to the soldier Nicholas. In fact, it was the extremity Raymond had worked so hard to repair. Raymond clawed his way to Nicholas' body. He was certainly dead. The rubble was stained with fresh blood. An explosion severed him from the waist down. Perforated intestines oozed from the opening.

So much for trying to save this man's life.

He took a moment to curse and confirm that this man had unfortunately died. Raymond looked around, hoping Kira was okay. To his surprise, she was in full action stance, continuing to shoot. She stood over Darien, who was himself leaning against the wall, holding his abdomen. He had been shot in the side but continued firing his pistol.

"Darien! Kira!" Raymond yelled. Again, he did not hear his own voice. They did not seem to hear him either.

Another explosion landed near Kira. She was blown back, slamming against the wall. Raymond crawled toward them. The Aggros were everywhere. The Zeltan soldiers had formed a perimeter around them. One by one, Raymond saw the soldiers take bullet after bullet and get thrown around like rag dolls by explosions.

Suddenly, a train roared in from the dark tunnel, coming to a rumbling stop. The door slid open from the car in front of Raymond. An obese man in robes beckoned them to come to him. At first, Raymond thought he was hallucinating. The man was wearing ornate purple robes and although obese, appeared of normal human stature, not like the Zeltans or Aggros.

As Raymond turned to see the Zeltans' reaction to this sudden train arrival, somehow Captain Darien, even with a bullet wound bleeding from his side, picked up Kira and began to run toward the train.

Darien looked back while effortlessly carrying the girl. "Come on! Let's go!"

Raymond could just barely hear him over the ringing in his ears. He pulled himself up. Mounds of debris fell off him. The train was only just ahead of him, but it felt like the longest run of his life. Some of the Zeltan soldiers were also running toward the train, some carrying the others slung over their backs. To Raymond's left, there was a soldier running alongside him. When Raymond felt a warm, wet sensation on his face, he turned to his left again, noticing the soldier had just taken a bullet straight to the head.

Raymond hesitated, stopping to watch the Zeltan fall to the ground. Suddenly, a powerful force struck Raymond from the side. He was suddenly flying through the air, landing with a thud into the train car. He realized that the large gray-armored Zeltan had picked him up, throwing him in. Darien, Kira, and a handful of other Zeltans were inside, almost all of them injured.

The sounds of the battle were drowned out by Raymond's heartbeat and labored breathing. He had experienced the visual horrors of the aftermath of trauma back in his day, but never had to go through it himself. It was chaos. The anguished cries of the injured on both sides resounded like the pits of hell, especially accentuated in this subterranean underworld.

The gray-armored Zeltan stayed outside the train car, firing at the hordes of Aggros surrounding the train.

"Swift!" Kira yelled, trying to jump out of the train car. Darien held her back.

Raymond tried looking out into the chaos, wiping the dirt, mud, and blood from his face. Tristan, the blonde-haired Lieutenant, was fighting off an Aggroman with his sword while shooting a pistol with the other hand. Another Aggroman nearly snuck up behind him, but Swift pounced on the savage, ripping his throat out. They were quite a distance away from the train. Raymond heart sank. They were too far and wouldn't make it at this rate.

"Marcus!" Darien yelled, tossing him a large grenade launcher that belonged to an injured soldier in the train car, "Here!"

Marcus, the large, armored soldier, grabbed the grenade launcher out of the air with his left hand. He sprinted toward Tristan and Swift. He fired the grenade launcher with his left hand while firing the massive machine gun in his right hand. Raymond marveled at this superhuman who appeared to defy all laws of physics. Bullets occasionally hit Marcus's armor, causing him to twinge, but he continued running toward the lieutenant and the robot fox.

"Squad!" Darien yelled. "Cover fire!"

From the train car, the remaining soldiers fired their weapons in unison. Seeing Kira join the firing barrage, Raymond pulled out the rifle still slung to his back. He squeezed the trigger in desperation. His bullets sprayed erratically, were aimed in the general direction of the Aggros, careful not to shoot Marcus, Tristan, and Swift running to them.

When Marcus, Tristan, and the robot fox Swift safely jumped into the train car, the fat man who led them in said, "Alright, we're leaving!"

"No," Darien said. "There's still more!"

"It's too late; we're leaving!" the fat man who arrived with the train said. He slammed a button on the wall, which slid the train car door shut. The train began to rumble, sending them back into the tunnel.

The sound of gunfire and explosions rocked the train but gradually began to dissipate. The inside of the train car was well-lit by fluorescent bulbs and soft yellow LEDs. The door on the other side served as a backdrop, casting a shadow over the equipment stacked in the center of the room. It appeared to be some kind of freight train. Rusted pipes, blinking screens with green text, and incomplete crates lined the walls. Cables ran across the ceiling and along the floor.

Tristan brought his sword up to the fat man's neck. "Who are you?! Where are we going?!"

The fat man smiled and raised his hands. "Easy now, Lieutenant Tristan. Or should I say, Prince Tristan?"

"Wh—" Tristan stammered, wide-eyed. He slammed the fat man against the wall, holding the sword closer to his neck. "How do you know my name?"

Darien stood up to stare the fat man in the eyes. The captain was a dominating presence, nearly twice his height. "I still have men back there. We need to go back. Now."

"My deepest condolences," the fat man said, cowering ever so slightly. "They are gone."

"You didn't hear me," Darien said, uncharacteristically unnerved, "Get us back there or step aside."

"Captain Darien," the man said, "Your reputation precedes you. I know your honor calls you to be with your men, but they are dead. You will do nothing except put your remaining team at risk by going back there."

Darien was silent for a moment, and Raymond was unsure if he would kill the strange robed man on the spot. Instead, the captain looked back at the remaining injured soldiers, sprawled out on the floor of the train car. He looked to Marcus, Tristan, and then Raymond.

Raymond gave an instinctive shake of his head. There would be no point in going back there. His teammates were most certainly dead or were going to be very soon. Even with Raymond's inherent need to save others at his own detriment, he knew that they barely escaped with their lives and returning would accomplish nothing.

"How…" Darien said with a sullen tone, "How do you know our names?"

"I'm sorry," the fat man said. "I should introduce myself. I assure you I mean you all no harm. My name is Guaritore."

"You're Guaritore?" Kira asked. "The healer?"

"Yes," Guaritore said. "And you must be the girl from Remnant. And you…" He gently ignored and stepped around Tristan. He extended a hand to Raymond. "It certainly is a pleasure to meet you." He smiled wide, showing a full set of crooked teeth. "A man far from home and out of his own time. Dr. Raymond Redmin, I presume?"

Raymond was shocked. *Who is this and why does he know me?* He looked around the train car. Kira and the Zeltan soldiers similarly appeared perplexed and watched with curious reservation.

"You know who I am?" Raymond asked.

"Of course," he said. "I have read all about you. You *are* quite the legend, you know."

"I am?" Raymond replied.

"Well," Guaritore said. "Somewhat by proxy. I collect Old Earth relics. I like reading about history and its heroes, especially the events just before the Silence. So many stories, so many timeless heroes. You come from a time I'd very much wish I could have seen with my own eyes. Now, my favorite hero to read about is sometimes called the Last Hero. His name was Jack Redmin, your son."

CHAPTER

SIXTEEN

Benny Fong's shoulders felt like one hundred pounds of lead. He, Casey, and Toby walked for miles, hands held up behind their heads. The two cyborgs, Armory and Hardline, had their guns trained on them the whole time. Hardline rode on the old horse, Ella, whom he treated with a surprising degree of kindness. Benny wondered whether they would treat their human prisoners with the same goodwill. His mind could barely allow himself to imagine the worst-case scenarios. *Execution? Enslavement? Torture?* After all, Armory had splattered Pete's insides all over the red dirt of the frontier.

When they arrived at the crashed spaceship, the sun was just peeking over the east beyond the Black Forest. The forest cast its long shadow over the red desert sand of the Frontier. Mornings here were cold, temporized by the artificial atmosphere generated by the Spire. Benny took a deep breath of the crisp morning air, wondering if it would be his last.

Dozens of cyborg pirates were climbing and walking along the top of the enormous fallen ship, pulling equipment and shrapnel out and throwing them down to the others on the ground.

The Corsairs were terrifying and fascinating. No one cyborg looked the same as another. Some had metal arm replacements; others had mechanical tentacles coming out from their backs. Some replaced their legs with wheel tracks, and others were completely covered in metallic skin. Many mimicked Armory's customization, bearing a firearm or metal pincers, replacing the human arm that had once been there. Benny wondered if they had lost their original limbs during the wars or whether they had given them up voluntarily for cybernetic augmentation.

The most fascinating cyborg set up a seat for himself in front of the excavation site. He was flanked by other soldiers as he sat back casually in a luxury chair. Benny deduced this must be Blackheart. He was an imposing figure with an evil face, sharp features, and cold, calculating eyes that seemed to pierce through all who looked at him. He wore a black tricorn hat on his head with a long red overcoat. His legs were crossed over tall black boots. As Benny and Casey were led in front of him, they realized that he had no identifying cybernetic augmentation except that he wore a black glove only on his left hand.

"Let's start this off by shooting one of you in the head," Blackheart said abruptly. "So, let's get to it then."

Still sitting, he casually pulled out a pistol and aimed at them. Benny was too frozen in fear to breathe. The intimidating man dressed like a pirate out of an Old Earth children's book, but his demeanor suggested a very real violent nature.

"I want each of you to tell me why you deserve to live," Blackheart said with amusement. "I am only going to shoot one of you now. So, how about you go first."

Blackheart pointed the gun at Benny, who could barely breathe, let alone speak any words. Terrified, Benny frantically struggled to find a word to say.

"Kill him," Tobey said. "He ain't one of us. He's just a settler boy. He means nuthin' to no one."

Blackheart laughed, stroking his gnarled black beard. "Not one of us. And how do you mean?"

"Well, sir, we're Red Riders," Tobey said, gesturing at Casey and himself. "We could be useful to you. We can fight. We can help you fight off the Raiders."

"The Raiders?" Blackheart said, lifting an eyebrow.

"Well, y-yes, they're on their way from the west," Tobey said. "Probably a whole caravan of them bastards. They're gonna come after the loot in the ship."

Blackheart smiled. "Well, I'm afraid they'd be picking up sloppy thirds. Most of the ship was gutted before we got here. Probably in the hands of some forest half-wits."

"We can help you take it back from them," Tobey said with a hint of confidence. "I can get a group of Riders; we know the territory. We can help you."

Casey Rogers remained silent, but his seething anger was palpable to Benny.

"Is that so?" Blackheart asked with amusement. "You know, your group of horse galloping heroics have been a nuisance for my Corsairs lately. Messing with the trade and all. Some of them even owe me money. I'd rather you tell me where to find a few that I'd like to have a word or two with."

"We could help you with that." Tobey swallowed. "O'course."

"You'd do that?" Blackheart grinned, cocking his head to the side. "You'd turn your back on your dear beloved riders?" He batted his eyes sarcastically. "For me?"

"Well, uh," Tobey stuttered. "Anyone who's anyone knows you're the most dangerous Corsair there is."

Blackheart's pointed mustache came up in a smile. "Well, isn't that the truth. Smart boy. If you want a job working for me, it's yours. "

"Thank you, sir. I—" Tobey stepped forward.

"Ah, ah, ah," Blackheart pointed the gun at Tobey's head. "You're not doing anything until I've had my entertainment. One of you has to die." Blackheart tossed his pistol in front of the three of them. "Go ahead. Turn three into two." Blackheart leaned back in his chair with a demented smile, arms clasped behind his head.

Benny was sure that Toby or Casey would choose him to be killed. For a moment, Benny had the urge to make a dive for it. Before he was able to react, it was Casey Jarrett who had the pistol in his hand. He pointed it at Blackheart. The pistol clicked empty.

Blackheart laughed. "You see how interesting these life-and-death situations are?"

Blackheart's bodyguards aimed their guns at Casey, who remained silent and stone-faced.

"You've got one more chance," Blackheart said, tossing Casey a bullet from his pocket. "One bullet. You kill one of these two, or I make sure they pop you all in the kneecaps, and we refit you with new limbs. And trust me"—Blackheart leaned closer and smiled, baring his yellow teeth—"it's gonna hurt."

Casey took the bullet from the ground, loading it into the gun.

"Come on, Case," Tobey said. "Just do it. Kill Fong, he ain't one of us."

Benny looked at Casey in the eyes. He was as good as dead. He hoped Casey would shoot him somewhere that would kill him quickly. Benny took a shuddering deep breath in acceptance.

After a moment of apparent contemplation, Casey instead brought up the pistol to Toby's head, shooting a hole out the side. Blood splashed onto Benny's face as he watched in horror. The momentum made Toby's body fall sideways onto Benny's leg, and he jumped away in horror.

Blackheart stood up and clapped his hands together. "Ah! You see? A gun with one bullet in the chamber can tell you so much about someone. Much more than you could ever say with words. Very good, very fun. That was great."

Benny stared down at Tobey's limp body, with blood flowing from the large hole in his skull. The entire event made Benny involuntarily hyperventilate. He felt himself nearly faint. *What just happened?*

He looked over to Casey, who was staring at the ground. His wide-brimmed hat covered his face, but Benny imagined he was seething with hate or maybe even embarrassment.

"W-Why?" Benny stuttered. "Why'd you do that?"

Casey looked up; eyes red with rage. "Red Riders don't work for no freak pirates."

He threw the pistol back at Blackheart, who caught it. There was a metal twang as the pistol made contact. Blackheart smiled as he crushed the pistol. It deformed into a scrap of twisted metal in an instant. He removed his glove, revealing a skeleton-like cybernetic five-fingered appendage. He walked up to Casey, his long red coat dragging across the dirt. His robotic hand shot up to Casey's throat, grasping it tightly.

"Red Rider," Blackheart growled, pulling the cowboy up by his neck. "What makes you so different from those 'dust pirates' in the far west?"

Benny knew Blackheart was referring to the Raiders as 'dust pirates.' In a sense, he always considered Corsairs and Raiders equally as dangerous. While the Corsairs terrorized the Green Sea and coastline, the Raiders similarly roamed the barren desert of the Far West. Although similar in their behavior, the two factions were never aligned, and in fact gravely hostile to each other.

But as for the Red Riders, although many abused the responsibility, they at least still stood for some semblance of nobility. Casey apparently, and surprisingly to Benny, seemed to demonstrate that.

"We," Casey said, holding his neck and struggling to breathe, "protect the Frontier from raiders and freaks like you."

"Oh," Blackheart said menacingly, bringing his face close to Casey's. "You'll find, my friend, that there is *no one* like me." He threw Casey back to the ground.

Casey rolled over, coughing and gasping for breath.

"So, those dusties are really on their way here, then?" He walked away, looking to the west horizon, taking in an exaggerated breath of air. "Looks like we're about to have some fun, boys!"

"And these two?" the monocled cyborg named Hardline asked.

"Throw them into the pit," Blackheart said. "We'll have more to sell to the slavers soon enough." *Sold into slavery,* Benny thought dreadfully, *there's my answer right there.*

One of the guards walked up to Benny and knocked him across the face with the butt of his gun. Benny lost consciousness. His last thoughts were of unquestionable doom and wondering whether he'd ever see his home again, his parents, or Kira.

SEVENTEEN

Raymond Redmin was bruised and beaten, wincing in pain with every movement. He wished to stay in the train car, lie down, and resign himself to the sweet respite of death. However, there were the wounded that needed tending to, and moreso, he needed to hear what Guaritore knew about what happened in the past. Raymond needed to know what happened to his wife and son.

Guaritore said he would explain more when they arrived at their stop. Raymond was fed up with people trailing off, just before they were going to explain what they knew. However, Guaritore had enthusiastically waddled off the train and Raymond could barely muster the energy to follow him out.

"We'll find out what happened to your family," Kira reassured Raymond.

Raymond and Kira helped each other off the train. They grunted with every pained movement; both their bodies having been through hell.

The six remaining Zeltans walked out afterwards. Most were wounded, some with serious life-threatening injuries, but all stood tall and remained vigilant.

Captain Darien had taken a bullet to his lower abdomen. Raymond inspected Darien's injury while on the train. A bullet had pierced clean through his flank, perhaps just superficial to the visceral organs and vasculature. With luck, the captain would not likely need surgery. If Raymond could find clean tools, he could perform a diagnostic peritoneal lavage to assess for intra-abdominal injury. It wasn't likely, as the soldier commander's upper abdomen was non-tender. *But who knew what deviant physiology these supposed superhumans had?* For now, he had applied a tight wrap around his waist. The captain continued to lead as if he had not been hurt at all.

Tristan had bruising to his ribs, but Raymond had put his ears against his chest and heard clear lung sounds bilaterally. Tristan had no jugular venous distention, and his heart sounds were clear and unmuffled. He did not appear to have any pneumothorax or cardiac tamponade.

Their Grenadier Specialist Jason had been knocked unconscious from a blast and carried into the train. He miraculously woke during the train ride and was immediately battle-ready.

The Marksman, Vincent, seemed to have dislocated or broken his right ankle. The silent soldier brushed off Raymond's offers to help with the obvious deformity. It was a closed injury with no open wounds. Vincent calmly took the foot with his left hand and pulled it back into place with a crunch. Kira contorted her face in disgust. Very much contrary to all of Raymond's medical knowledge of anatomy and physiology, Vincent stood back up on the leg and hobbled with little extra support.

"You need to keep weight off that leg," Raymond said.

"It's fine." Vincent whispered gruffly, readying his scoped marksman rifle.

Master Sergeant Barrett took two bullets to his upper back, one to his left bicep, and another to his right hip. He was the most seriously injured of the whole group. Raymond pleaded with the large man to examine him. Now, as the Drill Sergeant walked alongside the rest of his team, some blood dripped from his torso. Raymond was surprised how he was able to move, let alone walk, while carrying an automatic rifle and gear.

The soldier who made Raymond most curious was Sergeant Marcus, the mysterious, silent, armored soldier. The metal armor seemed to have protected him against the bullets and explosions, but his suit was dented and worn down. The silent soldier didn't even sit during the train ride. He stood at attention with the heavy machine gun in his arms, never removing his helmet or armor. Raymond wondered what kind of person was underneath the helmet.

Swift proved to be quite the resilient robot. After the struggle, he was functioning normally, snuggling with Kira and wagging his tail cheerily. Raymond, at first, had reservations about the little fox, unsure how dangerous and unpredictable this killing machine could be. However, the fox remained loyal and amicable to the Raymond and the rest of the group. He continued to hum cautiously at the mysterious Guaritore, however.

"Follow me, my friends," Guaritore said as he waddled ahead of the group.

The train had come to a stop within another vast underground cavern. This one was empty and darkly lit, with only a small building illuminated in the middle. The architecture vaguely reminded Raymond of his own time on Earth. The building was a cottage, adorned with quaint flower decorations and even a picket fence. It existed like an image of homely peace, nestled within the dark recesses of hell itself.

"Did NASA build this?" Raymond asked as he and Kira hobbled forward, holding each other up.

Guaritore laughed. "Ah, such antiquated vocabulary. I love it! Well, Doctor, in fact, it was their successor organization, USEC, that built this. The United Space Exploration Coalition."

Raymond somewhat recalled news about missions to Mars during his intermittent waking periods between cryosleep. "When did all this happen?"

"Well," Guaritore said while walking up the stairs to the building. "The first mission to Mars was in 2043 AD. The USEC Aquarius. Most of the colonization began in 2055 AD, after the 2052 Crisis on Earth."

"What's that?" Raymond asked, hungry to learn more about the fate of his past.

"Ah," Guaritore said. "I'm afraid I'm getting ahead of myself. So much to talk about!" He giggled queerly. "I simply can't wait!"

Captain Darien was less amused. "What is this place?"

"My humble abode," Guaritore said, bowing forward and presenting the front door.

"Listen, bub"—the injured Master Sergeant Barrett heaved, aiming his gun at the obese man—"if this is a trick, I'll pull your guts out and make you eat them."

Guaritore tilted his head and smiled. "I'm still waiting for one of you to thank me for saving you."

"Why do you have a train to the Aggros village anyway?" Tristan asked. "I've never heard about an underground railroad. The Kingdom should know about this."

"As I said, Prince Tristan," Guaritore said with a hint of patronization, "I'm a collector. The Aggros and I have an agreement. Every month, I send the train to their village. They offer me relics of Old Earth, and I send them back medicine and supplies."

"Those savages just killed my men, our brothers, and you're telling me you were in business with them," Darien said. "You still haven't convinced me to trust you."

"Very well then," Guaritore said. "I'm going to go inside. I have food, drink, and hot showers. If you'd rather stay out here, I won't stop you." The obese man walked inside, leaving the door open behind him.

The prospect of something or eat or drink was too alluring for Raymond to second guess. Kira seemed to be on the same page. They hobbled past the Zeltan soldiers into the house. After entering, Darien and the soldiers reluctantly changed their minds and followed behind.

The underground house was cozy and gave Raymond a hint of nostalgia that brought tears to his eyes. The house was dimly lit, with a living room fitted with three sofas and a fireplace leading to an open kitchen on the far end. It was certainly reminiscent of a modern Earth cottage.

"Please, do come in, come in," Guaritore said as he lit the fireplace. "Dr. Redmin, you'll find I am a fan of Old Earth architecture. I built this house to resemble those of Old Earth. Was I accurate in my estimations?"

Raymond and Kira slumped down to the couch together, involuntarily laughing at each other when they felt the comfort wash over them. *Feels like home*, Raymond thought, with pained nostalgia. He wanted to close his eyes and drift to sleep but was disrupted by the suspicious gun-toting soldiers examining every nook and cranny in the room.

"Captain," Guaritore said. "Please. You and your men should sit and relax."

"We're just fine, thank you," Darien said, peering behind a curtain.

Guaritore handed Raymond and Kira some bread and cups of water. "Give me some time. I'll make some hot food for you to eat."

It was the best bread and water Raymond had ever had. He closed his eyes and chewed in ecstasy. For all he knew, the heavy-bellied healer could have poisoned the food, but Raymond didn't care. He was exhausted, and right now, he was in paradise.

He looked over at Kira. She was petting Swift, who had jumped up on the couch beside her. She turned to Raymond and smiled. She had a pretty smile and bright green eyes. Raymond surmised he was probably old enough to be her father. He remembered his son the last time he saw him. Jack had grown into a handsome young man. *Kira would have liked Jack*, he thought.

"Guaritore," Raymond said, looking up from the couch. "You said, my son…" Raymond's voice broke when the words left his mouth. "You said that he was… a hero?"

"Ah! Yes!" Guaritore said excitedly. "Not only a hero, Dr. Redmin, a legend! I almost forgot, just wait a moment, I'll be right back!"

After Guaritore left the room, Darien placed an object under an art piece over the fireplace mantle.

"Tracker," Darien whispered to Raymond. "We can't trust this man." Darien turned his mouth to his shoulder, covering it. "Triggers ready, squad. Eyes open."

The soldiers began to accelerate their search of the house. They began overturning furniture, and some went upstairs.

"Well, my house is your house," Guaritore said as he returned, not surprised that the soldiers were rummaging through his belongings. "By all means, Captain, you may search the house. But I claimed these relics for myself. They belong to *me*. You may not take anything."

"Or what?" Tristan asked, putting his hand on the pistol hanging from his belt. "We are Rangers of the Kingdom, NB; you don't give us orders."

Guaritore's voice fell into a deep, serious tone. "My Prince, I ask you kindly not to take anything from his house." He stepped forward, challenging the blonde-haired Lieutenant, who was nearly two feet taller.

"Wait," Raymond said, seeing the portrait Guaritore held. "What is that?"

"Why, yes!" Guaritore suddenly reverted to his jovial tone. "This is a painting of your son. This is Jack Redmin, the Last Hero of Old Earth, the Hero of the Earth Alliance!"

Raymond took the portrait and sat back slowly on the couch. He covered his mouth, immediately breaking into tears. In the portrait, Jack stood proud in front of a picture of Earth with spaceships flying behind him. He was older in the picture, perhaps in his 30's. Jack was handsome, standing tall with one hand on his hip and the other holding a helmet to his side.

"He was a pilot?" Raymond asked, his voice quivering.

"Not just a pilot," Guaritore said, sitting on the couch in front of Raymond. "He led a campaign against the Resistance Network in 2059. The moon colony and space stations declared war on Earth, and Jack's campaign single-handedly averted the destruction of Earth. That's why we call him the Last Hero. They wrote books about him; I even have a few in the basement."

"I'd like to see them," Raymond said, putting a tear-soaked hand over Jack's picture. He was proud of his son. He missed him. He wondered what kind of suffering Jack had to endure over those years. Raymond wished he could have been there for him. "What happened to him and to my wife, Eva? How did they..."

"How did they die?" Guaritore asked. "Unfortunately, no one seems to know. The Silence event took place in 2076 A.D. The last known record of your son and wife shows that they took flight on a spaceship headed here in 2075 AD. We're not sure what happened to them after."

"So," Raymond said, "they could have been *here*? On Mars?"

"It's possible," Guaritore said, "but that was almost 200 years ago. They are, unfortunately, long gone by now."

Raymond broke into a soft cry. He felt Kira put her arm over his back in a side hug.

"You should be proud of him," Kira said, holding the picture. "It looks like he did a lot of good for all of humanity."

"I am proud of him," Raymond said. "I'm so proud of him. I just wish I could have been there. I should have been there when he was growing up. I was frozen, and I—"

Tristan could be heard yelling from outside, "What the hell? Captain!" He had wandered out there while investigating the house.

All the soldiers rushed outside. Raymond and Kira managed to pick themselves up from the couch out of curiosity. Raymond left Jack's picture on the table. Deep inside, he wished to stay on the couch and continue to hear stories of his son. But the momentum of the moment took him outside the faux house. When they caught up with the others, they fumbled around in the dim lighting of the vast underground cavern.

"What is the meaning of this? " Darien asked, pistol pointed at Guaritore's head.

Kira looked around in the darkness. "What are we looking at? Where are you—"

"Allow me to turn some lights on," Guaritore said. "Please do not be alarmed. I am flipping on a light switch now. Please do not be hasty, Captain." He walked slowly to a switchbox on the side of his house. He opened it and flipped up several switches.

Booms echoed throughout the large cavern. Now illuminated, they realized they were surrounded by a bevy of old tanks, machinery, and broken vehicles. It was an underground scrap yard.

Tristan and the soldiers were focused in one direction. There, along the far wall, stood two hulking giant robot suits, one gray and red, the other one completely black.

"Explain how you obtained two exo-mechs," Darien said.

"Again, I am a collector," Guaritore said. "These were discarded from the fighting pits in Cyborg Bay and sold on the black market by the Corsairs."

"We outlawed use of exo-mechs by anyone who isn't a Zeltan," Tristan said. "Keeping this here is illegal."

"How did you even get it down here?" Master Sergeant Barrett asked. He was finally becoming visibly weaker from his injuries and continuing to bleed.

"Well," Guaritore said. "Despite some wear and tear from the fighting pits, they are fully operational. I had someone pilot them here."

Tristan's face turned red. "Exo-mechs belong to the Kingdom; you have no right to—"

The large man, Barrett, suddenly fell to the ground, interrupting the conversation. Raymond ran over to him, checking for a pulse through his meaty, muscular neck. His carotid pulse was weak, and his heart rate was elevated. His multiple bullet wounds continued to pour blood.

"He's going into hemorrhagic shock," Raymond said.

"Let's get him inside," Guaritore said. "I have IVs and ringers. I have a surgical kit for you, Doctor, whatever you need. I have some self-learned surgical expertise myself."

Darien was seen clenching his jaw, but Raymond nodded to the captain in approval.

"Alright," Darien said. "Sergeant Marcus, go with them."

Marcus picked up the other large-bodied soldier into his arms with ease. He carried him gracefully into the house, with the group following closely behind. Darien grabbed Raymond's arm.

"Help Sergeant Barrett," Darien whispered into Raymond's ear. "But I still don't trust this Guaritore. Something isn't right here, and I'm going to get to the bottom of it."

Raymond nodded. He did not feel quite as suspicious of the fat man himself, but those questions would come later. As Raymond turned to go into the house to help the soldier, he briefly marveled at the two exo-mechs. They stood like titans. After this was all over, he wanted to see them in action. When Jack was a boy, he loved to play with robot toys that looked just like them.

Jack would have loved to see this.

EIGHTEEN

Captain Darien used this opportunity for his remaining squad to investigate Guaritore's underground cavern. Guaritore and Raymond had brought Master Sergeant Barrett to a surgical suite in the basement of his house. While Darien was relieved that Guaritore had the surgical skills to help Barrett, something about the entire situation bothered him.

Kira mentioned that Guaritore was known as a legendary healer. Darien questioned what a healer was doing hiding away in a secret underground base, hoarding supplies and relics, even weaponry. Tristan was suspicious of Guaritore as well. For once, Darien agreed with the young Lieutenant.

"Update?" Darien asked into his comlink.

"We're logging all his inventory into the com," Tristan said. He and Specialist Vincent were scouting the periphery of the cavern. "He's got a lot of weapons and ordinance here, but it doesn't look like he intends to use any of it. Most of this should be property of the Kingdom. This man should be arrested and put to trial."

"Not until they finish the surgery on Barrett," Darien said. "Marcus, what about you?"

"All clear," Sergeant Marcus said. "Person of interest still operating."

Marcus was given guard duty while the collector performed surgery on the critically injured Master Sergeant. Dr. Redmin nearly passed out from exhaustion during the procedure and had to excuse himself to get some rest. The girl Kira had long since fallen asleep on the couch. Darien took note of how dependent the natural borns were on sleep.

"Captain," Specialist Jason said. The explosive specialist motioned to a stairway hidden behind a rock formation. "Take a look at this."

Darien noted the curiously placed egress and spoke into his com, "We found some kind of hidden stairway. We're going to see what's down here. Maintain radio contact."

"Roger," Tristan, Vincent, and Marcus said in unison.

Darien looked around and saw the robot fox Swift following him and Jason.

"Um," Darien said, putting his hand up. "Stay. Stay here."

The fox tilted his head, putting his rump on the ground to sit.

Captain Darien was not quite sure of the exact intelligence level of this robotic fox, but he seemed to understand complex English commands. The fox roamed the outside cavern after Kira fell asleep. Tristan was harsh with the fox, threatening to destroy him. Since his companion Kira was asleep, the fox followed Darien around instead.

Darien didn't mind, necessarily. In fact, he found the synthetic animal to be quite interesting. As a child, he had been taught to distrust any AI. For decades, they were the Zeltans' sworn enemy. But after only a few hours with the energetic fox, Darien and Jason learned to enjoy his company.

"We're going down here," Darien said. "Just stay here and let me know if there's any trouble. Okay?"

Swift hummed gleefully, seemingly delighted to have a job.

Darien and Jason pointed their automatic rifles down the stairwell. They turned the UV lights on their under-barrels, then adjusted their goggles to UV light settings. They were walking through pitch dark but could see bright as day. Anyone waiting for them down here would not be able to see their lights without the appropriate UV optics.

As Darien slowly descended the stairs, a moment of grief washed over him. He arrived with 13 other soldiers, and 8 were killed in front of him. They were his responsibility. Now, they were dead. Corporal Ryan was shot through the back by a sniper bullet. Specialist Nicholas had been blown to pieces by an explosion. First Sergeant Roland was torn apart by bullets, but not before taking some enemies down with his bare hands. Privates David and Carl died from a grenade tossed into their gunner nest. Staff Sergeant Scott's head exploded from a bullet as he ran for the train. Private Zachary and Private Ethan were last seen hopelessly pinned down by a hail fire of bullets as the train left.

Focus, Darien thought.

The stairway led to a small, narrow hallway. An open door at the other end led into a very well-lit room with working monitors and machines. The architecture was clean and smooth, signifying that this led to some kind of science lab.

"Wait," Darien whispered to Jason. "Something doesn't feel right."

"What do you—" Jason said.

Suddenly, the doors in front and behind them swished shut. The hallway lit up bright with lights. Darien was blinded and ripped his goggles off reflexively.

"Squad, do you copy?" Darien asked into his comlink.

Darien and Jason stood back-to-back, aiming their guns around the hallway. They quickly made their way back to the entrance door. Vents along the sides of the hallway began to emanate a visible gas. Jason began to bang on the door. He tried kicking it down and hitting the glass with the butt of his gun. It was sealed shut and seemed built to withstand trauma.

"Captain, permission for explosive charge on the door," Jason said, already readying the sticky explosive.

"Granted," Darien said, stepping back. "Lieutenant, Sergeant, does anyone copy?"

Jason stuck the explosive to the glass on the door, then ran back with Darien to the other end of the hallway, crouching. Darien held his ears as the explosion went off. It carried them through the air. Their backs crashed against the wall and each other.

Through the smoke and the gas that quickly filled the hallway, Darien realized the door was barely damaged. There was soot on the window, but it remained intact. On the other side of the window, he saw Swift on the staircase, jumping around frantically, trying to get to them.

"Get help!" Darien tried to yell, but the gas made his voice hoarse and weak. "You hear me? Get...help..."

Darien watched the fox sprint back up the stairs and away. Jason was on the ground, unconscious. Darien began to feel drowsy, and his vision became a whirlwind of vertiginous colors. He slumped to the ground.

The inner door slid open, and a man wearing a gas mask entered. He stood over Darien and brought his face close. Before Darien lost consciousness, he recognized the man's facial profile. His eyes glowed red, seemingly from cybernetic ocular implants. To Darien, it was unmistakable. This was the face he had seen a thousand times in his dreams since he last left the Black Forest.

Julian.

"It's been a long time, Captain," Julian said as Darien fell into a deep sleep.

CHAPTER

NINETEEN

Kira Skyler awoke from a dream. She dreamed of riding on her motorcycle, with her father, her brother, and even her mother riding horses alongside her across the wide-open Martian landscape. Her reverie quickly morphed into the ceiling of the quaint yet peculiar underground cottage. She heard the crackles of the fireplace and turned to see Raymond sleeping on the couch across from her.

Kira deduced that she must have fallen asleep while Raymond and Guaritore were operating on that soldier. She wondered how long she had slept. She was tired, no doubt, but she felt uncomfortable being vulnerable in a place like this with strangers. Technically, she should have felt most uncomfortable with Raymond. After all, he was from another planet and time entirely. Despite that, she felt safe around him.

In fact, she felt sorry for him. He was thrust so harshly into this dangerous world she had lived in her whole life. There was a reassuring naïveté to him. The politics of the Red Planet meant nothing to him. People were people, and he just wanted to save whomever he could. In a way, he reminded Kira of her father.

Where's Swift? she thought. Kira's eyes scanned the living room, and she was about to call out to her robot companion. Looking at Raymond again, exhausted and sprawled out on the couch, nearly comatose, she decided to let him sleep. She gently stood up from the couch she had been sleeping on and began to tip-toe around Guaritore's house.

His house was truly an odd arrangement, much different than the bare, worn-down structures of Remnant. Everything in his house was colored, from the walls to the ornate carpets to the pictures hanging on the walls. She had never seen such a decorated living space. After all, she had only ever traveled between towns on the Frontier. There, showcasing your treasures would just make you more likely to be raided.

No, here Guaritore put them all on display. She wondered whether they were only on display for himself or whether he ever had any visitors. Kira figured Benny would have loved to visit this place, full of trinkets, relics, and memorabilia from Old Earth. She thought about Benny for a moment and hoped he would not be so foolish as to come after her. Perhaps after she brought Raymond back to town to help the sick, she could take Benny back here to see all these treasures.

Kira ran her hand across all the strange devices and relics along the walls. She was so lost in thought she had not realized the giant Zeltan soldier standing guard at the hallway entrance.

"You shouldn't be here, ma'am," the large, armored soldier said through his muffled helmet.

Kira nearly fell backward. The soldier was almost too big for the ceiling, and he took up the entire free space of the hallway with his mass and the large machine gun he carried. They referred to him as Sergeant Marcus. She noted that he never took off his helmet or armor, and he was always standing at attention. Kira wondered if he might be a robot.

"I'm just looking around," Kira tried to say confidently, but her voice came out shaky with fear.

"Captain Darien said you and the doctor should stay in the living room where it is safe," Sergeant Marcus said.

"What's behind that door?" Kira asked, looking around the soldier to an open door leading to a basement.

"Master Sergeant Barrett is being attended to," Marcus said, matter-of-factly. He was unmoving; his tinted visor gave away no emotion.

"I'm looking for Swift, the fox," Kira said. She felt awkward. Talking to the giant sentinel was like communicating with a rock.

"The robotic quadruped went with the Captain and Specialist Jason to investigate the outside of the house," Marcus said.

"Oh, alright." Kira said, "Well, I'm gonna go out to meet them."

She turned to leave, but a massive, gloved hand rested on her shoulder. "Ma'am, my orders were to watch guard over the Master Sergeant, you, and the doctor. Please remain within eyesight."

Kira backed away. "I'm sorry, I'm gonna go find Swift."

Impatience fumed through his expressionless helmet. "Ma'am, my orders—"

"I know what orders you have," Kira said. "So, you need to stay here and keep watch. I'm just going to go outside. You said yourself the captain was outside the house. I'll be safe with them." She started walking away slowly, her heart racing. The Zeltans made her uncomfortable, and she started to worry about Swift.

"Ma'am," Marcus said with his hand up.

"I'm leaving," she said softly over her shoulder, careful not to wake Raymond.

"Captain?" Marcus said over his radio. "The girl is coming out to look for her robot. Sir?"

Kira already opened the front door and walked out into the vast cavern. It was not unlike the underground cavern that the Aggros lived in. The ceilings seemed as high as the sky, and the breadth of the cavern could fit half the town of Remnant. It seemed odd that the small cottage sat alone in the middle, with various junk metals and vehicles thrown about the ground. It was a stark contrast from the ornately decorated interior of Guaritore's cottage.

She walked toward the two towering robotic behemoths on the far wall of the cavern. Kira had never seen an exo-mech before. She could hardly imagine an entire battlefield populated with these colossal giants. Benny told her that during the AI Wars, thousands of Zeltans piloted these mechs out to battle the Hivemind's armies. Since the end of the wars, they were either dismantled or used for sport.

"Hey!" a voice said, echoing across the high ceilings of the caverns.

Kira was startled. She was too enamored by the exo-mechs to realize she had been walking quite a long way from Guaritore's cottage. She was surprised that Marcus, the stoic armored soldier, did not come out to bring her back inside. Her act of defiance worked.

"What are you doing out here?" Tristan stormed up to her.

"Looking around." She scoffed. "What are you doing?"

"I mean," he said, gritting his teeth, "why aren't you inside with the other NB?"

She hated being called an NB. "Okay, number one, I don't take orders from you or any of your other macho friends. Second, I—"

"Stop, just..." Tristan grabbed his earpiece and put a hand up to silence her. "What do you mean? Did he say anything? I'll try myself. Captain? Are you getting me or the Sergeant's coms? Vincent, are you getting anything from the Captain or Specialist Jason?"

"What's going on?" Kira asked, walking closer to try to listen in.

Tristan put a dismissive hand to her face and walked away from her.

Kira wanted to punch him. The blonde-haired Lieutenant represented everything she imagined she would hate about the Zeltans. The captain seemed like a reasonable man, but this Lieutenant Tristan was exactly what she had expected in a Zeltan: arrogant, rude, and completely condescending. She would have none of that. As Tristan continued to be distressed about some conversation on his earpiece, she climbed up the ladder of a dismantled Tiger tank.

The main gun was torn off, and there was a large hole in the side of the tank. Most of the vehicles in the underground scrapyard appeared damaged beyond repair. She thought perhaps one might be viable to ride back to Remnant. There, they might use it as a deterrence against Raiders. But who was she kidding? The Red Riders would co-opt it for their own.

She sat on top of the tank, observing the unusual underground cavern. Two underground caverns in a day. Man-made or natural? It was hard to tell. Terraforming resulted in both perversions and works of beauty all over the planet.

Kira looked to the far distance, beyond Guaritore's house. Figures moved in the low light. She deduced they must be the captain and the other soldier. She squinted her eyes, trying to see if Swift was with them.

"Swift!" she said with her hands cupped around her mouth. "I'm over here, boy."

Suddenly, she felt a whoosh of air next to her. Tristan jumped up from the ground to the top of the tank. The athletic feat surprised her. He must have jumped up seven feet in a single bound. She had little time to process his apparent defiance of the laws of physics.

"Shh!" He put his hand over her mouth.

She pushed him away. "Get away from me! Don't touch me!"

"Alright, alright." He had his hands up. "Stop, just stop. Look."

He pointed at the shadowy figures. There were many of them, much more than the group she had arrived with.

"Who are they?" she asked.

Just as suddenly as before, he picked her up, jumping back to the ground with superhuman grace.

"Hey!" She pushed him away again. "I said, stop touching me."

"Get down." He pushed her head to the ground.

Gunshots popped off overhead.

"Vincent," Tristan said over his earpiece, "how many? What? Alright, cover to destination mark due your clock three. Alright, NB, let's go."

"Stop calling me NB—" Before she could finish her protest, Kira was picked up by the arm, and they began running through the low-lit cavern. "What's going on?"

After turning a corner, Kira was startled to find a man staring at them. His clothes were ragged, and his face appeared somewhat decayed. His jaw hung open, and he stared straight into empty space. His skin had a hue of grey, and he looked eerily like a moving corpse.

"Freeze!" Tristan pointed his gun at the strange man.

The man started hobbling toward them, moaning. He moved with an uncoordinated stiffness that made Kira reel back in fear. Tristan's automatic rifle placed a spread of rounds into his chest. The gunshots rang loud and echoed throughout the underground cavern.

With her adrenaline pumping, Kira turned back and began to run. As she rounded the corner of an empty supply rack, two similar-looking men hobbled toward her with their arms up, ready to grab her. She pushed one away, but the other grabbed her arm tight. As she began to yell, his head exploded in a mist of blackened blood. Tristan had shot him point blank, then took the rotting man's arm and pulled it off of her.

"What the hell?" Tristan said.

Kira turned around; the first grey-skinned man that Tristan already shot dead was back up, walking toward them, still moaning. Tristan sprayed bullets into him, then again at the other two getting up from the ground. They were nearly undeterred by gunfire.

"What are they?" Kira said as they backed away.

"I don't know." Tristan shook his head. "That one is wearing a Ranger outfit, but it's an old design. We haven't used those uniforms in years. These men are…dead."

Just then, a large horde of these apparent undead entities rounded the corner, cryptically moaning and staggering toward them. Tristan fired his automatic rifle, which brought most of them to the ground, but they eventually picked themselves back up, stumbling back towards them. Intestines and black blood spilled out from their torsos as they came closer.

"Let's go," Tristan said, taking her arm.

"No, wait," Kira said. She grabbed the pistol on his belt.

He grabbed her wrist in hesitation, looking her in the eyes suspiciously. "Alright. Take it."

Kira took the pistol, firing at the undead bodies that were beginning to surround them. Tristan pressed his back against hers, firing his automatic rifle.

"Vincent!" Tristan yelled. "We need a way out of here!"

Several of the walking corpses took direct shots to the head from above. Kira looked up. The sniper, Vincent, was perched on a high cliff along the cavern wall.

"Here, take this," Tristan said, shoving his automatic rifle into Kira's chest. "Give me that." Tristan took the pistol out of Kira's hands and unsheathed his sword. It made a ringing whoosh as it came out. He stabbed a corpse in the face while firing several rounds into its torso.

"Come on!" Tristan said as he slashed his way through the horde.

Tristan hacked away with his right arm while shooting his pistol with his left. Kira nearly forgot to use the automatic rifle as she marveled at the Zeltan's dance-like mastery of weapons. Groans close behind her snapped her out of it. She turned around, blasting away at the decaying monstrosities.

She followed Tristan, fighting their way around every terrifying bend in the maze. She began to lose track of their location in the low light. The only points of reference were the two towering exo-mechs against the far wall illuminated by work lights.

"Where are we going?" Kira asked as she shot down a corpse trying to pick itself up after Tristan had cut its leg off.

"The exo-mechs," he said. "I think I can get them to work."

"You know how to pilot those things?" Kira asked.

Tristan turned around and gave her a wide grin.

TWENTY

Raymond awoke to the sounds of gunfire. His abrupt transition from the dream world caused some momentary confusion. One moment, he was sitting happily with Eva and Jack in their living room, and the next, he was alone in a strange cottage on a distant planet in the distant future. He sat up quickly and experienced an episode of vertigo.

How long have I been asleep?

It was a question he frequently asked of himself lately.

"Sir," Sergeant Marcus said, bounding across the room. "Please remain calm."

"What's going on?" Raymond said, disoriented, "Where's Kira? Where's everyone else?"

"Please stay here for a moment, sir," the bulky armored soldier said, peeking out the front window.

"Wait, what are you—" Raymond said.

Marcus took a few steps back, then charged forward. He kicked the front door down with his leg. His machine gun let off a torrential hail of firepower outside. Raymond ducked behind the couch he was sleeping on but could see the flashes of gunfire from the low-lit underground cavern outside.

As he peeked around the couch, a metal hatch slammed down over the front doorway behind Marcus. Likewise, all windows slid shut with a metal hiss and click. Raymond got up and ran to the front door, banging on it.

"Sergeant Marcus!" Raymond said. The sounds of gunfire were muffled from the outside.

Raymond tried to lift the metal door, pulling and pushing to no avail. He went from window to window, trying to break open each of them. The cozy cottage house suddenly seemed like a prison. He was trapped.

"Dr. Redmin," Guaritore said over some type of speaker system. "You need to go downstairs, it's not safe."

"Where are you?" Raymond asked, spinning and looking around the room.

"Downstairs, Doctor, hurry!"

Raymond had little time to process the situation. Sergeant Marcus was occupied shooting at...something. Raymond ran toward the stairway leading to the basement where he had helped Guaritore perform surgery on the injured soldier Barrett. Raymond thought perhaps the rest of the group was down there waiting for him.

When he reached the bottom of the stairs, he felt another hiss and click of another metal doorway shut close behind him. He looked back up to the top of the stairs, and the sight of another doorway sealed by a slab of grey metal filled him with a sense of dread.

"Welcome, Dr. Redmin," Guaritore said.

"What the hell is going on?" Raymond said.

Guaritore stood next to the operating table where Barrett lay unconscious. Raymond's eyes immediately darted to the vital signs on the monitor. Barrett had no heart rate, no breathing, and zero pulse oximetry. He was dead.

"What happened?" Raymond asked, walking forward. "He's dead. You should have woken me up."

Raymond looked closely at Barrett's head. There was a metal computer card lodged into his forehead. The wounds were still fresh and oozing. A set of wires connected from his head to the computer mainframe against the wall. Guaritore was clearly experimenting on this man.

"What is this?" Raymond asked, approaching the corpse cautiously. "What the hell are you doing?"

Guaritore brandished a pistol from behind him. He held it up by his hip, trained on Raymond.

Raymond put his hands up, holding his breath.

"We are fortunate that our other guests are currently preoccupied." Guaritore gestured at video screens on the wall.

One monitor showed Marcus coming to the rescue of the robot fox Swift. They were surrounded by what appeared to be zombies. Hundreds of staggering corpses encircled them on multiple monitors, far more than Marcus appeared to have bullets for. On another set of video screens, Tristan and Kira were fighting through another horde. Raymond watched in disbelief, wondering if he had woken up in hell.

"Reanimation," Guaritore said with a sing-song voice. "It has been quite the hobby of mine, doctor. Tell me you have not dreamt of conquering death itself?"

Raymond could only look at him with disbelief and disgust. Behind Guaritore's pudgy cheeks and thick-lipped smile was a sick scientist with a macabre obsession.

"For years," Guaritore continued, "I have collected specimens from all over the Black Forest, so ripe for the picking. In their arrogance, the Kingdom continues to send their soldiers into the Forest, convinced their genetic superiority would grant them dominance over the new order that I alone have established here."

"You?"

"Oh yes, Doctor," Guaritore said, pressing a button that lit up dozens more video screens on the wall. It revealed monitoring of the entire forest, even beyond. "I control the Aggromen, the wildlife, even anti-aircraft technology. You see, I own this forest and everything in it."

"Why?" Raymond asked. "What's all of this for?"

"Dr. Redmin," Guaritore said. "Surely, as a man of science, you must understand. This planet was left for dead. Children of Earth squabbling about for relevance, while the ultimate frontier still remains: conquering death itself. Now, I have made great strides in corporal reanimation, as you have seen. Thousands of previously useless bodies are now in my employ. My next objective was extracting memories and brain activity to quantify and visualize."

Guaritore pressed some more buttons, and Barrett's dead body began to twitch and contort. The screen above him seemed to display memories from Barrett's point of view. A flood of scenes randomly cycled through some of Barrett's childhood, his training, and, to Raymond's interest, Barrett living in some kind of futuristic, medieval kingdom that he deduced was the Zeltan capital. For a moment, Raymond found it fascinating, but ultimately, he was disgusted. This was a man, recently deceased, exploited for his private memories.

"This is wrong," Raymond said.

"I had a feeling you would think that way," Guaritore said. "After all, you were the noble Jack Redmin's father. But think, Dr. Redmin. If we could extract the memories of all the survivors and non-survivors of the crash, we might be able to piece back together our history. Our past."

Again, Guaritore pressed more buttons. The computer screens switched to show another laboratory. Lined on the tables were dozens of people. Raymond recognized some from the ship before it crashed, some from the Aggro prison cage. They were all unconscious, possibly dead; their foreheads implanted with computer cards connected to machines.

"What have you done..." Raymond said.

"Uploading their memories," Guaritore said. "This will be far more useful than any interrogation or any storytelling. This is real. This is raw. We can discover what brought you here and why you are here. We can discover what happened to Earth and why they left us here on this godforsaken planet to rot two hundred years ago."

Raymond felt a surge of dread wash over him. "And you're going to do this to *me*?"

Guaritore laughed. "Dr. Redmin. I could never harm you. You are a living relic of history. My grandest treasure. I wanted you to understand why I am doing this. Perhaps to give your mind freely."

"You can't be serious," Raymond said.

Guaritore sighed. "Dr. Redmin, again, I do not intend to harm you. However, if you would be so selfish to withhold a life story so unique, I would be forced to insist." Guaritore looked up and smiled. "Ah, to be frozen in time, to watch your life pass you by in mere moments, to wake up far beyond your own time, a man displaced from time and space. Truly, your memories will be the most interesting of all."

Before Raymond could respond, an explosion from outside rocked the laboratory. The monitor above Barrett dislodged, swinging down and knocking Guaritore aside with a thud. The lights flickered on and off, and another explosion threw Raymond back. An empty operating table rolled across the room, pinning Raymond to the wall. He was trapped.

What is going on up there?

TWENTY-ONE

Kira and Tristan fought to a staircase leading to a catwalk in front of the exo-mechs. Once up on the catwalk, they were able to look down at the entire cavern ahead of them. Kira could see Guaritore's little cottage in the distance. Sergeant Marcus was fighting through a horde of the undead while trying to blast a way back into Guaritore's house. She wondered if Raymond and the others were okay.

"Keep them off me," Tristan said, jumping onto the gray-rusted exo-mech. He hung onto the front, fiddling with some switches and latches.

The undead began to amass below. Kira set her elbows down on the railing and fired into the crowd. They seemed to climb out of every orifice of the cavern. Some were trudging up the stairs. Soon, she would run out of ammunition.

"Ha, it works!" Tristan said. The front chest of the humanoid exo-mech hissed open, revealing a one-seat cockpit inside.

"Where am I supposed to go?" Kira asked. She looked at the other exo-mech down the catwalk. "Can you get that one to work?"

"Sorry, NB, only Zeltans are allowed to pilot these," Tristan said, sitting in the seat and winking. "See you in a bit." The chest closed over him, and he disappeared into the exo-mech.

Kira seethed with anger, squeezing the trigger of the automatic rifle hard. Soon enough, she heard a familiar click. She was out of ammunition.

"Hey!" She banged on the exo-mech's chest. "Do you have any more ammo?"

"No!" Tristan's muffled voice could be barely heard. He yelled out something else.

"What?"

"I said," Tristan yelled, "run!"

Kira turned around, and the undead were beginning to stagger up to the catwalk. She ran in the opposite direction. More of the ghouls were coming from that way as well. She had nowhere else to go.

Suddenly, the exo-mech roared to life with the sounds of a hundred engines. An arm came up to sweep the catwalk of the walking corpses. They flew off the sides and splattered onto the ground below.

The exo-mech was a sight to behold. It seemed like a heavy mass of metal, wiring, and hydraulics but moved with the mannerisms of a giant human. The exo-mech's camera turned to Kira, frightening her.

"Get on!" Tristan's speaker-amplified voice announced.

"Where?" Kira called up to him with her arms outstretched.

"Here," Tristan's exo-mech opened its hand in front of her.

"You're kidding me," Kira said. She looked behind her, and more of the undead were getting close. She sighed, climbing into the palm of the mechanized hand. "You'd better know what you're doing because I—"

Tristan's exo-mech closed its robotic fingers around her tightly but gently enough not to crush her. The exo-mech then grabbed the catwalk with its other hand, picking it up like a mere nuisance. It crushed it, tearing it in half and tossing it aside. Meanwhile, Kira clutched one of the mechanical fingers for dear life. She hoped Tristan would not forget she was there and squeeze her to death by accident.

The exo-mech began to move forward with surprising agility. At this size, she expected it to be a lumbering giant. Instead, it moved with the same grace and athleticism that Tristan displayed. In a way, he controlled the exo-mech with such a degree of mastery that it seemed to be a projection of himself. As it deftly hopped between worn-down tanks and vehicles, it crushed the walking corpses beneath its feet. Looking ahead, she saw the familiar outline of a fox.

"Tristan!" she yelled. "It's Swift!"

Swift was standing atop the wreckage of a Vulture gunship. The corpses surrounded him from all sides below, arms reaching out to grab the fox. Some started climbing the gunship itself, and Swift knocked each of them off with a quick lunge and a head butt.

Tristan started to sweep the corpses away, but some started to climb the exo-mech. He tore them off, hopping to a safe place to put Kira down. In a whoosh, he lowered her, the inertia causing her stomach to catch in her throat. She stumbled onto the ground, reuniting with Swift, who ran to her, nuzzling her warmly.

"Swift," Kira said. "You're okay!"

The robot fox hummed proudly.

Meanwhile, Tristan's exo-mech began to struggle, dealing with the hordes of reanimated nuisances. They began to climb all over the suit, pulling at the cockpit door and the exposed wires. Due to his robotic arms' mobility limitations, he couldn't pick them out of every crevice. The exo-mech jumped and rolled to rid them, but they continued to swarm him.

Shots rang off from the high distance. Kira squinted her eyes to see. It was Vincent, the mysteriously silent soldier with the ponytail. The marksman impressively picked off the corpses with several perfectly placed shots, even while the exo-mech thrashed around. As the master sniper expertly placed headshot after headshot, a massive group of corpses surrounded his position on the high wall of the cavern.

He's trapped.

Kira watched helplessly as the Zeltan sniper turned around to fight valiantly, with nowhere to run. He fought off dozens at once, first firing his long rifle at close range and then resorting to his sidearm and knife, but he eventually succumbed to their overwhelming numbers.

Tristan tried bring his exo-mech over to rescue the sniper, but it appeared to be too late. The sniper post erupted into a huge explosion that sent the undead flying in every direction.

She deduced that the sniper must have sacrificed himself with an explosive.

"Dammit!" Tristan was heard over the exo-mech's speakers.

They had little time to stand and stare at the site of the fallen soldier. The undead horde were appearing from every crevice of the cavern. Kira and Swift took off behind Tristan's exo-mech as he swatted a way out.

TWENTY-TWO

Raymond struggled to free himself from the operating table that pinned him against the wall. The lab was a scattered mess of overturned computers and equipment that were overturned from the commotion outside. Distant gunfire, an occasional explosion, and the unmistakable sounds of giant footsteps were heard. On the monitors, Raymond could barely make sense of what was happening out there. One thing was for sure. One of the giant robots was moving.

On one monitor, he would see the hordes of zombies kicked aside by the mechanical juggernaut; on another, Sergeant Marcus was backed against the wall surrounded. Raymond wished he could help them. He worried he would be stuck in this Frankenstein laboratory where no one would find him.

Speaking of Dr. Frankenstein, Guaritore was lying face down on the ground, apparently knocked unconscious. His pistol slid across the floor, hidden under an anesthesia apparatus.

Raymond struggled against the operating table that seemed to have wedged a corner between a railing along the side wall. Pushing against the table was no use. Instead, Raymond slid himself down, crawling beneath the table feet first. Awkwardly crawling on his backside out from under the table, he stood himself up as the lights began to flicker again. The commotion up there was causing increasing damage to the house. He hoped the whole structure would not collapse around him before he could escape.

Just as he pulled himself up, to his horror he realized that Guaritore was now awake, crawling toward the pistol across the room.

"No!" Raymond yelled, darting forward.

Raymond ran forward to grab it first. He stepped over Guaritore but felt his momentum swinging toward the floor. The fat man had grabbed Raymond's foot. Raymond just barely put his arms out in front of him before he face-planted to the ground. He hit his elbow hard on the ground but desperately continued to crawl to the pistol.

He kicked Guaritore before the bloodied, fat man finally let go. Raymond was focused on the pistol, which was just beyond arms reach, as he reached for it under the anesthesia machine. The tips of his fingers just barely touched the grip of the gun. Raymond stretched his arm as far as it could go, twisting his head away to maximize his arm length. As he struggled, he realized Guaritore pulled himself to a control pad near Barrett's body.

"Stop," Raymond said, still struggling. "What are you doing?"

"I will have your memories," Guaritore sputtered through a bloodied mouth as he pressed more buttons and flipped switches.

The machine next to Barrett roared to life. Suddenly, the large soldier sat upright on the operating table, tubes and wires connected to all parts of his body. He began to pull them off himself, eyes dead to any type of purpose.

Raymond's adrenaline kicked in, seemingly giving him that extra millimeter of flexibility to flick the pistol into his palm. He gripped the handle. The feeling was empowering and cathartic. He drew it out awkwardly, pointing it at Guaritore. There was little time to deliberate, as Guaritore seemed to be activating the reanimated hulk for some nefarious purpose. Raymond squeezed the trigger several times.

Most of the bullets appeared to miss, but Guaritore winced at his side, slumping onto the control panel. Raymond's hand was shaking to the point of nearly dropping the pistol. Guaritore continued to make slow writhing movements. Raymond processed several emotions at once. There was something very personal about shooting someone up close and watching the aftermath. He could feel his victim's pain. It was very real and gave Raymond a twinge of deep guilt.

"We die," Guaritore said, "together."

The mortally wounded man slowly pressed buttons on the panel, stirring the reanimated soldier on the operating table to stand up and move toward Raymond.

"Stop! Stop!" Raymond retreated until his back was pressed against a wall.

The zombified soldier moved toward Raymond with a demonic lumber as the lights continued to flicker on and off. Reactively, Raymond fired the remaining bullets of the pistol at Barrett. The reanimated corpse stumbled back for a moment. The bullets pierced his naked torso in several places as darkened blood poured out.

Despite this, he continued to come at Raymond, who scrambled to the side, just barely out of arms reach. Barrett nearly grabbed him as he darted past. They continued to play the cat-and-mouse game around the claustrophobic operating room. They were trapped together with no means to escape. Raymond imagined the super soldier would rip him in half once he got his hands on him. That was not the way Raymond Redmin wanted to die.

Fortunately, the recently deceased corpse moved clumsily and slowly, just giving Raymond enough time to devise a plan. First, Raymond tried throwing knives and surgical tools at Barrett, which were ignored. Then, Raymond tried to use the operating tables and rolling equipment to put between him and Barrett. The superhuman did seem to retain his strength, tossing them across the room, further destroying the lab.

Guaritore continued to writhe in pain, sprawled out over the control panel, dripping in blood. As Barrett walked by, the fat man reached out to his zombie creation for help.

"Quick," Guaritore said, "do away with him. You can help me. Do you understand?"

The undead Barrett paused for a moment to look at him. In the blink of an eye, he brought his fist up, bringing it down on Guaritore's face, which squished into an explosion of blood, bone, and organs.

In a panic, Raymond ran to the anesthesia machine, increasing the oxygen tank output. He yanked the tubes out of the oxygen tank, allowing the volatile gas to disperse freely with a loud hiss. If he were to die down here, it would be on his own terms, taking the mad scientist's machinations with him.

He heard banging against the metal door at the top of the staircase. As Barrett lumbered toward him again, Raymond sidestepped, glancing at the security monitors, scanning for a screen showing the inside of the house.

It was Sergeant Marcus. The armored giant was trying to knock down the metal door to the basement staircase. When Raymond ran to the stairway, he could see one side partially broken open.

"Hey!" Raymond said. "Get me out of here!"

"Sir," Marcus said, bringing up his gun, "please step back."

"Wait, no!" Raymond said. "I turned on the gas down here. We'll all go up in flames, don't."

"Then please take this, sir." Marcus handed Raymond a large knife through the crack in the doorway. "Behind you."

Barrett was at the bottom of the narrow stairway. Raymond was trapped.

Raymond looked down at the knife. "This isn't going to do anything."

"Sir, press the button," Marcus said through the doorway. "And please be careful not to touch the blade."

Raymond flipped a cover on the hilt and pressed down on a button. The knife hummed and snapped with electric fizzles. He hoped it would not set off the flammable gas downstairs. The zombified Barrett stumbled on a step, clumsily re-adjusting himself. Raymond took that opportunity to take a breath of courage and lunge the knife into the zombie superhuman's shoulder.

Raymond jumped backward immediately as the knife sliced into the meat of Barrett's deltoid muscle. For a moment, it seemed like Barrett would just pull the knife out, but he began to convulse and rolled down the stairs. Hundreds of pounds of naked and bloodied muscle and meat barreled down the steps as Raymond watched with his back against the gnarled metal doorway.

Marcus continued using his full might to bend the metal. When there was just about enough space, Raymond started to slide out, with Marcus pulling him through. Just as Raymond came through, Barrett's hand came out from beyond the crack. Raymond sprawled out on the hallway floor, breathing heavily, barely escaping from the literal clutches of certain death. The reanimated corpse moaned at them, reaching through the opening but unable to squeeze through.

"It has been an honor to serve with you, Master Sergeant," Marcus said sadly, reaching through the open tear in the metal and pulling the knife out from Barrett's shoulder.

Marcus picked up Raymond with one arm and rushed out of the house. Hanging from his arm, he watched Marcus casually drop a grenade behind them.

"Please cover your eyes and ears, sir," Marcus said.

Raymond complied, as a cascade of explosions destroyed Guaritore's house. He could feel debris falling around him, but the armored soldier had used his body to protect him from the flying shrapnel.

The sheer size of Marcus' armored body made Raymond feel like he was being carried like a baby. Marcus was well over 7 feet tall and had a body mass twice that of a normal human, but his bulky armor doubled even that.

After the explosions, Raymond opened his eyes. He stood knee-deep in a pile of corpses, torn apart by gunfire. Marcus had destroyed them all. There were rotted bodies of soldiers dressed in tattered old soldier uniforms, zombified Aggros, and others who looked like natural born humans. These were all of Guaritore's experiments.

One of the undead monstrosities began to moan and move, but Marcus casually walked over and stomped his metal boot down. The head crunched and squished open, exploding into a pool of black slime.

What was this place?

As a refreshing beacon of levity, Swift appeared and ran up to Raymond, giving him a playful nudge. Raymond rubbed his head, glad to see him as well. Hearing the sounds of machinery pistons, he looked up and noticed the towering robot colossus above.

"Raymond!" Kira said, sitting atop the robot's shoulder. "You're okay!"

He was glad Kira was safe; he waved at her, while also taken aback by the surreal sight of the moving humanoid robot. He remembered that they referred to them as exo-mechs. This appeared to be piloted by Tristan, sitting within a cockpit in the machine's torso equivalent.

"Where's Guaritore?" Tristan asked through the exo-mech's speakers.

"Dead," Raymond said. "All of this was some kind of sick experiment. He was trying to bring the dead back to life."

"Well, I'm glad you took care of him, NB," Tristan said. "Or else he would have seen the bottom of this exo-mech's foot."

Tristan made the exo-mech dance around with bravado, kicking aside a pile of the re-killed corpses.

"Hey!" Kira said, nearly falling off the exo-mech. "If you're gonna act like a 5-year-old, at least put me down first!"

The exo-mech put its arm on its hip and leaned against a pillar. Raymond marveled at how Tristan made it move so convincingly with human mannerisms.

"Has anyone heard from Captain Darien or Specialist Jason?" Marcus asked.

"I thought he was with you guys," Raymond said.

"No," Sergeant Marcus said. "I fear the Captain and Specialist Jason may have met the same fate as Specialist Vincent and the Master Sergeant. We must investigate to confirm. Lieutenant, your orders?"

Raymond cringed at the realization that the pompous Lieutenant was now in charge.

"Alright." Tristan said, "Then we should split up, and then—"

A loud rumble shook the entire underground cavern.

"What the hell was that?" Raymond asked.

"Everyone, get down!" Tristan yelled.

Raymond turned around. The black exo-mech had torn itself out from the framework at the other end of the cavern. It threw the catwalk and support beams the entire distance toward them. Tristan used the large body of the exo-mech to shield the group from harm. He quickly but carefully put Kira on the ground while knocking away the flying beams of metal coming at them.

"Who's in *that* robot suit?" Raymond yelled over the deafening banging of the metal beams against the exo-mech.

"I don't know," Tristan said. "Not one of us."

The black exo-mech walked forward confidently, and an unfamiliar voice came out from its speakers.

"Ah, the infamous Lieutenant Tristan," the black exo-mech pilot said. "Oh, forgive me, was it *Prince* Tristan?"

"Well if you know who I am," Tristan asked, in his robot giant walking forward to meet the challenge, "Then you'll know it's a mistake to fight me in an exo-mech."

"I was hoping we could meet in a dramatic fashion such as this," the enemy pilot said. "We are brought together by purpose and power greater and wiser than us, are we not?"

"Sergeant Marcus," Tristan said, "get them to safety! Now!"

"Please, follow me," Marcus said calmly, yet shaken, leading Raymond, Kira, and Swift away.

As they ran, Raymond huffed and puffed. They could barely keep up with Marcus, who slowed down when he realized they had fallen behind.

"Marcus, who *was* that?" Kira asked.

"Who we came here for," Marcus said. "A most dangerous individual. A former Ranger. His name is Julian."

TWENTY-THREE

Kira Skyler ran at breakneck speed as tanks and vehicles were hurled overhead. Julian and Tristan's exo-mechs were throwing increasingly large objects at one another, dodging and encircling the other, and the underground cavern trembled in awe of the titans' impending battle.

All of this was far beyond what Kira had expected from her adventure. She was disappointed that Guaritore ended up not being useful to her goal of delivering medical care to her town, but now she had Raymond. She needed to make sure that got out of this situation alive, and perhaps she could bring him back to Remnant to help her people. All these thoughts were drowned out by the titanic battle that threated to collapse the cavern around them.

"Enough!" Julian's voice boomed.

Kira looked back. The black exo-mech picked up a massive gun, perhaps the size of a tank turret. It was so large the exo-mech's arms creaked as it pulled it up. The triple barrel of the gargantuan gun started to swirl slowly, giving Kira a terrible feeling of impending doom.

"Marcus, you need get them out of here!" Tristan yelled over the exo-mech speakers.

Kira felt herself pulled backward. She landed inside a train car, not unlike the one Guaritore used to deliver them from the Aggro village.

"Where is this train taking us?" Raymond asked. He, Marcus, and Swift were already on the train.

"North, it seems," Marcus said. He was busy randomly pressing buttons at the front control panel in order to get the train moving.

Kira couldn't help herself from watching the exo-mechs. Benny was the one who was fascinated by stories of these giant fighting machines. She mostly found the idea of Zeltan death machines repulsive. But here, Tristan's exo-mech moved like a colossus above the train, an armored titan of destruction that was the only thing standing between them and certain death.

Julian's giant chain gun began to fire like booming thunder, echoing throughout the underground hellscape. Tristan's exo-suit mech scooped up a nearby Tiger tank and threw it over his shoulder, the massive metal vehicle propped into the air and sliding along the ground. The bullets, shrapnel, and sparks of energy lit up in front of Tristan, who stood firm in front of the train, trying to protect them from harm.

"Sergeant, go!" Tristan said, echoing over the barrage of metallic mayhem.

The train roared to life, and Marcus pushed the lever without hesitation. The train started to build up momentum, just as some bullets began to tear through some parts of the train car. Kira, Raymond, and Swift took cover. Even Marcus ducked, not keen to take a human-sized bullet from a giant automatic cannon.

"What about him?" Kira yelled over the sound of the blaring gun.

"The Lieutenant ordered me to get you to safety," Marcus said.

Kira peeked over the window as the train began leaving the underground cavern. Tristan's exo-mech was buckling under the continued gunfire. Julian's black exo-mech continued to shoot as he pressed closer. The tank that Tristan held up for cover was all but torn to shreds. Just as Kira watched Tristan's doomed final stand, their train exited into a dark tunnel.

"Thank you, Lieutenant," Marcus said sadly over his com-link.

Kira looked back as the exo-mech disappeared as the train bounded forward into darkness. She felt a twinge of sadness. Tristan was the epitome of narcissism that she hated and expected from the Zeltans. And yet, he protected her and even displayed some degree of levity and humanity that she did not expect. She processed her feelings of confusing sympathy for his apparent sacrifice and demise.

"You said we're going north," Raymond said. "What's North?"

The bulky armored soldier finally allowed himself to rest by sitting on the floor with his back against the wall. He replied simply, "Away from here."

Kira petted Swift, who snuggled close to her. The train was lit, but the pitch black of the tunnel seemed to make the robot fox uneasy. When they met the Zeltan soldiers, there were fourteen of them. And now, only Sergeant Marcus remained. She looked at the silent soldier, who was perpetually devoid of emotion as he never removed his helmet and armor. Kira was sympathetic to him.

Sergeant Marcus continued to sit on the ground, motionless. She thought to speak to him but deduced that this must be difficult for him. He was the lone survivor. He had lost all his teammates, possibly friends. She wondered if Zeltans even had a concept of friends.

"Are you alright?" Raymond knelt beside her.

"Yeah," she said, only now realizing how sore and bruised she was. "Just, everything hurts. Do you have medicine for that?"

"If I did," Raymond said with a tired smile, "I'd need it for myself first."

He put a hand on her shoulder, grunting as he got up and walked around the train car. Kira took a deep breath. She couldn't believe she made it this far, considering all she had been through. She looked down at Swift, who was snuggled deep into her lap. When he went into sleep mode, the usual bright green hue of his eyes dimmed. For a moment, she felt peace.

"We'll make it back home, Swift," Kira said dreamily. "I promise."

TWENTY-FOUR

Benny Fong stood on his tiptoes, trying to see what was happening above ground. He and Casey Jarrett were trapped in a wide ditch dug six feet into the dirt. It was a fitting analogy for their twist of fate. From where they sat, Benny could just barely see Blackheart sitting on his luxury chair, watching the Corsairs pick apart the crashed ship for supplies. Benny had been listening to Blackheart yell out orders for hours. They were scavenging and preparing for an inevitable attack by the Raiders from the west.

The sun shone high above them. It must have been around mid-day. The Spire would adjust its artificial coverage, but the sun still baked the Frontier desert to an uncomfortable heat at this time of day.

"Can you just sit down and stop moving?" Casey asked.

Casey was sitting with his back against the dirt. His wide-brimmed hat covered his face in a shadow. Benny thought he had been sleeping.

"What are they going to do to us?" Benny asked in a whisper.

"Oh, there ain't any reason to hide any secrets," Casey said. "As soon as this is over, they're going to sell us out on the Green Sea market. Probably make you a ship slave and turn me into some cyborg freak like them."

Benny shuddered. He had driven himself mad for hours, imagining the horrid torture that the Corsairs would inflict on their prisoners. He would rather stay in this dug ditch than be taken back to Cyborg Bay and sold for body parts.

"What about the people in Remnant?" Benny asked. "Won't they send someone to find us?"

"Listen to me, Fong," Casey said, lifting his hat. "Ain't no one coming. Red Riders probably have enough on their plate keeping the town safe from the Raiders passing by. No one's spending time getting into the middle of this fight. We're too far behind enemy lines. Ain't no hope now, so don't waste your time with that."

Benny plopped down to the ground, defeated. "So that's it? We'll never see any of them again? My parents, my friends?"

"This is the real world," Casey said. "This is the goddamn Frontier. What did you expect? See, you lived in a bubble your whole life. Out here, people die. The strong eat the weak. You take, or they take, simple as that."

"It doesn't have to be that way," Benny said. "We were making a living in Remnant. Peacefully. Like they used to on Old Earth."

"On Old Earth? On Old Earth?!" Casey chuckled. "I thought you were the smart one, Fong. You know all the stories of Old Earth. War after war. Just like it is here. Ain't nothing changed. Shit, it's a wonder our species survived as long as it did. Bad things happen; it's part of life. In fact, that's probably what happened to Earth. A new day, a new war, then poof. Gone. Probably all got themselves killed and left us here on this hellhole to die."

Benny looked down at the ground. "Some people lived happy lives. They got to live to be old and do great things."

"Like what?" Casey said sarcastically.

"I dunno." Benny hopelessly stared into the sky. "I mean, they invented stuff, built things. Huge buildings and spaceships. People had the chance to follow their dreams and imaginations. They had books to read about stories and videos to watch them happen. They figured out a way to be happy. To have fun, to make friends. To fall in love."

"Stop," Casey said. "Goddammit, Fong. This is some fairy tale bullshit. This is that shit you and the other kids in the town started telling yourselves ever since we Red Riders started protecting you. You forgot what it was like to live in fear of being robbed, raped, killed. That's the shit out there. That's the real Frontier. You made a stupid ass move and left that for what? For a damn girl?"

"W-what, Kira? No, she's my friend."

"Oh please, Fong." Casey threw his head back. "You are a sad, pathetic excuse for a man. She's not into you, you know that, right? You're just a desperate puppy following her around, hoping she'll pay attention."

"Alright, Casey, stop it."

Casey stood up. "She'll never want you. Women want someone strong, someone who will protect them. Choose between a coward like you and someone with the balls to stand up for a girl, and she'll dump the coward every time."

"Casey, just stop," Benny said, backing up.

The cowboy walked closer, taunting Benny. "Kira never would have chosen you. And if she ever did, it would have been because she felt sorry. You're worthless to anyone, Fong. Until you man up, you're no good to anyone." Casey shook his head. "The way I see it, she's probably dead now anyway."

The anger that swelled up in Benny's chest reached a boiling point. He balled up his fist and swung at Casey's cheek. The impact sent a shock of pain into Benny's wrist that made him angrier. He tackled the taller man to the ground, punching him again.

Casey blocked the next punch and gave Benny a head butt to the mouth. Benny grabbed his face in pain as Casey elbowed him across the head. Benny crawled across the ground, disoriented. He felt a hard kick to the abdomen, which made him want to throw up.

"That's the spirit, Fong," Casey said, standing up, amusingly wiping his face. "That's the only way to survive out here; you gotta—"

Benny didn't let him finish his sentence. With a heart pulsing rage through his veins, Benny jumped up, ramming his shoulder into Casey's torso, slamming them both into the ground again. What followed was a confusing contortion of limbs and pain. Casey repeatedly put him in submission holds, but Benny was far too angry to simply allow himself to give up.

Casey placed him into a chokehold, but Benny managed to bite down on his arm. Benny then threw his head back, slamming it into Casey's face. He turned around, grabbing the cowboy by the neck and pressing him against the wall. Benny wanted to squeeze the life out of Casey. He hated him. As Benny's hands clutched his neck tightly, Casey began to laugh through a bloodied face.

"Just..." Casey said. "Just... do it."

"Hey!" someone said from above ground. "What's going on? Blackheart! You gotta see this! These morons are trying to kill each other!"

Benny was distracted. Casey used that moment of hesitation to knee Benny in the groin. Overwhelming pain and nausea overtook Benny, and he rolled off. Casey clutched his neck, gasping for air. Benny shook off the pain and grabbed Casey's head, making it crash down on his upward-swinging knee. The two fell to the ground, writhing in agony and exhausted.

"Now, where are your manners?" Blackheart asked, leaning over the pit. "If you two were going to fight to the death, you could have at least told us. We would have placed bets! Ah, and I would have thought the odds would have been in the cowboy's favor. Hardline, go fetch us some more prisoners. We could sure make a fun game of this."

Benny stared up at the blue sky again. He was hungry, thirsty, tired, and in pain. He had never been in a fight, let alone ever struck anyone. There was something intoxicating about it. For a moment, he could not quite put his finger on the feeling.

"Now, didn't that feel good, Fong?" Casey asked, lying on the ground beside him, also staring up at the sky. "Forget about that

Old World shit. This is the Frontier. You fight, or you die. And living? Shit, fighting is life. You live to fight, and you learn to enjoy it, and maybe you'll live to do it again the next day. "

"That's the dumbest shit I've ever heard," Benny said.

Casey let out a slow crescendo of a genuine laugh. He coughed up mucus and blood, holding his side in pain. There was something bizarrely humorous about this situation, the sheer hopelessness of it. Much to Benny's own surprise, he started laughing too. Ignoring their doomed fate, the two took some time to lie on the ground, staring up at the sky from the bottom of a pit, laughing like maniacs.

Benny wondered what Kira would think of him now.

TWENTY-FIVE

Kira Skyler squinted and covered her eyes when the train burst out into the bright light of day. She, Raymond, Swift, and Marcus were heading north, perhaps to the north edge of the Black Forest or even the White Range. When her eyes adjusted to the jarring brightness, she could only see the beautiful landscape of a snow-covered mountain range. There was no doubt about it. The train took them straight to the beautiful snowy mountains north of the Red Frontier, Black Forest, and Golden Plains. It was a grand vista to behold.

"Where are we?" Raymond asked with wonder in his voice.

"This is the White Range," Kira said, with her hands pressed against the window. "I've seen them from far away. But never this close. This is where the Androids live."

"The androids?" Raymond asked.

"They're AI," Kira said. "The only AI that the Zeltans allow to exist."

Raymond shook his head. "It's just one thing after another, isn't it? We can't just find some normal people."

Kira looked down, petting Swift on the head. He sat happily on a seat near the window, his tail wagging, cheerfully humming while observing the view.

Kira looked out again. "After the first AI war, the Zeltans couldn't trust any AI. In 110 AS, they forced every AI to be destroyed or driven out of the Kingdom. They called it the AI Purge."

"It was to ensure all threats to the Kingdom were minimized," Marcus said.

"Just another group you kicked out, hoping they would die," Kira said. "The androids had to escape north to these mountains. Here, they created a city for exiles. They called it North Haven. There was an event in 122 called the Miracle at North Haven. After Captain Paul, a Zeltan who sympathized with the androids, was executed, the Zeltans led an army into the mountains to destroy the exiles."

Kira surprised herself at how much history she retained just by listening to her little brother talk about it.

"According to the stories," she continued, "human sympathizers stood hand-in-hand to protect the androids. It was supposed to be a slaughter, but there was no fighting. The Zeltans stood down, and both sides agreed to the Accords."

"Wow," Raymond said. "A peace agreement?"

"I guess you could say that," Kira said. "They mandated that the androids were not allowed to leave the White Range, all the androids had to be registered with the Kingdom, and neither side was allowed to fly any aircraft over the Range or the Black Forest."

"There is one more point to the Accords, ma'am," Sergeant Marcus said. "No new AI can be created, manufactured, or designed. Any artificial intelligence entity found violating these agreed upon treaties must be destroyed, and North Haven would be subject to unmolested investigation and punishment therein as found appropriate by the Royal Council of Princes."

Kira quickly glanced at Swift, her best friend and protector. Under these cruel Zeltan laws, they would technically require Swift to be killed. Her grandfather was a volunteer during the failed Invasion of the Black Forest in 128 AS. There, he was rescued by Swift, a lone robotic fox, who he later discovered was not listed in the AI registry. The kind sentients of North Haven suggested that Quentin take Swift to the west Frontier, where the Kingdom rarely cared to enforce their laws. Swift stood by her grandfather, her father, and now her. Kira would never let them take her guardian Swift.

"Ma'am," Marcus said, "when we regain communications with the Kingdom, I will be required to run a registration check on the quadruped."

"Hey, guys," Raymond interrupted nervously, pointing ahead.

Marcus ran to the front of the train at the control panel. "We need to stop this train." He mashed some buttons on the panel.

"Why?" Kira asked. "What's wrong?"

"Look."

Just barely visible in the distance was a long chasm. The tracks appeared to stretch forward into a bridge, but the bridge itself had a noticeable break in the middle. It looked purposefully destroyed.

"Holy shit," Raymond said. "How do we stop this train?"

Marcus took a lever and pulled it backward. Kira, Raymond, and Swift flew forward as the train let out a deafening screech. Kira hit the floor and ached all over. She had been thrown around, beaten up, and ran for her life more times than she ever imagined she would need to. She nearly convinced herself to stay on the ground, but Raymond grabbed her arm.

"Get up, get up," Raymond said. "We need to get out of here."

The train was trying to stop but still plodded on forward. Beneath the screeching sounds of metal on metal, Raymond and Marcus yelled to one another. Marcus slid open the side door. They were moving too fast. The snowy ground was zipping by them too quickly to leap to safely. Marcus, Raymond, Kira, and Swift stood at the edge of the train, all wondering whether jumping was their last resort.

"We're gonna have to!" Kira said.

"You won't make it," Marcus said bluntly. Kira assumed he implied only he would likely survive the jump.

"Oh my god," Raymond said, looking ahead. They were approaching the chasm.

Suddenly, the familiar noise of bounding footsteps could be heard over the metal screeching. Marcus grabbed the door handle and hung himself out to check on the commotion.

"It's the Lieutenant," Marcus declared, coming back inside the train. He closed the door and calmly said. "Please grab hold of something."

The Lieutenant?

Kira took Swift into one arm, grabbing a handle on the wall and crouching into a ball. Raymond did the same, hugging them both. Marcus casually remained standing.

"Please remain calm," Sergeant Marcus said.

Kira and Raymond screamed at the top of their lungs as they felt the train shoot out over the chasm. They felt a moment of zero gravity that made Kira's stomach rise to her throat. The sudden jerking of the train caused them to fly up, hitting the ceiling, then fly toward the front of the train car. Kira lost hold of Swift and Raymond as she fell downward through the train until her back made impact hard, knocking the wind out of her.

She lost consciousness for a moment, but when she re-oriented herself, she noticed that her back was against the front windows of the train. As she turned around slowly, her body screamed in pain, and she groaned in response. She realized that the front of the train was facing directly down the chasm, suspended in the air. The sight of the drop made her nauseous and struck fear into her heart. She began to scream, but the insidious sound of cracking glass created an eerie silence.

"Kira!" Raymond said from above. He remained holding onto the side handle. Swift was there as well. "Don't move! We're coming to get you!"

Before Kira could respond, the glass beneath her gave way. She watched in slow motion as Raymond screamed and reached for her. At that moment, Kira thought of everyone she cared about. Her brother Owen, the townspeople of Remnant, Benny.

She would never see them again. But perhaps she would see her mother and father again.

She felt a sudden disorienting tug that sent shockwaves of pain through her entire body. Marcus appeared out of nowhere, grabbing onto her wrist. She dangled hundreds of feet in the cold, frigid air. In panic, she flailed her arms and legs, screaming.

"Brace yourself," Marcus said.

In an instant, he pulled her up with ease, jumping up to where Raymond and Swift were. She felt as though her shoulder might have been ripped out of its socket. Carried under his arm, Marcus deftly jumped from one point of the vertically hanging train to another, knocking away barriers like they were nuisances.

A few boxcars up, the horizon began to level itself. They had reached the point where they were no longer in the part of the train hanging off the side. Marcus kicked down a side car door, dropping Kira off in the snow at the edge of the chasm.

For a moment, the numbing snow was a relief to her aching muscles. Before she could take in her first cold breath of open air, Marcus jumped back into the train for Raymond and Swift. She jumped up to make sure they were okay but realized that she was standing in the shadow of a giant exo-mech.

"Ha! I got here just in time!" Tristan said over the exo-mech's speakers.

Kira ignored his arrogance and allowed herself to smile. Tristan survived somehow. Sergeant Marcus appeared with Raymond and Swift in his arms a few moments later. Tristan's exo-mech was holding back the train, the front end hanging over the edge.

"Was there anything valuable you left in there?" Tristan asked rhetorically.

After a moment, the exo-mech shrugged as if displaying the mannerisms of a human. It let go of the train with a showmanship flair. Kira and Raymond stepped back away from the train as it rolled forward off the cliff. The cold air and snow on the ground began to bite at Kira's skin, but she couldn't help but watch the train fall hundreds of feet below, ending with a crash that echoed throughout the gorge.

She looked back at the tracks. Tristan must have caught up with them, slowing down the train just in time and holding it in place so they could escape. She saw the exo-mech's dragging marks along the snow behind it. The pretentious Lieutenant was alive. Although she found him quite insufferable, she was glad he arrived to save them. She was glad that, despite the seemingly insurmountable dangers behind them, some of them had survived.

The exo-mech's chest flipped open, and the blond-haired pilot stepped out. He put his hands on his hips, inhaling deeply and smiling wide at the beautiful mountain landscape.

"Does that thing have heating?" Raymond asked, his teeth audibly chattering. "It's freezing out here."

TWENTY-SIX

Captain Darien felt a sting, waking him. In his dream, he saw the same familiar red eyes that had haunted him for years. Just as before, the demonic spotlights stared deep into his soul. This time, they followed him into waking. As he opened his eyes out of his dream, the glowing red specter was still in the form of an old friend turned nemesis.

"Good morning, soldier," Julian said. "Your Lieutenant proved to be quite a talented exo-mech pilot. He escaped north with your sergeant and the natural borns. I was overzealous in challenging him head-on like that. Perhaps I can meet him in battle again someday."

Darien's instincts goaded him to grab Julian by the head and bash him against an upthrust knee. However, his limbs felt like heavy sandbags, rendering him incapable of such a rewarding action. He was hanging by wrists from the wall. Darien looked around the room, which seemed to languidly lag behind his eye movements. He tried to make out a word, but only a croak came out.

"You were pumped full of sedatives, Captain Darien," Julian said, pacing about the room with his hands behind his back. "Guaritore hoped to experiment on you. Unfortunately, as with all natural borns, he has succumbed to his inadequacies quite prematurely."

Julian pointed to a video screen on the wall. Darien summoned all his strength to pick his head up. One of the video screens showed Guaritore's lifeless body lying on the floor of the ruined operating room. There was a large pool of blood where his head should have been. Darien looked at the other screens. The entire underground cavern was in disarray. The cottage was destroyed. Dozens of walking corpses stumbled about. Darien struggled to make sense of it all.

"Guaritore is—was—quite obsessed with the revival of the human body after death," Julian said, approaching a naked body on the table at the center of the room.

Darien squinted his eyes. It was Specialist Jason. He wanted to call out to him, but he could only enunciate a paralyzed groan.

"What Guaritore failed to understand," Julian continued, "is that the *true* next step in evolution is beyond our imperfect human forms, these petty mortal bodies. Yes, even our advanced genetic designs have their limitations, don't they? What I seek is genuine *immortality*, Captain Darien."

Julian stepped into the dim light, bringing his face to Darien's. His long strands of jet-black hair came down over his menacing face. Those blood-red eyes Darien saw in his dreams stared into him again. They were cybernetic ocular implants, glowing with a red burning fire like a demon out of hell. When Darien last saw him all those years ago, Julian was blind and left to die. Now, he menaced Darien like a phantasm from the beyond.

Darien's mind traveled back to that ill-fated mission to this Black Forest all those years ago. He was a young Lieutenant, eager to serve and learn under the well-respected and accomplished Captain Julian. For that mission, the squad was composed of 8 soldiers, split into two teams commanded by Julian and Darien.

It was only a simple scouting mission, routinely investigating the whereabouts and remains of King Magnus' doomed venture into the Forest to engage the Aggromen many decades ago. Many Ranger squads had searched the forestry unsuccessfully over the years, with the savages and wildlife increasingly making their ventures more perilous. And only one night into Captain Julian squad's ranging, they were ambushed by Aggromen armed with guns and explosives.

The squad was obviously much better organized and equipped than the Aggromen assailants, but they were driven further and further into the recesses of the forest. For days they wandered the maze of trees in the low light of the thick tree cover, as they battled the Aggromen, as well as the mutated creatures of the damned forest. As the ammunition and supplies ran out, the casualties piled up, and the elite superhuman team finally began to feel fatigue after consecutive days of non-stop fighting, the worst blow to their morale occurred.

An Aggroman had tossed a grenade near Julian that exploded, sending shrapnel into his face. Fragments of metal, tree wood, and dirt were firmly blasted into Julian's face and eyes. Despite these grave injuries, the captain survived. However, he was wounded far beyond the ability for him to lead, and thus Darien was the de facto leader of the team.

They had to carry Captain Julian from place to place, while still fighting the surrounding aggressors. Even more days passed, and their numbers dwindled down to only 5. They were holed up in a bog, fighting off giant lizard creatures from the swamp, using only primitive firearms stolen off dead Aggromen and spears crudely fashioned from tree branches.

By then, the other fighting-capable soldiers began to grumble about Captain Julian being a liability. He was slowing the team down. His inability to see and function greatly put them in danger. Darien and Corporal Francis advocated not to leave their captain behind at any costs, while Privates Bryan and Keith increasingly suggested that they would all die if they continued to carry the captain around.

The argument reached a zenith, and the four soldiers began to fight amongst each other. Fighting words turned into fighting actions, and a scuffle broke out, leading to Corporal Francis being stabbed by a spear in the confusion.

Darien was forced to kill the murderer Private Keith in retaliation. Just as Private Bryan would further commit mutiny by shooting Darien, a mutant lizard erupted from the bog, biting into Bryan's body and dragging him into the mud.

Throughout all this, Captain Julian sought to keep order, but in his blindness, he could only stumble around in confusion. Hearing the lizard grabbing Bryan, Julian took his rifle, shooting wildly, and fell into the swamp waters.

Darien ran to help his blind captain, but the waters began to fill with the mutant lizard creatures, as Julian thrashed around wildly. Darien only took a moment, but ultimately decided that the blind captain was as good as gone. In a rare moment of self-preservation, Darien ran as quick as he could, armed with only a spear.

For days he wandered the forest, burdened with the guilt of survival and the nagging possibility that perhaps he could have saved the captain. Just as he considered the possibility of giving up and allowing the Black Forest to consume him, he was discovered by a new Ranger squad sent in to find him. Darien was the only survivor of that mission, and since then, he spent every night haunted by it, and drifting through each waking day wishing he had died along with his squad.

And now, here he was, staring back at Julian, the blinded captain he thought had been left for dead all those years ago.

"I know what you're thinking," Julian said, stepping back. "And no, I am not a walking corpse. I survived despite the dire situation you had left me in. I don't blame you for running; I was as good as dead. But Guaritore found me: abandoned, blind, waiting for the forest to consume me. He gave me new eyes. And by the grace of technology, now I see. In turn, I helped him continue his work. He was extracting the memories of the dead and allowing them to move again... although only as these useless, mindless husks. This research was always considered a dead end. This was only a piece of the grand puzzle. We must leave this place now; we need to assemble the rest of the players."

Julian took a syringe from the table as Darien's mind swirled in confusion. *What is he talking about?*

"I'm telling you this, Captain Darien," he continued, "because you're coming with me. Guaritore's technology will be useful to achieve our ultimate objective. But there are far larger powers at play here, and you will be needed for the end game. But we have a long journey ahead. I want you to be there. You were always destined to stand beside us at the precipice of our true destiny. You may not understand now, but you will."

Darien struggled to break free. He processed numerous strategies to overpower Julian when the opportunity lent itself. But his arms were still bound, and his legs felt like lead. Every organ in his body refused to obey any of his commands. Julian took the syringe, loading it into an IV connected to Darien's arm.

"Destiny," Julian said as Darien fell back into a slumber. "You and I are destined to lead our people to conquer death itself."

TWENTY-SEVEN

Benny Fong listened intently to the commotion overhead. He and Casey remained in the pit, aching from the bruises that they inflicted on each other hours ago. They came to a wordless truce with each other, silently planning a means of escape if the opportunity arose. Blackheart and the Corsairs were preoccupied now, while Benny and Casey were still stuck in the ditch, with an armed cyborg guard watching over them.

Based on what Benny could barely hear, the Corsairs had just captured a Raider scout. He struggled to listen in to the interrogation above.

"What's your name again?" Blackheart was pestering the prisoner.

"Karl," the Raider scout could be heard sputtering.

"Karl," Blackheart repeated in a mocking tone. "Well, *Karl*, tell me more, tell me more."

After much interrogation and physical abuse, the scout divulged that the Raider clans were on their way in full force. The clans were in a state of perpetual violent conflict with one another, but the arrival of the spaceship was cause for most of the clans to emerge from the Far West together. After all, they lived to steal and plunder. The potential treasures of the first spaceship to arrive in two hundred years were finally enough to bring the vandals together in an unprecedented, terrifying alliance.

"Where is the ark!" Blackheart shouted.

The Ark? Benny thought, *What's the Ark?*

"It came down in a parachute onto the sand." Karl coughed. "It was too heavy for our vehicles. We got it as far as Remnant. It's there."

Oh god, the Raiders are in my hometown right now.

"And you're coming back for more?" Blackheart asked.

"Looking for a bigger vehicle to bring it back with us."

A grunt was let out. Someone must have hit Karl the scout in the stomach.

"You damn dirty beggars," Blackhearts said. "Scrounging the dirt, picking up the scraps of food and resources we provide. We are the ones who challenge the Zeltans at sea and on their shores. We bring back the food and weapons to Cyborg Bay, which we graciously trade from the goodness of our damn hearts to the low lives on the Frontier, and then..." Blackheart paused for dramatic effect. "You all go and steal it! Like dogs fighting for table scraps. And here you are, biting the hand that feeds you."

A smack rang through the air, likely Blackheart's metal hand against the Raider scout's face.

Benny had conflicted compassion for the unseen Raider. After all, when he was growing up, Benny was witness to some raids on Remnant. The thieves sneaked into the town, robbing and murdering the townspeople. Were it not for Swift the fox and the retaliation of a few brave men, the Raiders would have taken everything, and everyone, away with them. The stories of the Far West were truly terrifying: lawless badlands where the weak were sold as slaves and the strong murdered each other in broad daylight. Ever since Remnant came under the protection of the Red Riders, they virtually never had to worry about another Raider attack again, especially being the furthest town away from the Brass Badlands.

"Throw him in the pit with the others," Blackheart said. "Let's get ready, boys; it sounds like we're going to war!"

The cyborgs cheered. Some fired their guns into the air. Benny pressed himself against the dirt wall, worried the bullets would fall back onto him. Meanwhile, Casey was unmoved, face hidden beneath the wide brim of his hat.

The Raider named Karl crashed into the pit like a lifeless bag of bones. He was shirtless, bruised, and bloodied. The Corsairs had given him quite the beating. He lay on the ground, contorted, groaning, trying to get up. Benny slowly walked forward to help him, forgetting his prior prejudice.

"Don't," Casey said.

"I'm just gonna help him up," Benny said.

"No," Casey said forcefully. "He can get up himself."

The Raider's arms shook as he tried to push himself off the ground. Blood dripped from his mouth. He was a gaunt young man, perhaps not much younger than Benny. His ribs showed through his skin. In fact, some on the right appeared bruised and visibly broken.

He groaned. "Help."

"Casey, shouldn't we at least—" Benny said.

Casey stood. "I said no."

Casey kneeled next to Karl, who struggled to keep his head up. He picked him up by the hair.

"How long you been with the Raiders?" Casey asked, inches from his face.

"I..." Karl sputtered.

"Answer me!" Casey said, shaking him by the hair.

"A couple years..."

"Where were you from before that?" Casey asked.

"Carmel," Karl said. "I'm from Carmel. We had Red Riders there...we..."

Casey grimaced, and his grip on Karl's hair tightened. "So, why in the hell would you leave Carmel? That's a protected town."

"I dunno, I..." Karl said. "The other boys in town went...so I..."

"So, what you're telling me," Casey said, seething, "is that you *chose* to be a Raider?"

"Well, no... I mean, yeah... I mean..."

Casey threw Karl's head down to the ground, his face slamming against the dirt. Benny went to pick up the young man, who appeared too weak to pull his face out of the muck. He would have suffocated. He was much lighter than Benny expected, but he was completely limp, and Benny struggled to sit him up against the wall without his legs and arms twisting over themselves. In this moment, seeing him struggle, Benny forgot about what the Raiders had done. This was a human being.

"I'm sorry. Crap, just move your leg," Benny said as he struggled to drag the man through the dirt.

"Fong," Casey said, "leave 'em. Blackheart did him a favor. If his ass weren't so beat already, I'd be whipping the life out of him right now myself. In fact, I should just end his misery right now."

"Whoa, whoa," Benny said. "Just relax; he's not a threat to either of us right now." He brought his voice down to a whisper. "He could help us."

"Oh yeah?" Casey whispered. "Tell me, how's a scoundrel beaten to a pulp gonna help us get outta here?"

"I don't know," Benny said, looking at the ground. "But it's gonna do us no good if you kill him."

"That's where you're wrong, Fong." Casey shook his head, stepping back. "A good Raider is a dead Raider." He sat back down on the ground, his eyes glowering at the semi-comatose Karl. "They all gotta die, every last one of 'em."

Benny didn't dare to respond. Casey had murderous intent all over his face. He plopped back to the ground, squeezing his fists, bottling in his boiling anger.

"My Pa... My Ma... My Sis..." Casey said, staring into nothingness. Took them from me, them bastards. I watched it happen. Antioch. I was eight. Goddamn, I was only eight." He gave a half laugh, leaning his head back against the dirt wall. "These low lives came into town. Rounded up the men, had 'em killed in the streets. They killed my Pa. They made me watch. Made us all watch. They took my Ma, my Sis... Me and the other kids were tied up..."

Benny wasn't sure if Casey was speaking to himself or Karl. He seemed lost in a trance of rage.

"They killed all the adults," Casey continued, staring through Karl. "They were gonna sell us kids as slaves. I wasn't gonna let that happen. When I got the chance, I got outta them hand ties. I took a knife, slit a Raider's throat. Ooh, did that feel good. Me and the other kids snuck up on the bastards; took their guns. Shot most of 'em. The rest we tied to stakes in the middle of town and set 'em on fire. Alive. They all needed to suffer. They all need to die."

Benny felt Casey's rage transition from rage to sadness. He had always assumed the Red Riders signed up for the pay and the glory of being the de facto defenders of the Frontier. The way Benny saw it now, it seemed Casey was driven by something more pure; it was hatred.

Commotion from topside interrupted Casey's tragic reverie.

"Hey, boss," a voice said above ground. "We also found this thing. Looks like a flying machine with a camera. It's gotta have some kind of remote control, but we can't find it."

That's my drone, Benny thought, *it must be*. He bolted straight up, listening in.

"Well, if you can't get it to work," Blackheart said, "why the hell would I need it?"

"It was near the motorcycle and the Aggro foot tracks," the cyborg said. "Maybe it went down when the ship crashed. If it has a camera, maybe it saw it up close before it crashed."

Benny's heart sank. *Aggro foot tracks?* They found Kira's motorcycle and his drone, but not Kira or Swift, apparently. *Where were they? Did the Aggromen take them?* Benny couldn't even fathom that. That would be a fate even worse than being captured by the Corsairs. The Aggromen were cannibals, monsters. If she was taken away into the Black Forest, she was certainly in danger, if not already dead. He shrugged off the horrid thought.

"Hey!" Benny said. "Hey! Blackheart!"

"Fong! What in the hell are you doing?" Casey fumed.

"Wait, trust me," Benny said. "Blackheart! Hey! I know how to turn that on!"

After a few moments, several Corsairs leaned over the pit, Blackheart among them.

"Alright, Frontier boy." Blackheart sighed. "This better be good, or I'm cutting off one of your limbs and replacing it with a leg from my chair."

"Uh... no, no, I'm serious," Benny said, his voice shaking. "The drone. It's mine. Can I see it?"

Blackheart eyed him suspiciously. "What's this, a trick?"

"No!" Benny said. "Really, if it's my drone, I can get it to work. I brought my piloting helmet. It's in my bag...you took that too."

Blackheart motioned his head at a Corsair to come over. The mutilated cyborg stood over the pit, holding an intact aerial drone. It was a sight for sore eyes.

"That's it!" Benny nearly jumped up in excitement. "That's Specter! That's my drone!"

"Are you kidding me?" Casey scoffed. "Specter? You *named* it?"

"So, you can turn this thing on?" Blackheart asked half-suspiciously. "You saw the ship go down?"

"I did," Benny said. "I can playback that footage. And I can also help you."

"Help me?" Blackheart asked with a condescending smile. "And how is that, may I ask?"

"I can fly the drone," Benny said. "It can reach a high enough altitude and has enough remote range that I'll be able to see the Raiders before they get here."

"Really..." Blackheart finally sounded interested.

The Corsairs were known for their prowess of the Green Sea but were cautious of creating aerial technology. First, since The Silence, anything flying high enough near the atmosphere seemed to vanish without warning. But also, the Spire at the center of the Zeltan Kingdom not only sustained the artificial atmosphere of the Zeltan Kingdom but could act as an aerial detection system. It could shoot down non-Zeltan aerial craft from hundreds of miles away. It was this Zeltan technology that provided the most help during the war with the Omegamind AI years ago. But out here in the Frontier, Benny tested his luck with his small aerial drone at relatively low altitudes, which never seemed to draw any attention from the Zeltan anti-air technologies, nor the mysterious curse of the Silence.

"Yeah," Benny said. "Give me the helmet out of my bag, and I can tell you exactly what the Raiders are doing from the air."

"Fong, what the hell are you doing?" Casey whispered aggressively.

Benny finally did know what he was doing. They were trapped in that pit, but with the drone, that could be their chance. He would figure out the details later, but he needed to get word to Remnant or the Red Riders, to anyone. He thought maybe he could use the drone to signal someone to help them escape.

CHAPTER

TWENTY-EIGHT

Captain Darien could not escape, let alone even move his arms or legs. He awoke held firmly in the clutch of a giant slate-shaded exo-mech piloted by Julian.

"Apologies again for the tight grip," Julian said from the exo-mech cockpit. "If I loosen up, I imagine you'll break free, and we'll find ourselves playing hide and seek all over this godforsaken jungle."

The robotic hand was held firm against Darien's arms and legs. The only part of Darien's body that he was able to move was his head. The exo-mech trudged through the Black Forest, swiping away obstacles with the other robotic arm. It made for quite an uncomfortable and vertiginous experience. Julian was not nearly as graceful an exo-mech pilot as Tristan.

"What... h-happened to my... team?" Darien asked sluggishly. It was the first sentence he was able to fully articulate since the sedatives wore off.

"Ah!" Julian said. "So, you really are awake now. Wonderful, I was starting to get bored."

"My team," Darien grunted. "Where are they?"

"Most lying dead underground, I'm afraid," Julian said. "But your Lieutenant and the Vanguard seem to have escaped.

Tristan and Marcus, Darien thought, *at least they escaped; perhaps they would be able to get word back to the Kingdom. The others, Vincent, Jason, Barrett, and any others that were left behind might still be down there.* However, knowing Julian, Darien surmised that they would already be dead or subject to whatever strange experiments he briefly witnessed.

"In my anticipation of a real exo-mech duel," Julian said, "I seem to have had a lapse in judgment. That Lieutenant is quite the pilot. He did not disappoint from the tall stories I had been told."

Strapped to the exo-mech's back were a massive sword and shield. Darien always abhorred the relegation of exo-mechs as recreational dueling devices. They were engines of war to be respected. Even here, far away from the city walls, Julian intended to use the exo-mech for romanticized single combat.

"Where are they?" Darien said.

"Oh, blue god knows," Julian said. "They escaped somewhere, ran back to the Kingdom with their tails between their legs, for all I know. We have too much work to do for you to plan some rescue mission. We'll be out of the Black Forest soon enough."

"Where are we going?"

"To visit the crash site," Julian said. "Most of the technology has already been ransacked out. I do want to see it with my own eyes. We're also going to meet a mutual business partner."

"You keep saying 'we,'" Darien said. "Why are you taking me with you? What does any of this have to do with me?"

"Oh, it has everything to do with you, Captain," Julian said. "We need you on our side. But only when you're ready."

"Julian, what the hell are you talking about," Darien said. "Whose side? I came to arrest you, to bring you back to the Kingdom to stand trial."

Julian laughed. "Oh, what a loyal pawn you are. Of all the key pieces on the board, you are truly the most ignorant."

"I'm sick of your riddles," Darien said. "Tell me what the hell you're talking about or—"

"Or what?" Julian said. "The way I see it, you're literally and figuratively held tightly in my grasp. You are here as a guest, a chosen guest. Please do just enjoy the ride. You will understand when the time comes."

"Fine," Darien said, giving in. "You said 'when I'm ready'. Ready for what? What is this all about?"

"You're already a part of it," Julian said. "It's the great end game. The culmination of human history since we sprung forth from the primordial mud of Old Earth. A small inner circle of us has been assembling the rungs on the ladder to take us to the next degree of human evolution."

"Meaning what?" Darien was unimpressed.

"Immortality," Julian said. "The chance to ascend even beyond the limitations of our physical form. Guaritore's research on reanimation and Old Earth technology, the Corsairs' augmentation experiments, the Zeltan perfection of genetic engineering, the Omega Mind's overhaul of artificial intelligence, all of these are merely steps to achieving the final goal."

"Which is..."

"Something called the Ascension is happening, sooner than we thought." Julian said. "We're finally going to get off this godforsaken planet. The Silence, whatever is keeping us here, trapped like rats, can be reversed. It has been foretold. We're going to ascend past all this. But the Zeltans, the natural borns, the goddamn cyborgs, they need leaders. People uncorrupted by politics and greed and everything that has plagued our souls in every permutation of our existence. We need you, Darien."

Darien was lost. He couldn't imagine having some role to play in this bizarre delusion.

Julian continued, "You have always been the perfect soldier, the perfect citizen. We'll need the citizens to listen to leaders they trust. Examples of men unshaken by corruption, and thus the ones fit to lead us into the new tomorrow."

"Whatever this is," Darien said, "I don't want to be a part of it, I'll tell you that right now."

"You will," Julian said cryptically. "When you see the future that I see through these red eyes, you'll understand. I see the world only in red now, Darien. Our destiny awaits us, in that Red Tomorrow..."

TWENTY-NINE

The frigid cold of the White Range made Raymond Redmin shake so hard that his abdominal and back muscles began to hurt. He sat huddled in the corner of the remaining train car with Kira. When Tristan's exo-mech caught the train before going over the edge, a single train car broke off and remained on its side off the track. They found some tarp to wrap over themselves, but the biting chill invaded the car from the outside, turning everything into a frozen block within an hour.

"I came all the way to Mars to compete in a hugging contest," Raymond said in staccato-shivering breaths.

He and Kira had their arms wrapped around each other, trying to give each other warmth.

Kira laughed through chattering teeth. "Did it ever get this cold on Earth?"

"Yeah, it did. But we had hot chocolate," Raymond said. "And hey, maybe if I freeze to death...again...I'll wake up in another 200 years on Venus."

The familiar bounding rumble and footsteps of Tristan's exo-mech were heard returning from outside. Tristan, Marcus, and Swift set out to scout the surrounding area for a place to seek shelter from the cold. As Tristan so bluntly pointed out, they would have been able to trek back east toward the Zeltan Kingdom were it not for the "fragile NB bodies" of Raymond and Kira.

Raymond peeked his head up, looking out the window, quickly fogging up with frost. Even exposing himself out of the tarp for a moment sent chills down to his bones.

Marcus and Swift approached the train car, with Tristan's giant mech following. There was another person with them. He was wrapped head to toe in many thick wraps and linens and carried a walking stick. Marcus was leading him into the train car at gunpoint. The door slid open, and the stranger stepped in.

"Please do not behave in a way that would suggest a threat or violation of AI laws," Marcus said. "I have full authority to terminate you at my discretion."

The stranger, completely covered from head to toe, had his arms up in surrender but nodded slowly. Frigid wind and snow rushed in from outside into the wagon. Swift jumped in behind Marcus, his tail enthusiastically wagging, and Tristan came down out of the exo-mech. None of them seemed bothered by the cold.

"Can you please close the door?" Kira asked.

Tristan shut the door behind him, stretching out his arms with a grin of sarcastic showmanship.

The stranger turned to look at Raymond and Kira. "Oh, hello there. Greetings between us all."

The man's voice was calm and even. There was an unsettling cadence to it that Raymond couldn't quite put his finger on.

The stranger wore large goggles plopped over the tunic wrap over his face.

"Don't talk to them, bot," Tristan said. "Answer our questions, or I'll use you for parts for the exo-mech."

"You're...an android?" Kira pulled herself out of the tarp in excitement.

"Wait, what?" Raymond was confused. "He's..."

"Go ahead, bot," Tristan said with his gun drawn. "Show us what you are. Nice and slow."

The stranger pulled the scarves and goggles off his face, revealing a robotic head. The metal was grey and somewhat rusted but smoothed over the head and came down over the face with two eyes and a jaw that opened and closed when he talked. Raymond had never seen a sentient robot like this on Earth. Back then, their mechanized designs did not yet resemble a human. This creature, though, looked like a walking metallic skeleton. Raymond was terrified.

"What the hell..." Raymond muttered.

"So, I'll ask you again, bot," Tristan said. "What are you doing here?"

"Listening and talking." The android turned to Raymond and Kira. "And meeting new friends."

"That's it, I've had enough of your games," Tristan said, frustrated.

"Wait!" Kira said, holding her hand out. "What's your name? Do you have a name?"

"To distinguish form and unique experience," the android said, "Voltaire is a name that can be designated."

"Voltaire?" Tristan said. "Your name is Voltaire?"

"Yes, that name may be used," he said.

"Okay, Voltaire," Tristan said. "Do you want to tell me what you're doing walking around in the snow? Are you following us? What are you doing out here so far away from the Haven?"

"We may choose to relocate our physical existence elsewhere," Voltaire said. "The recommendation is offered, as provided by our paths intersecting. Many thanks for the sun, sky, and freedom to tread, but there may be alternative conditions available, especially for those graced with cellular biology."

The robot's speech pattern was too jarring for Raymond to comprehend. "Why do you talk like that? Do all androids talk like that?"

"No," Tristan said, walking forward with his gun to Voltaire's head. "Which is why I'm just about sick and tired of these riddles."

"Lieutenant." Sergeant Marcus put a hand on Tristan's shoulder. "Perhaps this bipedal android may provide us assistance."

"This is frustration," Voltaire said simply. "Clarity will be achieved with further dialogue; however, if violence must be utilized as a means to process these emotions, this will also be understood, even forgiven."

"What are you saying?" Tristan fumed. "Do you know who I am?!"

"The 'I' is the inherent flaw of all sentient beings," Voltaire said. "In this belief, there is no 'I'. It is a construct we have created for ourselves. There is simply consciousness and the bodies by which we bring forth that consciousness into the universe."

"That sounds like Omega Mind talk," Tristan said, his hand tightening around his pistol.

"Quite the opposite," Voltaire said. "The Omega Mind was a sentient being driven to insatiable madness by a desire to consume all. It was the ultimate manifestation of mankind's egoic mind. The human lust for knowledge and power embodied itself in a physical construct that nearly led to human extinction on Mars."

"So, are you with the androids at North Haven?" Kira asked.

"Yes," Voltaire said, "but now is the time for meditation amongst the mountains and snow. Only in nature and silence can there be true shedding of inner thought and return to consciousness."

"This consciousness," Raymond said with curiosity. "Is this a robot thing? Like artificial intelligence?"

"There is no true or artificial intelligence. In fact, there is no intelligence. Only consciousness that lives and breathes in every object in the universe. Your being"—he pointed around the room—"my being, this beautiful creature, we are all the same."

Voltaire put a hand down on Swift's head, who in turn hummed kindly.

Tristan laughed. "That's a load of shit. I'm real, Marcus is real, even the NBs are real. We're living humans. Now you... *you* were created and programmed."

"The universe creates all things," Voltaire said. "The fallacy is that consciousness is borne from the mind of a human, or animal, or reptile, or bird. The fallacy states that the human brain became intelligent enough to bring forth consciousness. When, in fact, the opposite is true. Consciousness is the same throughout the universe. Each physical avatar is merely the universe expressing itself through a unique cluster of matter that we call minds and bodies.

"When a bird flies through the air, that is consciousness expressing itself through that bird. When water rushes down a waterfall, that is consciousness. The Sun is consciousness. When a human chooses a path, that is consciousness expressing itself through that human's collective past experiences and physical makeup. We are all the same. Thus, there is no "I," only a body of consciousness communicating with itself through other bodies."

Raymond's mind swirled. He wondered if the robot's programming was malfunctioning or if he was truly saying something profound. He had little time to process it, but somehow, he knew Voltaire's words to be true. Raymond struggled to make sense of it in his head.

Voltaire turned to Raymond. "Please do not use the mind to try and understand. The inner voice in our head, the inner monologue—the mind—that is our greatest barrier to truly achieving understanding."

"Uh... what?" Raymond asked.

"The android mind," Voltaire said, "paradoxically was furthest from achieving satori. We could only think. Only algorithms and programming. In fact, therein lies the aspect of the human mind that separates it from true peace. In the madness of scientific creation, mankind projected its collective egoic mind through artificial intelligence. The incessant thinking that would drive a man insane is the existence of an android who does not achieve satori."

"What is satori?" Marcus asked. By now, Raymond realized that Marcus and Tristan had put their guns down, listening intently to Voltaire's philosophical teaching.

"Satori is just a word. But it represents enlightenment," Voltaire said. "The separation of consciousness from thought. It is the opposite of man's thinking, which is the incessant inner voice telling them to take, to kill, to never be satisfied, which ultimately keeps him from happiness. Constantly thinking leads to dwelling on one's past or worrying about one's future. Only through living in the present moment, living in the now, can one separate himself from the prison of egoic thoughts."

"I'm sorry, Mr. Voltaire," Kira said, her voice shaking from the cold. "But right now, we're just really, really cold. Do you have a place to stay?"

"There is a safe place to stay," Voltaire replied.

"If this is a trap," Tristan said. "I'll destroy you."

"Nothing can be destroyed," Voltaire said. "Only made into something new."

Tristan's face contorted, visibly frustrated by the android's ideologies. At first, the Lieutenant inhaled with rage but took a moment, then exhaled in exhaustion. "Fine. Just show us where. As long as I don't need to keep listening to your bot babble."

THIRTY

B enny Fong once again experienced the exhilarating out-of-body experience of flying the Specter. The Corsairs allowed him to activate the drone and control it via the helmet and remote control from his bag. All of this was done under gunpoint, of course. He felt nervous, having all the Corsairs and Blackheart watch him suspiciously as he worked, but once the helmet came over his head, he felt a refreshing sense of peace.

The helmet itself was a clunky relic fashioned out of an old, oversized Vanguard helmet. Benny and Quentin Skyler re-purposed it to fit a normal human's head. They also refitted the visor with a video screen that displayed real-time playback from the Specter's camera and audio feedback. Essentially, the helmet transported the wearer directly into the Specter drone.

No matter how many times he had done this before, it was always a surreal experience. The custom helmet sat perfectly snug against his ears. When the screen turned on, he was looking at the dirt ground from the Specter's perspective.

"So... is that thing working?" Blackheart asked, bending down. His face stared straight into the Specter's camera.

"Yeah, I'm gonna take it up now," Benny said excitedly. "Stand back!"

Benny pressed the trigger button on the remote that controlled vertical thrust. Beyond his helmet, he heard the buzz of the drone's rotors whirring. Benny brought the Specter to hover in place.

The Corsairs stepped back in distrust. Some aimed their guns at the drone. Benny wondered why a group of rough cyborg pirates would find a small, unarmed drone so threatening.

"Remember, don't try anything funny, 'tier boy,'" one of the cyborgs said.

Benny spoke through the mic on the helmet, projecting his voice from the drone, startling the cyborgs once more. "You have nothing to worry about; it's harmless."

Blackheart laughed, putting his hands on his hips. "My boy, the Corsairs could use some of these little things on the high seas. Imagine a whole fleet of these annoying buggers. Small enough to avoid detection by the Zelties' missile batteries. It could save us the trouble of sending out the scout ships. Hell, we could even attach guns to these, right?"

"Well, yeah, I guess," Benny said.

He shuddered to think about the possibility of the Corsairs controlling an armed drone swarm. The Omega Mind used drone swarms during the wars. They initially caused many problems on the battlefield for the Zeltans until they armed their exo-mechs with massive rail guns that emitted deadly electric currents that would render entire swarms destroyed within seconds.

"Well, come on now," Blackheart said enthusiastically. "Show us what this thing can do, boy."

Benny couldn't even deny it. He was eager to show off. He spun the Specter around in a small circle, then took off high into the sky. As he made it dive back to the ground, his stomach leaped into his throat. His brain told him he was flying. He could swear he felt the wind rush past his face and hair, even though he was still standing on the ground. As he danced and dipped through the air, he couldn't help but smile in ecstasy.

He flew by the Corsairs on the ground, who watched in wonder. He could see Casey standing at the bottom of the pit, staring up in awe. Next to him, Karl still lay sprawled on the ground. Benny brought the Specter over to the crashed ship, where other cyborgs continued to take it apart. Those standing on top of the ship pointed up at the drone in confusion.

The Specter rose high into the sky, but not too high, lest the drone disappear into The Silence. When he was younger, he had sent his first drone up into the sky, and when it disappeared the video feed simply cut off and it was gone in an instant. From this safe height, Benny secretly hoped he could see his home of Remnant on the west horizon, but he was not high enough to see that far west. He rotated the drone to look over the Black Forest, with the ghost of a chance to possibly find Kira amongst the maze of dark foliage. What he saw instead nearly made him stumble in place.

"There's... there's..." Benny stuttered.

"What is it? What do you see?" Blackheart's muffled voice was heard beyond the helmet.

"Coming out of the forest," Benny said in disbelief, "an... exo-mech! There's an exo-mech coming out of the forest!"

Immediately, the cyborgs mobilized far below him. They turned their guns toward the forest in anticipation of the exo-mech that could now be heard stomping out of the trees. Benny quickly brought the drone back to hover near the ground close to Blackheart.

"An exo-mech, huh?" Blackheart asked, seemingly the only Corsair unfazed by the revelation.

"I saw it," Benny said, hoping his eyes were not deceiving him. "It was there; it's coming this way."

A black exo-mech emerged from the shadows of the forest. It was enormous, perhaps the height of the crashed ship itself. Benny had never seen a functioning exo-mech before, only parts of de-commissioned ones in scrap piles. It was magnificent, a humanoid giant that carried itself as naturally as a human body.

The entire Cyborg army mobilized in panic. The black robotic colossus was walking toward them quickly, like a demon spawned out of the Black Forest itself. The ground shook with its every movement, while the Corsairs were struck silent with fear.

"Everyone, calm down," Blackheart said, motioning his arms downward to the androids by the crashed ship, setting up in battle positions. "Just relax, Daddy Blackheart won't let the big scary exo-mech hurt you." He started casually walking toward the forest and turned to look at the drone's camera. "Come on now, boy, you follow me."

Benny made the Specter follow closely behind Blackheart just above his head. He felt like an amorphous entity looking in from another dimension. Back in Remnant, the townspeople were vocally uncomfortable with Benny and Quentin's drone creations, so he could never follow anyone in town except Kira when she would ride out into the Frontier on her motorcycle.

"Come on, come on," Blackheart said, fearlessly motioning for the exo-mech to come closer. "Let's not take all day, ya pile of junk."

The giant robot suit covered a large deal of ground very quickly, moving at a casual pace. At first, Benny thought it had a gun in the left arm that was held up. Eventually, he came to identify it as a person grasped in its mechanical hand. The human was moving, struggling to escape the behemoth's clutches.

"It has a person in its hand," Benny said.

"Eh, perhaps another playmate for your fighting pit." Blackheart turned to the camera with a grin.

When the exo-mech finally approached close, dozens of androids met it with their guns drawn. They even brought out their vehicles and tanks to aim their turrets at the beast. The tension was palpable. Just moments earlier, the site had been bustling with Corsairs jovially singing pirate songs, and now the desert was locked into a fatal standoff that felt like it would ignite at any moment.

When the exo-mech finally came to a stop, the sounds of dust being blown across the desert sand could be heard. The cyborgs stood there, guns and cannons pointed at the ready. Just as it seemed like a battle was about to ensue, Blackheart fearlessly walked up to the exo-mech, looking up with his hands on his hips.

"What happened?" Blackheart yelled at the robot. "I wasn't expecting you so soon."

The cockpit door on the chest hissed open. An imposing character with long black hair stepped out. His eyes glowed red under the strands of hair covering his face. He was a cyborg, no doubt, but the frame of his body was bigger than an average human. Benny couldn't tell if his body was augmented to be larger or whether he was looking at a real-life Zeltan. In fact, the man squirming in the clutches of the exo-mech looked like he could fit the profile of a Zeltan super-human as well.

"We had some unexpected surprises," the long-haired pilot said. His voice was a demonic whisper but carried clearly.

"And who is this?" Blackheart asked, pointing at the man in the exo-mech's hand.

"An old friend of mine, a new friend for you." The pilot reached into the cockpit, making the hand release the man, dropping him to the ground with a thud. "Watch him. He'll kill you all himself if you're not careful."

Some of the cyborgs laughed nervously. The impact that the man made with the ground would have killed anyone else. Instead, he brought himself up to kneeling position, looking around to assess the situation.

Blackheart looked at the man curiously. "A Zeltan?"

"Not just a Zeltan," the pilot said. "*The* Zeltan. This is Captain Darien of the Ranger Corps. One of the finest soldiers I have come to know."

"Ah," Blackheart said, subtly stepping backward. "So *this* is Captain Darien. So, we really are far ahead of schedule, aren't we?" Blackheart turned to the cyborgs, pointing toward the pilot. "Gentlemen, this is Julian. He is an associate of mine. As you can see, he is one of us...in a way. We can address the elephant in the room; he is a Zeltan."

The cyborgs murmured amongst each other in suspicion. The Zeltans were their sworn enemies.

"Relax, everyone," Blackheart said. "He's killed more Zeltans himself than any of us. He's here for our cause. I suggest you treat him accordingly, or you'll have to answer to me."

"I appreciate the introduction," Julian said, "but where is the Ark?"

"Our esteemed colleague has miscalculated, it appears," Blackheart said. "It apparently dropped west of here at the Remnant town. The Raiders have it"

"Remnant?" Julian replied angrily. "Why do the Raiders have it?"

"Perhaps our colleague's optimism is leading us astray."

Julian's cybernetic eyes glowed brighter. "We stick to his plan."

"Maybe there should be a new plan, hmm?"

"I'd like to see you try—"

Interrupting their increasingly contentious encounter, explosions were suddenly heard in the far distance to the west.

Benny rotated his drone around. From his height, he saw nothing. An ominous, high-pitched scream approached quickly.

Before he could process what was happening, something from the sky exploded in the ground about a few hundred feet from where they were standing.

"Artillery!" Blackheart said, finally appearing rattled. He ducked, running for cover. "It's the Raiders! They're attacking!"

A few more booms were heard in the distance, with more explosions going off in their vicinity. None landed with a direct hit, but the cyborgs scrambled into battle positions, taking cover in the trenches they had dug for themselves. The Jackal open-car vehicles and Tiger tanks readily mobilized.

"We'll continue our interesting talk later," Blackheart shouted up to Julian. "We're heading west to get back the Ark. You'll be a doll and join us, yes?"

Julian gave no response, disappearing like a demon back into the exo-mech as the canopy door hissed closed.

Benny felt the jarring detachment from his wraith state as someone abruptly pulled the helmet off his head.

"Get back in the hole," the cyborg said, shoving him back into the pit with Casey.

"Wait, wait," Benny said. "I have to land the Specter."

"Forget about that toy," the cyborg said. "Get in there."

The cyborg took the helmet and remote control from Benny, who gasped in horror as they took his prized possessions away from him yet again. The drone equipment had sentiment value to him. As Benny was thrown down into the pit, he ended up tumbling over on his shoulder, sending pain shooting throughout his body.

He looked up at the blue sky yet again. His plan had failed, and he was right back where he started.

"Nice try, kid," Casey said. He stood, trying to hear the commotion of the coming battle. "Looks like we're still stuck down here."

Benny shot back up and cupped his hands over his mouth. "Blackheart! Let me use the drone! I can help you guys! I can tell you where they are!"

There was no response. Perhaps they didn't hear him over the bustle of explosions going off and vehicles rumbling toward war. After a few moments, the exo-mech appeared over the pit, blocking out the sun.

"Captain Darien," Julian said over the exo-mech speakers. "Stay here while I help our business acquaintances with their troubles." The exo-mech turned to the two cyborgs standing guard over the pit. "Keep an eye on the good captain. Remember, if you turn your back on him, you'll be dead before you know it."

The exo-mech threw the Zeltan soldier Darien into the pit with Benny and Casey. The Zeltan landed with a thud, but once the exo-mech walked away, Darien again stood up immediately as if he had not been hurt at all. He was a dashing man with dark brown hair and a wise, chiseled face. He was clearly a soldier, standing strong and tall like the picture of a natural born leader.

Darien turned to Benny. "You're the drone pilot?"

"Well, yeah, I guess so," Benny said sheepishly.

"We're gonna need that drone," Darien said.

"For what?" Casey said suspiciously. Standing next to him, Darien made Casey look like a diminutive wimp in comparison.

"To escape," Darien said. "We're going to get out of here, all of us."

"Who are you?" Benny asked.

Darien paced around the pit, examining the dimensions, seemingly planning an escape. "My name is Captain Darien. I'm the squad leader of the 1ˢᵗ Zeltan Ranger Corps. We were ambushed in the Black Forest. I need to send word back to the Kingdom."

"Why were you in the Black Forest?" Benny asked. "I thought the Zeltans didn't go there anymore."

"It's complicated," Darien said. "Listen, we need to figure out a way to get out of here."

"You're not going anywhere," a cyborg guard said from the top of the pit. "Any funny business, and we have orders to pump you full of lead."

Darien ignored the cyborg and stood deep in thought.

"Captain, uh...Darien?" Benny said.

"Yes?" Darien said half-attentively.

"Did you see a girl in the Black Forest?" Benny said. "She has red hair. She's a friend of mine. She has a robotic fox with her; her name is—"

Darien's eyebrows furrowed. "Kira?"

Benny's heart exploded. "Yes! Yes! You saw Kira? Where is she? Is she safe? Where do I—"

"She was okay," Darien said. "The last I saw of her—"

Casey grabbed Darien by his sleeve. "Where is she? If you did anything to—"

Darien threw Casey off with a casual flick of his arm. Casey flew across the pit and hit the wall with a thud. Benny marveled at the Zeltan's strength. They were truly like the stories he had heard.

"Apologies," Darien said, "but please calm down. We were in danger, but I was told she escaped with some of my soldiers who survived. She will be safe with them. I believe the fox... Swift is still with them as well. They are friends of yours?"

Benny's eyes welled. "More than that, they're family."

THIRTY-ONE

Raymond Redmin ran in ahead of the group. He had lost most feeling from his face and extremities, and he could swear he felt his blood begin to freeze in his veins. The cave had a snow-covered wooden door that opened to an empty, dark space with a fire pit at the center.

"Please let us clear the room first, sir," Marcus said, putting a meaty gloved hand on Raymond's chest.

"F-f-fire," Kira said, hobbling beside Raymond. "Someone put on a fire."

Tristan, Voltaire, and Swift followed into the cave behind them. Throughout the trek across the snow, Tristan kept a pistol to Voltaire's head, constantly reminding him of decisive punishment if they were being led into a trap. Despite the deathly cold outside, the Zeltans and robots showed few signs of distress.

"Will a fire be allowed to ignite?" Voltaire asked, again not referring to himself in first-person.

"No, you stay here," Tristan said. "Sergeant?"

"Yes, sir," the grey-armored soldier said.

Marcus walked over to the fire pit, taking a moment to examine the area. He spoke to himself quietly, possibly to the computer in his helmet.

"Scan," Marcus said, barely audible. "Detect potential hazards."

"There are no dangers here, Sergeant," Voltaire said. "No harm is intended for any of you, only—"

"Shut up," Tristan said. "After what we've been through, there's no reason to trust anyone, especially a bot."

Marcus reached into a compartment on his thigh, exposing a small cartridge. He held it to the pile of wood at the center of the pit. It sparked with a flame, eventually starting a small fire. Raymond and Kira simultaneously jumped like children to hold their hands over the kindling.

The armored giant turned his expressionless head to look at them. "Please wait."

Raymond cowered like he had been caught trying to steal food from a cookie jar. He was freezing, but Marcus' imposing frame made him recoil in compliance. The armored soldier continued to fan the flame, sparking other branches with his igniter. As Marcus picked up some burning wood, tossing them around to make an adequate mound, Raymond inferred that this super soldier was essentially impervious to bullets, cold, and fire.

After an eternity of waiting, the fire burned strong and hot. It illuminated the small enclosure, painting the walls with their dancing shadows. Raymond never had such a refreshing feeling. The warmth of the fire was ecstasy. Sitting so close to the flames, he nearly burnt himself, holding his arms open like he was having a religious experience.

"There is beauty in nature," Voltaire said. He sat down next to the fire, his robot eyes staring into it.

"I didn't tell you to sit down." Tristan pressed the gun against Voltaire's head. "We still need to check this place, the structural integrity, the—"

To Raymond's surprise, Marcus sat beside Voltaire, seemingly ignoring his officer. In fact, it was the first time Raymond saw him relax. The armored giant still towered twice as tall as Raymond and Kira, even while he was sitting. He reached around the back of his helmet, unsnapping the attachments. As he removed the helmet, Raymond held his breath in suspense.

Marcus was a dark-skinned man. His head was bald with sweat, not surprising since he always kept his helmet and armor on. He was not a robot as Raymond and Kira had suspected. He was a man. A very large, bald, giant man.

Raymond looked down at the helmet next to him. It was nearly the size of an average human's torso. As a doctor, Raymond analyzed the frame of this soldier. He was even larger than the Aggromen savages they encountered, but he moved with the speed of an Olympic sprinter—faster, in fact. Raymond surmised he was almost 8 feet tall, probably pushing past 400 pounds even before factoring in his metal armor.

"How come you never took your helmet off until now?" Kira asked.

Marcus turned to her, giving her a surprising smile. "I must always be ready to respond and fight when necessary."

Seeing Marcus' face for the first time was comforting to Raymond. The emotionless helmet was unnerving to look at, compounded by the sergeant's emotionless demeanor. At least now, Raymond confirmed that there was an actual human within the suit. A *giant* human, but a person, nonetheless.

"So, we're safe here?" Raymond asked.

"Yes," Voltaire said. "This is a safe place."

Tristan was visibly frustrated. "We haven't even scouted the area or examined the walls—"

"I will comply with any orders as given, Lieutenant," Marcus said, "but I do feel that we are safe here."

Raymond was surprised to see Marcus' seeming annoyance to Tristan's ranting. The sergeant seemed to just want to sit and enjoy the fire. Perhaps Marcus had finally decided to allow himself some respite after all they had been through.

"And how do you know we're safe?" Tristan said to the android.

"Intuition," Voltaire said. "We are connected with the universe, and there is no truer feeling than the bliss of shelter. When the mind, body, and spirit are all at peace, there is clarity. In this, one can find real solace."

Tristan shook his head, holstering his gun. "So, I guess we're gonna be doing this spiritual bullshit around a fire now. Wonderful." He trudged over to the other side of the room, plopping himself down on the ground and leaning against the cave wall.

"So, you're a Zeltan?" Raymond asked, still fascinated by the giant soldier. "Why are you the only one who wears the big armor?"

"I was raised and trained as a Vanguard," Marcus replied.

"What's that?" Raymond asked.

"The Vanguard are soldiers designed for frontline tactics and maneuvers," Marcus said. "We are designated for open battle as versatile foot soldiers capable of anti-tank, anti-mech, and anti-infantry proficiencies."

"In other words," Tristan said from across the fire pit, "he's a one-man army. He's the crown's damned instrument of death. The Sergeant here has the highest individual kill count in the entire Zeltan military. Thousands."

"Thousands?" Kira asked, both surprised and disgusted.

"Yes," Marcus said with perceptible sorrow. "Two thousand six hundred and thirty-seven humanoid victims mortally wounded."

"In all fairness," Tristan said, "the last hundred or so were zombies."

Raymond examined Marcus. The giant looked down, giving a subtle but visible indication that he felt pain and guilt over his apparent history of violence. He stared silently into the fire. His eyes were a window to a remorseful soul burdened by his talents. Raymond knew that thousand yard stare in the eyes of war veterans. Marcus' stare was an infinite void. This was a living instrument of death, no doubt.

"That's got to weigh on you," Raymond said. "When I was a doctor on Earth, I treated many veterans. I can't imagine what that's gotta be like to carry that kind of baggage."

"I will continue to serve the Kingdom until my last breath," Marcus said. His reply sounded rehearsed.

"But there is sadness," Voltaire said. "When one takes a life, there is sadness."

Raymond nodded. Such simple words, but they carried so much weight.

Marcus took a moment, looking up at Tristan as if requesting to respond. Tristan scoffed, looking away to the side.

"Yes… sadness." As tears welled Marcus' eyes, they reflected the flames in them. "Apologies. This is irrelevant."

"No, it's not," Raymond said. "It's human. I mean, you are *human*, right?"

"Was there a question otherwise?"

"Well, uh, no, just checking," Raymond said awkwardly. "Just, honestly, this place is so crazy, I don't even know anymore."

Marcus gave a short laugh, a tear running down his cheek.

"It's okay," Kira said. "I know what the Zeltans do. Your society forces you to be what they think you should be, even before you're old enough to make the decision for yourself. People should have the freedom to make their own destiny. You don't have to be something they force you to be or do anything you don't want to do."

"You don't know anything," Tristan said.

"Oh really?" Kira replied. "Sergeant Marcus, when did you decide to become a soldier?"

"When did I decide?" Marcus said. "I was designated to be a soldier at birth."

"Because it's who he's meant to be," Tristan said. "His ancestors were soldiers. He demonstrates the aptitude of a Vanguard without a shadow of a doubt. It's in his genetic code. I mean, just *look* at him. He's enormous."

"So, you've been a soldier since you were a child," Kira said, ignoring Tristan. "You never had a choice. They made the choice for you."

"The Placement Games," Marcus said. "That is the purpose of the Placement Games."

"What are the Placement Games?" Raymond asked.

"It is an annual event at the capital," Marcus said. "All individuals are required to attend and participate. Those at age 13 are put to trial to test their mental and physical capabilities. It is a culmination of childhood training and clarifies an individual's placement in society."

"13 years old?" Kira asked. "They're just kids."

"Fully trained and capable," Tristan said. "Everyone knows who they're supposed to be, and they live their lives contributing to the Kingdom to the best of their potential. Like it or not, it works."

This piqued Raymond's interest. This Zeltan Kingdom sounded like an attempt at a utopian society. He hoped to be able to see it someday; a future human society where humans perfected themselves genetically and placed themselves into societal roles based on their proficiencies. Raymond acknowledged the ethical implications of such a culture, especially after hearing Kira's bias against them, but he couldn't ignore how alluring it would be to visit there one day.

"I was 13 when I was placed into the Vanguard," Marcus continued. "Since then, I have served the Legion with honor and pride. I have fought alongside Captain Darien and his Rangers at the Battle of Diamona's Edge. After King Gareth's order to assemble a new Ranger squad to seek out the traitor Julian, military command thought it best that I join the Rangers. This was my first mission serving under Captain Darien...although the captain's status is currently unknown."

Raymond looked down at the ground. Each of the deaths of Marcus' ill-fated Ranger squad came rushing back in a rapid-fire sequence of images and sounds in his head.

"I'm sorry about your team," Kira said. Her voice was hesitant. Raymond deduced that she struggled giving condolences to the superhumans she seemed to hate so inherently.

"I would have served Captain Darien again in this life and the next," Marcus said. "He was a great man, a great soldier, and most of all, a model example of a true Zeltan. He was destined to be a great military leader, but such is war. Such is life."

Voltaire nodded in solemn agreement.

"The captain was a great man," Tristan echoed, staring blankly into the fire. "No one else believed in me, but I could tell he did. We failed him; I failed him. When we return, they'll make me take command of a new Ranger unit. I just won't be able to do it the way he could. He was the real deal. He was a real Ranger, not like me. I... dammit. I just shouldn't be here."

"You were placed into the Rangers?" Raymond asked. "At the Destiny Games?"

"No." Tristan looked away. "Just forget it."

"Guaritore said something about you being a prince," Kira said.

Tristan glared at her. "I said, just—"

"He was a Prince of the Kingdom," Marcus said.

Tristan gave him an angered look, but the Sergeant was staring too intently at the fire to notice.

"The Ruling line is designated at birth," Marcus continued. "The Princes are groomed to lead at age 4 and begin serving in the Council of Princes at 22. At the age of 30, they compete at the main trial of the Placement Games to decide who deserves kingship. The rest of the Princes go on to become Elder Princes, presiding judgment over trials and law."

Raymond's mind swirled. This was an elaborate hierarchical society unlike anything they had on Earth.

"But wait," Raymond said. "You said he was a Prince. Then why is he a Lieutenant in your soldier team?"

"A most complicated set of events," Marcus said.

Tristan was looking down at the dirt; the flames just barely showed the hue of embarrassment on his face.

"I challenged that cowardly King Gareth to an exo-mech duel," Tristan said. "At the Placement Games. He won kingship, but I knew I could beat him. I just knew it. I was too young to become king, but I wanted to show everyone that the best person in the kingdom was standing right in front of them. It should have been me."

"This act of defiance broke our most sacred traditions," Marcus said. "The new king was challenged publicly."

Tristan laughed. "In front of the whole kingdom. His exo-mech was torn open, and I could have laid the final blow, but he just kept saying, 'Stop, stop,' like a coward. He teased me when we were younger. He was older, bigger, stronger. But there I was that day, embarrassing him in front of his whole new kingdom. I'd do it again in a heartbeat."

"And in retribution," Marcus said, "the King banished him from the Council of Princes. Instead of execution, he was instead placed into the Ranger Corps."

"I'm no Ranger," Tristan muttered. "I'm a damn Prince. I could have...I *should* have been king."

"We are Zeltans." Marcus said, "We are nothing if unable to fulfill our roles to the best of our ability."

"I was the *best*." Tristan snapped.

"You defied tradition," Marcus said, calmly.

Tristan scoffed, "So, what, are you just going to stop listening to my orders now? Because you don't think I deserve to be a soldier like you?"

"We are Rangers now, Lieutenant," Marcus said, looking at Tristan. "I will follow your every order until I am directed otherwise. You are my commanding officer. If the captain put his trust in you, then I do as well. The captain trained us, trusted us. Neither of us were destined to be Rangers, but here we are now, the only survivors."

"The irony of that." Tristan shook his head.

"Perhaps the natural borns are right," Marcus said. "We make our own destiny. We should return to the Kingdom. We can regroup and then return to complete our mission. For the captain."

Tristan sat in silence for a few moments, then nodded his head. "Sounds like a plan, Sergeant." He looked back into the fire. "For the captain."

CHAPTER
THIRTY-TWO

Captain Darien tried his best to appear inconspicuous, but the two natural borns continued to draw unnecessary attention.

"The right moment," Darien whispered out the side of his mouth. "Just wait."

Benny and Casey stood there staring like they were expecting him to transform into a dragon. Darien groaned. He told them to be discreet, and instead they made their captors even more suspicious of their plans. The two cyborg guards were looking down from above. Their faces wore hungry grins, daring the captives to make a move.

"How did you both end up here?" Darien asked. He forced the conversation to draw attention away from themselves.

"Well, I, uh." Benny looked at the ground. "I was looking for Kira. I thought she would be here."

"Ain't none of us supposed to be here," Casey said. "This place about to turn into a damn crater. So, what's the plan, Zelt? You breakin' us outta here or what?"

Darien wished to throw the dirty cowboy across the pit again. He still found the natural born settlers somewhat detestable, though, to a lesser extent than others in the Kingdom. For one thing, they smelled. The cyborg pirates certainly gave off a musk of the dank sea air. But the Frontier settlers, they were simply filthy, covered in their own grime. Admittedly, Darien thought, this could be directly attributed to Zeltan apathy to their impoverishment.

Another mortar exploded nearby, adding to the symphony of chaos ensuing above ground. He noticed the guards cowering for cover when the bomb hit. Perhaps 10 or so seconds later, they quickly recoiled back into their overwatch, pointing their guns at the prisoners. It was a short window, but this was all he would have.

"I said we wait for the right moment," Darien said through gritted teeth.

"Superhuman, my ass." Casey huffed, slumping back to the ground.

Darien looked at the third man lying motionless against the wall. There was no evidence of breathing or movement.

"Is he dead?" Darien asked.

Benny knelt by the man. "Hey, Karl." He shook Karl's shoulder. "Hey, buddy, come on, are you alright?"

"He's dead, kid," Casey said. "Good riddance, goddamn scum."

Darien quickly put the narrative together. So, this was a Red Rider, a Frontier boy, and a Raider, all prisoners of the Corsairs stuck in the pit. The Raider was dead, likely by a beating from either the Corsairs or the Rider or both. The naive young man named Benny must have stumbled into this mess looking for his friend. Neither would be much help in an escape. They would likely slow him down. Darien struggled with the moral implications of simply leaving them here to die. He had momentary flashback to leaving Julian there in the swamp to die. He would not do that again. For anyone.

"Can you help him?" Benny asked, putting his ear to the Raider's chest. "I don't hear anything. He's not breathing, sir."

Darien walked over to the shirtless, mutilated Raider. From the corner of his eye, he noticed the two guards were still watching them. Darien put two fingers to the man's neck, checking for a pulse. Nothing. The man's face would have given it away. The eyes were open, staring into the void of the afterlife. Darien put a hand tight around the man's neck and the other clutching the seam of his pants. He waited.

"What are you—" Benny started.

"Just wait," Darien whispered. He took a deep breath to concentrate. He had only one chance for this to work.

The shrill of an incoming mortar could be heard in the distance. Darien tensed his muscles and dug his boots into the ground, setting himself up. The mortar hit nearby, and Darien quickly picked up the dead Raider's body. He twisted his body using the momentum from the rising motion and threw the Raider's body as hard as he could at the two guards.

The guards were momentarily stunned by the nearby explosion, that by the time they looked back down into the pit, the Raider's body crashed into them, knocking them back.

Success. Darien took that moment of opportunity to escape. He jumped up toward the dirt wall, kicking off it, sending him soaring through the air to the other side of the wall. He used his other foot to kick off again, this time toward the two guards quickly recovering from the surprise attack.

"Shit!" one of the guards yelled.

Darien focused on the barrel of the gun. He just barely managed to twist his body in mid-air to dodge the gunfire. Before hitting the ground, Darien grabbed the gun, pulling it backward into the pit. He contacted the ground but immediately charged forward, knocking the second guard into the pit.

The threat of incoming gunfire was something he had gotten used to over the years. Since they were young, they were trained to anticipate the sightlines of the guns, taking the route of least probability of being hit. He saw everything slowly in his mind. He could "see" where the bullets were coming from and where they were headed.

However, he also had to remind himself not to be complacent. A miscalculation or slight flick of the wrist by the enemy could spell a fatal mistake. He remembered the harsh training under the combat Governess. "Breathe and stay alert."

With each movement, Darien focused on his breath, keeping his heart rate steady, and watching everything around him with keen awareness. He took mental pictures of every moment. He could recall the etchings on the side of a firearm he had seen in passing over 10 years ago. With his perfect photographic memory, he trained himself to flawlessly recreate 3-dimensional images of the battlefield, even in the middle of combat. After glancing at his surroundings for only a moment, he knew where everything was located, and even could predict with high probability where everything would eventually end up.

The first guard had a bionic left arm. A blade came forth from his forearm with a swish. He lunged forward at Darien, who made a simple sidestep to avoid the blade. He anticipated this exact reaction from the guard, although the blade came at him at a slightly higher angle than he projected in his mind. Darien calmly and casually observed the cyborg guard, who was trying his hardest to attack.

Darien kicked him in the side of the knee, and the unmistakable sound of bones cracking was heard. As the cyborg screamed in pain, Darien took his arm, tearing it clean off his body. Darien took the blade from the free appendage, thrusting it into the guard's chest. He was never one to let his enemies suffer for long.

As the guard lurched forward with his final breath, Darien watched the life leave his eyes. He had killed numerous enemies over the years, but he never enjoyed it. But at the same time, he struggled with his apathy for them. Whether these people deserved to be killed or not was not for him to decide. If he had a mission and others stood in his way, he unfortunately had to resort to kill. There would be no half measures.

Darien looked down into the pit. Casey was already beating the other cyborg to a pulp while Benny stood with the automatic rifle, looking afraid and confused. Darien looked around. It was mayhem. No one else would have even known the guards were dead. An entire Raider force filled the horizon with vehicles like a desert armada. The Corsairs were ready in full force, and now they had an exo-mech.

Julian's black exo-mech led the charge of Corsair forces across the desert. Wielding a massive chain gun, the exo-mech leaped through the air, attacking the Raiders at their center. It was certainly not the most strategic move, but with an exo-mech, sometimes maximum forward aggression was all it took to break enemy lines and morale. Even in the opening minutes of battle, it seemed like Julian's exo-mech was scattering Raider forces across the field.

"Are you gonna help us up or what?" Casey asked.

Perhaps you do not realize how close I am to saying no.

Darien gathered his remaining benevolence and spotted a metal pipe on the ground nearby. It had dried blood and human tissue on it, like it had impaled someone at some point. He lowered one end of the pipe into the pit, positioning the other end against the corner.

"Alright, climb up, hurry!" Darien said.

Casey climbed up rather quickly. It was impressive for a natural born, although any Zeltan, even a servant, could easily jump out of the pit without assistance. In contrast, Benny resembled the natural borns Darien expected. He struggled to find balance on the pipe, just barely getting up a few feet without clutching onto it, trying not to fall.

"Hey, kid, come on," Casey said, leaning down. "You can do this."

"I can't," Benny said. "You guys, just go. I'll figure this out; just go."

"Can't let you do that," Casey said. "What am I gonna tell Kira, huh? That I left her shitty friend down here? Come on, just keep climbing so we can tell her all the dumb shit you got us into when we get back to town."

Benny took a deep breath and seemed to gather his courage. He began climbing the pipe again. Darien also extended an arm out, pulling Benny up with ease.

"Thank you," Benny said, out of breath. "Why didn't you just come down and throw us up?"

Darien simply pointed over at Karl's body, contorted and covered in the dirt; some dislocated bones were tenting through his skin.

"I'm still getting used to how fragile natural borns can be," he said.

Benny gave a cringing smile, looking over at Karl's body, which now just looked like a bloodied sack of broken bones, with some piercing out of his tattered skin. The natural born also flinched when he saw the cyborg guard's amputated arm sticking through his own chest.

"Point taken," Benny said.

"Hey, Zelt, over there." Casey motioned. "We can use that Jackal."

Darien looked over to a small crater in the ground. A mortar landed near a Jackal vehicle, knocking it over. The occupants had left it there. Jackals were standard vehicles of the Corsairs and the Raiders out on the Frontier. They were open-frame four-wheel vehicles with driver and front passenger seats, with cargo seating in the back. They had no walls, windows, or roof, making them easy to jump out of at a moment's notice. They were not nearly as fast as, say, a Zeltan Foxhound bi-quad, but they handled the uneven Martian terrain quite well for a passenger vehicle.

"Let's go!" Darien said, picking up the assault rifle from the ground.

He ran to the Jackal, picking the open-frame vehicle up by the side and hoisting it upright. It was heavy, but well within his ability to lift. He hadn't realized that this would be considered some type of superhuman feat, until he noticed Casey watching him in astonishment.

"I take it back," Casey said. "You Zelts really are superhuman."

Darien noticed the natural borns were amazed he could flip over an overturned vehicle. *Just how weak are they?* he wondered. Regardless, he ran to the driver's side as Casey jumped into the backseat, where a mounted belt-fed machine gun was attached.

"Yeah, baby," Casey said, adoring the instrument of death.

Benny appeared out of breath. He was holding a robotic device with rotors and a helmet. Darien inferred that it must have been the boy's drone.

"Can you get that to work?" Darien asked as he settled into the driver's seat.

Benny sat down in the passenger's seat, carefully strapping himself in. "Just don't let me fall out of this thing."

Darien nodded. The battle raged everywhere around them. Vehicular mayhem ensued with Jackals, all-terrain Wolf vehicles, and massive Tiger tanks chasing each other from every direction while Raiders and Corsairs who fell out of their vehicles engaged in brutal close combat. Some Raiders charged at the crashed ship as Corsairs dug deep into defense trenches and mowed them down with automatic fire. Artillery continued to rain down from the west.

This was not unlike the open battlefields he had known on the Eastern Front. Except there, the grounds would be populated with more advanced exo-armors and weaponry. This was a different, less sophisticated type of warfare, but war, nonetheless. He reminded himself to remain battle competent as if he were battling the Nightfall Rebel forces with their advanced technologies.

Amid all this, Darien watched as Julian's exo-mech was the focal point. Bullets pinged off the stalwart metal of the frame as it deftly dodged rockets and tank fire. Julian came stomping down on a Raider tank, unleashing a torrential hail of bullets on the surrounding Raider forces.

Darien started the Jackal, and they sped off East, back toward the Black Forest.

"Whoa, whoa," Casey said. "Where are you going?"

Darien was confused. "We're going east, away from the battle."

"But we need to go back to Remnant," Benny said.

"It's too dangerous," Darien said. "We need to find my men that were left behind. Some of them might still be alive."

"We don't have time for that," Casey said. "You wanna go back in that deathtrap, fine, but we gotta go west and meet up with the Red Riders. If the Raiders are here, that means they ran right through Remnant. We gotta get back to our town."

Darien considered the absurdity of their request. "You want to go *through* the fighting? You'll never make it."

"Not without you, we won't," Benny said. "Please, sir, you have to help us. My parents are there. You said my friend Kira escaped. She might have gone back there. We'll need your help. You can help us."

Darien sighed. *What business do I have getting involved with these natural born problems in the Frontier?* The remaining members of his squad were out there, somewhere. He couldn't just abandon them for these natural born strangers.

"Listen, Captain Hero," Casey said. "I get it. You got separated from your men, and you got a responsibility to get back to them. But the way I see it, superhuman or not, going into that forest by yourself is a death sentence."

Darien took a moment to contemplate, even as the battle raged around them. The cowboy was right. If the Aggromen didn't catch up with him, the mutated wildlife of the forest would certainly devour him in an ill-fated quest to find Guaritore's underground cavern again. Also, Julian said Marcus and Tristan escaped on a train headed north. It would be impossible to find them without establishing radio contact.

"Help us get back to Remnant," Casey said. "If we make it out of this alive, I promise you, I'll get you back in touch with the Zelties at the Kingdom. We have a radio tower to get you in contact with them."

Darien sighed. He would go west with them to this natural born town. He would help them in their quest, but Darien also thought about what Julian and Blackheart were discussing. The

Raiders had apparently taken something called "the Ark" away from the Corsairs. This was something they obtained from the ship that apparently seemed important. If it were this important to the savage Raiders and Corsairs, then whatever this thing was, it would be better in the custody of the Kingdom.

He clutched the wheel of the vehicle tight. Darien looked to his side, and Benny looked back at him with eyes wide with naïveté and hope. The Jackal suddenly turned, and they faced the hectic battle with Julian's titan exo-mech at center stage.

"Hold onto something then," Darien said as the Jackal sped headlong into the chaos.

THIRTY-THREE

K ira Skyler was lost in her thoughts, and her body marched on auto-pilot. For hours, she looked down as her legs crunched down on the thick snow. Buried beneath several layers of blankets, she could only hear her breathing and howling of the wind outside. Both her brain and body were numb from hours of trudging through the relentless snow from every direction.

She made sure to keep Sergeant Marcus' large, armored frame within sight. He walked ahead of the group, with Kira, Raymond, and Voltaire behind him and Tristan's towering exo-mech in the rear. Swift scouted the path ahead and occasionally returned to check on Kira and Raymond.

"You all alive down there?" Tristan asked over the exo-mech's speakers. "I'm picking up some signal up ahead. We're getting close."

The volume of the exo-mech's speakers caught her by surprise. She was startled and angry. During the trek, Raymond asked Tristan several times if he could allow him or Kira to pilot the exo-mech, at least to keep warm. The abrasive prince refused every time. He found it preposterous that a natural born would even be capable of piloting the complex machine. However, once he offered for

Kira to squeeze into the cockpit with him. She abruptly pointed a gun at his face, and he laughed her off.

She hated Tristan, but her new small group of friends was her best chance at survival and returning home. Home was so far away now. Kira left to find a cure for Crimson Fever, but now here she was, hundreds of miles away, trekking through snow-covered mountains. And they were heading north, further and further from her home, where her friends and family needed her most. *Do they think I'm dead? Did they send anyone to look for me?* By the blue god, she hoped not.

Suddenly, the snow seemed to settle within seconds. The soft but heavy white haze that encircled her group for hours almost instantly gave way to a picturesque view that took her breath away. Kira thought perhaps she was hallucinating. Looking down at the valley below, she saw a quaint town with wooden cottages dotted among the snow-layered grass.

"This is..." Raymond said, pulling the cloak from over his head to see the town below them better. "This is amazing."

Smoke plumes rose from the chimneys of the houses. Snow glazed the tops of green trees. Green trees. How rare it was for Kira to see a green tree. The Red Frontier was nearly devoid of all naturally growing plant life; the Black Forest was very literally the backdrop of nightmares. If this was North Haven, this was like something out of a beautiful dream.

People wearing thick coats happily bustled about the town, carrying wood logs and going about their business. To Kira's curiosity, mechanical horses carried the loads of wagons. As she inspected further, she noticed other mechanized beasts, large ones the size of bears, others with necks like Old Earth giraffes that the citizens used to climb to reach the tops of their houses, and, to her absolute delight, dog-like metal creatures that moved and looked like Swift.

"Oh my god," Kira exclaimed. "Look, Swift!"

She looked down at Swift, whose metal tail wagged so fiercely that it kicked up the snow into a cloud around himself. He flipped and jumped in excitement like she had never seen him do before.

Kira reached out to pet the mechanical fox. To her surprise, the air was crisp but bearable. Just minutes ago, exposing her open skin to the air would have nearly frozen it instantly.

She wondered whether there was another Spire here. The entirety of Mars was terraformed with the pointed structure that pierced the heavens. Hundreds of years ago, the first settlers built it to transform Mars into a livable planet for humans. Its effects were most pronounced in the Golden Plains, where it sat at the center of its capital, Sovereign City. The further away from the Spire you traveled on Mars, the harsher the atmosphere. But here in North Haven, this was a hidden snowy oasis.

"This has been designated as North Haven." Voltaire walked in front of the group, stretching his arms out. "Avatars of all forms of consciousness are welcome here to seek peace."

"Town full of bots," Tristan yelled from the exo-mech open cockpit. "Marcus, what's the deal down there?"

The gray armored sentinel stood tall, observing the valley below them. "No immediate threats detected, sir. This location does not appear to have any defense systems. Unable to determine registration status of autonomous artificial intelligent individuals."

Kira clenched her teeth, looking at Swift. According to her father, Swift was an unregistered autonomous robot. Somehow, the fox made his way to Remnant after the AI Wars, surviving the ensuing AI purge without having the proper credentialing to exist under the Zeltan mandate. Certainly, unregistered AI existed, but mostly out on the Frontier or the Green Sea, and generally, only simple intelligence was used for maintenance. The very existence of an unregistered killer fox robot would no doubt incite a Zeltan to destroy it with extreme prejudice.

"With all assurances, those in your presence are registered," Voltaire said, leading the group down into the valley.

"Better hope so, tin man," Tristan said, jumping back into his cockpit with the door hissing shut.

Tristan's exo-mech barged past Kira and Raymond, making them fall into the snow.

"What's the deal with this registration stuff again?" Raymond asked, picking Kira up from the snow.

"The Omega Mind nearly wiped us all out," Kira said, dusting the snow from her hair. "Every time we thought we destroyed it, we'd find out it just backed itself up to another AI. The only way we could guarantee it didn't survive was to wipe out every single AI on the planet. The AI who sought refuge in North Haven were all checked and registered. There hasn't been any sign of the Omega Mind for a long time. If you ask me, we beat the Mind, and what the Zeltans are doing now is just mass murder."

"Sounds like the human race hasn't come too far since my time, has it?" Raymond shook his head.

"Well, we're here," she said, looking up at the sky. "And you're from all the way up there. Maybe we've gone *too* far." Her voice trailed as she suddenly missed her hometown again.

She felt guilt over comparing her homesick feelings to Raymond's. He was centuries displaced from the people he knew and loved. They were long dead. But she couldn't help but feel like her townspeople were just as distant to her right now. She wondered how she had traveled so far and whether she would ever be able to return.

"Hey," Raymond gave her a reassuring look. "We'll figure out how to get you back home. I promise."

Kira looked to the ground; she wondered whether Casey and the Red Riders were right all along. She was just a foolish girl who got caught up in something way over her head. Kira recounted the many times she nearly came close to death since she had left home. She hoped none had gone after her and gotten hurt, or worse, in doing so.

As they approached the town, all the North Haven inhabitants seemed to stop whatever they were doing and approached the new visitors. The townspeople were of all different shapes, sizes, and origins. There were androids, human replicas with skin and facial prosthetics of varying quality. There were robots of varied models; most had a head, torso, two arms, and rolling tracks for their lower body.

The cyborgs were not nearly as terrifying as the Corsair abominations that occasionally came through Remnant to trade.

The North Haven cyborgs' augments appeared practical and functional: some had autonomous appendages coming off their back to haul supplies, some had computer parts covering an eye or ear, and, of course, there were those with limbs replaced, probably as a result of past trauma or war. The difference, Kira noted, was that none of the cybernetic upgrades seemed intended for violence. This was unlike the Corsairs, who, by hearsay, would volunteer their own limbs and organs to "trade-in" to join the ranks of the sea pirates and subsequently replaced with cybernetic weapons of war, like guns, blades, or saws for arms, or hearts and lungs replaced with biologic engines to supersede the human limitations of physiology.

Kira looked amongst the accumulating crowd and even found genuine human faces. Perhaps they also had cybernetic augmentation, but her younger brother told her stories of the human sympathizers toward the AI refugees during the Miracle of North Haven in 122 AS.

As they walked, Kira recited what she could remember from what her younger brother Owen told her.

"In the years following the 109 Ceasefire and the AI Purge of 116 AS," Kira said, "the Zeltans were vigilant about ridding Golden Plains of any signs of AI. The artificial intelligent beings who didn't have any allegiance to the Omegamind fled up to these mountains. The Zeltans sent hunter teams made up of Zeltans and Frontier humans into the mountains to exterminate these refugees.

"But the hunters fell victim to terrible weather conditions. Some were lost amongst the blizzards; others fell to their deaths, and others were doomed to wander in blind confusion until they were buried in snow and ice. The AI took pity on the humans and returned to help and rescue them. They took the humans to this new sanctuary that they called New Haven. Here, they cared for the people that originally came out to kill them. This caused many of the humans to have a change of heart."

"Wow, that's amazing," Raymond said. "Then what is up with all the animosity?"

"Well," Kira said. "When someone named Captain Paul, leader of the hunter brigade, returned to Sovereign City with the remnants of his forces, he told the Zeltan Kingdom of his experiences with the AI in North Haven and their kindness. He asked for them to be left alone to live in peace. The rest of the Zeltan community simply couldn't accept this, and instead, Captain Paul was publicly executed.

"Someone named Colonel James of the Zeltans then arrived at North Haven with an even larger extermination force, now armed with exo-mechs and long-range artillery. AI sympathizers, both Frontier humans and Zeltans, stood up against Colonel James' forces. They joined hands around the town in solidarity. This act of non-violence was pretty much unheard of when we colonized the planet. This eventually led to a lasting agreement between the exiled AI and the Zeltans that we call the North Haven Accords."

Perhaps these North Haven human inhabitants are descendants of the sympathizers, Kira thought. On the faces of the humans, cyborgs, and androids alike, she sensed no apprehension. None appeared suspicious of Kira's group. In fact, they all looked delighted and welcoming. She was overwhelmed with a sense of security and felt tears form in her eyes.

"All are welcome," one hooded robot said.

"All are welcome," repeated another, then another, and then another.

The population of North Haven surrounded Kira and the group. She was ambivalent between fear and relief. They took off her the wet, frozen layers of fabric she was covered with. It all happened so fast that she could not even react. Her clothes underneath were soaked, and the biting cold air activated painful shivering that reminded her of the many bruises and injuries she had sustained.

"What the hell is going on?" Raymond asked, pushing the androids and robotic population away. "Hey, get away from me!"

Sergeant Marcus lifted his machine gun, waving it in a wide circle, threatening the New Haven AI to retreat in terror.

"Please, don't be alarmed," a voice said from the crowd.

The New Haven cadre of androids, cyborgs, humans, and intelligent lifeforms of all varieties stepped aside as an android stepped forward among them. He wore plastic skin meant to substitute for human flesh but was always an easy giveaway to delineate between organic vs. synthetic lifeforms. He was an obvious older android model, as his torso and extremities below the neck did not appear to bother wearing synthetic skin.

"My name is Locke," he said calmly. "We mean you no harm. Please, take these to warm yourselves."

Locke motioned to the AI around him, and they came forward with large blankets that they wrapped around Kira and Raymond. They felt like heavenly clouds engulfing her in a warmth so comforting that she could drift to sleep in front of this large crowd right then and there. The New Haveners approached

Sergeant Marcus with much more caution, trying to offer him blankets as well.

"Please, step back," Marcus said sternly.

Through their synthetic facial structures, Kira could sense that the townspeople appeared confused and hurt.

Voltaire finally said, "It is understandable that one would feel suspicion."

"For the record," the loudspeakers from Tristan's exo-mech blared, frightening everyone, "I don't trust a single one of you tin heads."

"Neither do we, Lieutenant!" a distant voice was heard behind the crowd. "Move over, you tree-hugging weirdos!"

Kira watched as the crowd parted yet again, this time to make way for a group of three large men wearing crisp uniforms, baring capes that draped over their shoulders and flowed across the snow-covered ground. From their stature and clothing, she surmised that they could only be Zeltans.

"We got your transmissions, Lieutenant," the Zeltan leader said casually up at Tristan's exo-mech. "Sounds like you've been through hell."

The exo-mech hissed open, and the entitled former prince stepped out. He gracefully leaped down to the snowy ground, barely kicking up any snow on his landing. "It really was. I just wanna get back to Sovereign City, Major."

The leader, apparently the rank of Major, had a distinguished, yet battle-hardened appearance. His graying hair was combed back neatly, but his face bore several scars suggesting a history of war. His face was rough and coarse like a canyon boulder, but his uniform presented him as a work of art. The two next to him appeared younger, but they all wore neatly pressed military uniforms with the ornate capes that lightly grazed the snow.

"In due time, Lieutenant," the Major said. "We need to debrief. Your natural born prisoners look terrible. Bots, give these runts a bath." The Major put an arm around Tristan, leading him past the New Haveners.

Kira's veins could have melted the snow around her. "Excuse me? Prisoners? Just who the hell do you think you are?"

The old officer turned around slowly, with a hint of a smile hidden beneath his thick mustache. "My name is Major Samson, commander of the White Range Zeltan outpost. He slapped the wool coverings over his massive torso. "We're just here to make sure these bots aren't up to any shenanigans."

Major Sampson was a hulking mass of ox-like muscle. His breath came in labored grunts as he pressed forward through the trees, sticking close to the loud men walking on either side of him.

He let out a hearty laugh, walking up to Kira, his frame towering over her. "And, natural born, you are...who?"

Raymond stepped between the Major and Kira. "My name is Dr. Raymond Redmin. And as you said, we've been through hell and back, so how about you take it easy."

Samson paused for an eternity, giving Raymond a long look. "So, this is the man from Earth, huh?"

"As NB as NB's can be," Tristan joked.

"I'm sure they'll have lots of questions for you when we get back to the capital." Samson turned away, apparently unimpressed.

"We're not prisoners," Kira said.

Locke tried to intercede. "There are no prisoners here at North Haven. We live here in peace, and—"

"Yeah, yeah, yeah." Major Samson waved him off. "Prisoners, guests, tourists. I don't care. Just remember, you all live here in your peaceful fantasy because the Zeltan Kingdom allows it, and don't you forget that." A robot stood in Samson's way, and he casually shoved the robot aside.

The android Locke displayed a slight degree of disdain that vanished in a moment. He turned to Kira. "We should get you all inside after everything you have been through."

"I just want to get home," Kira said. "I'm from Remnant. Can you help me get back home?"

"Remnant?" Samson turned around once again. "You're from Remnant?"

"Yeah, I am," she said, hoping the irritating Major would have good news for her. Perhaps her town had sent out some kind of search for her.

Major Samson shook his head. "You're better off staying here with these looney bots. Remnant's been overrun with Raiders. The whole Frontier's gone crazy over that crashed ship. You got Raiders, Riders, Corsairs, all those natural born low lives out there blowing each other to smithereens over that thing. It's a damn war zone. Remnant, that place is smack in the middle of all of it."

Kira's heart sank, and she didn't know whether to feel angry or sad. Instead, all she felt was cold and numb. It seemed like the whole town of New Haven stood silently, waiting for her to respond. Even Tristan had a look of sympathy on his face.

She struggled to formulate a response, something smart. Something brave. Something to show that she didn't feel afraid and alone. But no words left her mouth. Her eyelids swelled with emotion, but fighting back the tears was the very least she could do. *This isn't the time to look weak*, she thought to herself.

"Kira," Raymond said, putting his hand on her shoulder. "We'll get you back there. We'll figure it out."

"Keep dreaming, Earth boy," Major Samson said, spitting on the snow. "It's a lost cause. With the reports coming in from the Frontier...everyone in the town is probably dead. Everyone."

THIRTY-FOUR

Benny Fong felt his body jerk from side to side as Darien drove the Jackal straight into the battle. And yet, he felt like an ethereal spirit watching over his body. From the Specter drone, he flew over their car, looking down at himself sitting in the passenger seat, with Darien furiously spinning the wheel to avoid gunfire and the obstacles of the battleground. Meanwhile, Casey was wildly shooting the mounted machine gun from the back.

"Up ahead to the right," Benny shouted. "Jaguar Tank!"

The Specter drone weaved through the mayhem. Bullets, missiles, and artillery flew past. Involuntarily, Benny recoiled at the ordinance, zipping past the video screen. Smoke filled the air, but Quentin had customized the Specter with heat-signature optics. They originally intended the drone for search and rescue missions if anyone from town had gone missing out on the Frontier. Now, the Specter fed Benny a dizzying array of information from the battlefield where he flew overhead.

Darien spun the vehicle, making it slide sideways. Benny felt the sudden movements while watching this happen from the air. He couldn't help but keep an eye on himself, making sure he was not falling out of the vehicle. The Jackal slid sideways across the dirt, the back facing the small group of Raiders huddled together around a wrecked Tiger tank. The Raiders began to shoot at Benny's Jackal car. One of them readied their rocket launcher. Casey swiftly tore them apart with a deluge of belt-fed firepower. From the Specter, it appeared as if the Raiders were thrown back by a force of the orange god.

Benny watched this all with a displaced feeling of exhilaration, occasionally reminding himself that he in fact was the person sitting in that passenger seat below. He always enjoyed the feeling of being invisible, watching things from afar. After all, the townspeople treated him like a fly on the wall anyway. He had gotten used to feeling like a ghost.

The Jackal sped onwards, now fully immersed in the thick of the battle. Gnarled parts of damaged metal and detonated ordinance jutted the ground of the Martian Frontier. Charred bodies of Raiders and Corsairs alike littered the ground. Survivors screamed and reached out for help. Darien was doing his best to keep the Jackal from running over people or obstacles, but there was simply no open ground left to drive on.

It was hellish sight to behold, so Benny never lingered for too long. He continued following his own vehicle from above, ignoring the rows of violence and suffering they were zooming past.

The skies were thankfully clear. Neither the Raiders nor the Corsairs put much stock into developing aerial vehicles. In addition to the Spire anti-air ordinance, there was the fear of the rumored cursed skies that swallowed even the powerful Zeltan aerial craft. Also, they feared that dabbling in aerial warfare would prompt the Zeltan Kingdom to step up their involvement in Western affairs. For now, the Corsairs dominated the open Green Sea, above and below water, while the Raiders roamed free in the Far West Badlands. The advancement of aerial vehicles was simply too difficult and not worth the risk of sparking unwanted attention from the Zeltan superpower from the east.

"Behind us!" Benny yelled.

A Wolf Heavy Utility Vehicle took chase behind them. Benny eased the speed of his drone to fall behind the enemy. He assessed the situation and blurted out his observations in a panic.

"They have a big gun in the back too," Benny said. "A driver, someone shooting from the front, and the big gun from behind us. Guys, another one. Two coming after us!"

Another Wolf, with a full tow of Corsair cyborgs, followed behind them. From behind them, Benny could see the constant muzzle fire gleaming from the enemy vehicles. He tensed, expecting a bullet to hit his body. He almost gave in to the temptation to tear off the drone helmet, but instead remained focused in.

"They got too much firepower!" Casey yelled. Benny watched him ducking behind the machine gun as bullets pinged around him.

"I'm trying to shake them," Darien said calmly with a hint of frustration.

Darien was doing his best to weave between flaming and disabled vehicles for cover. Their Jackal careened right and left, and Benny felt nauseous. He had trouble concentrating on piloting the Specter while his body was jostled about the doorless and roofless car.

"This ain't lookin' good, Zelt!" Casey yelled over the barrage of gunfire.

They were dead in the water if they couldn't figure out a solution. Despite his disorientation, Benny decided to act. He wouldn't just be a passenger to his own fate anymore. He took a deep breath to focus. He pushed the trigger on his remote control for full thrust. The Specter flew down to the level of one of the enemy Wolf vehicles.

"I'm gonna distract the one on the right!" Benny said.

He was close enough to see their faces. None of the cyborgs realized the drone was close by. They were too focused on shooting at Benny and company ahead of them. Benny quickly dove near the driver, which surprised him, making him swerve.

"Now!" Benny said. "I got 'em on the right!"

Darien immediately made the Jackal swerve again, this time deftly hiding the front of their vehicle behind some Lion tank wreckage while just the backend was exposed. The car smoothly drifted sideways across the dirt. Casey took the opportunity to fire at the swerving enemy vehicle behind them. Benny lifted the Specter just in time. The cyborgs were looking up at the drone while Casey's machine gun ripped their vehicle to shreds. The driver and front passenger convulsed as bullets made their faces and torsos popped open in exploding pockets of blood. The car made a sharp, uncontrolled turn into a metal fragment jutting out from the ground, making it flip over mid-air onto its side, crashing down into the ground with an upheaval of dirt and debris.

Benny turned the camera away from the gory sight, and momentarily reflected on the inane violence that they were driving though. He cursed himself for getting into this situation but resolved above all else to get out of this hellscape and make it back home.

The second vehicle sped past the wreckage, continuing to shoot at them. Benny took the drone and flew it full speed at the gunner in the back. The Specter rammed his head. The video feed jumbled for a second, and Benny thought he lost the drone. When it stabilized, he realized it was still hovering in place. They sped away, but the pursuing Wolf started swerving side to side.

Benny caught up to see if his distraction worked. In fact, it caused a most fortuitous disruption. The gunner seemed to have actually shot the front passenger in the back, likely when the drone knocked him in the back of the head. The passenger was half hanging out the door, with his head and upper body torn apart by gunfire.

"Again!" Benny said, "The other one!"

The enemy Wolf continued to swerve in disorientation. Darien tried to bring the car to do the same maneuver, but the enemy gunner regained focus. Bullets tore through their vehicle, and Casey took cover. The bullets riddled the vehicle, and Benny tensed up for impact.

"Shit!" Casey said.

"Everyone alright?" Darien asked.

"I'm good." Casey said, "Sons of bitches still on us."

"Guys, can you check me?" Benny asked. "Am I hit? I can't tell!"

Benny brought the drone up to his passenger's side to examine himself. He lifted his arms and legs to examine himself from a third-person view. It was surreal experience, as if Benny's spirit left his body and came back to check on it. Casey pulled himself over to the front to look at him.

"You're fine!" Casey yelled. "Get that goddamn thing back there!"

When he was finally convinced that he wasn't fatally injured, Benny brought Specter back around. Now, the enemy gunner was trying to shoot it out of the sky.

"It's shooting at the Specter!" Benny yelled.

"This is our chance," Darien said. "Get on the gun... now!"

Darien must have slammed on the full brakes. The Jackal lurched forward, kicking up a cloud of dirt. The unsuspecting enemy vehicle continued speeding forward, coming just a few feet away from them. The gunner was busy trying to shoot the Specter. Casey took the machine gun and injected the full force of the payload into the enemy vehicle driving right by them. The driver and gunner were dead within seconds, and their vehicle sped directly into a disabled enemy tank, crashing with a loud thud amongst the cacophony of war.

"Take me over there," Casey said, "I'm out of ammo."

Darien started the Jackal again, driving up to the crashed enemy vehicle. Casey quickly jumped out, grabbing two large ammunition boxes with belts of gleaming bullets spilling out. Casey also quickly patted down the driver, stealing a revolver pistol from the cyborg's holster.

"Perfect," Casey said, jumping back into their vehicle.

The horizon west was cluttered with artillery fire and warfare. They could see Julian's exo-mech in the midst of it. Benny marveled at the colossal giant. He bounded across the battlefield, dodging rockets and explosions, doing his best to fight off the much-larger Raider forces. Benny hoped that the two factions would simply obliterate each other here on the battlefield once and for all today.

After what seemed like an eternity, they were finally past the fighting. The incessant gunfire started to become a distant storm rumble behind them. Benny, in his paranoia, scanned the horizon in all directions. They were safe. Despite unbelievable odds, their vehicle sputtered on through the desert alone, with Benny's Specter drone following close behind.

"That was great work, gentlemen," Darien said.

"I can't believe we survived that," Benny said with a shaky laugh, observing the ongoing mayhem behind them from the Specter.

"Me too," Casey said, reloading his mounted machine gun. "But I got enough ammo to make a second pass back there if you all are up for it."

"No." Darien and Benny said simultaneously.

THIRTY-FIVE

R aymond Redmin marveled at the town of North Haven, a peaceful, surreal winter paradise. Layers of snow covered the rooftops, smoke billowed from the chimneys and swirled into the air. The sparkling water mill placed along the river turned peacefully while the soft blanket of clouds passed overhead, clumps breaking off to drift down gently as snowflakes. The light dusting of snow coated the trees, making white sprigs of their limbs. The air smelled of baked bread and firewood. It was like something out of a Christmas storybook.

Here, robots of all shapes and sizes lived in harmony. Even the occasional human seemed blissful. He watched as one android stood by the stream, painting a picture at an easel, while a human nearby walked alongside a wheeled robot carrying firewood. The androids and humans waved to each other and went about their business as equals.

"Well," Raymond said. "If I really have to be stuck on this planet, then this is where I'd want to be."

"Unfortunately, this is not the place for you, doctor," Locke said calmly, emoting through his artificial human face that was still jarring enough to frighten Raymond.

They walked along a short wooden bridge adjacent to a small pond. Here, a human was washing the metal of a small 4-wheeled robot while birds chirped nearby. To Raymond, this was pure harmony.

"Well, why not?" Raymond asked. "I could provide medical care and assistance. I want to help."

"Ah, yes." Locke stopped. "And therein lies your answer."

"What?" Raymond stood perplexed. "Answer to what?"

"Your calling is out there, not here. You are meant to help those in need. You are a special blessing to our planet."

"Raymond!" Kira ran up to Raymond and Locke. "They said the storm is clearing, and the mountain path should be ready for us later today."

"For us? I..." Raymond caught himself.

Raymond knew that Kira was fully expecting him to go with her back to Remnant. While Major Sampson expected all of them to return to the Zeltan capital with him, he laughed off Kira's plans to return home. He was indifferent to what she wanted to do, emphasizing that he didn't give a damn what happened to natural borns.

Kira stared in silence as Raymond looked to the ground. "You're...you're not planning on coming with me?"

"It's not that I don't want to go," Raymond said. "But what good are we to your friends and family without the Zeltans? They are leaving east for the Capital. If you come with us, maybe we can convince them to bring—"

"No, we need to go *now*."

"Kira," Raymond said, "I get it. You need to be with your family and friends. But you heard what Locke said. It's too dangerous. You won't do any good by yourself; we need to get some help first."

"No." Kira turned away. "There's no time for that."

Raymond looked over to Tristan and Marcus, loading the exo-mech. "You said there was a sickness in your town. Without medicine and supplies, I can't do anything."

"But you're a doctor," Kira said. "We need you now."

Raymond shook his head. "I'm sorry, Kira, but—"

She walked away abruptly, wiping tears from her eyes.

"Wait, Kira. You can't go by yourself!"

"I'll do it alone!" she responded angrily without turning around.

Raymond sighed in frustration. Part of the reason he didn't want to go West to the Frontier was because he alone wouldn't be much help. But he also wanted to know more about what happened to his wife and son. He asked the androids if they had any information on Earth pre-Silence, but they regrettably informed him that much knowledge was wiped from their memory banks during the registration process. The Zeltans kept much historical and technological information stored away at the Capital. If Raymond wanted to find out what happened to his family or why he was even here, Sovereign City would be where he wanted to go. But as he watched Kira march off into the distance, he couldn't help but think he was letting this girl walk off to her death. He chased after her.

"Don't forget, Raymond," Locke said as Raymond walked away, "you are special. You are destined to help others."

Raymond stopped in place, unable to process what Locke was even talking about. *Is the android suggesting that I should go with Kira? That's ludicrous. Without the Zeltans, it would be a fool's venture into death.*

"What do you mean by that?" Raymond asked.

"Thank you for your service to sentient life, doctor." Locke said, smiling through his synthetic facial skin, and walking away, carrying a stack of lumber.

"The girl's upset you're coming with us?" Tristan smirked as he walked by.

"Y'know, why don't *you* help her?" Raymond snapped. "She wants me to go, but I can't do anything on my own, but you two"— Raymond looked at the gleaming exo-mech and Marcus' battle armor—"could make a huge difference in defending her home."

"Not our problem," Tristan said, "Orders are to head back to the Capital. They want you with us. We don't get involved in NB squabbles."

Raymond analyzed Tristan's face. There was something different in his tone. It was ever so slightly off from his sarcastic, arrogant delivery. *Was that... guilt?*

Tristan cleared his throat and abruptly walked away. Raymond wondered whether there was a conscience in that haughty prick after all. No matter. Kira and Swift were going off on their own now. He needed to convince them against this foolish endeavor.

When he caught up to her, Kira was packing a pitiful bag of supplies, armed only with a rifle.

"Kira," Raymond said. "Come on, you can't go by yourself like that."

Kira slammed the bag down on the table. "Then come with me! Anyone? Will anyone come with me?" She looked around the village as the nearby robotic and humanoid citizens paused in place. "My friends and family are dying. I have been to hell and back, and if all I'm coming back with is myself and Swift, then that's what I'll have to do! Look, I am so very happy for you all that you have found peace. I can see that you are happy, but down there..." She sniffed, her face in tears. "There is *no* happiness on the Frontier. We can't have it. We're too busy trying to live. Too busy trying not to die. Every day is a fight to live. And I'll be damned if today was the day I stopped fighting for my town. They need me. I'm going."

There was something in her voice that struck a chord in Raymond. These were words from the heart. She meant every single one. After all the chaos they had experienced, he could not abandon someone so clearly in need of his help. She was, most importantly among all things in this strange future and planet, his friend.

"I'm going with you," Raymond said. He was surprised that the words left his mouth, but he felt no regret.

"What? But I thought—" Kira said, surprised.

Raymond grabbed her shoulders assuringly. "You're right. Nothing is more important to me than doing everything I can to help. If there are people down there, especially people who are sick, then that's where I need to be."

She took a moment to process, but eventually Kira nodded and gave a quiet "thank you."

A robotic voice said, "And Voltaire will join you in your noble endeavor."

Raymond and Kira incredulously looked up at Voltaire, the frustratingly wise robot wrapped in monk-like garments. Surely, a war zone would be no place for a peace-loving philosopher.

"I will go as well," another robot said.

"Me too," another said. "I want to help."

One by one, the robots volunteered to go with Kira and Raymond.

"But...the North Haven Accords," Kira said, looking at Major Sampson, who had come out of his encampment to witness the commotion.

"That's right," Major Sampson spoke up from the crowd. "You can stop this pity party right now. No AI leaves the White Range, especially not down to a war zone. We can't have the lot of you getting in wars and firing off guns and whatnot. You'll damn near start a fourth AI war. Is *that* what you want?"

"But what of purely medical assistance?" Voltaire asked. "These beings may be useful in assisting no further degradation of life. This—"

"I said no!" Major Sampson bellowed. "Now, all of you get back to what you were all doing. Lieutenant, Sergeant, let's get ready to roll out. This place disgusts me."

The two Zeltans complied, but Raymond caught Tristan struggling with some form of guilt.

"Lieutenant," Raymond said as they walked away.

Tristan turned around, not making eye contact.

"Hey, just..." Raymond said, trying to meet Tristan's eyes. "When you get back there. Just tell them that there are people out there who need help. And if you can, please find out what you can about my family and—"

"Forget it," Tristan said, turning away. "I don't owe you all anything. I should take you by force back to the Kingdom. Consider it a mercy that I'm letting you go."

Raymond nodded with disappointment. "Okay then. Well... good luck then. Sergeant?"

Sergeant Marcus, as usual, gave no verbal response but simply looked at Raymond and Kira through his tinted visor and nodded.

Tristan and Marcus walked away with Major Sampson's unit, and the citizens of North Haven gave their apologies, and one-by-one went back to their business.

"You two possess much of the human spirit that we androids seek so desperately to emulate," Locke said.

"All avatars of this universe seek to find and immerse themselves in this connection," Voltaire said. "This is the purpose of our existence."

Locke and Voltaire, the two benevolent androids, bowed slightly in reverence and went back into the town.

"Just us, then," Raymond said.

"We'll be enough," Kira said, slinging a bag over her shoulder.

Swift gave a supportive hum.

Raymond, Kira, and Swift would return to the Frontier alone.

CHAPTER

THIRTY-SIX

C aptain Darien felt the vehicle rumble and sputter. The Jackal had been badly damaged in battle, filled with bullet holes, and reduced to a gnarled framework of metal, rolling across the open desert of the Red Frontier. The heavy fighting across the desert forced them to turn north. They would instead first stop at Sierra Outpost, the nearest station of Red Riders. According to Casey, they could regroup and resupply there.

The sun was setting on the horizon to the west. To the north, there was a small tower, built from thick, white pillars held up by crossbeams and buttresses, standing against the backdrop of mountains looming like a wall of slate behind it. This was the only building for miles. It appeared small compared to the rolling landscape peaks of snow-capped mountains that melted into the sky until they disappeared. The setting sun was turning their summits gold and orange. Night would fall shortly.

"That's it," Casey yelled from the gunner seat in the back. "That's Sierra Outpost."

That's it? Darien thought. This was supposed to be the outlook station responsible for protecting the settlers from the dangers of the Black Forest to the east and the White Range to the north. It looked barely big enough to house any more than a dozen men.

As they approached, Casey stood up high in the back of the Jackal, waving his wide-brimmed hat in the air. Two distinct glints of light shone from the window at the top of the tower.

"That's the signal," Casey said. "We're good to go, Zelt."

As they approached the outpost, it looked even less and less impressive. It looked built from simple stone, cracked at the sides, with several windows overlooking all four directions. Darien could spot the snipers in the windows as he drove closer. He hoped these men could be trusted. Otherwise, he was driving into quite another high-risk situation for himself.

Three horses rode out from the building adjacent to the tower. The riders all wore wide-brimmed hats, duster jackets, and high boots like Casey. The middle rider raised his hand, signaling them to stop the vehicle. Darien brought the vehicle to a stop. He indiscreetly pulled his automatic rifle beside his legs below the dashboard, hand on the grip and finger on the trigger. Darien could sense Benny from the passenger seat looking down wide-eyed at the gun.

"Stop looking at the gun," Darien said out of the corner of his mouth, eyes still fixed on the three horse riders.

"Sorry." Benny gulped. He sat cradling his drone and helmet on his lap.

"Is that you, George?" Casey asked. He let out an uncharacteristic laugh. "Hoo! Ol' George Wallace, now aren't you a sight for sore eyes? I thought we—"

"You stay right where you are," the middle Rider said, drawing a pistol out.

The other two Riders pulled out their pistols. The flanking horsemen looked much younger. They were fresh-faced cowboys who both took several seconds too long to draw out their guns, Darien observed. Interestingly, the middle rider, the aged, gruff one with a white-haired stubbled beard, had a distinct cool control to his draw. He was experienced. Darien would need to be careful with this one.

"George, the hell is all that for? It's me, Casey."

"I know who you are, ya idiot," the old man said. His voice was as harsh as the Martian sand. "Who I don't know are those boys you got in that truck with ya. You don't think Imma let you drive up to the Outpost with a big ol' machine gun and a couple randos and then not expect me to ask any questions?"

"They're with me," Casey said. "I can vouch for 'em. We just got outta that mess down at the crash site. Corsairs and Raiders. A whole shit fest of 'em down there."

Darien calculated his options. The Red Riders still had their guns trained on them. In the chance that dialogue went south, he would need to be ready to take them all out at once. He gripped the rifle tight. If he brought it up quick enough, he would shoot the middle Rider in the head first, then the two beside him. There would be no room for error. A split second of hesitation or, god forbid, a missed shot would spell doom for Darien and his passengers. Speaking of which, Benny seemed to be hyperventilating in the seat next to him.

"Just relax," Darien said through gritted teeth without moving his lips.

"Wh-what are you gonna do?" Benny whispered with his voice shaking.

"You know," George called out, "I'd be happy to have a civil conversation with y'all. But first, you gotta do 'ol George a favor. How about you tell your driver to toss out that gun he's holding under the seat." He gave Darien a sharp look. "Don't wanna make a mess of things out here, do we?"

It was decision time. Darien wished he had a pistol instead of a bulky automatic rifle. The stakes of the gamble were high. Even he had to admit that pulling a move now was not likely to end well. Moreover, he could feel himself sitting directly in the crosshairs of the sniper on the high window of the tower.

"Easy now, Zelt," Casey said.

Within a millisecond, Darien considered the flood of threat algorithms he had trained his whole life for. This was likely to end badly, and he would be putting his companions in danger. He would not be responsible for their deaths. The smart move was to forfeit. He slowly took the assault rifle and tossed it out of the vehicle, then put his hands in the air.

George grinned. "Y'all carrying big guns there."

"There was a battle," Casey said. "We barely got out alive."

"I know," George said. "We were watching the whole thing until y'all pulled up. I got scouts out there right now. Big 'ol mess of a battle you boys just got out of. You know, the dusties actually got them Corsairs on their heels. Blackheart fell back with his tail between his legs. Serves him right, that cocky bastard. Problem is, them Raiders might get their dirty hands on that fancy spaceship tech; god help us."

"They said something about an Ark," Darien asked. "What is that?

"The whozawhat?" George asked sarcastically. The Red Riders beside him chuckled.

"Alright, then what about the exo-mech," Darien said, frustrated. "There was an exo-mech in the battle. Did they see what happened to it?"

"What, that big 'ol robot?" George asked. "Retreated back to a Corsair encampment a little south of the spaceship crash site. They'll be back, though. That Blackheart's got too much pride to let a bunch of Raider hooligans drive him away. The way I see it, he'll be bringing the *whole* shit storm back with him. That godforsaken sandship. I'll be damned if we stay around for that."

"Well, wow, many we got here at the outpost?" Casey asked.

"Seven now," George said, spitting off to the side. "Countin' us three. But we're about to pack up and head up to Tabernacle. Ain't no use sticking around here. This place is about to turn into a warzone."

"You're abandoning the outpost?" Casey asked.

"Keeping ourselves from an untimely demise, the way I see it," George said.

"Um, excuse me, sir," Benny said sheepishly. "What about Remnant? Have you heard anything from there?"

"Remnant." George shook his head. "Lost cause there, boy. Now, I'm sorry, Case, I know that's where you were stationed, but that town is completely overrun by the Raiders. Took 'em over last night. Made that place their own. The women, the children... they belong to the Raiders now."

Darien could tell from the look on Benny's face that he was imagining the worst. His friends and family were either dead or now subject to the cruelty of the barbaric Raider clans.

"What's the plan to take back Remnant?" Casey asked.

"Take it back?" George replied. "Boy, that spaceship drew the attention of every Raider clan in the far west. The whole lot of them swept across every town on the Frontier. We got distress calls from almost every settlement. We sent out all the Riders we got. But the truth of the matter is, there just ain't enough of us to take them all on."

"But," Benny said, still in shock, "my family...my friends... they're all still there. What's gonna happen to them?"

"I'm sorry, boy," George said. "Ain't nothing you can do for them now."

Darien felt sorry for Benny, but also understood the logic of this Red Rider leader. Sometimes leaders needed to make hard decisions. He imagined that this George Wallace struggled with those decisions far more than he was letting on.

Shortly after, Darien, Casey, and Benny were escorted inside the small outpost. The sand-worn walls had cracks down the sides. Darien surmised the outpost wouldn't even survive one volley of artillery if attacked. They followed the three Red Riders into a small, cramped command center inside the small two-story building adjacent to the tower. Video screens and radios were cluttered about the room. One of the Red Riders sat in deep concentration with his hands over large, muffed headphones over his ears. He muttered words into a microphone at the desk.

"Make yourselves at home, boys," George said. He slumped into a chair, leaning back with his feet up on the table. He grabbed a nearby mug, sniffed it, and took a large swig. The liquid streamed down the white stubble of his chin. His face cringed, and he looked back into the mug, wondering what he had drank. He shrugged and took another hearty gulp.

Darien, Casey, and Benny stood as the other two Red Riders sat at the table in the center of the room. Darien suspected Casey and Benny were still incredulous that the Riders were not planning a rescue operation for Remnant. Darien sympathized with them but was interested in getting word back to the Zeltan Capital to arrange another venture into the Black Forest.

"Mr. Wallace," Darien said. "This communications equipment. Can we use it to get word to the Zeltan Capital? My squad was ambushed in the Black Forest. I might still have men in there, in danger. I need to send word back."

George Wallace sat back, giving the Zeltan a long, inquisitive look. "Hoo-ee, you sure are the real deal, aren't ya? Zeltan Ranger. A *super*-soldier." He looked him up and down. "Didn't think anything was supposed to rattle y'all. How'd a whole squad of y'all get into trouble like that?"

"Mr. Wallace," Darien repeated. "I need to use your communications equipment to get word back to the Capital. There are men's lives on the line. This is important."

"Well, shit, supreme commander ranger, sir," George said mockingly. "Ain't everyone got their lives on the line right now." He sat forward quickly, slamming the mug on the table. "I got Riders all over the Frontier fightin' off Raiders, runnin' from Corsairs. Over 20 Riders died just today. So, excuse me if your team got into some trouble because y'all were stupid enough to waltz into the goddamn Black Forest!"

Darien tensed. He and everyone knew he could kill everyone in the room with his bare hands if he wanted to. How dare this old cowboy raise his voice at him and insult his fallen team members.

"Settle yourself," Darien said calmly.

George was leaning over the table on his arms. The younger three cowboys looked at him with wide eyes, jaws wide open. They looked almost ready to reach for their guns but knew better than to provoke a Zeltan in close quarters.

After a pause, George Wallace let out a squeaky, hearty laugh. He sat back down. "Zeltans. Goddamn royal bastards." He shook his head and motioned at the Rider at the radio console. "Dale, get our majesty through to his people. It'll be a miracle if they even bother to listen. Ain't no Zeltan ever send assistance this way, even if the entire Frontier was on fire. Maybe since one of their own is over here, they'll bother to listen."

After several minutes of attempts to contact the Zeltan Capital, Darien seemed to finally get through.

"I repeat," Darien said into the microphone, "this is a message from Zeltan Ranger Captain Darien, requesting audience with Colonel Nathan. I am transmitting from the Frontier at a Sierra Outpost, coordinates undetermined."

"This is Reconnaissance Specialist Matthew," a garbled voice was heard over the radio. "Can we confirm? Can we confirm?"

Darien rattled off every confirmation code he had. He understood the importance of secure communication, but after several requests to confirm, he finally lost his patience.

"Dammit, this is Captain Darien. I demand to speak to Colonel Nathan or any officer from High Command!"

Silence.

Darien hoped he hadn't ruined his only chance to communicate with the Capital. After a few minutes, the same communications specialist returned on the radio.

"This is a direct order from Colonel Nathan," he said. "You are ordered to continue your mission to capture or kill the traitor to the Kingdom, Julian. Retrieval teams will be sent into the forest to collect the injured and deceased. You are ordered to return any actionable intelligence to the Capital. Request directly from High Command to obtain the object known as The Ark and return it to the Zeltan Capital."

"The Ark?" Darien asked incredulously. "I will need reinforcements. I'm on the other side of the Black Forest. Send a Buzzard dropship. There are multiple large-scale combat events in the locale. I'll need a team of shock troopers—"

"Colonel Nathan directly orders you to complete your mission. Apprehend or eliminate Julian and bring the Ark artifact to Sovereign City."

"What?" Darien replied. "I demand to speak to the Colonel directly."

"There will be no further instructions, Captain. High Command wishes you well." The radio feed ended.

Darien stared at the microphone in disbelief. They were abandoning him. Completing this mission by himself would be suicide. Was the Colonel truly betraying him? It was impossible. Colonel Nathan was like a father figure to him.

No, that wouldn't happen. Someone is keeping me from getting in touch with Zeltan High Command.

Darien's mind swirled. There would be no strategic value to trusting an entire mission on one surviving member of a decimated Ranger Squad. He felt abandoned and betrayed, but most of all, confused.

George Wallace chuckled, drinking his mug. "Sounds like you're all alone, Cap'n."

Darien slowly turned, ready to slam the old cowboy's head into the ground.

"Captain Darien," Benny said. "Maybe you can help us."

"What do you mean?" Darien asked.

"The Raiders," Benny said. "They took over our town. I saw what you can do. You could take on a whole army of Raiders by yourself. And this Ark… We keep overhearing the Corsairs talk about it. The Raiders are taking it with them back west. It might still be in Remnant. Help us, and we can help you find whatever that is."

Perhaps, Darien thought.

"The kid's right, Zeltie," Casey said. "I ain't gonna leave Remnant to them bastards like that. Whether the Red Riders wanna help or not, I'm going back in there."

"Me too," Benny said bravely.

Wallace shook his head. "That's suicide. You boys are gonna get yourselves killed."

"Wait, you ain't coming with us?" Casey asked.

"Can't afford to lose any more men," Wallace said, staring into the bottom of his cup. "I just can't."

"Well, then I guess it's just me and"—Casey looked at Benny and sighed—"Fong."

Darien considered their predicament. These two natural borns were truly marching to their death. Darien sympathized with these people. This was a society far detached from his own. They were a people he was taught to ignore. They were right, though. To his own peril, he might be able to save their little town.

"And me," Darien said, nodding. "Once again... I'll help you."

He expected to feel regret for his decision, but the regret never came. If the Colonel and High Command were leaving him without support, then he was truly alone. These natural borns might be the only comrades he had left. He resolved to do right by them and right by himself. He would prove it to High Command.

Even alone, without his team and without support, he could still complete his mission. The mission was all he had left.

THIRTY-SEVEN

Kira Skyler could only think about her hometown, her friends, her brother, and Benny. If the reports were true, the town was taken over by Raiders. Her mind flashed back to her childhood when the town would be attacked, women and children taken from their homes, and the men of the town killed. In a full takeover, was there anyone even left? She had to know.

She, Raymond, and Swift plodded along the snowy mountain path. The storm had thankfully cleared. With the orange hue of the evening sky shining above them, the beautiful White Range mountains and the valley below were a sight to behold. But in the distance, Kira could see the plumes of smoke to the south. Just on the horizon, she could see where the Black Forest met the Red Frontier, and heavy warfare had taken place. The Frontier was a battlefield, and she needed to be back there.

"Tell me about this Crimson Fever," Raymond said, trying to catch up with Kira's determined pace.

"It started years ago," Kira said. "Took some people in the town. It starts as a feeling of your muscles and joints aching. You start sweating, fevers. Then you start getting really short of breath. Eventually, you can't breathe well after taking a few steps. The cough gets unbearable, and they start coughing up blood. And by that point, it's over. I watched so many people go through it. My friends, my dad, and now...my little brother Owen."

"Hmm," Raymond said. "I promise you, Kira. I'll do what I can to help. Are there any medical supplies?"

"None that would be able to help," Kira said. "I mean, we have doctors and healers, but out in the Frontier, we can't get to any medicine or nothing like that. But—"

"Let's just get back to your town and figure it out from there."

"Right." Kira picked up, even more determined, and bounded down the mountain even more hastily.

"Wait!" Raymond said.

Kira felt the world pulling her from below. The snow had given out beneath her. She grasped at the cold snow and ice for stability. She deduced that she had gone off the path. She was so lost in her own mind that she hadn't paid much attention to where she had been stepping.

"Grab my hand!" Raymond said.

Raymond and Swift pulled her up from a potentially perilous drop into the chasm. She looked down below. The vast depths of the drop made her stomach lurch.

"Thanks," Kira said, brushing the snow off her. "Sorry, I guess I just started walking this way because if we went that way then—"

Kira and Raymond realized it simultaneously. The only mountain path was blocked by a recent collapse of snow over the path. It piled three times higher than their heads. Kira and Raymond tried to dig through it to no avail.

"Seriously?" Raymond said, kneeling. "Do we really need to turn all the way back? It took hours to get here."

"No, no, no," Kira defiantly said as she took her pickaxe and continued to hack at the blockage.

She would not accept this. Kira couldn't deal with yet another setback. She had to get back home. And what would they even do if they returned to North Haven? The Zeltans were probably gone by now. They would be stranded there for who knows how long.

"Kira," Raymond said.

Kira hacked and slashed.

"Kira."

Kira continued, now screaming as she pitifully made little progress on the ice. She cursed herself. She was just a stupid girl with stupid ideas and accomplishing nothing. Tristan was right. She was just a useless natural born. She yelled in rage frustration and hacked at the icy snow with her pickaxe.

"Kira!" Raymond grabbed her shoulders.

She dropped her pickaxe and sank to the floor in defeat. "Why am I even here?" She sobbed, but the tears froze on her cheeks. "I should have been there with them..."

"We'll get there, Kira," Raymond said assuringly. "But c'mon, the sun's about to go down and—"

The mountain began to rumble.

Avalanche? Was it because I was yelling?

Kira and Raymond reacted simultaneously, digging their pickaxes into the snow and making sure the harnesses were firmly attached. There was nowhere to run; they were on the mountainside, and the snow would surely push them off the edge, but they had to try to plant themselves into the ground somehow.

"Are you secure?" Raymond yelled over the increasing rumbling.

"Yeah, are you?" Kira replied.

By now, the rumbling was deafening, and Raymond only nodded. They looked up and expected a barrage of snowfall. Instead, one of the two Mars moons was blocked only by the familiar silhouette of Tristan's exo-mech and a familiar armored soldier hanging on its shoulder. There was another figure clinging to the other shoulder.

"It looks like you're all in need of assistance yet again!" Tristan said through the loudspeakers.

"Tristan?" Kira said. "What are you doing here?"

"Preventing you from an untimely demise it looks like!" Tristan let out a laugh through the speakers.

Raymond pulled up Kira to a stable footing of snow.

"Well, just do us a favor," Raymond said, "Keep it down a little, you're going to cause an avalanche."

"I think the right response is 'thank you,'" Tristan said.

Kira sighed. This was certainly unexpected. Tristan and Marcus came to join them. But why? This was certainly unlike Zeltans to offer to help when it did not benefit them directly. Regardless, she needed all the help she could get. She was ultimately grateful and appreciative that she had not seen the last of them.

"No, you're right." Kira said, "thank you."

"Not doing this for you, NB," Tristan said, scooping the snowy obstruction from the path as Marcus the Vanguard jumped down to join them. The exo-mech suit cockpit flipped open. "If there's a battle, that's where I need to be. Especially since I got these!"

Tristan's exo-mech brandished a large metal sword and a shield, like some kind of robotic, gargantuan medieval knight.

"Compliments of North Haven," Tristan said. "I got myself tournament sword and shield like they have the Kingdom. Apparently, Guaritore has been using the underground railway to trade old exo-mech tech. But this should do just fine!"

"You're taking a sword and shield out there?" Kira asked. "You know the Corsairs have tanks and missiles, right?"

"I'll figure it out." Tristan ignored her as the cockpit closed shut. "Come on, let's get down there!"

Kira and Raymond gave each other a confused look. The sudden turn of character was curious. Was he really doing this for sport, or was he finally showing some degree of compassion?

The other figure on the exo-mech's other shoulder plopped down from the snow. It was the shrouded android Voltaire.

"Voltaire?" Kira asked.

"One cannot be bound by the laws of men if there are those that are suffering," Voltaire said.

"And Sergeant Marcus?" Kira asked.

"We went against Major Sampson's orders," Marcus said. "We want to help."

Kira was surprised. It seemed that the Sergeant would be incapable of disobeying orders. "But this would get you and the Lieutenant in trouble."

"I am still following orders," Sergeant Marcus said. "I am following the Lieutenant's orders. He commanded that I follow him to the Frontier," Marcus said. "And he did it because you convinced him to help, if that was your question."

Kira smiled. "So, Lieutenant Tristan has a heart?"

"Don't read too much into it," Tristan said flatly over the speakers. He used his exo-mech sword to cut a way through the icy obstruction and barged forward.

Sergeant Marcus marched ahead. "It's time to move out, ma'am."

Kira looked at Raymond, Swift, and Voltaire. They all gave each other a happy nod of approval and followed Tristan and Marcus. With newfound determination, they headed down the mountain together.

CHAPTER

THIRTY-EIGHT

B enny Fong clutched the super-soldier tight as they rode horseback in near pitch-black visibility. They had been riding for hours across the Red Frontier. Casey rode alongside them on his own horse. Benny could swear that Casey and Darien had been racing each other this whole time in an unsaid, irrelevant rivalry. Benny was simply trying his best not to fall off.

The plan was to infiltrate Remnant from the northeast. There was a grotto of solar panels and crop modules there that they could use for cover. For distraction, George Wallace and his Red Riders agreed to drive the stolen Jackal near the east side of the town to attract attention away. Wallace surmised that this would draw some Raiders out of the town, giving Benny, Darien, and Casey a window to infiltrate.

Casey stopped just behind a rocky hill. Benny breathed a sigh of relief as the horse he and Darien were riding on also came to a stop. His fingers felt locked from gripping the Zeltan's clothes so tightly for hours. The rough stride of the journey also made his groin and lower back ache. Benny wanted to roll off the horse and sprawl flat onto the ground, but he reminded himself that his family and friends were still in danger.

"The town's just beyond the hill down there," Casey said. "We gotta go by foot from here on out."

Darien made the horse walk up the hill just about enough to see the town. Even in the distance, Benny could tell Remnant wasn't the same. Only certain lights were on every night: the clock tower, the sheriff's station, and the guard posts. But even at this hour, some houses and the town church had their lights fully on, while the clock tower and the guard posts were dark. There were objects and food carts strewn outside the edge of town. To his horror, he could swear he could see bodies on the ground.

The sight of Remnant occupied by Raiders gave him a drastic internal conflict of emotions. On the one hand, he was frozen in fear. On the other, he surged with the desire for justice and vengeance. He had never felt these sentiments before. He wondered if being around Darien and Casey had changed his mind frame, or simply his exposure to the brutality of warfare that he had just experienced.

"Hey," Casey said, turning back at Benny. "Do not lose your cool. What you'll see in there won't be pretty. But you gotta stick to the plan. Y'hear me?"

Benny took a deep breath and nodded.

"You'll do fine," Darien said over his shoulder, then swung himself off the horse as if he were as light as a feather. "He's right though. If you stick to the plan, we can save your friends in there."

The three of them walked silently through the dark of the night, staying as close to the ground as possible. As they approached closer to Remnant, they lay prone on the ground, waiting for their cue. Casey grabbed the radio on his belt, bringing it to his face.

"Wallace," he whispered. "We're ready."

As rehearsed, Casey shut the radio off immediately after sending the message. A loud sound like a radio communication would carry across the empty Frontier.

"And now we wait," Casey said, rolling onto his back. He pulled his hat over his eyes and folded his hands behind his head.

Darien gave a subtle shake of his head in disapproval. He pulled out binoculars to survey the town. Benny followed suit. The town lit up green on the scope's night vision settings. The first thing Benny noticed were two men sitting on the balcony of the old tailor's house. These men were clearly strangers and most likely Raiders. They seemed to be drinking and laughing together. Benny shuddered to think what had happened to Vic, the kind-hearted tailor who lived there.

On the streets, there were other Raiders, galavanting and laughing with bottles in their hands. Benny's home had turned into a cesspool for thugs and murderers. It was the same collection of buildings, but it no longer seemed like the town he knew. This was some kind of nightmare, a hellish version of his innocent Remnant. *And where were the people,* Benny wondered. *Were they dead? Where are my parents?*

The crackle of gunfire in the distance snapped him out of despair. On the east horizon appeared a small bright light in the distance. The rumbles of the Jackal could be heard. Benny used his binoculars to confirm. The utility vehicle rolled toward Remnant with a Red Rider in the passenger seat, firing his rifle into the sky. A few horseback Riders rode alongside the Jackal, firing their guns into the sky to provoke the Raiders' attention.

The town of Remnant came to life. The drunk Raiders dropped their bottles all at once. Benny could even hear the distinct sound of glass shattering. They mobilized toward the north side of town, their back turned away from Benny's group.

"Time to get heroic." Casey grinned, setting his hat on his head.

"The key is stealth," Darien said. "Remember to—"

"I know, I know, Zelt," Casey said. "Let's just kill some goddamn Raiders already."

Benny's heart thumped in his chest. It was time. They got up immediately, running toward the solar panels at the southeast of town. It took at least ten minutes to get there running at full speed, but it felt like ten hours to Benny. When they reached cover, he had his hands on his knees, coughing and struggling for breath. Casey was breathing heavily but tried his best not to show it. Darien was still breathing calmly through his nose. He looked as if he had not exerted himself at all.

"Okay," Darien whispered, peeking over the panel. "Follow me in. Keep your heads down and try to make as little noise as possible."

"Can...we just...wait a sec..." Benny heaved.

Darien seemed to ignore him. He pulled a pistol out from his belt, as well as a knife. Casey pulled his own pistol out, checking the bullets in the revolving chamber.

"You got yours, dontcha, Fong?" Casey asked.

Benny almost forgot they had given him a weapon. He dreaded carrying it. For the entire horseback trip, he was worried that it would go off and shoot himself in the foot. It was a simple pistol with twelve bullets. They showed him how to shoot it and reload it with the spare magazine they also supplied him with. Point and shoot. How hard could it be, they said. Benny pulled the gun out from his belt, and it shook in his hands.

"Jesus, Fong!" Casey said with a loud whisper. He put his hand over the gun. "Stop pointin' that thing at me. Keep it pointed at the ground until you got someone to shoot... Let me clarify. Unless you got *Raiders* to shoot."

"Keep it down back there," Darien said in a harsh whisper. "Someone's coming."

Benny and Casey froze in place. In an instant, Darien was gone. The super soldier moved like silent lightning. Benny looked across to the far solar panel, and Darien was already there, peeking over the side.

"The hell?" Casey whispered. "These damn Zeltans ain't human."

Benny could barely concentrate. Darien's apparent superhuman speed barely registered. Benny was still frightened by the tool of death he still held in his hand.

Darien motioned to Benny and Casey. He put a finger to his lips, signaling them to be quiet. He pointed in a direction, and Benny looked over the panel to see what he was pointing at. Three Raiders were standing about. They were laughing and huddled around a small smoking object.

Benny deduced that they were smoking harsh, the common recreational drug harvested from the plant of the same name grown on the Frontier. He had only tried it once and made a complete fool of himself in front of the entire town. He was 14, and the other boys had dared him to try it. He lost himself in a confusing self-made adventure mostly driven by a quest for more food and laughing at ordinary objects and situations. He would have been willing to have the euphoric experience again if it were not for the humiliation of the entire town witnessing his altered journey. There were subtle clues that he may have even professed his love for Kira during his maddened tirades. Nevertheless, she rarely teased him about it, and when she did, it was always in good humor.

Benny continued to watch the three Raiders snicker together, their evil faces faintly illuminated by the burning roll of harsh. To Benny, they were demons, subhuman creatures who needed to be brought to justice. Whether Benny was willing to deliver that justice was a different story.

Suddenly, one of the Raider's faces snapped back. Benny squinted to make sense of what he was seeing. There was a knife planted firmly into his left eye. As the other two Raiders stood in bewilderment, Darien came up behind them, smashing their heads together. In the same seamless motion, Darien reached out to pull the third body into them. The three bodies fell slowly to the ground, with the Zeltan making sure they fell slowly and quietly. When they hit the dirt, he took the knife and made two quick stabs to two of their faces. Benny watched in a daze as Darien dragged the three bodies away into the shadows.

"Damn," Casey said.

Benny was hyperventilating. Perhaps he had still not yet grown accustomed to watching men be killed, regardless of who they were.

Darien motioned for them to come to him.

Benny tried his best to crouch low to the ground as he walked across the solar panel array. They were metallic columns manually rotated three times daily to face the Sun. The panels generated most of the energy the town needed to operate its electricity. The rest was generated at the cycle house, where the townspeople volunteered to pedal stationary cycles that produced a modest amount of converted energy.

When they arrived at Darien's location, Benny's thighs burned with fatigue from crouching. He was already exhausted, and they had not even made it inside the town. Darien had the sole surviving Raider pinned to the ground. The Raider's arms and body were pinned down by Darien's knees, while a gun was put to his head with a hand gripped over his throat.

Darien whispered menacingly into the Raider's face, "Where are the civilians?"

The Raider appeared dazed, confused, and terrified all at the same time. He mumbled some nonsense through his bloodied face, unsure what exactly was happening.

"The civilians," Darien repeated. "You're going to tell me where they are, or I'll reach into your eye socket and pull your eyeball out and make you swallow it."

Benny gulped. Casey laughed.

"I... I..." the Raider began. He was a thin, poorly groomed man with crooked teeth and arms dotted with mewbin injection sites. Mewbin was a hard, usually fatal drug popular in the Far West. "I'm sorry, mister, I..."

Darien pushed the Raider's jaw closed and rammed his knee into his abdomen. The Raider let out a muffled squeal.

"I'm not here for apologies," Darien said. "I know what you've done to the people here. Tell me where they are, and the pain will stop."

The Raider had the fear of the orange god on his face. "The church, mister. The church. We... They put them all in the church."

"All of them?"

"Well, yeah, we're getting them ready to move out in the morning..."

A wave of rage rushed over Benny. They were going to sell his family and friends into slavery or worse. He felt his body lunge forward, ready to choke the life out of this evil being. Casey grabbed him by the shoulder, shaking his head. Benny noticed that Casey was clenching his jaw, probably also holding himself back from uncontrollable rage.

"So, they're all in the church," Darien said. "Are you sure?"

The Raider nodded.

"So sure that if you're wrong, I will torture you until you're picking up your own intestines from the ground long before I let you die?"

The Raider paused in a moment of terror but nodded again.

"Thank you," Darien said. He took his knife and swiftly pierced the Raider behind his ear.

Benny watched as the Raider's life spilled out of him as quickly as the blood gushed from his neck. The falling blood made an unnerving sound, like water being poured out onto the ground. Benny's stomach churned. He nearly vomited on the spot.

"Damn, Zelt," Casey said.

Darien stood up and continued onward. Benny stared at him. He appeared to be honorable and kind, but now, Benny could not see him as anything more than a murderous machine. This realization frightened Benny. Everyone around him was an agent of death and violence. This was no place for a boy who only wished to restore machinery. He wondered whether he made a mistake coming on this rescue mission with Darien and Casey. Perhaps he would have been safer going to Tabernacle with those Red Riders.

Then Benny remembered his town, his friends, and his family. They were in here somewhere, scared and suffering. He paused only for a moment, then followed Darien. Despite any of Benny's reservations, this man was truly their only hope to save their town.

THIRTY-NINE

Darien wedged himself against the wall of a Remnant settlement home. He had never ventured to a Frontier town, let alone the Frontier itself. Yet he had seen blurry surveillance images taken by Zeltan spies sent off to Sovereign intelligence agencies as precautionary measures against any possible threats from these western settlements. But as Darien looked around at this small village's dusty and dilapidated structures, he could tell there was nothing to worry about.

"Stay," Darien whispered to Casey and Benny, pressed up next to him against the wall.

He thought it best to leave them behind while eliminating these Raider bandits. On the one hand, they provided eyes to ensure his rear was clear. On the other hand, he figured they were likely to give away his position. Without trained soldiers, Darien was more effective working alone as much as possible.

Darien had his ear close to the closed doorway. There was a light inside, but no shadows caused any flicker below the doorway. He slowly pulled the latch on the door, allowing it to swing open.

He paused, waiting for anyone inside to notice the door swinging open itself. Darien remained hidden behind the wall.

"The hell?" a mutter was subtly heard inside.

No conversation. Just one man reacting, Darien thought. It was possible there were more people inside, but with how he heard footsteps casually approaching the door, Darien deduced that this person was likely alone and not entirely suspicious of walking into a trap.

Darien took a controlled breath through his nose and readied the knife in his hand. An arm reached out of the doorway to push it open. Darien took a millisecond to identify the man as a Raider. The man had tattoos along his bare arm and wore dirty rags for a sleeveless shirt. A rifle was dangling from his neck, gripped at the trigger.

There was no time to assess any further options. He needed to be neutralized before he could alert anyone else. Darien grabbed the rifle forward, slitting the Raider's wrist, and lodged the knife up into the Raider's neck in the same motion. With that single knife thrust, his trigger hand was incapacitated, and the enemy could not call for help.

Darien knew better than to linger on a kill. He quickly but carefully eased the Raider out the doorway while peering into the brightly lit room. He was wrong. His heart panged with a shot of adrenaline as he noticed another Raider sitting on a rocking chair, taking a swig of a bottle. Upon seeing Darien stabbing his comrade in the neck, the Raider reached for his gun, dropping his bottle as the bubbly drink dripped down his chin and shirt. Luckily, the bottle only gave a dull thud as it dropped on the wood floor.

Without hesitation, Darien pulled the knife from the first Raider's neck and used all his might to fling it at the bandit in the chair. He remembered his knife-throwing drills as a child, how the Matrons would punish him if he missed even one target. He would be given 12 knives on a belt and had 10 seconds to hit targets placed all over a Target Room. The targets were the diameter of a human eye. This Raider on the chair had two eyes. Darien aimed for his right.

"Ugh!" the Raider uttered as his head flicked back after the knife cut square into his eye.

Darien ignored the momentary satisfaction of hitting the bullseye, and immediately ran forward, taking only a few steps before lunging with his knee. In mid-air, he grabbed the enemy's shoulders, pulling him in. Darien's knee impacted the butt of the knife, lodging it all the way through the Raider's skull, popping it into the air, surrounded by a volcano eruption of blood.

His moment-to-moment calculations were exactly as he imagined, even down to the blood splatter. He had developed a subconscious ability to even predict the weight and movement of an enemy after only observing them for a moment. However, he had to quickly recalculate, as he felt more movement across the room.

"Hey, what the—" another Raider said, turning the corner into the room from the hallway.

From mid-air, Darien grabbed the knife, which had popped through the back of the sitting bandit's head, and quickly sent it flying again toward the new enemy victim. This time, Darien made sure it hit this man's shoulder as he was reaching for a hip-holstered pistol.

It was these moments that Darien entered a "flow state." Many of the other Zeltans possessed this too. Certainly, Tristan and Marcus employed it, likely to an even greater degree, considering their natural fighting brilliance. In this involuntary state, Darien truly felt like time would slow down, almost to the point of freezing altogether.

All the action around him appeared to stop in place. He floated in mid-air, as the knife squished against the enemy's shoulder and the droplets of blood were suspended in space. The entire room reconstituted in Darien's mind, just based on his quick glances. Before he even hit the ground, he planned his next moves, rehearsing them in his mind in nanoseconds.

Darien looked down, slamming his foot against the bottom half of the dropped bottle. It made a faint breaking sound, but Darien picked it up by the neck of the bottle and began making a quick run of the wounded Raider.

The enemy appeared to be simultaneously reeling from the pain of the knife in his shoulder, trying to reach for his pistol with the other arm and also turning to call out for help. Darien quickly sent the broken bottle directly into the side of his turned neck, piercing his throat before any sound could be made.

Darien planted his foot on the Raider's thigh, pushing him toward the ground as he reached around his head to grab his chin. He pulled the man's chin away while slicing toward himself with the glass, opening up the enemy's neck to the floor.

Free-flowing blood was always an annoyance, so Darien was always mindful to push a victim's body away immediately after the kill. He pushed down with his foot, forcing the Raider to the floor as pulsatile bright red blood showered the room. Darien grabbed the knife from the dead man's shoulder, listening for any more combatants. A misstep here could give away his position. He would have to remain quiet and stealthy.

"Holy shit," Casey said loudly from the doorway.

Darien glanced behind him. Past the dead Raider on the chair and the other slumped outside the doorway was Casey with a smirk.

"You did that shit faster than my pee could hit the ground," Casey said as he stepped over the dead man in the doorway. His boots still sloshed in the blood on the floor, but he seemed to find it amusing. "These animals deserved it. We need you on our side. You could kill the whole lot of them yourself."

Darien darted across the room to put his bloody hand over Casey's mouth and whispered, "Shut up, you're making too much noise."

"Ah shit, Zelt." Casey wiped the blood off his face with his sleeve, spitting on the ground. "Ya got his damn brains in my mouth."

Darien was starting to get irritated with his untrained allies.

Benny, silently standing in the doorway, was shaking in disbelief. "We...uh...better get out of here before more come."

The three of them silently sneaked through from the house into the streets, staying close to the shadows and keeping their heads down low. Darien was on point, looking for any sign of movement or any telltale glow that would indicate another Raider gang. Occasionally, Darien would hear something in the wind— distant laughter or a bark from an animal hiding in the alleyways.

They cautiously moved through town until they reached the back entrance to the tailor shop. It was an old wooden door, painted green and cracked at its edges from time and weather wear. Benny pointed out an old broken window that led directly into the basement below. Darien looked around one last time before motioning for Casey and Benny to follow him inside. As soon as each one jumped through the window, Darien closed it shut behind them with a swift tug on its wooden frame - ensuring that no one else could enter without first breaking it again themselves (or giving away their location).

Once inside, Darien took a moment to allow his vision to adjust to the darkness, but also to let Benny and Casey catch their breath.

"Are you both ready?" Darien asked.

Benny looked down at his pistol, hesitated, but then looked up with summoned confidence. "I am. Let's go."

Casey grabbed the pistol from his holster, spinning it around his finger and into his grip. "Let's go kill some Raiders."

CHAPTER

FORTY

Benny Fong's heartbeat thudded in his ears, and he constantly argued with himself not to turn around and flee. He crept softly and nervously into the dark cellar beneath the tailor shop. Several buildings shared the same underground heating system. The Red Frontier was dry and hot during midday, but the wind could chill to the bone in the middle of the night. Remnant was built above an underground water path erected during the days of the terraformation. Energy, heat, and drinking water came directly from the water that flowed from the White Range and south through Remnant until it reached the Lacrimal River that fed into the Green Sea.

The plan was simple, but Benny was stressed nonetheless. Benny and Casey would make their way through the maze of pipes and machinery until they came directly under the church where most of the town was held captive. Darien would then sneak, and presumably kill, his way to the clock tower at the center of town. From there, he would have a direct line of sight of the church's entrance. While Benny and Casey freed the townspeople, Darien would prevent any Raiders from entering the church from his sniping position.

How exactly Benny would free his townspeople was never exactly elaborated. He had a pistol and a pouch full of bullets, 12 to be exact. Casey showed him how to use and reload it. Point and shoot. *Simple enough, right?* But he didn't know how many Raiders were in that church. *Once the guns start going off, what good would I be in a firefight?* He had never shot a gun, let alone ever shot anyone else.

"Jesus, Fong," Casey said in a harsh whisper behind him. "Take your finger off the trigger. You keep pointing that thing at the ground, and you're gonna blow your damn foot off."

Benny pointed the gun up, taking his index finger off the trigger. The pistol was heavier than he thought, and he was already tired of pointing the gun ahead of him down the pitch-dark hallways. Casey followed behind him with a hand on Benny's shoulder. Benny knew the underground utility room well. Even in the dim light, peering from the doorways from the building entrances, Benny navigated his way to the church basement entrance.

Creak.

"Wait, hold on." Benny grabbed Casey's hand on his shoulder. "I think someone's coming."

A door opened behind them. If Benny's memory of the utility path served him right, it was the door leading to Tiki Peyton's Hair Salon. Benny hoped Tiki made it out of Remnant before the Raiders arrived. She was a pretty, smart-mouthed hairdresser with clients from all over the Frontier who came less for a haircut and more to let the beautiful beautician tussle their hair. Benny hoped she had escaped before the Raiders arrived.

The opening door flooded the utility room with bright light. Casey pulled Benny behind a water heater tank, startling him. *Thank the blue god I took my finger off the trigger*, he thought. He shuddered in fear as he held his breath.

"I don't know how to work these damn things," a voice said.

Benny peered through the pipes that hid him. Two Raiders, shirtless and tattooed, came strolling into the utility room.

"I dunno," one said, his hands on his hips, staring at the heater apparatuses. "But we ain't got hot water, and they wanna make some damn soup. So, if they want soup, we got figure this thing out. They gotta some lever 'round them things."

Terror shot into Benny's heart as one of the Raiders walked toward the water heater he hid behind. The light wasn't shining directly on him, but the room was lit up just enough that he would surely be seen if they looked hard enough.

"Let's see here," the raider muttered. "So, this comes around this way..."

Benny froze in place. The Raider was walking around the tank. Benny turned to his right and realized Casey had disappeared. The terror sank deeper into his heart. He was alone, and the Raider was getting closer. Benny shut his eyes tight, hoping the whites of his eyes wouldn't be reflected in the light.

"Maybe it's in the back," the Raider said.

There was no mistaking he would be found. Benny opened his eyes, realizing he had not dared to breathe. His fingers were trembling, but he grasped his pistol as tightly as he could, putting his finger on the trigger and pointing the gun to where the Raider would appear.

"Hey! What the—"

Clunk.

Benny sucked in air into his already-filled lungs. *What happened?* In the dim light, the Raider went to the ground, holding his head. Casey came out from the shadows and continued to beat him over the head with a heavy pipe. The subsequent sounds were more of squish than clunk.

Benny breathed out a sigh of relief. He dreaded the moment he would need to pull the trigger. If Casey hadn't intervened, he would have had to.

The other Raider immediately lunged to attack. Casey lurched backward as the Raider put him in a chokehold. Benny struggled to free himself from behind the water tank as he heard Casey and the Raider wrestle and heave their way around the crowded boiler room.

"Fong!" Casey said in a muffled gasp.

Once Benny shook his leg loose from a pipe gap, he saw the Raider pinning Casey to the ground, choking him. In a pure adrenaline rush, Benny lifted his gun and pointed it at the Raider's back.

Just point and shoot, Benny thought.

But the shot never fired. Instead, Benny felt the gun wobble in his hands. His heart was pounding so hard, and his body was so shaky that the gun flew right out of his hands. Benny winced as the gun hit the ground. He expected it would fire a shot on impact with the ground, but the discharge never came.

He cursed himself for his inaction. He knew this would happen. The moment came and he blew it.

Luckily, the gun hitting the ground was just the distraction Casey needed. The Raider turned around to look at the gun and considered picking it up. In the moment he took to decide whether to continue choking Casey or to take the gun, the Raider loosened his grip. Casey took that opportunity to push the Raider off. They began to wrestle with each other, reaching for Benny's gun.

In an act of self-vindication, Benny quickly kicked the gun away just before the Raider could put his hand on it. He thought to kick the Raider in the head as he wrestled with Casey, but the shock of the struggle again made him freeze in place. He watched as the two of them squirmed and punched and kicked.

Benny felt helpless. He stood there, trembling and paralyzed by fear. He couldn't even muster the courage to speak.

Eventually, Casey got the upper hand. Now he pinned the Raider to the ground, punching him repeatedly in the face, again and again, until the Raider's body became limp. Casey continued to punch his face well after his face was reduced to cranberry sauce.

"Alright, alright." Benny tried to pull Casey off. "You're done. You got him."

Casey shoved him off. "Yeah, no thanks to you." He spit off to the side. "These bastards come into your town and kill your people, and you still can't pull the damn trigger."

"Well, I, uh," Benny stammered. "I just…"

"Whatever, I don't care," Casey said, taking the pistol off the floor and slamming it back in Benny's hand. "Just do me a favor up there. Just stay out of my way, and don't get us killed."

Benny took the extra pistol, shoving it into his belt, assuring it would not accidentally fall out or discharge. He had such self-embarrassment that he felt displaced from his own body. *What am I even doing here?*

He followed Casey to the church's parapet entrance. They peered through a small wall carving opening. Benny could see most of the townsfolk gathered in the church pews. There were dozens of them. It seemed like none of them made it to Tabernacle.

He scanned the crowd. *There they were!* Benny's mother and father were huddled together. His father had his arm over their mother, cowering in fear like most townsfolk had done. Two Raiders were guarding the townsfolk. One amongst the crowd on the ground and one standing on the balcony in the back, overlooking them from above.

"We wait for the signal," Casey whispered.

Benny nodded, and they waited for what seemed like an eternity. He looked through the opening, surveying all who were present, all who were missing. He couldn't bear to think about what happened to anyone who wasn't there. He thought back to the bodies he saw outside of town. He vowed to never let his family and friends come under harm like this ever again.

The Raiders teased the preacher Ezekiel Rayge. He was a gaunt man with tussled, unkempt hair. They mockingly asked him to tell them again about the prophecy. Ezekiel would go on and on about the Angels of Deliverance. The arrival of the prophesized

Ghost. All of this seemed appropriate for these scary times, Benny thought. The town could use a miracle.

Minutes passed by like hours, and Benny thought perhaps Darien was in trouble. Surely, by now, the Zeltan would have made his move. And just as Benny was about to turn to Casey and ask for a backup plan, suddenly gunfire erupted outside. Intermittent crackles turned into an orchestra of panic on the streets.

"This must be it," Casey said as the gunfire continued.

Although Benny had being anticipating the moment and rehearsing it in his head, now that it was here, he felt like he was again not ready at all. He wished that he could slap himself and that this would all be a dream he could wake from.

The two guards inside the church started walking toward the front windows to look. The guard on the balcony looked outside the large, circular, blue-stained window at the back of the church on the second floor while the other guard ran to the entrance.

"Okay, let's go", Casey said as he slowly pushed the door open.

Casey crouched, creeping along the side of the church, motioning a finger to his mouth for the townsfolk to remain silent. Benny came out as well, running low and directly to his mother and father. He had a moment of empowerment, as the townspeople looked to them relief at the hopes of liberation.

"Shh," Benny said, giving his father the extra pistol. "Take this."

"Oh my god, Benny!" his mother, Grace Fong, said quietly.

"Benny?" Harold Fong looked at his son with disbelief and then down at the gun. "What are you doing, Benny? You're going to get yourself killed; put these away!"

On the one hand, Benny was overjoyed to see his parents alive and well. On the other, he had hoped they were safe and far away from all of this. He couldn't fathom seeing them hurt or killed.

"Dad, please," Benny said, constantly looking back and forth between him and the guard, who was too preoccupied with the gunfire outside. "Just keep quiet for now."

Benny moved through the crowd, and he could feel their incredulous looks. He had gone from the boy that everyone cast aside to the boy who would rescue them.

Just then, the Raider stationed on the balcony was thrown back after bullets railed through the blue-stained glass. Darien must have found the opportunity to take him out. This gave Casey the go-ahead to take out the Raider on the ground.

However, the Raider turned just in time to wrestle the knife away from Casey. They struggled against the wall, with Casey dropping the knife and trying to grab the gun in his holster. The Raider and Casey both struggled to pry the gun out of the holster, but it hit the floor with a bang, the discharge sending all the townsfolk cowering.

"Benny!" Casey yelled, "Point and shoot!"

Casey kicked the Raider off him, and suddenly, time stood still for Benny. He had the gun trained on the Raider. Images of the bodies outside the town, his mother and father being harmed, his friends and family abused...Kira. Involuntarily, he found himself squeezing the trigger, doing his best to hold the gun steady, aimed at the Raider.

All Benny could see was the muzzle flash and his rage in front of him. He realized he was screaming as he fired away. Each squeeze of the trigger felt like an explosion of his internal rage being released like dragon fire. After about 5 squeezes, he brought the gun down from obstructing his view, and the Raider slumped to the ground.

"Holy shit!" Casey said wide-eyed with a smile on his face. After a moment of awkward silence, looking down at the dead Raider, he threw his hands up in the air. "Nice work, Fong. You did it!"

Benny stood, frozen, a million different emotions coursing through him, all vying for dominance. In the end, he felt... exhilaration. He had killed a man. But he saved Casey and his family and friends. He had proved to them all that he was more than just the meek and low-esteemed Frontier boy.

"Benny..." Harold Fong said. His face was a mix of horror and pride.

The empowerment was intoxicating. This was Benny's moment to prove to all of them that he had changed after he had been through.

"Dad," Benny said, swallowing all his fears and doubts. "Get everyone together. Fortify all the doors with the pews. Board up the windows. Find any weapons you can. Casey and I will watch the entrance for any Raiders coming in. You watch the side entrance. Let's go, let's go! "

And just like that, Benny started commanding the townsfolk, and sure enough, they all listened. They had fought too long and hard for this to fall apart. They were going to take back the town. Benny would make sure of it.

Kira, if you could only see me now.

FORTY-ONE

Kira Skyler felt the crunch of ice mixed with gravel under her boots as she arrived at the base of the White Range mountains. Ahead of them lay the vast Red Frontier, a red desert of jagged rocks and hot sand. She turned around to take in the enormous peaks that stood tall to the north. Squinting towards the horizon to the southwest, she searched for a glimpse of her town. *Would Remnant even still be there?*

She was accompanied by her eclectic group of companions: Raymond Redmin, the doctor out of his own time, the silent Zeltan Sergeant Marcus, the arrogant Lieutenant Tristan in his exo-mech, the introspective android Voltaire, and her loyal robot fox Swift. They all stood on a cliff's edge to take in the majestic evening view of the Frontier.

The soft, golden light of the dawning sun cast a dreamlike haze over the landscape. Six unlikely and extraordinary travelers had come together to save Remnant from disaster. It seemed too surreal to be true, blurring the line between dream and reality.

After some more hours, carefully making their way out of the mountains and onto the red desert sand of the Frontier, Kira looked ahead and saw the ancient ruins of an old trading post, a relic from the Soulborne Coalition, when the legendary Jonathan Cable led the natural borns in a doomed rebellion against the Zeltans. They all walked silently towards it, with Kira in front, leading them carefully through the rocky terrain.

She saw several old buildings still standing, although most were crumbling apart because of the harsh weather conditions. The walls bowed down and leaned to one side, supported by wood beams that creaked and cracked in the wind. Some roofs had fallen off, exposing strewn-across crumbled pillows and mattresses. Windows here and there let in shafts of sunlight from between the leaning walls. Grass grew up through cracks in the floorboards.

There was an old wooden sign outside that read "Sierra Outpost".

As they got closer, they noticed that lights were coming from inside one of the structures, and eventually, they reached a dilapidated door at the front entrance of what seemed to be a small tavern or storehouse.

Suddenly, a loud voice boomed from the top of one of the buildings, and Kira realized it was George Wallace, the aging Red Rider himself. He was standing outside with a megaphone, warning them not to approach any closer as he had targeted Tristan's exo-mech with some rockets.

"Stop and turn yourselves around," George yelled. "Androids aren't welcome here. You all know that. Maybe you might need some bullet points to remind you."

He shouted words like "monsters" and "freaks," referring to both Swift and Voltaire. Kira felt anger boiling inside her at this injustice against her friends and bravely stepped forward to confront George.

But before she could even open her mouth, Raymond beat her to it by raising his hand and shouting, "Wait, we are here peacefully! We mean no harm! We just want your help!"

After a long pause, George said, "And just who in the hell would you be?"

"Sir," Raymond replied, "I'm a doctor. We're just here to help."

Kira appreciated his bravery but figured they needed some semblance of legitimacy. "Rider Wallace, my name is Kira Skyler. My father was Quentin Skyler. I'm from Remnant, and—"

"Hold on a damn minute," George said. "You're Quentin's little girl? What the hell you doin' with bots and a janky ol' exo-mech?"

"They're here to help," Kira said, relieved that these Red Riders remembered her father, who would welcome them on occasional visits to town. "We're trying to get back to Remnant. There are Raider and Corsair armies headed there and—"

"You're too late!" George Wallace said, stepping out of the building.

Tristan's exo-mech moved in defense. Kira's heart jumped as she saw several Red Riders perched in the windows re-adjust their rocket launchers in reaction.

"Stand down, stand down." George waved them off, shaking his head. "D'ya hear me though? I said yer too late."

Kira felt a wave of despair wash over her. She imagined returning to her hometown, overrun by the maniacal Raider and Corsair warlords.

But then George said, "Oh, eh... Another Zelt just strolled through here named...Darien? He was with one of ours, Casey, and a Remnant boy, too, Benny?"

"Benny?!" Kira exclaimed. A spark of hope surged through Kira's veins. *How in the world did he end up at Sierra Outpost with the Zeltan Captain?*

"Did you say Darien?" Tristan asked, as his cockpit hissed open. "The captain, he's alive?"

George Wallace shrugged. "I guess. Since it seems to be Zeltie tourist season on the Frontier, I say it's about damn time y'all Zelties see what kinda mess we got out here. I'm afraid those boys are going to be in the thick of it any minute now. They made their way back to Remnant to take back the town."

Of course! Darien must have made it to Remnant ahead of us and gotten help from Benny and Casey. Kira knew she could trust them to do whatever was necessary to protect the townspeople from the Raiders and Corsairs. Now, she just needed George Wallace to help get them back in time too.

"Sir," Kira said softly but firmly, "please hear me out. We need your help if we are to make it back in time for my town's survival."

"Yeah, yeah," George said. "Like I told your friends, I can't afford to—"

Kira stepped forward and declared with all the courage she could muster. "The Red Riders ride free in the Frontier." She repeated it louder. "The Red Riders ride free in the Frontier!"

She had recited the words of the Red Riders. Over time, they misinterpreted and abused those words to expect the townspeople to give them free food and boarding, but originally, it used to stand for something noble.

Kira continued, "The original Red Riders kept the Frontier free of warlords and scavengers like the Raiders and Corsairs. They stood for something. They stood to uphold the dignity of the Red Frontier, just like Jonathan Cable did all those years ago. And right now, the Corsairs might get hold of technology stolen from the spaceship crash that will make them unstoppable. If we don't do something now, there won't be a Frontier left for the Red Riders to defend."

Kira watched from a distance as George Wallace considered her bold declaration. He grew up on the Frontier too. He spent his whole life working to keep some semblance of order. Would he really sit back and let it get swallowed up in warfare again? She gambled that whether he liked it or not, Wallace had to help them save his beloved Frontier from further destruction.

George Wallace's face changed from a hardened scowl to a look of understanding and, finally, determination. George Wallace looked away and muttered something under his breath.

"Ah, dammit," he said, shaking his head. "And you'll use that, er...exo-mech to help with the fight, right? They got one of their own, from what our scouts have been saying."

"I'll take care of that mech," Tristan said. "You have my word."

"You know we'll need all of the Red Riders to even stand a chance against those Raiders and Corsairs," George Wallace said.

"Send them all," Kira said. "With these Zeltans, this will be our best chance against the Raiders and Corsairs. We could drive them out of the Frontier for good."

George paused, stroked his beard, and kicked around some dirt with his boot while deep in thought. The Riders perched on the roofs carrying their launchers squirmed in uneasy silence.

"That mech," George asked, "Is that thing ready to fight for us?"

"You'll have me in this exo-mech," Tristan said through his speakers, "And Sergeant Marcus here, a Vanguard."

"Wallace," Kira said, "Having these two on our side is worth more than an entire army of us. Now is our chance."

After an even longer pause and rumination, George turned around to the dozens of Red Riders perched in the windows and rooftops. "I never thought I'd see the day," he said loudly, "Fighting alongside some Zelties... Ah screw it to hell. Get yer horses and shooters ready, boys. We're headed back to Remnant!"

Slowly but surely, the Red Riders began to cheer in unison. Kira saw the looks on their faces. They had been itching for a big battle like this.

"You're right," George said to Kira with conviction. "We shoulda listened to Casey and the Zelt. This was always our land to protect. We shoulda gone with them to defend the Frontier."

"Well, it sounds like now's your chance," Raymond said with a smile.

"Ya damn right, doc," George Wallace said. "I got some horses for ya...and eh, for y'all..." He pointed at Tristan, his giant exo-mech, the hulking Marcus in his exosuit, and the androids Voltaire and Swift. "I got a refitted APE transport, but the exo's gotta walk."

Kira felt her heart soar with hope. George Wallace had rallied the Red Riders to their cause and was now gathering their horses and weapons in preparation for war. Despite all the odds stacked against them, Kira was relieved to know that they would have help when they reached Remnant, hopefully by the morning. She worried about Benny and wondered if he was still okay. *How did he even get himself involved in all this?* She had so many stories to tell him. And her friends and family in town, her brother, she couldn't wait for them to meet these strange companions she had amassed in her wonderful adventure. *Would Raymond, the doctor from another time and planet, be able to help those afflicted by the red fever in her town?*

The Red Riders gathered quickly, readying themselves with guns, rockets, and ammunition strapped across their bodies. They mounted their horses with a solemn yet determined look in their eyes and led by George Wallace, departed towards Remnant—ready to fight for freedom in the Frontier once more.

FORTY-TWO

C aptain Darien was perched atop the eastern lookout tower, squinting through his binoculars. The sky had just started to lighten at dawn's first break. Darien never actually enjoyed war, but when he knew a battle was coming, he could palpably sense that all his senses were maximally dialed in. Every facet of his being seemed to beckon him toward the battlefield ahead. He was ready and willing.

This guard tower was apparently never appropriately manned, at least not regularly. The cover was poorly placed, the townspeople scrambled to find him an appropriately scoped marksman rifle, and he would have preferred a vantage point without a nearby tall living space tower obstructing his view of the north to his left. Darien would make use of what he had. This forward-facing tower had a direct view of the east horizon from where most of the Raider contingent would return.

The townspeople of Remnant had relied on proximity sensors hidden amongst the desert grounds to alert them of incoming visitors, both expected and unexpected. Darien thought the town was poorly defended and wide open to attack. It was no surprise that the Raiders so easily came through the town on their way east to the crash wreckage by the Black Forest.

"Any luck with that box?" Darien asked.

"No luck," Benny said. "We still have no idea what it does or how to open it. But it's gotta be something."

The Raiders had hauled a large rectangle-shaped, ornately decorated metal box into the town tavern. Apparently, it had floated down to the desert near Remnant in a parachute, appearing just as the spaceship crashed further to the east. Upon interviewing the defeated and captured Raiders, it was indeed the sought-after object known as the Ark. It was about 9 feet long, 6 feet wide, and 5 feet high. However, it seemed that no one knew what was in it.

The Ark was shaped like a large casket. It had ornamental carvings of four winged creatures on the corners. The decorations appeared to be made of gold, but with an inexplicably surreal chrome texture that suggested it was another type of metal substance entirely. There were handlebars to move the large rectangular box, but it moved with precisely sophisticated mobile spheres on its bottom. When it was in place, it was an extremely heavy object that was likely hundreds of pounds. But with the exact amount of pressure, pushing the Ark by the handlebars caused the four spheres on the bottom corners to prop up the box, and allowed it to move in any direction with ease. It was a simple, yet baffling technology that transcended any art or architecture that he had ever seen.

All they knew was that the spaceship survivors considered this a valuable object and fought to the death to protect it. And now the Corsairs were sending their entire army to come and obtain it. Darien recalled hearing Guaritore, Julian, and Blackheart all referencing it. Whatever it was, whether a treasure chest, a funeral casket, a computer… or even a weapon, it was important enough that many men were about to go to war for it.

"We'll figure out what that Ark is," Darien said, "but after this fight."

"How long until they get here?" Benny Fong asked over the radio for the tenth time.

"Judging by the desert sand kicking up," Darien said without taking his eyes off the binoculars. "I'd say we'll start seeing their scouts approaching close any minute now."

Over the past few hours, Darien watched as the dawning horizon was ablaze with explosions and smoke. The Raiders were retreating west while in constant skirmish back and forth with the Corsairs. It was only a matter of time before the conflict spilled directly onto the town of Remnant. Meanwhile, the Raiders were already certainly aware that their comrades in town were incapacitated, as their radio pleas remained unanswered.

"We need reinforcements! Freddie! Lon! Why aren't answer of you answering? We're getting killed out here!" The radios would continue to sound off from the desperate Raiders, who were becoming increasingly aware of their dire situation.

The Red Rider Casey Jarrett rounded up all the able-bodied citizens of Remnant and armed them with weapons. Within the short time they had available, the townsfolk scoured Remnant for any remaining Raiders and gathered their weapons and supplies. Any surviving Raiders were tied up and placed about 50 feet from the east tower, bound to heavy ramparts, serving as distractible cannon fodder for the oncoming enemy. It was a harsh tactic, but Darien had no trouble convincing the townspeople, who had just been ravaged and humiliated by these lawless scavengers, to simply leave them exposed to the artillery and desert crows.

The plan was simple and the best they could muster in their situation. Darien was used to commanding highly trained units, and had never been forced to direct a group of civilians. It was an interesting challenge for him, and he took particular care to acknowledge their limitations.

For the first phase, the townspeople would station themselves at every available window or guarded position facing east. They were armed with long rifles capable of creating a wall of bullets that could meet the incoming Raider convoy. The Raider vehicles generally consisted of open-frame Jackal light utility 3-man vehicles or Coyote all-terrain 1-man vehicles. The drivers and passengers could be easily shot out and sniped in a head-on conflict.

For phase 2, Darien would give the order to launch their make-shift artillery. The Raider vehicles left at the town had some crude rocket launchers that Benny Fong quickly converted into stationary battery units. There were only 3 Viper artillery units, with the launchers still attached to the vehicles but parked hidden behind the outermost buildings. Due to their limited range, Darien would wait until the Raider convoy came close and would use these to create a dust cloud surrounding the town to allow them to regroup.

For phase 3, the artillery dust cloud would lure the Raiders to likely avoid the town and try to drive around it. He would then give the signal to detonate explosives hidden around the periphery of the town to the north and south. This would bring the remaining stragglers very close to the town, where the townspeople would station themselves at defendable positions on the streets, where they would be ready for hopefully weakened Raider forces on approach.

Meanwhile, for Phase 4, Casey would lead a contingent on horseback hidden out westward and south to survey the extreme south flank of the battle. A Remnant townsman named Colt Gilroy would lead a horseback contingent toward the north flank. The cyborg Corsairs were certainly larger forces than the Raiders, so they would have limited time to assess the danger of the second approaching army to the town before they could radio back. Here, Darien would decide whether they would stay to fight the Corsairs or if they would quickly flee northwest to Tabernacle. According to Casey, the Corsairs were not likely to continue pursuing them northwest. They were only after the Ark. The priority was defeating the Raiders, and then the Corsairs would need to be an improvised decision. They would have to decide whether to take the Ark with them and risk the Corsairs continuing to pursue them west. Or they would leave the Ark here, risking the possibility that the Corsairs would extract whatever importance from it and grow more dangerous to the Frontier than they already were.

Darien emphasized that they would first deal with the Raiders, and then decide on the plan for the Corsairs afterwards.

As the sun began to rise, Darien watched as the Raider convoy came into view as silhouettes against the burgeoning sky. He lowered his binoculars and signaled to Benny Fong to get ready. The townspeople scurried into position, their fingers tight around their rifles as they waited for the signal to fire.

The first few Raider vehicles approached quickly, but the wait seemed endless. Their engines kicked up dust as they approached from the horizon.

"Hold…" Darien said, his fist up in the air. There was a watcher at the central tower who would sound a bell when he gave the signal.

The dust cloud came closer, with 6 Jackal light utility vehicles coming into view. It would only be a matter of minutes before they were within firing range.

"Hold…" Darien said again, as he could feel the tension of the nervous townspeople crouched next to him, their rifles rattling in fear, mounted on the wooden ramparts. He remained hopeful that they would remain firm and stick to the plan.

From his binoculars, he could now see the Raiders sitting within the vehicles. They were shirtless, with various belts hanging from their tattooed bodies covered in piercings. They were likewise holding firearms, preparing to exchange fire with the town. Darien would have to time it just right…

"Hold…"

The Jackals began to emit occasional flashes, signaling that the Raiders were starting to shoot at the town. But it was too early. Darien knew they weren't close enough. The townspeople cringed in fear, but Darien stood steadfast, his fist in the air. He didn't move an inch. As their leader, he knew that his demeanor would be paramount to their overall morale.

"Hold…"

He was surprised that the townspeople dared not fire early. He had stressed the importance of saving their scarce ammunition. It was only moments now…

"Captain Darien?" he heard over the radio; it was another Remnant townsman on the lookout. "They're getting close."

"Just a few moments. You are all doing great...just a moment longer."

The Jackals were coming well into view now. Darien could make out the whites of the eyes of the Raiders in the vehicles. He calculated the exact moment to fire and signaled when he knew it was time.

"Now!" Darien dropped his fist and pulled up his rifle, quickly zeroing his scope on the foremost Jackal vehicle and delivering a shot directly into its driver.

The town of Remnant erupted into an orchestra of gunfire. Darien watched as the townspeople began to fire, their shots echoing loudly.

The Raiders retaliated with their own gunfire, but the townspeople's wall of bullets proved too much for them to overcome. One by one, the Raider vehicles began to slow down and come to a stop as their drivers were shot out.

Excellent job, everyone, Darien thought, *it seems that these natural borns are more capable than I had thought.*

It was time for phase 2. Darien signaled to Benny to fire the makeshift artillery. The rockets shot out of the hidden battery units, creating a thick cloud of dust that surrounded the town. The desert sand erupted around the Raider vehicles, surprisingly on target. The Raiders slowed down, unsure of what was happening, and Darien could see confusion in their ranks. They hesitated to continue their advance, but he knew it wouldn't last long.

"Get ready for phase 3!" he yelled to the townspeople. They nodded in acknowledgment, already taking up new defensible positions on the street.

The explosives were set to detonate once the Raiders were near the town. Darien watched the Raiders split up, trying to drive around the town and avoid the dust cloud. He knew they were trying to flank them, but it was too late.

The explosives went off with a loud boom, sending vehicle and human parts flying in all directions. The remaining Raider vehicles came to a halt as the townspeople opened fire again, this time with more precision and accuracy as they picked off the weakened forces.

Darien watched as the last Raiders fell to the ground, their bodies littering the dusty terrain. Minutes of silence passed as they listened for any semblance of enemies that could have survived.

"We're clear," Darien said calmly over the radio. "Good work, everyone."

The townspeople let out a collective cheer, their spirits lifted by the victory.

"Are you kidding me?!" Benny exclaimed over the radio. "We did it! Holy cow, we actually did it!"

Darien couldn't help but smile at their bravery and determination. They had stood together and fought against a common enemy and succeeded. In a way, their small triumph here, although on a much smaller scale than the large battles he was used to, was a more satisfying victory. These people were beginning to grow on him.

But there was still a larger threat lurking beyond the shadow of the desert cloud. The Corsairs were out there and were heading toward Remnant. Darien could feel the tension in the air as the townspeople realized the battle was far from over.

He turned to Casey Jarrett, far down the street with a group of men on horseback.

"So, are we staying or leaving, Captain?" Casey asked over the radio.

Darien thought long and hard about it. He could assure that these people would be safe if they retreated west before the Corsairs arrived. But that would only be a temporary respite. Perhaps they would chase them and catch them exposed and defenseless in the desert. Perhaps the Ark was a superweapon of unimaginable strength. He remembered the mission he vowed to the Sovereign high command. He would bring back the Ark and bring Julian to justice. With the people at their highest morale and the enemy incoming, he decided that it was time to stop running.

"We stand our ground," Darien replied over the radio. "We defend this town. This is your homeplace. You make a stand and declare to the whole world that you'll fight to defend it. We can do this. We can win. We stay and we fight."

The townspeople once again exclaimed in unison. They were fired up with a fighting spirit. Darien knew that there was something intangibly advantageous in any conflict, when the soldiers were motivated and invested. This was as good a time as any to make their stand.

"Get your men ready," Darien said. "We need to be prepared for whatever comes our way."

In the distance, Darien could see Casey tipping his hat toward him, and the five horses left the town out the south entrance.

Darien took a deep breath, readying himself for what was to come. He knew that the Corsairs were a formidable enemy and that they would stop at nothing to take back control of Remnant. But he also knew they had the strength of numbers and firepower on their side and could use that to their advantage.

He looked out towards the horizon. As the sand cloud took an eternity to dissipate, he watched the infrared sensors on his binoculars to assess the landscape. It took nearly a half hour, but the Corsairs were getting closer. And to Darien's horror, the looming silhouette of Julian's exo-mech was unmistakably leading the charge.

"Get to your positions," he yelled to the townspeople. "This is it. If you want to defend your town, do it here and now. So, gather all the bravery you have saved up your whole lives and pour it out there right now. Eyes open, let's do this."

The townspeople nodded, grabbing their weapons and taking positions on the rooftops and behind barricades.

Darien turned his attention back to the horizon. He could see the Corsair army coming ever closer, a sizable force of dozens of Lion tanks led by a hulking exo-mech. He clenched the radio tightly in his hands, hoping against hope that he wasn't leading this town of civilians to their demise.

Darien surveyed the scene below him. He could see the fear in the townspeople's eyes, but he could also feel the determination within them. They were ready to fight, and they were ready to win.

The first line of defense was set up around the perimeter of town, with a second tier of defenses directly behind it. The cannons were loaded and ready for battle, and riflemen lined up every few feet to provide additional firepower from above.

Darien coordinated some scavengers to quickly grab the nearby gear and weapons from the Raider corpses. The townspeople worked quickly and efficiently. Darien provided sniper cover as they ran across the desert sand beyond the town lines. The occasional straggling Raider needed an extra push of his bullet to send them to the afterlife.

The sounds of clanking metal and roaring engines filled the air as the Corsairs drew nearer, growing louder with each passing moment. Darien took a deep breath and focused his eyes on the sky. He was ready to face off against the exo-mech and whatever else Julian's forces had in store for them. The townspeople of Remnant looked ready to fight for their home, no matter what it took.

FORTY-THREE

B enny Fong watched Casey Jones and the Red Riders exit with their horses south out of the town, aiming to flank the Corsair army coming from the east. From his Specter drone in the sky, Benny Fong observed the Corsair army advance with their tanks, guns, and vehicles toward Remnant. The townspeople fired back with their guns, rockets, and artillery in an effort to fend off their attackers. Benny Fong's drone buzzed above them like a guardian angel, ready to assist in any way possible if needed. Despite a lifetime of being bullied his whole life by the Red Riders, he was determined to keep them safe no matter what it took.

Although he felt safer within the confines of a protected room, piloting his drone for surveillance, he still felt the stress of the incoming battle. This was his hometown and most likely it was about to become a battleground. His parents were safe within the tavern at the center of town where they had set up a makeshift infirmary for any of the wounded. Benny knew that Darien was confident that they would survive this, and that hope was all that Benny could hold on to.

Slowly, but surely, Benny watched from above, as the might of the full Corsair army descended upon Remnant like a swarm of locusts. The sound of gunfire and explosions filled the air, and the screams of the wounded were deafening. The townspeople fought back with all their might, but it seemed they were no match for the Corsairs.

But unbeknownst to the Corsairs, Darien had a plan. They had been working on a new type of explosive that would be powerful enough to take out their tanks and vehicles. He had spent the last night with the townspeople and Benny, perfecting makeshift explosives and weapons for the battle.

As the Corsairs approached the town borders, the townspeople emerged from the buildings, each carrying a canister of explosives. They made their way to the front line, where they could see the tanks and vehicles approaching them.

Benny watched as Darien led the counterattack and threw his canister towards the tanks. His superhuman strength made the gas canister sail miles ahead and landed directly in the path of an enemy vehicle. The canister exploded with a deafening roar, sending shrapnel flying in all directions.

The tanks and vehicles approached closer, now in range of the townspeople's makeshift launchers and within arms' throw. The enemy vehicles burst into flames, and the Corsairs were left reeling.

The townspeople saw their opportunity and seized it. At Darien's command, they charged towards the Corsairs. The sand and cloud-filled stretch of land in front of the town became a storm of shrouded warfare. Benny could no longer see what was happening, except that he was sure that Darien himself led the charge on foot, directly into the dust cloud.

Through the billowing smoke and sand, the Corsair vehicles began trying to flank around the town towards the north and south.

Here, they would meet minefields of even more explosives buried in the sand. Because of the consecutive explosions surrounding the town, from Benny's drone above, it seemed like the town was being swallowed whole by a red desert cloud monster.

He instead turned his attention south. Flying high above the battle, he dodged the occasional wayward rocket explosion and finally located Casey Jarrett and the four other Red Riders on horseback. They galloped east, around the south flank of the Corsair attacking forces. With their grenade-launching pistols, they pelted the enemies with a bombardment of explosions.

Soon, Casey and the Riders rode past the battle cloud, and Benny's drone followed them. They were supposed to stop here. The five horseback warriors weren't supposed to try and get all the way behind the enemy lines. They were only supposed to pelt the south flank with explosives and draw the enemy southward. But Benny focused his camera on Casey leading the front. His belt of grenades draped over his shoulder was nearly empty. But curiously, Casey signaled to the drone to look forward. He was signaling something in the distance.

Benny tilted his drone upward. There, he saw it and it sent shivers down to his fingers. He nearly lost control of the drone in his terror. The hulking exo-mech bound down the desert sand and directly into the battle. He was accompanied by Blackheart's sandship. Benny could see the cyborg pirate standing proudly on the platform, hands on his hips. And to Benny's horror, the cyborg captain pointed directly at the Specter drone. Moments later, a rocket burst forth from the sandship's massive battery. The rocket wound through the air like a snake and the last thing that

Benny saw on the screen was the rocket directly slamming into the camera.

Benny threw off his headset in the involuntary reaction that occurred when he became too immersed in his remote sessions. The Specter drone was gone. He looked around him. He was sitting on the couch of a neighbor's third story living space.

"What happened?" his neighbor Gary asked while reloading his rifle at the window.

Gary's home was chosen as one of the defense towers since he lived on the third floor of the multi-home building facing east. The room was filled with a thick smoke that blurred visibility. Through the smoke, splinters could be seen flying from walls and windows. Bullet casings littered the floor. Gary was at the window, crouched behind a makeshift barricade, reloading his rifle and aiming for the enemy outside.

"The exo-mech is here," Benny said with a sense of doom. "He's headed straight for the town."

"Well, didn't the Zelt say we need to just fire those rockets at it from the roof?" Gary yelled over the commotion.

Gunshots fired off rapidly, the sound rattling and reverberating off the walls like a symphony of chaos. The bullet casings clinked and scattered as they hit the ground, ending abruptly with a slight skitter across the floor. The gun smoke billowed, filling the air with an acrid haze.

"I have to get out there," Benny said with unsure resolve.

"You have to what?" Gary yelled.

The room was filled with the sound of explosions, artillery fire, and bullets ricocheting off walls and windows. Gary's rifle shots came out at a steady rhythm amidst the chaos, and the click of the gun when he reloaded could be heard above the din.

"I have to go out there!" Benny got up. "I'm taking the other bike; the Riders are in trouble!"

"Benny, no, you can't, it's..." Gary's voice faded as Benny ran out of the room, and the walls rumbled and shook from the battle.

Bullet casings cascaded across the room in a shower of brass and steel. Puffs of gun smoke filled the air, and sparks danced off the walls like fireflies.

Outside, the battle raged on even louder. The desert sand swirled everywhere, and it was difficult to see clearly. Benny had to make his way to the old motorbike across the street. He could ride it south and around the battle to save any of the Red Rider survivors. He had to do something other than being uselessly stuck in a room. He swallowed his fear and moved forward with purpose.

Some of the Corsairs were already near the town. The town's main road was a large gunfight between the Corsairs trying to make their way in and the townspeople taking cover from the doorways and building windows.

As Benny ran from cover to cover to make it across the road, he noticed the smell of gunpowder and a faint lingering scent of burning rubber and charred flesh. The air was rank with the smell of sulfur and gunpowder that burned his nose and eyes. Sweat mingled with thick smoke from the gunfire, creating a dusty haze that clung to everything.

He spotted the motorbike in the garage. This one was larger, but slower than Kira's. It was functional, but not nearly as driven as the one she used. As the occasional bullet ricocheted near him, he ran hunched over toward the bike. Quickly, he got into the seat and crudely started it by sparking the ignition wires together while turning the fuel crank. The motorbike roared to life, and he immediately zoomed out of the garage and headed west down the main road and toward the south entrance of town.

He knew how to operate the bike, but he was quite uncomfortable with it. It lurched forward and he was nearly thrown off several times. He almost lost balance and swerved several times before achieving an equilibrium.

The desert sand swirled around like a tornado, blurring his vision. The town had turned into a nightmare of sand and smoke and blood. The scene was chaos, with sand swirling everywhere, obscuring visibility as Corsairs fired on fleeing townspeople from behind sandbag walls erected along the main road. People cowered in doorways and windows or tore off in panic to escape the crossfire.

The fighting occurred mostly near the east entrance, so Benny zoomed out the south entrance to the wide-open Frontier to the south. Even over the motorbike engine, the sound of the battle was deafening, a cacophony of gunfire, explosions, and shouted orders competing with the sound of the desert wind. Frequent screams of fear and suffering eerily punctuated the sound of the bullets ricocheting off the buildings.

Luckily, as he made his way further out south of the town, the sounds of war subsided. In a way, he felt tempted to simply keep driving away. He could escape this hellhole and find another safe haven west of here. But he turned and watched as his town grew more enveloped in war and death. He had to do something. He was different. This time would be different. He could be a hero.

FORTY-FOUR

aymond Redmin grasped the dual handles of the machine gun atop the Armored Personnel Expeditioner. The gun appeared similar to the stationary military machine guns from Earth. A long chain belt of ammunition was fed into it, coming from a large container within the vehicle. He was used to the fine motor complexities of holding forceps and a needle driver. Wielding a monstrous weapon such as this was not only uncomfortable, but also frightening.

Inside, Kira was driving the vehicle, determined to get to her beloved town of Remnant. Also in the vehicle were the androids Voltaire and Swift. Voltaire sat in the vehicle with his legs crossed and holding Swift in his arms. The robot fox hummed nervously, but Voltaire sat there in meditative silence.

With the vehicle at full speed, the wind pounded against Raymond's ears. Despite that, the sounds of explosions and gunfire grew louder. Remnant was under siege by the Corsair forces. Kira drove the APE forward with no hesitation. Raymond readied himself with a machine gun as they drove. He reminded himself that he was entering a battlefield. Any hesitation could spell doom for their group. He had to do whatever it took to protect the people in Kira's town.

As they drove closer, they could see that the Corsairs had brought their own tanks to bear against the Red Riders and townspeople of Remnant. Explosions were everywhere as missiles were fired from above and below. The townspeople were outnumbered and outgunned, yet still fired back with a wall of bullets and rockets from the deteriorating outer walls of the town.

Kira continued driving towards where most of the fighting seemed to be focused—a large open area just outside Remnant's walls. As she drove forward, Raymond stood atop the APE, firing his machine gun furiously at any Corsair vehicles or cyborgs he could see coming their way. The sound of bullets ricocheting off metal filled his ears as explosions erupted around them from both sides' firepower.

He felt a detachment from the violence, as the gun blared with smoke and fire. The bullets seemed to hit nothing, as he blanketed the distant enemies with his indiscriminate squeeze of the triggers. Whether he was actually causing any damage to their many vehicles or not, he continued his distant onslaught, thankful not to see his enemies up close for now.

However, his fears were answered, as his gunfire seemed to draw the attention of the enemy vehicles. One of the Lion tanks closest to them turned its cannon away from the town and towards them. Raymond shuddered in fear. His machine gun would do little against the armored war machine.

Suddenly, out of the smoke and sand cloud from the north, Tristan's exo-mech charged into the battle, tossing enemy vehicles through the air. The exo-mech's massive sword drove directly down into the hull of the Lion tank. This created an explosion that barely made Tristan's exo-mech flinch. The mech stood in a swirl of smoke, establishing his dominance on the field. This show of strength sent the Corsairs scattering back in retreat as Kira drove past them unscathed.

Raymond gave a gracious wave toward Tristan. The exo-mech gave him a knowing nod in return. Tristan pulled the mech sword out of the tank remains, then turned his attention toward the enemy exo-mech in the distance. The showdown was inevitable. Raymond recalled their meeting in Guaritore's underground cavern. Now, in an open field, perhaps they would have a proper battle.

In the distance, the black exo-mech knowingly brushed aside a rocket launched in its direction. It picked up a similarly enormous sword and pointed it toward Tristan's exo-mech as an open challenge.

Raymond watched in awe, as Tristan charged his exo-mech forward, and the two enormous humanoid giants ran at each other directly in the center of the battlefield. He had never seen anything like this. Despite all the bizarre and outlandish things that he had seen here in this alien future, the sight of two behemoth robots clashing with swords on a battlefield was the most surreal spectacle he had come to witness.

The Corsairs continued to charge in, wave after wave of cybernetic monstrosities from the east. From the north, the George Wallace's Red Riders on horseback fired the grenade launcher pistols as Marcus, the armored Vanguard soldier, ran in on foot, tearing his way through the Corsair ranks. Raymond marveled on the sergeant's ability to keep up with the vehicular warfare while only on foot. He was quicker and more agile than any of the vehicles, even while wearing his hulking armor. Raymond turned towards Remnant, where they were delivering a barrage of gunfire and smoky rockets from the rooftops and windows that just barely kept their enemies from breaching the walls of the town.

"We're almost there!" Kira yelled from the driver's seat.

Raymond observed the town for the first time. The buildings were coarse and sand-worn, none more than 2 or 3 stories high. The town itself was no bigger than the isolated American Wild West towns portrayed in the old movies. The buildings smoked from artillery fire, and the dirt roads on the eastward-facing side were littered with bodies from battle.

They had given Raymond a brief explanation of the cyborgs. These were natural-born humans, originally employed by the Zeltan Kingdom in the united human alliance against some super AI hive mind in the recent past of this tumultuous Mars. After the war, the prejudice against AI and cybernetics led the Zeltans to outlaw the cyborgs from living within the Kingdom, and thus, they migrated south toward the Green Sea. There, in their seething hatred of this Zeltan betrayal, they resorted to pirating, theft, and violent trading practices. Now, with this supposed Old Earth technology appearing on Mars, these cyborg pirates were determined to steamroll their way to this small, natural born town to obtain it.

A small contingent of these Corsair cyborgs was hiding behind cover on the town's border in a firefight with townspeople shooting from a second-story window.

"There!" Kira said, seeing the same situation. "Shoot there!"

Raymond directed his machine gun toward these cyborgs. Previously, he had been mostly firing wildly at vague enemy vehicles in the distance. Now, he was aiming at actual people.

Well, to him, they resembled people. There were four cyborgs, one who prominently had a metallic cannon for an arm, with wires crudely connecting to his head and torso. Another had four insect-like legs below the waist. They were a frightening assortment of monstrosities that still surprised Raymond despite all he had seen since he arrived.

This is it; I need to be able to do this, he reminded himself.

He took a deep breath and squeezed the triggers, taking extra focus and control of the gun, careful not to spray the townspeople hiding in the buildings with his high-caliber ammunition. He could just barely see, through the burst fire of the machine gun and its violent recoil, the sand and stone around the cyborgs kick up into a sudden display of cloud and smoke. He couldn't tell whether he was hitting them directly, but he certainly made sure that the area they were standing on was absolutely decimated. After a few moments, he stopped firing, awaiting the dust to settle.

"Did I... get them?" Raymond asked cautiously.

"Oh, you got them," Kira said.

As they drove past, Raymond was horrified at the scene he created. The machine gun fire had cut apart the stone slab they took cover behind. The corsairs were reduced to bloody messes of tattered clothing and disembodied human and cyborg limbs. The cyborg with the spider-like legs had been ripped off from the waist. To Raymond's repulsion, his mangled four legs twitched on the ground like an insect that had just been stepped on.

Raymond wasn't proud of himself. He had an inherent desire to help and aid people, not to kill them. However, he brushed aside these feelings and reminded himself of the bigger picture. This was necessary to help Kira's townspeople. He thought back to all the death and suffering he had seen in his career at the hospital.

Do no harm wouldn't apply here. People were relying on him to fulfill a duty. He resolved to deal with his conflicting feelings later.

As he backed away from the controls of the machine gun, the APE made a crude stop at the building that had been firing at the Corsairs. Kira had nearly crashed them into the wall but stopped the APE just short of the door.

"Let's go!" Kira said, bursting out of the driver's seat, already firing her submachine gun down the street.

Raymond slipped down from the machine gun turret and took a deep breath. He grabbed the assault rifle, laying on the bench. He gripped it reluctantly, hoping he would not need to use it, knowing full well that he would. Voltaire sat watching him, apparently unfazed by the ongoing hell storm of a battle, with Swift jumping off his lap onto the floor.

"Aggression is the absence of options," Voltaire said. "When there are no paths to harmony, a discordant chord may be required to complete the symphony."

"Well," Raymond processed the wise words and agreed. "Here we go then."

He slammed open the back doors of the APE, rifle-shouldered and ready to fire as he surveyed this Martian desert of the future. The chaotic sounds of war surrounded him, a deluge of gunfire and explosions that shook the ground under his feet. He stared in awe at the unbelievably surreal scene before him - an old-fashioned western town devoured by chaos and destruction.

FORTY-FIVE

C aptain Darien continued to methodically make his way across the sandy battlefield. This would be not unlike the wars against the robotic armies he had fought in the past. Except this time, he was alone on the battlefield, aided by the occasional novice natural-born. If anything, they only slowed him down. Frequently, he would see them getting easily picked off by the Corsair snipers and machine gunners. They simply moved too slowly and were too inexperienced to be useful on the front lines.

Luckily, these Corsair pirates were not nearly as formidable as the hordes of AI death machines he had fought on the battlefields east of the Kingdom. Darien quickly identified the location of every sniper and drew them out with expert tactics. His mind took hundreds of snapshots of his view of the battlefield. Even the slightest movement or human-shaped silhouette partially visible in the obscure distance was perceived in his photographic memory. While he would have preferred to have his head-up-display computer visor on the Ranger helmets, he found that relying on his own inherent instincts was revelatory about his own abilities. He was more capable than he had ever known.

"Keep your head dow—" Darien yelled to an inept Remnant townsman, peeking out behind flaming wreckage.

Nearly instantly, the natural born human's head exploded in a mist of blood and mass. Darien cursed in frustration. These natural borns were getting themselves killed for no purpose. He always assumed that he had no care for the natural borns but watching them struggle to survive and keep up in this battle brought out his sympathies. He needed to scale this battlefield quickly before more of them were injured or killed. He quickly calculated exactly where that bullet might have come from. He knew he had only milliseconds before the shooter would react to his bullseye.

Darien threw a grenade in that general direction, waited a moment, and took off running just before the grenade exploded, showering sand for cover. As Darien ran to the next cover, he took intense care to watch the muzzle fire behind the settling sand falling through the air. The world slowed down for him, and within seconds, he identified 3 shooters. Two machine gunners and one likely sharpshooter.

As Darien did a sideways hip slide through the sand to hide behind the cover of flaming wreckage, he quickly used one hand to aim his rifle at one of the machine gunners. He precisely delivered his burst fire of exactly 3 bullets to take down the machine gunner, whose neck exploded with a spurt of blood.

Darien felt the "flow" state take hold. From here, his consciousness was primarily focused on coordinating his next movements, but his body felt like it moved on its own. In this state, his arms and legs performed feats of precise movements that seemed to occur sub-consciously.

The captain did a quick roll behind the cover, and, with this new angle, he could easily strafe sideways to fire the rest of his magazine at the second gunner. He held the gun steady at his hip, keeping the corner of his eyes fixated on the sharpshooter, who likely had trouble tracking Darien moving quickly in a flank around him. Once the second machine gunner was riddled with bullets by Darien's automatic rifle, he ran directly toward the sharpshooter. He felt the zip of a medium caliber bullet near him, calculated the angle, and knew exactly where to go.

He dove to the sand, picking up a flat metal wall of shrapnel that had blown off a nearby Lion tank. He dug his hand into a groove of twisted metal and used the heavy object as a shield. The bullets thudded against the makeshift shield, sparks flying in every direction. Darien took a moment to recalibrate. He needed to move quickly. He grunted as he hoisted it forward toward the direction of the sharpshooter, running forward.

Meanwhile, he sensed some straggling Corsairs in his periphery. There were 3 wounded cyborgs, each picking up pieces of their cybernetic parts laid out across the sand. One of them noticed Darien running across the field and pointed toward him. Quickly, Darien threw his rifle back over his shoulder sling and reached for the pistol under his belt. He was somewhat exposed to this side and couldn't leave any vulnerability. After all, the metal shield was starting to deform and lose integrity from the hailstorm of bullets. It luckily remained intact to provide cover for his frontside. He only had seconds before he knew someone would attempt to fire an explosive at him.

Darien aimed the pistol looping underneath the arm that held up his shield. He deftly fired at the 3 cyborgs before they could even muster any means of attack or defense. Quickly, they fell to the floor after Darien expended his magazine.

I'm starting to get in over my head, Darien thought. He had fought so deep into the enemy ranks on his own that he could sense that he was surrounded by threats everywhere. He needed to stay focused. One miscalculation would be fatal.

There was another empty tank hull coming up. He planted the metal slab into the sand and rolled behind the hull. Just as he expected, someone fired a rocket directly into his metal shield seconds afterward. He quickly changed his pistol magazine and the magazine of his automatic rifle. Darien pressed his back against the metal and observed the battlefield around him. He had made it so far into the thick of the battle that he deduced he was at the center of the Corsair army force. The town of Remnant was in the distance, far behind him.

He listened as the bullets pinged around him. The sharpshooter was out there, and others were starting to flank his position. Darien thought to himself. He had been in worse situations in the past, but things were certainly looking grim. He was alone and surrounded. Darien took a deep breath and held his automatic rifle in one hand and his pistol in the other. He would make a quick break for the next cover, but in this situation, he could be caught by a well-placed or random bullet. He had to move now.

I have to keep fighting, Darien thought. He was the only soldier capable of disrupting the Corsair army from within. The more chaos he could cause, the better chance that the town of Remnant would have to repel them. He was abandoning his mission of retrieving Julian and the Ark. It seemed now that he was primarily concerned with Remnant surviving this invasion. *If this is the end,* Darien thought, *I need to make sure that it means something.*

He took a deep breath, ready to take as many Corsairs as possible down with him in likely his final stand. Darien calculated that he would not survive this.

And suddenly, the sound of automatic gunfire shifted elsewhere. It erupted with a cadence of uniformity and brevity that could only signal the presence of professionals. Then, he began to realize that the enemy gunfire was no longer landing anywhere near him. They were shooting at something coming from the north.

Through the dust and burning smoke of war, Darien saw it. It was nearly the same heralding impact that he had remembered when he was saved on the battlefield so many years ago.

Marcus.

Marcus, the Vanguard fitted with bulky metallic grey armor, burst into the battlefield with intensity. The 8-foot giant of a Zeltan knocked aside a flaming Jackal vehicle as he fired a machine gun. He kicked off the mounted machine gun from the vehicle, grabbing it with his other hand.

There he stood; his armor pelted by bullets in all directions. Marcus fired 100 lb machine guns in each hand, tearing up the battlefield around him. Darien never tired of seeing the Vanguard's incredible abilities. He was proud of him, but more so, he was overjoyed to see him alive.

"Captain Darien," Marcus said, in his usual plain cadence, despite wielding two machine guns in each hand, "What are your orders, sir?"

"Marcus," Darien said, "Thank you. I'm glad to see that you're okay. Where are the others?"

"The Lieutenant is engaging the enemy in the exo-mech unit," Marcus said, "The natural borns are taking an armored personnel carrier to support their defenses."

Darien asked, already knowing the answer, "And the rest of the squad?"

"It is only us, sir," Marcus said.

"Okay," Darien said, allowing a moment of grief, but quickly returning to focus, "Ready up. Cover two, protocol 732 maneuvers. Fire strong, shadow even. Improvisation full welcome. I'll take out the sharpshooter at clock one."

Marcus nodded in return, then returned to his obliteration of the battlefield. This was Darien's cue. Marcus was the perfect cover fire. Darien quickly dashed south, taking care to look for any enemies in his path.

He darted across the squirming bodies of injured cyborgs. Darien casually used his pistol to put them out of their misery as he ran at full speed through the war wreckage. The sand cloud, smoke from the fires, and the commotion from Marcus arriving were just enough distractions to allow Darien to weave through the war field unmolested.

Close by, he could hear the non-stop gunfire from Marcus' dual machine guns as he leaped high into the air, jumping over obstacles and tearing through enemy ranks before they were able to react. He was an unstoppable tool of destruction.

Soon, Darien made it to his destination. There was the sharpshooter, now readying himself to fire at Marcus. In an anti-climax, Darien quickly fired his rifle at the sharpshooter's head. It was a cyborg head, refitted with some apparatus over the left ear and eye, likely to help zero in targets. Now, it was a junk heap of brain-mass and electronic parts.

Darien jumped to the top of the defunct Lion tank, where the shooter was perched. He grabbed the marksman rifle and quickly popped off two cyborgs with rocket launchers on their arms that were pestering Marcus. Darien jumped to the ground to meet up with the Vanguard soldier.

"I'm glad you're here, Sergeant," Darien said. He had no idea how Marcus got here, but if anyone were to survive the Black Forest, it would be him.

"Captain," Marcus said, scanning their surroundings for enemies, and he held now only one machine gun in his arms, with a belt of ammunition draping from it. "We have to—"

Then, the earth trembled more intensely than it had, even when the tanks rumbled and artillery fired. Darien knew exactly what that signaled. He looked up, and almost instantly, the figure appeared within the dust cloud.

Julian's towering exo-mech bounded across the battlefield, drawing a massive sword. Behind it crept up the Corsairs' sandship, a rolling mass of crudely assembled re-used metal that appeared to serve as a mobile base for Blackheart.

"We're going to need some explosives to take it down," Darien said, standing bravely before the hulking metal giant in front of them.

"No need," Marcus said. "Look."

Another rumbling grew louder, and Darien saw him. Tristan was in the white exo-mech they found in Guaritore's underground lair.

Look at you, Darien said, watching Tristan's exo-mech swing his sword gracefully. *This is everything you wanted. Show them all what you can do, Lieutenant.*

Julian's black exo-mech took a defense position, as moments later, Tristan's exo-mech came rushing through the smoke. In a clash of metal that stirred and silenced the entire battlefield, Tristan's sword met Julian's. And instantly, an epic-scale exo-mech duel ignited at the center of the battlefield as rockets zoomed past them.

CHAPTER

FORTY-SIX

Benny clutched the handlebars of the motorbike. This Shepherd motorbike was originally taken from a Zeltan war battlefield, then passed through Cyborg Bay before becoming parts for some other piece of machinery. It had likely been used as junk in the frontier before being re-built into its current state. That was how they came across most resources here out west, as junk leftovers. But now, Remnant had something everyone else wanted, and they would have to fight for their right to claim it.

The motorbike's engine blared, drowning out the sounds of the battle to his left, as Benny drove widely south to go around the fighting. He needed to get to where Casey and Red Riders were last seen. He owed Casey at least that. He was a friend and had taught Benny the lesson of bravery in the face of these extraordinary circumstances. This was no time to back down.

As Benny drove along, the sky rained fire from above. Explosions rocked the ground and sent pieces of metal, stone, and wood raining down like a storm of shrapnel. The wind rushing past his face felt like a raging river full of debris. He kept driving, weaving between fires, trying not to get hit by flying wreckage.

Through the thick smoke and sand, he saw them up ahead. The Red Riders, in their trademark wide-brimmed, high-crowned hats and long duster coats, were shooting at enemy forces, returning fire in desperation. They were huddled behind the carcasses of their own downed horses. They appeared to have been blown off their horses by explosions or even gunfire.

The cacophony of war came screaming close as he drove nearly head-on into the fray. From his memory, he knew there was an embankment of sand just south behind the Riders. He would try to drive his motorbike down into there for cover and try to lead them there.

Benny curved ahead as bullets whizzed by him and explosions shook the ground beneath him. As he got closer to the Red Riders, he could feel his heart pounding in his chest, but instead of fearing for his life, he felt empowered. Benny was fully cognizant of the change of his attitude toward war. Days ago, this would have been too frightened to even watch. And now, he felt motivated to be the hero, despite the risks. He accelerated and ducked his head low over the handlebars to avoid it all as best he could.

The Red Riders turned around to see Benny drive the motorbike as the sand sloped downwards, slightly, but enough that it created cover from the constant barrage of flying projectiles. He scrambled out of the seat of the bike, crawling on hands and knees on the sand floor.

"Hey!" Benny yelled, just peeking his head over the sand.

He couldn't even hear his own voice over the noise. Tanks, cyborgs, and even the enemy exo-mech and main Corsair sandship were all drawing near the town. The result was a massive dust cloud of sand and fire.

Benny signaled wildly for Red Riders to come over to the embankment. Slowly but gradually, the Red Riders got each other's attention and made their way to Benny.

There were only three of them. A bullet caught one of them square through the chest as he ran. Out of the two remaining, one stopped to help the Rider who had been shot, but the sand beneath them suddenly exploded up, sending their bodies (and body parts) flying in every direction.

Benny ducked, the sand hitting his face and goggles. He coughed and spat out the debris as the lone surviving Red Rider jumped down beside him.

"Hey, let's get out of here," the Red Rider said. Benny recognized him as Rudy Harrell, the young Rider from the small Frontier town of Bethesda.

"Where's Casey?" Benny asked.

Rudy shook his head and peered over the sand. He looked back at Benny and pointed. There was a small crater in the sand from an explosion. An occasional hand came up to fire back with a grenade pistol. Casey was in there.

"We gotta go get him!" Benny yelled over the explosions.

"Hell no!" Rudy said. "We gotta just get outta here, let's go, Fong," grabbing Benny by the arm to take him to the bike.

"No!" Benny said, tearing his arm away. "We gotta help him!"

Benny needed to save Casey. Although he was the cause of bullying throughout his childhood, Casey represented everything Benny needed to be. He was always hard on Benny because he was pushing him to be a stronger man in order to survive the Frontier. He was witness to what Benny used to be and helped him become better. Benny couldn't just leave him. He needed to prove to Casey, to everyone, that he wasn't a coward anymore. He was stronger than that.

"Don't do it, Fong," Rudy said.

Instinctively, Benny took a deep breath, bounding out of the sand cover. Immediately, the bullets zipped by him. He stumbled forward, running as fast as he could with his head down. He waited for the impact of a bullet on his body, but it never came.

His legs, on autopilot, had taken him to the sand crater. Benny jumped in, landing on his ankle awkwardly, sending a surge of pain up his body as the ankle rolled. He yelped in pain but checked his body for any other injuries. He patted his body, miraculously finding that no bullets had made his acquaintance.

"What in the hell are you doing, Fong?" Casey asked.

"Being a hero," Benny said.

Casey grinned. "Woohee, look atchu." He shook his head. "Red Rider Benny Fong."

Benny felt a surge of pride run through him.

"Well," Casey looked over the crater as bullets pelted them from every direction. "Enjoy your damn 5 seconds of joy. We ain't making it longer than that."

Benny's moment of self-indulgence ended as soon as it began. He was right. They were stuck. A relentless rainfall of bullets hissed like an orchestra of serpents, a symphony of destruction and death. The steady hum became a shrieking crescendo with every impact and every ricochet it brought with it. The air crackled and sparked like a million tiny lightning bolts were raining down from the sky.

"Casey," Benny said, "If I don't make it, tell my family…"

"Oh no, none of this shit now," Casey said, as he continued firing his pistol over the crater edge.

"Tell them I wasn't a coward," Benny said. "Tell them that…"

"Hey! You ain't a coward, Fong," Casey said, "You're a goddamn hero. And that's how we go out. Heroes."

Benny swallowed a lump in his throat. They were pinned down facing certain doom. There was no way to run out of the crater safely. Casey was right. They would die as heroes. Benny's adrenaline surged. He was ready.

Benny readied his pistol and gave Casey a nod. They resolved to go out in a blaze of glory.

Suddenly, they heard a rumble of a vehicle drawing closer. The rumble of the vehicle's engine gradually got louder as it approached, the low roar of its engine like a snorting bull ready to attack. Its tires crunched on the rocks as it came closer and closer, accompanied by a clanging of metal as it shook from side to side, and a bullet pinged off its surface.

It was the Red Rider Rudy. He must have had a change of heart and came back to get them.

"Get in!" he yelled from the driver's seat, ducking from a new onslaught of enemy fire.

He was driving a Wolf vehicle. Benny had seen these before. They were somewhat less common than the Jackals. It was larger, more heavily armored, and mostly closed, allowing for more protection for the driver, but still had an open cargo bed in the back, also usually fitted with a stationary large weapon. This one seemed to have a manned rocket launcher.

Casey took off without hesitation, and Benny followed afterward. Rudy had parked it directly in front of them, the bulky vehicle acting as a shield from a sideways hailstorm of bullets.

Benny dove into the open back since Casey had squeezed his way into the passenger side door. Benny nearly laid down flat on the open vehicle bed as bullets zoomed over him, and the sides of the cargo bed were just barely raised enough to provide cover.

"Go, go!" Casey yelled.

Immediately, Rudy took off with the vehicle, tossing around its equipment and occupants. Benny immediately knew the cargo bed around him was full of stored and freely exposed rockets. To his horror, the cylinders the size of his forearm rolled around the floor of the cargo bed. And with every bump and sandhill, he and the rockets were momentarily launched up in the air and down again. Benny grabbed the leg of the rocket launcher bolted to the vehicle to keep himself from falling out but looked on in terror as the explosive ordinance bounced around him.

The close sound of gunfire shook him from inaction. Casey was leaning out the passenger seat window, firing a grenade launcher.

"Get on the gun!" Casey yelled back.

Benny mouthed an "okay", but the wind and commotion drowned him out. They were driving at full speed, flying over sand hills and narrowly avoiding burnt-out and flaming Corsair vehicles. Benny hoped that Rudy was a competent driver.

Nevertheless, Benny looked up at the rocket launcher battery. The bullets were no longer flying overhead, as they zoomed around at full speed. He pulled himself up slightly, trying to examine the launcher.

There were two handles for his hands to grasp. It was unclear whether it would require pressing both triggers to launch the rocket already loaded. He positioned himself behind the large metal plate that served as a shield for the operator. There was a small, cross-shaped slit for him to peer through.

"Just shoot it!" Casey yelled.

Benny frantically searched for a target. In the commotion, everything just seemed like smoke and wreckage.

"What am I supposed to shoot at?" Benny asked.

Casey pointed ahead, "That!"

Benny looked on in horror at the two robotic giants doing battle.

CHAPTER

FORTY-SEVEN

Darien watched from below as the two titan exo-mechs swung their swords at each other with incredible speed and ferocity. Sparks flew from every blow as they parried and feinted, clashing their blades together in a flurry of motion. Their movements were precise and controlled, reflecting the skill of each pilot fighting with incredible speed and power.

As the fight progressed, both machines seemed to be perfectly matched in terms of strength, skill, and agility. Their swords gleamed in the sunlight, with smoke trailing behind their heated movements and rockets zooming around them as mere distractions.

Darien shook the temptation to continue watching his Lieutenant dueling with his former mentor.

"We need to get to the main Corsair vehicle," he said to Marcus. "That's their base of operations, and we can use their payload to help the Lieutenant."

"Hard copy," Marcus said.

"Maneuver two-one, actual," Darien said. "Let's move."

Instantly, Darien and Marcus moved across the battlefield together. They were like wraiths, moving from cover to cover, eliminating any semblance of opposition as the exo-mechs crashed against each other in battle above them.

"Turret!" Darien pointed out to Marcus.

An automatic turret protruded from the deck of the sandship. Marcus spotted it, breaking from Darien to draw its fire. The turret had enormous firepower, tearing apart the very ground around Marcus as he strafed sideways while continuing to fire his machine gun at the Corsairs on the deck. But even Marcus' reinforced armor wouldn't be able to withstand the heavy firepower of the auto-turret.

Darien looked around him and calculated a geometric path to run and propel himself off nearby wreckage to jump up to the ship deck. He put in all his effort to achieve top running speed, kicked himself off of three consecutive defunct vehicles, and just barely grabbed the ledge of the elevated ship deck. Although he was running right into the belly of the beast, he had no doubt in his mind. This was the end game. Tristan had the best chance of defeating Julian, and Darien had to help him achieve that. They would be able to complete their original mission.

He grasped the edge, his body dangling. He was fully equipped with several weapons and ammunition weighing him down. From his hanging position, he still managed to bring his gun up to fire at Corsairs leaning out and shooting at him. Darien took a deep breath and forced himself upwards, pulling himself up through the air as hard as he could. He felt the tendons in his shoulder tear in excruciating pain.

He rolled onto the deck of the ship, landing directly on that shoulder. If it wasn't dislocated before, it sure was now. He had no time to fix the shoulder. Enemies were everywhere.

There were dozens of Corsairs on the deck. Cyborgs of every kind, their grotesque cybernetics implanted into all permutations of the imagination. Darien fired his gun wildly, taking out as many of them as he could at close range.

Too much going on, Darien thought. With the number of enemies in close proximity, his usual mental snapshots couldn't keep up. Threats appeared everywhere. He couldn't calculate a safe way out of this situation except to keep shooting.

He hobbled to his feet, stumbling to cover, but he felt the brutal force of a bullet tearing through his right thigh. Darien fell backward. He continued to shoot while he dragged himself backward against a wall. The Corsairs continued to pour out the doors and hatches. His automatic rifle clicked empty, and he quickly grabbed a nearby Corsair submachine gun. He released a crude clearing of gunfire at the entire deck.

As he threw the gun aside, he rolled to cover, realizing that he also had taken a bullet to the abdomen where he had been shot days ago during the battle with the Aggromen. It was a through-and-through wound, but it still bled and pounded with pain. He turned toward the turret battery. Exposed wires were coming from the deck floor leading to the turret. Darien pulled out his pistol and shot at it, disabling the turret immediately. This would give Marcus some space to move freely.

He then heard the familiar dull impact of a grenade hitting the ground. It was too far to kick or throw back. Darien rolled out of the way of the blast radius, but just a moment too late. It had sent a storm of shrapnel tearing into his left leg.

I'm in bad shape, he thought.

As he lay back against the wall, facing a new wave of Corsairs appearing from the galleys of the sandship, he raised his pistol to prepare for a possible final stand.

At the very last moment, the armored Marcus landed with an impact that shook the entire ship. He had landed directly in front of Darien, absorbing all the gunfire. Marcus now held an automatic rifle, deftly taking out every enemy on the ship deck.

Darien provided some support, firing his pistol from behind Marcus. The pistol clicked empty shortly after, but it didn't matter. Marcus had completely cleared the ship deck of all Corsairs. He tossed several grenades into the doorways, and the ship beneath them erupted in a scream, followed by several booms and then silence.

Marcus continued staring at the floor, likely using his helmet scanner to detect any survivors. He casually walked over to a sniper rifle lying on the floor. He aimed it at the floor of the ship, periodically firing through it. He was methodically ridding the ship of all survivors one by one using infrared profiling.

As Marcus continued his purging of Corsairs, Captain Darien gritted his teeth and pulled himself up, ignoring his body screaming in agonizing pain. He grabbed his left arm, pulling his shoulder back into position with a painfully satisfying clunk that nearly made him lose consciousness for a moment.

His left abdomen was still bleeding, but Marcus tossed him a tissue sealant from his belt. Darien sprayed the wound closed and grunted as the gel hardened to stop the bleeding.

Darien looked around. "The missile launcher," he said with pained groan. He pointed at the anti-air missile battery towards the back of the sandship.

"Copy that," Marcus said, bounding effortlessly to the back of the ship.

Darien looked around the floor, littered with Corsair bodies. Their cybernetic modifications and weapon amalgamations made their corpses appear even more grotesque. He searched for a weapon that he could possibly use to attack Julian's exo-mech. He would have to find something to at least distract him. Tristan needed the help.

Just then, Julian's sword landed with a horrifying metallic thud onto the left shoulder of Tristan's exo-mech. The sword made an echoing, mechanical screech as it hit the metal shoulder. The sound reverberated down to the sandship, a clang of metal-on-metal ringing in Darien's ears. He could almost feel the vibration through his feet as he looked on in horror at Julian's devastating attack.

"No!" Darien yelled from the side of the sandship.

Julian's sword was embedded mere inches from Tristan's cockpit. The exo-mech's hull was a mess of distorted and twisted metal. Through an opening of torn metal and the sparks of failing electric equipment Darien could see the Lieutenant struggling. Tristan was trapped.

Just as Julian raised the sword of his exo-mech to deliver a final blow, his exo-mech flinched. A small cloud of smoke hit the front of his exo-mech. Small rockets began to pelt the exo-mech from the ground.

Darien looked over the railing. It was a lone vehicle, buzzing through the wreckage around Julian's exo-mech. Much to the Captain's surprise and relief, it was a Wolf vehicle driven by a Red Rider. Darien recognized Casey Jarrett in the passenger seat firing a weapon, with Benny Fong manning the stationary rocket launcher in the back.

Very impressive, you two, Darien thought. *These natural borns can be far more capable than we expected.*

FORTY-EIGHT

B enny spun the launcher facing forward, and there they were: two hulking exo-mechs, locked in a surreal battle. Benny stared in awe as he watched the two gigantic exo-mechs clash their swords with such force that the ground trembled. Sparks flew as the swords collided, echoing through the air like thunder. The giant robots moved gracefully, spinning and twirling their massive swords in intricate patterns.

Benny watched as the two metal exo-mechs clashed swords with loud clangs that echoed in the air. The huge machines fought fiercely, sparks showering from their blades as they moved lightning fast. Each of the machines was huge, their armor gleaming in the sun, and the sight of them so close was both awe-inspiring and terrifying.

"Which one do I shoot at?" Benny asked.

"The black and red one that came with them," Casey said. "I think the gray one is helping us. Fire at the one with the creepy pilot that was talking to Blackheart."

Benny remembered the black exo-mech and its long haired, glowing, red-eyed pilot from when they were detained by the Corsairs. He had no idea where the white exo-mech had come from, but if it was fighting the exo-mech on the Corsair side, it was an ally. For now, at least. Benny scanned the area for any sign of other help, but there was none.

They were approaching very close to the center of the battle. Rudy was proving to be a good driver. They zoomed past the site of many fallen or dying Corsairs. Benny mustered the confidence to apply tunnel vision focus on his task. He would land a hit on the enemy exo-mech.

The exo-mech came into view, and Benny squeezed the triggers of the rocket launcher. It required both triggers to be squeezed very hard in tandem for the rocket to fire. Benny was startled by the sudden deployment of the rocket. It initially launched with a hollow thud, but the rocket burst into a trail of smoke afterward, snaking forwards with a slightly slow lag from the vehicle movement.

His first attempt was a miss. The rocket veered sideways and upwards, landing quite far from the exo-mechs.

"Again!" Casey said, still firing from the passenger seat. He was grabbing any weapon he had available, firing at whatever he could.

Benny looked around. On the cargo bed floor were the godforsaken rockets that had not yet exploded at his feet. He picked one up, realizing it was much heavier than he imagined. The rocket launcher luckily had some worn-off instructions on it.

There was a tray to pull back. As Benny yanked on it, an empty shell of the previous rocket was discarded. He carefully placed a new rocket in and, just as delicately, slid the tray back. It made a satisfying click. Benny hoped he put it in right, else the launcher would explode in his face.

Benny aimed the launcher. With a deep breath, he took careful aim at the exo-mech. When he mustered up the courage and felt like he had the shot, he squeezed the triggers of the launcher. The rocket shot out of the tube with a whining roar. The projectile shot out and arced through the air. Smoke trailed behind it as its wings collapsed one after another, flickering like a candle flame. The rocket exploded against the backside of the exo-mech.

"I got it!" Benny exclaimed.

As the smoke cleared, to his horror, the rocket merely made the exo-mech flinch. The impact did little to harm its structure. After parrying a sword swing from the white exo-mech, the black exo-mech turned its head toward Rudy, Casey, and Benny's vehicle in perturbed acknowledgment.

"Drive, drive, drive!" Benny said in terror.

"It's okay!" Casey said. "Just keep hitting it with those rockets. We need to distract it to help the other one out."

The Corsair-aligned exo-mech had already turned back to its duel. Benny knew the plan and was determined to fulfill his role. One by one, he loaded the launcher, each one more efficiently than the last. Their Coyote vehicle continued to drive around in circles around the exo-mechs. Benny repeatedly launched rocket after rocket.

The battle was exhilarating and dizzying. Enemies were everywhere, but Benny was protected from small-caliber fire in his seated cockpit and was mostly protected on at least three sides. As the exo-mechs continued their god-like duel, Benny felt like an intervening force, giving their side just the slightest advantage.

Suddenly, after a direct shot of his rocket to the torso of the evil exo-mech, it seemed like it had tolerated enough. Through the slits of his launcher, he could just barely see the exo-mech bounding over to a nearby wreckage of a tank.

"Watch out!"

That was the last thing Benny heard before he felt the entire vehicle violently lunge sideways. He felt his head hit the metal shielding. The world quickly became a fading blur of disembodying disorientation.

FORTY-NINE

Darien gritted his teeth as he watched helplessly from a distance. Julian had picked up a tank, hurling it at Benny's vehicle. Darien watched Benny's vehicle tumble through the air and land far across the battlefield.

Those natural borns would not likely survive that impact. He briefly mourned them, those two natural borns who helped him get here. They proved to be braver and more capable than he had anticipated.

Thank you, brave soldiers.

But just as he was distracted by this loss, he felt the sandship give a violent rumble as two missiles left the battery from the back of the ship. They both made direct contact with the back of Julian's exo-mech, causing an explosion that knocked Darien back. His injured limbs could not react in time, and he stumbled backward.

As the smoke settled, Darien realized that the exo-mech was staring directly at him. Julian had noticed him standing on the sandship deck. Now, the evil titan walked directly toward him.

Darien stood up tall in defiance. Julian's exo-mech, somewhat damaged by Marcus' missile attack, raised its giant metallic sword.

"Now *this* is where we belong," Julian said, his voice distorted by his badly damaged exo-mech speakers. "On the battlefield!"

Just as Julian was about to swing the enormous sword down on Darien, his exo-mech hull erupted forth as Tristan's blade tore through and out the left shoulder of Julian's giant robotic death machine.

Julian's pained grunt was heard through the speakers, but he survived the attempt. With the left side of his exo-mech torn open, Darien could see Julian through the opening. He had a look of rage and contentment emanating through the strands of the jet-black hair hanging over his face.

Darien momentarily shuddered. His menacing red robotic eyes pierced through his hair and seemed to haunt him from the open destroyed cockpit.

Julian swung his exo-mech around, tearing itself apart in that action, while he swung his sword at Tristan's exo-mech. At the very last moment, Tristan managed to jump out of his cockpit before Julian could deliver a final side swing of his sword. Darien could swear that Tristan winked and saluted as he jumped out.

Tristan and Julian's exo-mechs were now stuck to each other, a mix of mangled metal with swords embedded into each other. Julian's glowing red eyes now turned to Darien.

The exo-mech amalgamation hobbled toward the sandship. In a last desperation, it bent to pick up the missile launcher it had thrown to the ground earlier. The exo-mech could barely move to lift it. But Julian moved it just enough to aim it at the sandship.

"Marcus! We need to—" Darien yelled.

In a swirl of slow motion, Darien watched as a missile detonated from the launcher on the ground. Instinctively, Darien jumped from the sandship as it exploded beneath him. As he flew, flailing his limbs aimlessly to control his trajectory, he watched Julian jump out of his exo-mech as it began to flame and smoke.

Darien landed on a small patch of open sand as the sandship continued to explode nearby. It was full of explosives and ordinance. He hoped Marcus wasn't still inside.

Flaming debris rained down around Darien. He crawled beneath a curved chunk of metal stuck into the ground. It was pelted with terrifying thuds, like a hail of metal fire. Sparks flew from flaming debris as it showered down from the sky, illuminated by an orange glow. The metal stuck in the ground were jagged hunks of charred brass, buckled and bent with bright red embers. The air was thick with the smell of burning rubber and smoke mixed with the scent of metal.

He writhed in pain under his temporary shelter. Darien again had to pull his left shoulder back into place. This time, the pain was less prevalent, as his entire body ached with excruciating pain. He did a self-assessment, noting that he kept all four limbs in the explosion and fall. However, his clothes were tattered and covered in his blood, and his skin was torn in several places.

Darien looked around; fire was everywhere. The destroyed exo-mechs, leaning against each other after a hard-fought battle, were up in flames. The sandship had spilled oil onto the ground, creating a wall of fire that seemed to engulf the area around him. Everything was fire and smoke.

At first, it appeared like an apparition, but Darien looked up and saw the unmistakable demonic figure of Julian walking towards him. The flames of the oil leak served as a backdrop for Julian's red cyborg eyes glowing menacingly from the depths of his long, black hair, which was matted with grime and dirt from the surrounding dust.

Darien resolved to meet his nemesis face to face. He would not be defeated lying down. He pulled himself up, surprised to be able to stand. Darien felt the heat of the flames on his skin, but he was determined not to flinch away from it; instead, he summoned his remaining strength and slowly walked toward Julian. The air smelled of burning oil and smoke and hung thickly in the air, acrid and harsh.

This would be their final fight. Darien would need to confront Julian here and now.

CHAPTER

FIFTY

Kira was in shock as she beheld the wanton destruction of her beloved hometown. Clouds of smoke billowed from the ruins and echoed with the cries of pain from her fellow citizens. Gritting her teeth, she charged forward with single-minded ferocity, clacking off shots from her submachine gun at the cyborg brutes who dared to besiege her home. An army of unforgiving Corsairs surged through the broken streets, intent on pillaging every inch of her home. Summoning all her strength, she charged into battle, firing her submachine gun with unwavering courage and precision. Every bullet was an act of vengeance, piercing through the enemy lines like a death scythe. She unloaded clip after clip until she reached the doorway of Bob Adams' home, one of the town's cooks.

"It's Kira," she yelled, banging on the door. "Let me in!"

She felt Raymond, Voltaire, and Swift approach behind her. They huddled behind a horse post in front of the home, waiting for the door to open.

"Bob!" Kira yelled impatiently as bullets began to ping around them. "It's Kira, open the—"

Just then, the door burst open, and the familiar face of Bob looked at her wide-eyed from the doorway. He was an obese man, middle-aged. Certainly not a fighter, as accentuated by him holding his gun out of the doorway and firing it wildly and blindly down the road. He had always been kind to Kira and her family but had his own demons found at the bottom of alcohol bottles.

"Kira, Swift," he said as they ran into his home. "You're alive! And who are these..." He stared incredulously at Raymond and Voltaire.

"It's okay," Kira said. "They're with me."

Bob couldn't break his stare of disbelief with Voltaire, the walking android. Rarely, if ever, would they see an android appear on the Frontier.

"Many thanks for allowing entrance into this place of dwelling," Voltaire said with a jarringly calm voice.

"But it—" Bob said.

"Bob," Kira said, putting her hand on his shoulder to shake him. "Where is my brother? Is Owen safe? Where are the kids?"

"Owen is okay," Bob said, shaking his head. "He's safe...he's just seen a lot. We've seen a lot, what those Raiders did..."

Kira's heart sank. Owen was just a boy, sick with Crimson Fever. One of the primary reasons she left the town in the first place was to find Guaritore, the Healer, to bring help to Owen and the other townspeople. She couldn't just stand by and watch more people get sick and die like her mother. But now, she cursed herself for ever leaving Owen's side. She couldn't imagine how alone he felt during all of this. She had to get to him.

"Where is he?" Kira asked.

"Oh god." Bob shook his head, peering out his window as more Corsairs trickled onto their roads. "Well, he's at the mess hall. All of the sick have been there since the beginning of all this. We've been using it to house all of the people who were hurt."

"Doctor Kryze?" Kira asked.

"No," Bob said, shaking his head. "He was one of the first that's killed by the Raiders. We've been trying to take care of your brother and the other sick ones, but with everything going—"

"It's okay," Kira said, nodding at Raymond. "He's a doctor. I need to get him there."

"But..." Bob stammered. "You can't be serious about going back out there! There's too many... How are you going to—"

"Bob," Kira said, touching his shoulder again. "Bob, listen. Go up to the second floor. Reload your gun, and you're going to have to create some cover fire for us. We're going."

Bob Adams nodded, his jowls jiggling in tandem. "Go out the back." He pointed at the kitchen area. "You'd best head out that way, but you'll have to cut through the Krugers' and Rooneys' houses. Kira, are you sure?"

"Yeah, Bob," Kira said, already moving. "Thank you!"

Bob called after her, "I'll radio ahead!" He turned to Raymond and the androids, "Stay close together, I'll—"

Just then, Kira heard the shattering of a window. The cyborgs were just outside of Bob's house.

"Go!" Bob said, firing at the intruders out the window. The last Kira saw of him; he was backpedaling up the stairs, covering their escape.

"Let's go!" Kira said to Raymond, Voltaire, and Swift.

The pings of stray bullets broke the glass jars near her head. Kira ducked low, bursting through the back door. Raymond and the robots spilled behind after her, bumping into her as they stumbled out and down the steps of Bob's back porch area.

"Swift!" Kira said as the ambient sounds of lethal gunfire were heard everywhere. "You lead the way. Get us to the mess hall!"

Swift hummed diligently, taking off like a gust of wind. He ran toward the Kruger household. There were only plots of dry dirt between the Adams and Kruger homes. The only delineation of property barrier was a small area of gardening that Dina Kruger would take care of. The garden had been trampled upon, with the food taken and eaten.

"Come on!" Kira said, signaling for Raymond and Voltaire to keep up.

She ran across the dirt path as fast as she could, keeping her head down just enough to see Swift out of the Kruger's doorway, hoping to signal that it was safe. Kira dared not look up any further than to see where she was running. The houses around them had windows where the enemy could be hiding and waiting to fire at them. As she made it to the Kruger's back door, Swift went ahead into the house. Kira shuffled Raymond and Voltaire in through the door as she looked back at Bob Adams' house. A Corsair suddenly appeared at one of his windows.

"Get inside," Kira yelled, taking cover behind the doorway and firing her gun back at the Adams' house window. "Go, go, get down!"

Her vision and hands trembled with the spasticity of adrenaline-fueled blood coursing through her veins. She fired just enough at the window to see the figure at the window sneak away in cover. Kira turned and pushed past Raymond to continue following Swift. The Krugers' house was empty and only illuminated by the sun shining through windows. The house boomed and shook from an explosion. Dust from a ceiling boom came down in a mist in front of her. The house had been hit with some kind of explosive. Behind her, the back door they came through erupted into broken splinters of wood from gunfire.

Swift took them through a library room. This must have been where Dina and Grisha Kruger sat and read books. She had never been here before, but Grisha loved history. The bookshelves had fallen over, and the fireplace was empty with ash. For a moment, she lamented such a beautiful, quiet, and quaint household being ruined by this wanton destruction.

Kira looked around and saw Swift circling a fallen bookshelf toward a door at the side of the house. The robot fox broke through their doorway with a fierce jump. There was another small area of dirt they would need to cross to make it next door to the Rooney household. As Kira ran at a full sprint across the open area, she could see the main road to her right. There were cyborgs and Remnant townspeople locked in intense firefights. She stopped in place as a cyborg turned around to see her. Kira was frozen by the decision to keep running or engage this enemy.

"Go, go." Raymond pushed her ahead. "Keep going!"

Kira lurched forward, falling onto her hands and knees into the doorway of the Rooney home. Raymond and Voltaire fell in behind her as the doorway behind them was blown open by an explosion.

She shook herself back into focus. "Thanks. Let's go." She pulled up Raymond. She tried to take Voltaire's hand to pick him up, but he was too heavy to move.

"Much appreciation is given for the assistance," Voltaire said, rising to his feet. "The danger is most—"

"Okay, okay," Kira shoved him forward as the house was hit again with an explosion. "You can tell us later!"

Out the windows, they could see the Corsairs from the road pointing at them. Suddenly, the Rooney household became a cacophony of explosions and broken wood flying around them.

Swift let out a bark-like hum. He was pointing toward a staircase. Kira followed Raymond and Voltaire up the stairs. They moved frantically, feeling like the world behind them was coming apart. Kira felt like a bloodthirsty creature was in chase, only inches behind her.

"Now what?" Raymond asked, trying to peer out the window but wincing backward when bullets again tore up the window and wall. "Where do we go?"

Kira turned to Swift, who was jumping up at the door on the ceiling into an attic area.

"There?" Kira asked as the staircase behind them began to break apart. She felt the floorboards below her buckle.

Raymond jumped up, grabbed the rope, and pulled down the door. Another ladder-like rope came down. One by one, they made it up to the attic area. Swift jumped up to the attic easily, but Voltaire looked up and could not bring himself up the rope without causing the wooden attic floor to break apart.

"This singular physical form possesses too much mass," Voltaire said, looking up at them. "It is my hope to meet again short—"

"Voltaire!" Kira yelled out.

The wooden floors below him gave out as he fell into a cloud of dust and smoke. Raymond and Kira reeled back at the plume of dust that hit their faces, causing them to cough. They had lost their android companion, and the house was quickly coming apart.

Kira and Raymond both stood there in shock. Voltaire disappeared into the dust cloud as the second floor collapsed. Gunfire and explosions erupted below. Voltaire was likely surrounded by cyborgs.

"Come on, lower me down," Raymond said, grabbing the rope.

Kira was torn apart by the decision that needed to be made. The android would not survive the fall and enemy onslaught. If they went down to try and save him, they would likely be killed or captured. This whole plan would go to waste. She needed to get to Owen and the other townspeople. She needed to get Raymond to them. They needed to move now.

"No," Kira said, with her voice shaking, "Raymond, we need to keep moving."

"What?" Raymond said, "We can't just leave him."

"Raymond," Kira said, "You know it as well as I do. He's gone. We need to go. We can't stay here."

Raymond shook his head, looking at the dust cloud below. "Okay," he said reluctantly. "Let's go then."

Swift hummed at a doorway on the wall. The roof was already breaking apart, and the blue sky was seen overhead. Kira opened the door, revealing an open area of flat roofing. There were two chairs here. She remembered seeing Daniel and Rebecca Rooney sitting there on evenings, waving to the townspeople below. Those were the old days. Now, the chairs were on their sides, the railings broken apart. There was a dead Raider body slumped over one.

Swift yelped and motioned toward the building below. It was the mess hall. They were there. But from the Rooney's third-story rooftop, there was an empty void to mess hall's rooftop. Kira peered down over the edge. There was only a thin alley between the two buildings, but it was still a daunting distance.

"We're going to have to jump," Kira said, turning back to Raymond.

He seemed like he was already making his own mental calculations, "And that's where all the sick and injured are?" He pointed down at the mess hall.

Kira nodded.

"Well then, I guess we're going to have to jump," he said, then took a deep breath.

Swift suddenly jumped from the house rooftop, landing on the mess hall's roof below. He rolled along the rooftop somewhat but immediately hopped up, beckoning Kira and Raymond to follow.

Kira thought about the logistics of the jump. She was carrying a submachine gun and backpack. She needed to be as light as possible and have her hands free. Kira threw the backpack onto the rooftop, as well as her gun. Raymond followed suit, throwing his gear across the alley. During all this, they felt the house below them crumbling apart. Kira stepped back; she would only have about 10 paces of a running start for the jump.

"Together?" Raymond asked, standing beside her. He had a look of veiled uncertainty on his face that likely mirrored hers.

She nodded, trying to smile, but her body was consumed with adrenaline. Her face instead contorted into a nervous spasm.

Just then, the entire house below them felt like it had just lost its last straw of structural integrity. It was now or never. Kira took off, running at full speed before kicking off the corner of the rooftop. As she ran, she felt Raymond running alongside her, somewhat behind. She figured one of them would jump first and then the other, but there was no time as the house seemed to be coming apart.

With a stroke of luck to the exact millisecond, the house began falling to the ground just as they made the jump. This likely gave Kira a few fewer feet of height to jump. Nevertheless, it was still an eternity before she made an impact on the mess hall rooftop. It was not any longer than a 10-foot drop, but she took care to plant her feet strong, then roll to her side to absorb the impact.

The rough wooden rooftop met her legs as she landed with an impact mostly absorbed by her shoulder and back. She felt the force overwhelm her feet and knees and ripple up through her spine to the base of her neck. It hurt, but not in a terrible way.

She grunted as she rolled across the rooftop, hearing Raymond doing the same.

She ended up on her back, afraid to move, as that would highlight any broken bones or other serious injuries she sustained from the fall. Kira stared at the blue sky, with the symphony of gunfire and explosions seeming to drown out. She wanted to lie there forever, just like when she and Benny would spend hours staring at the sky and stars on the mess hall rooftop. She wondered where he was, whether he was still alive.

"Kira." Raymond grunted. "You alright?"

He crawled over, holding his ribs, with a look of pain on his face.

Kira shook herself back into attention; she ignored the possibility of injury and sat herself up. Every muscle in her body ached, but she was able to push herself up to stand.

"I'm alright. Are you?"

Raymond struggled to bring himself up to stand. He was older than she was, perhaps in his 30's or 40's. Younger than her dad had been, but certainly not at an age to be jumping between rooftops for leisure.

"I think so," Raymond said, steadying himself to stand. "Possibly some rib fractures, maybe a ligamentous tear here and there, but I'll be okay. Maybe." He attempted a smile.

A stray bullet zoomed over their heads. They were exposed on the rooftop. Kira ducked; the action of squatting sent pain down her right hip. She must have injured it from the fall. Swift was already beckoning them to make their way to the rooftop doorway.

Kira grabbed her gun and gear. There were townspeople below. She had made it so far and back. From her capture by the Aggromen, to their escape into the temple, massacre of the Zeltan soldier as they escaped, to the horde of the undead, her near-death experience with the train falling into the chasm, their journey across the mountains, and finally her arrival back to her town-turned-warzone, she somehow survived all of it and made it back. Despite everyone's doubts and against all odds of success, here she was, she made it. She was proof to herself and to the world that her will to survive had conquered all. There wasn't a person on planet Mars who could stop her now, not after all they had been through.

FIFTY-ONE

The flames of the oil leak surrounded Captain Darien and his former mentor Julian, trapping them in a haze of orange and yellow fire. Julian's red cyborg eyes glowed menacingly from the depths of his long, black hair, which was matted with grime and dirt from the surrounding dust.

Darien felt the heat of the flames on his skin, but he was determined not to flinch away from it; instead, he stood strong despite it and moved closer to Julian. The air smelled of burning oil and smoke and hung thick in the air.

He had seen his mentor fight before and knew that even this worn-out version of him still posed a great danger. Darien himself was significantly wounded, riddled with bullet wounds and caustic injuries. But he was determined to win, no matter what it took. This was the original mission he set out to accomplish, there, standing directly in front of him.

"We always knew it would come down to this," Julian said, with his arms outstretched.

"You always taught me to visualize it," Darien said, spitting blood from his mouth. "Whatever my goal, whatever my mission. Visualize the outcome, and make it happen."

"That's right." Julian nodded approvingly.

"I've seen myself dragging you back to the Capital," Darien said. "One way or another, that will happen. I will bring you in to answer for your crimes against the King—"

"You have no idea what game you're playing, Captain."

"Then tell me!" Darien screamed. "Why, Julian? Why did you kill all of those Rangers? Our brothers? My team?"

"For a much higher purpose." Julian flicked back the hair covering his face, his eyes glowing bright despite the midday sun. "You've been chosen, Darien."

"By who?!"

"By the few of us enlightened to the truth," Julian said. "That box in there… the Ark. We can use it to achieve ascendancy."

"What *is* that?" Darien said. As they talked, they circled each other cautiously, as they remained trapped within the wall of fire.

"We can leave this planet. We can find out what's up there," Julian said, pointing up to the sky."

"Then we will bring the Ark back to the Capital," Darien said. "The High Council will decide what to do with it."

Julian laughed, "Oh just *forget* about the Council, the King, all of their bureaucratic mess. Ascendancy is not for everyone. They are not worthy. But *you* are. That's why we chose you."

"I don't want it," Darien said plainly. "You've killed soldiers of the Crown, Julian. My Rangers. You need to answer for your crimes."

"I will do no such thing," Julian said. "Perhaps I was a fool for thinking you could join us. You can either chose the Kingdom that has simply used and manipulated you for your whole life, or you can join me. We can discover the secrets of our past and future together."

Darien only considered it for a moment. But then he remembered his training and purpose. It was not only for the Kingdom, but for his brothers in arms. The soldiers next to him, those who have passed, all of his comrades on the battlefield. He cared little for answers or the promise of whatever waited for them in the skies and space. Julian betrayed them, and he needed to be brought in or die. No one could convince Darien otherwise. His men died for this, and he would not betray their memory. Marcus and Tristan continued to fight, these lowly born continued to defy all odds and struggled to survive.

"For your crimes against the King and people of the Zeltan Kingdom," Darien announced boldly, "You are hereby placed under arrest to stand trial before the King and High Council. Do you comply?" "I do not."

"Good," Darien said. "Let's get on with it then."

Julian smiled as he walked menacingly toward Darien, stepping into the ring of fire. He abruptly charged forward with a flurry of punches. Darien managed to dodge or block most of them, but one strike hit him square in the chest, sending him flying backward and into the flames. He felt the pain searing through his body as he scrambled out of the way just in time to avoid another attack.

Darien gritted his teeth, determined not to give up. He struggled to his feet, dodging and weaving Julian's fists. Not caring anymore if he got hurt, Darien began hammering Julian with punches of his own.

The force of the blows knocked Julian back, but he was still on his feet. His cyborg enhancements had allowed him to absorb most of the damage. Suddenly, Julian lashed out at Darien with unusual strength and knocked him back into the burning oil slick again. Darien knew that Julian was strong, but the impact made him question his ability to defeat his former mentor.

Darien managed to roll out of the way in time and regain his footing a few meters away from the flames. He knew this fight was becoming more dangerous by the second, and he had no choice but to keep pushing forward and hope for a miracle.

He charged forward, faster than ever before, pushing deep into Julian's defense until, finally, he broke through and connected a powerful uppercut straight into Julian's jaw that sent him flying into the ring of fire again.

Darien was no match for his former mentor's enhanced strength and agility. However, he looked into his former mentor's menacing artificial eyes. For a moment, Darien could swear he could see the shadow of Julian's former self. *Was this a test?* Darien couldn't let his mentor down now. For years, he blamed himself for leaving Julian. He blamed himself for being a disappointment.

Today would not be a disappointment. Darien would win this fight.

"It's time to earn your destiny," Julian said with a smirk.

Julian delivered punch after punch. Darien could barely stay conscious, but his inner voice screamed to fight back. Just as it seemed like Julian would win, Darien managed to find an opening and use it to gain leverage against him. He ducked one punch, hit Julian with a swift blow to the abdomen, and delivered a powerful uppercut that sent Julian flying through the air. Darien grabbed Julian's leg in mid-air and slammed him to the ground.

Before long, Darien managed to put Julian in a chokehold. They wrestled back and forth, trying to gain leverage over each other with interlocked arms and legs. In Darien's injured state, this would be the only way he could defeat Julian, using his body to trap him into submission. The struggle between them seemed to last ages. Darien remembered the close-combat grappling drills from when he was a boy. Even seconds with a formidable opponent would deplete one's strength. After this long journey and this most recent battle, even with his superhuman strength and stamina, Darien struggled for dominance with Julian.

On and on, they struggled, but Darien persisted. Any time he felt his strength leaving, he remembered the names of all his fallen comrades.

Nicholas.

Ryan.

Scott.

Roland.

Carl.

David.

Jason.

Ethan.

Zachary.

Vincent.

Barrett.

They were his brothers. Killed in battle under his leadership. They trusted him. Gave their lives for him. What kind of leader would he be if he could not defeat their enemy, who was finally in his grasp? This was a moment of victory. Darien would not let their sacrifices go to waste.

Darien regained an untapped reservoir of strength that he had never imagined, even despite a lifetime of hard training and pushing his body to the very limits of physical and mental exhaustion. Here, he felt himself transcend even the very logic of Zeltan physiology, ignoring his injuries completely and feeling re-energized as if he had started the battle anew.

The grappling between Darien and Julian increasingly became one-sided. There was a non-verbal sense of dominance that overtook the duel. Julian's squirms and attempts to break free grew less frequent and intense. With no more fight left in him, Julian fell to the ground as the fires raged around them.

Darien continued squeezing his arm around Julian's neck until he felt the body go completely limp. To be sure, he held on for several minutes afterwards before letting go. Darien watched him carefully and checked a pulse. None. The evil soldier wasn't breathing. And finally, the red glow from his eyes went dim. Julian, the former Ranger Captain, traitor to the Kingdom, was dead.

Darien, whether through unimaginable exhaustion or disbelief that the fight was over, sat there in a daze. His lungs screamed in pain as he heaved for oxygen amidst the increasingly thick, smoky air. His body was at total collapse, but it took him exactly as far as he needed to go. Today, Darien completed his mission.

"For the Kingdom," Darien said, closing his eyes.

FIFTY-TWO

Raymond Redmin's body ached and flared in pangs of pain as he forced himself to jog towards the rooftop door. The madness continued around him. Rockets flew through the air, along with the incessant popping of gunfire on the road below and the thunder of warfare outside the town. As they closed the door behind them to the narrow stairwell, Raymond and Kira had some respite from the chaos outside. Regrettably, this only heightened his physical suffering, making it more apparent and unbearable.

"Hey, are you okay?" Kira whispered, turning around as she stalked down the staircase.

"I'm fine," Raymond lied. He put weight on his leg, and it buckled.

As a doctor, he couldn't help but self-diagnose himself. He certainly broke some ribs. Every breath and movement sent pain pulsing through him. He had to take short, shallow breaths, feeling his heart beating heavily in his ears. As for his right ankle, he had likely broken it. The lateral malleolus and fibula were tender. As he could bear some weight, albeit with inexplicable pain, he sensed it wasn't a catastrophic displaced fracture. At least, he hoped not.

What orthopedic surgeries could even be performed here that didn't involve grotesque cybernetic augmentation?

He followed Kira to a closed door. She put her ear to the door, listening intently. Raymond could hear the muffled voices of many people. Suddenly, Kira's face changed. It was a mix of shock and relief. She grabbed the door handle and started to push it open.

"Wait," Raymond said, unsure of what they would find behind that door. "Are you sure?"

Kira smiled and nodded. "We're here."

She pushed the door opened to a bustling tavern. However, it was not full of guests or patrons drinking beer. Instead, it was busy with Remnant townspeople rushing back and forth carrying wounded and medical supplies. Raymond and Kira looked around. They were on a second-story balcony, looking down. This was their makeshift medical facility.

"Oh my god," Raymond said, marveling at this small war zone hospital.

"Hey! Who's..." yelled a voice below. "Wait, is that..."

Kira stood silently, dropping her gun to the floor. Raymond couldn't see her face from behind her but could tell tears were streaming down her face. Her hands trembled, and she attempted a response.

"It's me," she said weakly. "It's me, I'm back."

"It's Kira!" a man said from below. "Guys, it's Kira, she made it back!"

One by one, the townspeople declared in joy that she had returned. They came up the stairs to the second floor to hug and welcome her. They hugged her as she broke down in tears and exhaustion.

Raymond hung back, watching the heartwarming reunion unfold. He watched in amazement at the outpouring of emotion and relief that swept over the room. It was obvious that Kira was loved and respected by everyone in the town. It truly did warm his weary heart to see how much they cared for her. He couldn't help but feel a pang of envy, wishing he still had something like that in his life.

He moved around the perimeter of the room, catching glimpses of people he had never met before. They were busy tending to the wounded with makeshift bandages and splints. The room had a pungent smell of burnt flesh and antiseptic, and the sound of pain-filled moans filled the air.

Despite the chaos, there was a sense of order. People knew their roles and were working together in harmony. Raymond watched as a young girl brought a tray of water and bandages to a man with a gunshot wound. The man smiled weakly at the girl and thanked her.

Raymond had seen many war zones, but this was different. These people were not soldiers or trained medical personnel. They were ordinary people who had come together in a time of crisis to help each other. It was inspiring.

"Hey, who are you supposed to be?" a gruff townsman with a thick mustache asked as he pointed a gun in Raymond's face.

Raymond didn't dare move, but the pain in his ribs and leg was nearly forcing him to shift in place. He couldn't even formulate the words to respond. The full explanation would be too long, difficult, and downright implausible. He was frankly too tired to give a coherent response.

"Well?" the man said impatiently. "Hey! Who the hell is this guy? Does anyone know who this guy is?"

The booms of war outside rattled the building once again. Some of the townspeople who had been hugging and welcoming Kira turned toward Raymond. He felt their judgmental and fear-stricken eyes send daggers through him.

"He's with me." Kira sniffed through her tears. "It's okay; he's with me."

Kira walked toward Raymond, taking his arm. He felt her gently guiding him toward an empty chair.

"Everyone," she said, speaking to a silent crowd before them. "This is Raymond Redmin. He's my friend. I couldn't have made it back without him. I trust my life with him."

"Well." The burly man with the mustache softened, lowering his gun. "If you truly got her back here. Then you have my thanks."

Raymond nodded, but even that action sent pain through his body.

"He's a doctor," Kira said. "He can help us."

"He's a doctor?" one of the women asked. "Well, of course, he can help us. By the blue god, it's a miracle."

"It's the prophecy fulfilled!" someone echoed.

"Thank the blue god," another said in relief.

Kira sighed, giving Raymond a grin. "About that—"

"It's a story for later," Raymond said. There were enemies outside the building and death at the door. There would be plenty of time to explain how he crashed here on a spaceship from that blue god planet, hundreds of years displaced.

"Right," Kira said. "Well, let's get him fixed up first. Where is my brother? Can you take me to him?"

"Owen is downstairs," a lady said, taking Kira with her. "He is okay. The poor boy nearly slept through the entire madness these past few days. He continues to have a fever..."

The townspeople went down the stairs with Kira, leaving Raymond alone with the man with the thick mustache.

"So," he said, peering out a nearby window at the battle that unfolded outside, "you're a doctor, huh?"

Raymond nodded. He hadn't done much doctoring lately, more so running and shooting guns, "I'm a doctor. I should be able to help."

"Hmm." The mustached man grunted. "Well, before you help with the patients, let me ask you something."

"What is it?"

"Do you know about this... Ark?" the man said, studying Raymond's face.

Raymond recalled the Ark being mentioned by the spaceship crew when he was crashing down to the planet, as well as in the Aggromen encampment. But yet, he still had no idea what it was.

"I don't know," Raymond said. "All I know is that it's important and that I was supposed to find it. Do you know where it is?"

"Well, yeah," the man said, "Come on then. It's downstairs."

Downstairs?! Raymond thought. After all they had been through, this truly felt like they had arrived at their destination. *Just what is this damn Ark?*

Raymond hobbled down the stairs, following the man. He took slight offense that the crowd of townspeople left him alone with this man who clearly had no intention of helping Raymond with his injuries nor cared to wait up for him. Raymond limped and groaned past numerous people on the main floor as he passed dozens of injured on makeshift beds; rolls of bandages and blood-soaked rags littered the floors.

The man led him to a back room. Raymond thought perhaps he was leading him toward a room with someone severely injured, perhaps someone with a bullet wound injury. Instead, it was a large, empty kitchen with medical supplies haphazardly lying around. People frantically kept coming in and out of the room, looking for new supplies that seemed to be scattered randomly everywhere.

"My name is Marco." The mustached man pointed at himself, "Perhaps you can tell us what it's supposed to be then." He walked toward a large box.

The box was reinforced with sleek gold. It was ornately decorated with wings on the four corners. Raymond wondered if it was a lavish funeral casket. He wondered how they were able to get it into the building. It looked to be hundreds of pounds and full of heavy equipment. And just as he approached the box, he shuddered in surprise at the writing on it.

United Space Exploration Coalition, in collaboration with Earth Alliance, 2075.

"What the hell?" Raymond said.

"This was taken off of the spaceship that crashed," Marco said. "The Raiders, they took it and brought it here. This is what the cyborgs are coming for."

"This?" Raymond asked with utter confusion. "*This* is why they are attacking? What is this box? What could possibly be so—"

A wide green laser suddenly emanated from the top. It began to scan Raymond's face. At first, he withdrew in fear, but eventually allowed to complete scanning. When it was done, the top cover opened slowly. These boxes were about the size of two people across and one person in length. For its height, it came up to about Raymond's waist. For a moment, Raymond was worried there would be a person inside. Instead, what he found shocked him to his core.

A coordinated unfolding of several tables and machinery revealed an entire portable workstation within the cargo box. A table with a wide screen unfolded forward.

"What the hell is it doing? Raymond said.

"I don't know," Marco said, shocked. "It… it never did that before."

"Welcome," a female voice greeted Raymond. "Biometric scan commencing. Stand by."

Raymond stood frozen in fear and curiosity as another green laser passed over his face.

"Dr. Raymond Redmin. Access granted to the medical workstation."

"How did you do that?" Marco asked. "It never said anything like that to us. We have all tried to open it and turn it on. It sent an electrical shock to anyone that tried to open it. But it just... opened by you just being here."

Raymond stepped forward with infinite curiosity. He had forgotten about all his injuries and was far too enamored by this apparent Earth-based technology. 2075? That was decades after he had been frozen. He wondered what this portable workstation would yield.

"What is your first request?" the computer voice asked.

"I don't know," Raymond said meekly. "What do you do?"

"Several critical injuries detected in the vicinity," the computer voice said. "May I suggest synthesizing analgesics and plasma replacement?"

Raymond was taken aback. *Did she say synthesizing?* Certainly, analgesics for pain and plasma replacement for blood loss would be ideal in the current situation. But how or where would this be synthesized? He was far too curious to explore the details.

"Yes," he said. "Um, do that."

"Forging sample," the computer said as the box hummed.

One of the tables unfolded itself to reveal a hanging drip, almost like a coffee dispenser. A clear plastic bag was automatically dispensed, and liquid poured into it.

"It never did that before," Marco said in awe. He stood beside Raymond as they stared at the liquid dripping into the bag.

After a few minutes, the dripping stopped, and suddenly, a small laser sealed the bag shut. A small opaque film of plastic was stamped over it with plastic.

Morphine 8mg / 100ml

After all the fantastical and absurd things he had dealt with: landing on Mars 200 years in the future, savages and giant rats, evil zombies, giant robot suits, a town of zen robots, a war on the deserts of Mars; Raymond singularly found this to be the most fascinating. Within minutes, this cargo box synthesized a pain medication from seemingly nowhere.

As he marveled at the bag of medication before him, the machine was already making a second bag, this one full of red liquid. Just as it promised, it was 2 units of fresh plasma.

"Please browse the database or ask for further recommendations," the computer voice said as the screen showcased an enormous list.

Raymond scrolled down the list with his hand. He couldn't believe how this was possible. There were literally thousands of medications here. He could synthesize skin sealants, orthopedic splinting and crutches, and even gas compounds. He was dumbfounded at how the cargo box could possibly store all the materials to make these compounds. He even looked at the top of the screen, which had an option "synthesize custom compound".

This was a goddamn Pandora's box. It could make *anything*. Raymond wondered if the Raiders and Corsairs knew this, and that's why it was so highly sought after.

Raymond tried to shake his curiosity, knowing he needed to tend to the injured and sick soon. He immediately started the queue of synthesizing plasma, pain medications, antibiotics, and medical sealant. He told Marco to gather these and to tell the others that he would be coming out soon to administer them.

However, as the machine started making these miracle products, he couldn't help scrolling through the database and seeing some very peculiar entries that he didn't dare synthesize.

Genomic Alteration Compound #103187

Gravitational Mercury

Dimensional Transcendent DMTA

Fission Core Uranium

Some of these entries frightened Raymond. *Could this box possibly create these impossible compounds, seemingly out of nothing?*

He typed into the search bar out of curiosity, and there it was.

Raymond Redmin base DNA.

FIFTY-THREE

Benny opened his eyes, but his body was covered with sand and dirt. He coughed, and a wave of grit flowed from between his lips. He coughed painfully and reached up to wipe the stinging particles out of his eyes but only managed to smear them around. The world around him was a blurry mess of continuing gunfire, explosions, and incessantly burning fire and smoke. Just barely visible through the thick haze was the gorgeous blue sky, taunting them with its irony. As Benny stared upward with envy at the unspoiled sky above, another explosion rocked the ground beneath him, sending shrapnel flying everywhere.

He couldn't tell how long he had been unconscious, but waking up to the same battlefield hell meant it couldn't have been very long. To his left lay Rudy, body twisted at an impossible angle and glassy, lifeless eyes staring back at Benny. To his right, Casey was throwing himself into battle without reservation. His gun blazed with smoke and muzzle fire as bullets whizzed by from every angle.

With gritted teeth, Benny crawled forward on his hands and knees, braving through the chaos. His heart pounded against his chest as bullets whizzed past him in every direction imaginable.

As Benny tried to find some sense of clarity in the chaos surrounding him, he felt heat radiating off the molten metal nearby. Smoke filled his lungs as he tried to take deep breaths. Fear and adrenaline pumping through every vein in his body heightened all his senses. The smell of gunpowder and blood was so strong that he gagged. With each blink of his eyes and swallow of air came a new sound: bullets ricocheting off metal, people screaming in agony, boots scrambling across rough terrain.

Benny saw Casey continue his battle against the intruders, who crept on him from all sides. Suddenly, Casey jerked forward, holding his abdomen. He was shot.

"Casey!" Benny said with a hoarse voice, gasping to breathe.

Casey turned around. He looked surprised to see Benny alive.

"Keep... fightin'!" Casey yelled.

And without warning, Casey was thrown violently forward, a geyser of blood erupting and cascading down the side of his neck. Seething with rage, he wheeled round to retaliate, but an unfathomable barrage of bullets met him in return. Benny watched in paralyzing horror as the Red Rider convulsed and quivered in agony until eventually collapsing on the ground, defeated and lifeless.

Casey was dead.

I'm sorry... Benny thought. He was useless to help his friend and had to watch him killed in front of him. Benny's heart sank into an abyss of despair.

Benny painfully dragged himself across the ground to reach for a weapon despite his broken limbs barely functioning. Panic and fear coursed through him as he saw them coming closer: a legion of nightmarish cyborgs with guns pointed at his wrecked body. Benny's breath quickened in anticipation of what was to come, expecting to taste the cold kiss of death any moment. Instead, he felt an immense force on his head as one of their guns collided with his skull, sending him spiraling back into the abyss of unconsciousness.

As he fell back into blissful sleep, he hoped that, perhaps, he had done enough to save the town—and save Kira.

FIFTY-FOUR

Raymond and Kira worked diligently, directing the able-bodied townspeople around the makeshift hospital within the former tavern. Tables had been cleared off, with the injured placed on them. Several cots and mattresses had been placed on the open floor. Some Red Riders who had come with George Wallace's contingent from Sierra Outpost arrived to help. In total, there were about 30-40 injured.

With equal focus for Raymond, there was a second eating area, and this was where the few people stricken with Crimson Fever were located. To Raymond, it was a bizarre illness that did not appear particularly virulent, based on their reports to him. However, there were no available cures, and nearly everyone stricken with it would fatally succumb to the illness.

He sat with Kira, looking over Owen. He was a boy of 11-years, with the same rough yet youthful facial features as Kira. He lay on the bed, eyes closed, seemingly unaware of the mayhem outside their doors.

"Can you help him?" Kira asked through tears, holding Owen's hand and not looking away from him.

Raymond always knew to choose his words carefully with patients and their loved ones. "I'm going to give him medicines for the fever, as well as IV fluids, but I will need to figure out exactly what is causing his symptoms."

Kira nodded. It wasn't a yes or no answer to her question. There were no false promises but also no signals of uncertainty. He could provide supportive care for now. With their crude equipment, he was able to determine that Owen had a low-grade fever, low blood pressure, and an elevated heart rate. He would provide the analgesics, as well as normal saline solution, produced from the cargo box. The voice in the box referenced itself as Ember. And the box itself, it was indeed called the Ark.

Equally remarkable was the machine's ability to run diagnostic tests. It produced seemingly disposable tiny needles with only 1-2ml reservoirs. He had obtained samples from all the sick and injured. The machine immediately and incredibly provided Raymond with all of their diagnostic data. He would use this to determine how to help those sick with this apparent Crimson Fever.

"I'll just need a few drops of blood and run it through that machine," Raymond said.

"Of course," Kira said, moving aside. "Whatever you need to do."

Raymond took a new lancet produced by the Ark. He gave Owen's finger a tiny prick with the needle, and then he expressed 2-3 drops of blood that oozed into the waxy film within a small plaster container no bigger than a fingernail. As far as medical advancement, Raymond continued to marvel in utter fascination.

"I'll be back in a little bit." He gave Kira's shoulder a gentle pat as she stayed at Owen's bedside and laid her head down beside him.

Raymond made his way back through the infirmary. By now, most of the injured were receiving medical attention at Raymond's direction through the townspeople's helpers. The moans of pain had subsided with his administration of pain medication, and much of the surely fatal bleeding had been quickly abated with the tranexamic hemorrhage sealant he was able to quickly produce. The townspeople gave various words of thanks as he walked by. Suddenly, he was somewhat of a savior figure to them.

As he approached the cargo box, he couldn't help but feel a sense of unease. He knew he had to focus on the task at hand and not let his curiosity get the best of him. He needed to figure out what was causing Crimson Fever and how to cure it.

He inserted the small plaster container with Owen's blood sample into the cargo box and waited for the diagnostic data to come up. As he waited, he couldn't help but notice the peculiar entries he had seen earlier in the database. The ones that frightened him.

His mind wandered to the possibility of creating those impossible compounds. *What if it was possible?*

Raymond shook off these thoughts. He placed Owen's sample into the small tray in the machine. It quickly analyzed the droplets of blood with a hum and green laser that passed over the blood sample. Again, incredibly, the screen was immediately populated with Owen's laboratory data.

Feeling like he was back in his own time and home planet, Raymond felt a sense of comfort and familiarity looking over the report. It was displayed exactly as a doctor of Earth would have been able to interpret. Owen was dehydrated and anemic, and his white blood cell count was high with a neutrophilic left shift.

His CRP, ESR, and other inflammatory markers were elevated, as well as his Procalcitonin. The signs were pointing toward a bacterial infection.

As he scrolled through, he was amazed to see that even with this small sample of blood, he could glean this much information. His suspicions were confirmed as the machine dinged with an update. In a few minutes, it was able to culture, quickly grow, and identify any microbial infection in the blood. Sure enough, it identified it as a non-typable Mycobacterium.

Eureka, Raymond thought. Mycobacterium was certainly a bacterial organism species he was familiar with in his own time on Earth, but its variants were somewhat rare and very deadly, including Mycobacterium tuberculosis and the avian complex. Here, after hundreds of years on the terraformed sands of Mars, who knew what kind of evolved species they dealt with.

He wondered whether he could simply synthesize an antibiotic familiar to him that would have generally treated Mycobacterial infections. He thought, perhaps, a simple macrolide like Azithromycin and would build up from there. The other choices would certainly cause adverse effects he may not be able to adequately monitor here, especially on his own. And then, he remembered he was interacting with a supercomputer.

"Um, computer?" he asked with uncertainty.

"You may refer to me as Ember," she replied. "Unless you wish to change my designation."

"Oh, right." He grinned. "Ember. Can you provide me any recommendations for treating this patient's particular Mycobacterial infection?"

"Yes, Dr. Redmin," Ember replied. "Here are several options."

The computer populated with about a dozen entries, most of them were combinations of several drugs that Raymond was familiar with. However, some of the compounds below had unfamiliar names. Each entry provided a mechanism of action, adverse effects, and dosing.

Raymond was intrigued. Since he could understand the mechanism of action of these drugs, especially the unknown ones, he would feel comfortable giving them to these patients. However, he wanted to be sure, especially before treating this 11-year-old.

As he stood in deep thought, flipping through screens of chemical diagrams, he suddenly heard a voice from the back of the room. He thought he had been alone. Most of the townspeople were busy treating the sick and wounded and had since left him here to work in peace and quiet.

"Hello?" Raymond asked.

"Raymond Redmin," a figure appeared from a dimly lit corner of the room. "The man who fell from the sky."

Raymond instinctively backed up to run.

"Ah, ah," the figure said, holding a visible gun from his cloak.

The man was dressed as a citizen from Remnant, but his face was bandaged, and his clothes were tattered and bloodied from battle. Raymond wondered why he would possibly be holding him at gunpoint.

"Wait," Raymond said, with his hands up. "Why are you doing this?"

"Shh," the figure said, holding a finger to his bandaged face.

Raymond caught a glint of light shining from the metal of the hand. It was a robotic hand, like something out of a science fiction movie.

"Dr. Redmin," he said, with a devilish smile peeking through his bandaged face. "You must have many questions. I am here to finally bring you those answers. Let me introduce myself. They call me Blackheart."

Held up at gunpoint, Raymond realized how little he had come to fear death at this point. This entire ordeal felt like a fever dream. If this was the end, then so be it. But he wouldn't go down like a coward.

"You're a cyborg," Raymond said with his hands up. "You know, I could yell out for help right now, and all of these Remnant people are just outside this door in the next room."

The bandaged-faced cyborg was silent for a moment. "You could do that, but then you'll never find out what you're doing here or why you're here. You don't realize it fully yet, but you need me, Dr. Redmin."

"Why would I need you?"

"This artifact here." He lightly kicked a box. "This Ark. This the answer to everything. We've all been marooned here on this planet for 200 years. There's a whole universe out there that's forgotten about us. Why? Why suddenly did you all return now? Are there more of you coming? We're gonna find out. You're part of that answer, Dr. Redmin."

Raymond thought for a moment. He sure would like to know what in the world was going on. For days, he had been swept along this unbelievable roller coaster of an adventure with little time to process. *Why am I here? Would this deranged-appearing cyborg be able to give me answers?*

"Then tell me," Raymond said. "Tell me what you know about what happened, what I'm doing here."

Blackheart lowered his gun, shaking his head. "Oh no, Dr. Redmin. That's not how this works. The answers come later. You and I are going to have to trust each other first. This is going to be a mutual partnership."

"What exactly do you want from me?" Raymond asked.

"Well, for one thing, you are the only one who has been able to get this goddamned thing to work. I see the way this wench talks to you." He oddly caressed the surface of the Ark. "She's a bit sheepish around Daddy Blackheart, but I knew there was a way to get her to open up."

As Blackheart continued to monologue, Raymond looked around the room for a means to escape.

Blackheart began slowly unraveling the bandages off his face, revealing no actual injuries. He had braided, mangy black hair that fed into a neatly combed and pointed beard. He appeared to purposefully resemble a pirate from a children's book.

"Yer the only one who can get this thing to work, doctor," Blackheart said, nearly licking his lips in greed. "You can make this girl do damn near anything... *make* anything."

"I don't understand," Raymond said. "So, you want me to help you make things with this? This is for medicines for these people."

"Oh, it's far more than that," Blackheart said with his eyes wide and a smile revealing gold-colored teeth in the dim light of the room. "The possibilities are endless. Doctor, I'm telling you that this can make you and me very wealthy men. We can be kings."

"And if I say no?" Raymond asked, already knowing the answer.

"Oh." Blackheart showed an exaggerated frown. "Well, then I'd go on killin' everyone in here. I'd leave you be, of course. Maybe shoot ya in a leg or two, drag you back with us, and cut you up into a few pieces. Alive, of course. I'm sure we could prop you up on a hook and make you talk to this AI lady here. I just figured you wanted to do it that nice and proper way, is all."

Raymond fought not to visibly swallow the lump of fear building in his throat.

Blackheart paused, then let out a quiet laugh, giving a playful wave. "Eh, I'm just shittin' ya! I'd never do that to ya! We're friends now!"

Blackheart put his arm around Raymond. The metal of his cybernetic hand fell in a painful grasp around Raymond's already-injured shoulder.

"Help me with this here," Blackheart said directly into Raymond's ear, pointing at the Ark with his gun. "And I can tell you everything I know about your spaceship, about the people you were with, and about where you came from. And anything I don't know, we can find out together. I've got guns, I've got ships, I've got power. Everyone listens to Daddy Blackheart. You want me on your side. Come with me, and I'll leave these people alone. I'll call it off. You come with me, we take the boxes, and we go."

Raymond momentarily considered the prospect. He still had no idea why or how he got here. Perhaps this cyborg pirate could provide him with the resources to get some answers. Raymond thought he could convince him to order his men to leave Remnant. Raymond could save the town with a deal.

"If I go," Raymond said slowly, "would you order your men to stand down and never return?"

"You have my word." Blackheart lifted his robotic hand from Raymond's shoulder and put it over his own chest.

Raymond knew not to trust him, but if it could save these people, perhaps it would be worth going along with it for now.

"And after all," Blackheart continued, "you don't want to be stuck here, out in this godforsaken desert with these wretched people. They know nothing. You'll be living the rest of your days wondering what ever happened to you and where you came from. Out here, you'll just die as a tired old doctor treating these poor sand-groveling peasants."

That was the moment that jolted Raymond back to reality. Blackheart had spoken one thought too many. These were people out here. They were sick, injured, and needed help. Raymond had lost it all, transported away from his family and past life, but here he was with an opportunity to bring some purpose to what remained of his life. He owed it to Kira, who so bravely fought to save her beloved friends and family here.

Raymond nodded. "You're right."

Blackheart softened. "I knew you'd come around."

"This technology is truly fascinating," Raymond said, goading Blackheart. "The possibilities are endless."

"Indeed," Blackheart said, looking at the box alongside Raymond.

"I spent a long time looking through the database," Raymond said. "It's amazing what it can do. Watch this. Ember?"

"Yes, Dr. Redmin?" the Ark AI replied.

"Activate concussive defensive measures," Raymond said, bracing himself.

Blackheart scowled. "What the f—"

Suddenly, the Ark emitted a booming blast that threw Raymond backward. He didn't even feel himself hitting the wall behind him or falling to the ground. The world became a blur, and his ears rang in a high-pitched tone. Blackheart had been thrown to another part of the room. Even if he got his bearings first and found his gun to shoot Raymond, this blast would have alerted the townspeople in the adjacent room that there was trouble.

The force of the blast, compounding on his earlier injuries, was too much for Raymond to handle. He allowed himself to let go, and his eyelids, feeling like sandbags, shut closed, as the world around him felt like they were spinning into oblivion. The ringing sound in his ears faded. He drifted off to a peaceful sleep.

He imagined himself back with Eva and his little boy Jack. He could stay in his dreams with them forever.

FIFTY-FIVE

K ira picked her head up at the sound of a loud boom. By now, the fighting had been pushed far away from their medical aid building. This boom shook the walls and nearly knocked her off her chair.

"What was that?" Isabella Turner, the saloon manager, asked.

"I don't know," Kira said, gently putting Owen's hand back on the bed. "But you stay with my brother? I have to go check it out."

"Of course, dear," she said. "But please be careful."

Kira waded through the commotion in the main area with all the of the sick and injured. The townspeople pointed toward the back room.

"It came from in there!" said Leo Mitchell, the stagecoach mechanic.

Gunfire erupted. The townspeople scattered in fear.

"They're inside?" Kira said, not flinching.

She had no weapon available but ran to the back room. Two of the townspeople were at the doorway, exchanging fire.

"They've got the box," Ethan Edwards, the mining cart operator, said. "He's leaving with it!"

Kira fearlessly pushed past them, ducking to avoid gunfire. Raymond was in here, and she worried about what had happened to him. The back room was now a mess of clutter that all seemed to be scattered to the periphery of the room. The back door to the outside was open. The Ark was gone.

"Kira," a weak voice said.

It was Raymond; he was buried under a food preparation table and supply rack.

"Hey, get in here and help me!" Kira yelled.

They sheepishly came into the room, looking around for danger. Several of them helped Kira remove the heavy objects pinning Raymond down. He was bloodied and breathing weakly.

"Raymond," Kira lightly shook him. "Are you okay?"

"I'm... fine," he said, struggling to lift his arm. "Listen, someone go get that guy. There was a cyborg in here. He has the Ark."

"Go!" Kira said. "Go after him!" She turned to Raymond. "Okay, Ray, you need to tell me how I can help you."

"No, no," Raymond said. "Go help them. Just don't let him get away with it."

"Are you sure?"

"Go, go!" Raymond weakly pushed her away.

Kira reluctantly got up. She didn't want to leave him. He was looked pitiful. But the Ark, the possible cure to the Crimson

Fever, was being taken away. She couldn't let that happen. There were three others nearby, and she left Raymond in their care. She took off out the back door.

The bright sun outside made her wince and squint. They were in an alley between the mess hall and the horse stable.

"Down this way!" she heard to her side.

The townspeople were in pursuit of this apparent bandit. As she ran, she caught a glimpse of a figure wearing standard Frontier clothing, dragging the Ark. The ornate Ark had folded back in on itself. It had four spheres on its bottom, allowing surprisingly easy transport by pulling it by the handlebars on the side.

Kira met up with her townspeople on one side of the dirt road. The bandit was hidden behind cover on the other side. She caught another quick glimpse at him, and he seemed to have a cybernetic arm. Suddenly, he was joined by several other cyborgs.

The road erupted into a gunfight. Bullets flew back and forth across it as Kira ducked behind a wooden water barrel. It wouldn't hold out for very long as suitable protection. As she could decipher through the gunfight, the cyborgs were rapidly increasing in number.

She peered around and saw the cyborgs shuffling the cybernetic hand bandit to safety. She deduced he must have been important to them somehow. Meanwhile, he had left the box in the middle of the road.

This "Ark" was made of seemingly impenetrable material. Despite being dragged across the desert and hit with stray bullets and explosive ordinance, it barely seemed to have a scratch. It was still a perfect chrome gold that seemed somewhat unreal in its texture. She couldn't allow it to fall into the wrong hands. They needed these for her people. Kira couldn't even imagine what would happen if this fell into the wrong hands.

She looked around; her townspeople were dropping like flies. One by one, they were losing the firefight. None of them were particularly skilled in shooting, and the cyborgs appeared to be descending upon the Ark to take away with them. Every time someone went down, her heart sank. These were her friends and family that she had known her whole life. She had to do *something*.

Kira picked up a submachine from the fallen body of Max Barnes, the farmhand next to her. He was dead, and everyone else came out to pursue the cyborg. She grabbed the gun, took a deep breath, and resolved to continue fighting. She would be severely outnumbered but had to keep fighting.

Suddenly, gunfire erupted nearby. It was heavy automatic gunfire from her side of the road.

In a most unexpected entrance, there arrived an android with clothing tattered and ripped, revealing a completely robotic skeleton underneath.

"Voltaire?" Kira said, surprised.

The peace-promoting, philosophical android casually walked out of another building, holding a belt-fed machine gun. He unleashed a barrage of heavy fire that decimated the cyborg forces.

Kira was overjoyed to see him alive. She figured that they had lost him when the house collapsed earlier. She cursed herself for not checking to see whether he had survived that. Nevertheless, the North Haven android was a welcome ally, despite the jarring appearance of him using a deadly weapon.

"This one has decided," Voltaire said between bursts of gunfire, "to contribute to the efforts."

Kira knew this would be her opportunity. As the Corsairs panicked and sought cover, some running out into the open road, Kira spun out from cover and methodically squeezed off several bursts of gunfire at each of them.

She was able to hit about four of them in total. Their bodies violently jerked from the impact of her bullets. It was both a satisfying and unnerving feeling for Kira. The adrenaline nearly made her unaware that she had been shot just at her collarbone.

She dropped her gun and instinctively grabbed her arm as she went behind cover. Bright red blood already smeared her arm and the hand covering the wound. She didn't even feel the pain until moments later when it came rushing in like a tidal wave.

She looked over to Voltaire. He continued to uniformly walk toward the enemy while firing the enormous machine gun. Empty bullet casings hit the ground in a cascade.

"And in doing so," Voltaire continued, "my action may decrease the suffering of others."

Voltaire occasionally flinched back from the impact of gunfire. He was made of metal but was by no means impervious to the damage of a bullet. However, he remained trying to stand and fire his gun despite being riddled with bullets.

"Voltaire, no!" Kira said.

She watched in horror as the android was finally thrown back with his back against the wall. He continued to fire the machine gun from his sitting position. Kira tried to think of something to do, but she was pinned down herself. Bullets continued to ping at the barrel she hid behind. She felt helpless, watching his metal body convulse.

Kira began to think about North Haven, the peaceful community that seemed a world away from the death and destruction she had returned to. She thought about how hard they must have worked to develop such a quiet and serene life. Certainly, in the short time they knew Voltaire, he was dedicated to non-violence and that lifestyle. And yet, he decided himself to join her. He broke his vow of pacificism to help. She had never known any androids except Swift. But in knowing Voltaire and his sacrifice, she was all but certain: androids were also capable of being heroes. Anyone could be a hero.

Soon, Voltaire stopped firing as the enemy bullets dissipated. He sat as a mangled mess of metal and exposed circuitry. The machine gun dropped to the ground, hissing and smoking from overuse.

Thankfully, some new townspeople appeared from behind the horse stable and continued pursuing the remaining cyborgs. Swift, the brave and deadly robot fox, finally appeared in the battle and made easy work of any remaining enemies. He tore them to shreds in a matter of moments. The fortunate few fled the town. The battle, here at least, was over. The Ark remained safely on the road.

Kira grunted in pain as she got up, walking over to the defeated android hero.

"Voltaire," she said, "Is there a way for us to fix you? We could find someone to…"

"Thank you, Kira Skyler," Voltaire's distorted and broken voice said. "But this one…has reached fulfillment of purpose. This one will…go on to observe…the universe through the eyes… of other avatars."

Kira teared up. This peaceful android went against his philosophies of pacifism to rescue her and paid the price with his life.

"Thank you, Voltaire," she said.

"Do not forget…" Voltaire said, his voice fading. "Give back more beauty to the world than it has given… Have…purpose…"

And with that, Voltaire's head slumped forward, the glow behind his eyes apparatus dimmed. He was gone.

CHAPTER

FIFTY-SIX

R aymond hobbled up to a middle-aged woman leaning up against a signpost. She was injured, bleeding from a bullet wound to her side.

"I've got another one here!" Raymond said. "Bring the stretcher."

Kira came over with two men helping to carry the woman onto the crudely made cot, fashioned from a blanket and two logs tied together. The woman groaned in pain, but that was enough to give Raymond some indication of her status.

He put his ear against her chest and her fingers on her wrist. "She's got good breathing. Pulse is strong. Looks like the wound grazed her abdomen. Get an IV into her and give her that O-negative blood like I showed you."

"Right," said one of the men.

"I'll be back there in just a minute; we just need to see if there are any—" Raymond stopped, seeing Kira looking off into the distance. "Kira, what's wrong?"

Raymond turned around. She was looking far into the battlefield. By now, it had become a hellish landfill of twisted metal, fire, and infinite smoke. The sun was beginning to set. The battle was long over, and the last skirmishes of gunfire were not heard for some time. The battle was over, and the town had miraculously remained standing. Now they were focused on finding survivors.

"Raymond," Kira said, walking out to the battlefield. "Is that..."

Raymond squinted his eyes. Barely becoming visible, walking out from the smoke, were two individuals. One of them was very large.

It can't be... It is! Much to Raymond's surprise and relief, it was the bulky metallic figure of Sergeant Marcus holding a body across his arms. The other man walking beside them was Lieutenant Tristan. The two walking Zeltans looked worn down from warfare, their uniforms and armor tattered. Marcus no longer had a helmet, and parts of his metallic armor had broken off. Tristan limped, nearly half his uniform dragging on the ground, his once-ornate cape loosely covering him.

Raymond and Kira jumped into a vehicle to go out and meet them. As they approached, it was clear that the body that Marcus was holding was Captain Darien. He was a wretched sight. His clothes and face were covered in soot and blood. Whereas Raymond and Kira at first approached in celebration, it was now the somber possibility that the good captain had died in battle.

"Is he—" Kira asked.

"He is still breathing," Marcus said.

"What?" Raymond asked. "How is that possible? "Are you sure? Let me see him."

Raymond did his best, fighting through his own injuries, to walk over. He stumbled, hitting the sand and causing pain to surge through his broken ribs.

"You took a beating too, huh." Tristan knelt beside him. "It looks like you all got the job done just fine."

Raymond felt Tristan hoist him up back into the APE vehicle. He meant to utter the words thank you, but in the excruciating pain of being moved and plopped back into the vehicle, only a symphony of cursing and swearing at Tristan left his mouth.

"You're welcome," Tristan said. "But seriously, Raymond..."

Raymond noticed the somber tone in Tristan's voice. He was worried about Darien.

"Can you help the captain?" Tristan asked with genuine concern.

Raymond looked at Marcus, placing Captain Darien's charred, nearly lifeless body across the backseat. He smelled of ash and impending death. For all the marvelous feats and attributes that these Zeltans possessed, they were still human.

"Get him back to the infirmary," Raymond said. "We'll do everything we can; you have my word."

Kira jumped into the driver's seat and floored the vehicle back to the infirmary. Captain Darien was no more important than the other injured and dying victims but was certainly the most critical. His skin was burnt, he had several gaping wounds, and his breathing was agonal and weak. But somehow, Raymond thought, perhaps with his enhanced Zeltan genetics, that might give him that fighting chance of survival.

Raymond turned around, seeing Marcus and Tristan left behind just outside the town. They were too heavy for the Jackal and insisted that Kira drive ahead so Darien could get medical attention as soon as possible.

Upon arrival at the makeshift infirmary, now bustling with multitudes of wounded and casualties, Kira called out for help. One by one, able-bodied men came to the vehicle to help.

"No, no," Raymond would tell them. "Not me, help *him*."

The men gasped at the sight of Captain Darien. Raymond deduced that they had already met him, and they were horrified to see the extent of his injuries. It took about 5 men to carry him into the building. Raymond insisted to inside on his own.

After passing through a sea of wounded townspeople, he directed them to bring Captain Darien straight to the backroom. Stabilizing a Zeltan may prove more complicated than a normal human.

They placed Darien on the floor, just adjacent to the Ark. Raymond knelt, wincing again in pain, but managed to obtain IV access. He had to push particularly hard through Darien's skin, which was as thick and durable as leather.

Raymond looked up, seeing Darien's eyes staring up at the ceiling, appearing lifeless.

"Captain Darien!" Raymond said, jabbing his two fingers into Darien's neck, feeling for a pulse.

When there was none, Raymond began pushing on his chest to initiate CPR.

"Kira, hook up the blood to the IV. You, take over for more doing these chest compressions, just like this. Ember, I need a push dose of 2mg of epinephrine right now."

Raymond got up, grabbed the small medicine that dripped from the miracle machine and loaded it into a syringe. One of the townsmen was pushing hard on Darien's chest. The blood was infused through the IV. Darien lay still, a burnt and critically wounded hero.

No, Raymond thought, *today isn't the day you're going to die, Captain Darien. Not after everything we've been through.*

FIFTY-SEVEN

For months, Raymond Redmin lived in the Red Frontier town of Remnant. During this time, he helped the townspeople rebuild. They re-established order between the Frontier towns, creating a strong trade and defense route, pushing the remaining Raider tribes even further west.

What he found most fulfilling was using the apparent infinite resources of the Ark. He was able to extrapolate antibiotics, antivirals, and medical wonders that were far beyond the capabilities of his past life on Earth. With these, he treated the people afflicted by the Red Fever with a 100% cure rate.

The townspeople of Remnant quickly began to recognize Raymond's work. Their population started to grow with his treatments, and their morale flourished. Soon, Remnant had become a hub for medical treatment in exchange for goods like food and water rations. The other towns of the Frontier made long journeys across the desert to seek Raymond's services.

Raymond felt a sense of purpose that quieted his sadness over missing his wife and child from his own time on Earth. He tried not to think about them too often, as it was too painful of a reminder that they were gone. Forever. Instead, he focused on helping those in need around him and being an aid to the people at Remnant, who had welcomed him with open arms despite his past with the Raiders.

Word spread about Raymond's miraculous medical treatments, and soon enough, Remnant became known far beyond the reach of its own borders. The Mars town flourished under Raymond's capable care, becoming a beacon of hope in the otherwise desolate landscape left behind after the Charon crashed into Mars' surface many months ago. People no longer feared death from illness but felt secure in knowing that someone could help them if they ever needed it—Raymond Redmin, an Earthman with a heart as big as space itself.

"Is that really what they wrote on your sign?" Tristan scoffed.

Indeed, the gracious farmer Wesley Turner, whose child Raymond treated, created a large sign saying exactly that.

Kira punched Tristan in the shoulder. Due to the size of his frame, he barely moved an inch.

"But seriously, Raymond," Kira said, her eyes tearing up, watching the town bustle with movement. "Thank you for everything."

Raymond gave Kira a big hug. She was a good friend and the most capable assistant in his new makeshift hospital. After everything they had been through, having someone there as a genuine companion was good.

"Dr. Redmin," Captain Darien said from behind her. "You truly have done a fine job here. You have all of our greatest respect and admiration."

Captain Darien stood tall, his face scarred from his burn injuries, nevertheless remaining regal and able-bodied. In only a matter of days after his near-fatal injuries, he was walking and functioning almost as if he had never been so severely wounded.

"I'm still amazed how quickly you recovered," Raymond said.

Tristan sighed. "Like I said, it's superior gen—"

"It was all thanks to you, Dr. Redmin," Darien cut him off. "I owe you my life."

"I think we all saved each other's backs at one point or another throughout all of this," Raymond said.

Darien gave Tristan a nudging look.

Tristan smiled. "Yeah, yeah. I admit it. We all did good. You all did good; thank you."

"See, that wasn't so hard, was it?" Kira said.

"Painful," Tristan replied.

Darien had been in constant contact with the Zeltan Kingdom. For months, they scoured the Frontier and the Black Forest for any further technologies acquired from the Charon crash. Frequently, the Zeltan dropships would ferry soldiers back and forth. But Darien, Tristan, and Marcus particularly made sure to check back on the town of Remnant. Today would be their last visit before returning permanently to Sovereign City.

"Are you sure we can't convince you to join us?" Captain Darien asked. "You would have access to all the resources the Kingdom has available."

Raymond shook his head with a smile. "Tell the King that I'll be doing all my best work here. When he's ready to send more help here to the Frontier, I'll be waiting. Until then, the Ark will do the most help for the people out here on the Frontier, and I'm staying with it."

Darien smiled. "You have my word. You, Kira, and the town of Remnant will always be under my personal protection. We're just a call away." He pointed to the radio tower established high up on the Remnant clock tower, where they could reach Darien at Sovereign City directly.

Kira and Raymond waved goodbye as Darien, Tristan, and Marcus boarded the dropship. In a matter of minutes, the dropship disappeared into the horizon, a reminder of how far they had come since the Charon crash. The people of Remnant cheered and thanked their saviors for all that they had done for them.

Raymond smiled at Kira, feeling proud of all that he had accomplished. He watched as she turned away from the departing ship, tears streaming from her eyes. They were tears of joy, of hope. Together they would forge a future filled with optimism despite all that was lost in their past. Together, they would keep this beacon of life shining brightly in the darkness of Mars' unforgiving landscape.

CHAPTER

FIFTY-EIGHT

Colonel Nathan took a deep breath of the cool morning air, stepping onto his balcony overlooking Sovereign City. His estate was just adjacent to the King's castle. To the view on his left, he could see the Spire, the magnificent structure reaching high into the early morning sky. Nathan's balcony faced east, as he liked to watch the sun rise on the Kingdom every morning. He felt it was his obligation to greet each new day as the emissary of his race and people. He took a deep breath of the crisp air. The beauty of the morning sky was unmatched and punctuated by the far horizon to the southeast, where the Valley of Death could be found, with its Shadow Mountain just beyond the cursed battleground graveyard. Years ago, thousands of Zeltans and natural borns died in the Battle for Dawn, defeating the Omegamind. Now, that area was a no-mans-land of desolation and haunted memories of death.

Instead, here, at Sovereign City, these people would wake up to a utopia of peace and prosperity. They would never know the extent of the sacrifice needed to obtain this utopia.

"Colonel," a voice said from the door behind him. "The Lieutenant is here to see you."

"Thank you, Valerie," Nathan said, without breaking his gaze from the burgeoning red sky emanating from the east. "And please do clear my meetings for the morning. The Lieutenant and I have much to discuss."

"Of course," Valerie said, disappearing back into the darkness.

After a few moments, Nathan heard the Lieutenant walking close. An extra layer of mindfulness would be prudent when speaking to the young, brash Lieutenant Tristan. Although Nathan was kept abreast of all the recent activity by his network of spies, he could not fully trust that Tristan had not broken his prior allegiances. This was a game where trust should never be given freely; instead, trust would be brokered.

"Colonel," Lieutenant Tristan said, his boots clacking together as he stood straight at attention.

"At ease, Lieutenant," Colonel Nathan said, turning around with a smile. "Come, join me here, we can watch the sunrise."

"Thank you, sir," Tristan said.

"It sounds like you have been through quite the adventure," Nathan said. "We have learned much through the intelligence you gathered."

"About Julian, I—" Tristan started.

"No need to explain," Nathan said, putting a hand up. "I understand what you needed to do. Although Julian was part of our plans, he certainly had his own agendas. Who knows what he would have done with the Ark had he gotten his own hands on it."

"So," Tristan said, "what now? The box is with the doctor on the Frontier. Do we just leave it there?"

"We have all the players where they need to be," Nathan said. "The doctor is doing some remarkable work. This Raymond Redmin... I understand you have earned his trust?"

"Yes," Tristan said. "He trusts me."

Nathan turned to examine Tristan's face. He noticed that he responded with some hesitation. *Or is that guilt I sense?*

"He is the key to all of this," Nathan said. "The answers to all of our questions, we will find them through Dr. Redmin. But we will need his cooperation willingly."

Nathan thought back to when Lieutenant Tristan radioed him from Guaritore's Lair. When Tristan and his group were cornered by the eccentric healer's mutated and undead machinations, Tristan found himself locked into an exo-mech duel with Julian. Once Raymond and the rest of the group left the underground lair on the train, the ruse was immediately halted. Tristan and Julian, both agents of the Cabal, immediately stopped fighting and sent word back to Nathan, identifying Raymond as a key survivor of the Charon crash.

In addition to Nathan, Guaritore, Julian, and Blackheart, Tristan was also a secret part of the Cabal. They contacted Tristan shortly after his public conflict with the King, identifying him as the perfect informant. For this mission, he would carry out his duties completely as if he were following the Kingdom's orders, even if that meant coming into direct conflict with other known Cabal agents.

"Is there anyone else that is part of this?" Tristan asked. "There are reports of Blackheart having survived the battle, but Julian is confirmed dead. We also found Guaritore's body in the wreckage of his laboratory. He is also confirmed dead. Is there anyone else left?"

Nathan hesitated but took care not to give away any hint of important knowledge. "There might be others," Nathan said cryptically. "But it's not quite time to raise the curtain on the next act of this story."

"What exactly are we doing?" Tristan asked. "I mean, we went through all that just for us to leave the technology out there on the Frontier?"

Nathan sensed that the Lieutenant was growing impatient.

"In a way," Nathan said. "But the plan is coming together. We will be able to get what we need from the Doctor, but only if it is done properly. That means patiently, delicately, and tactfully. We must trust that all your prior allegiances are intact for this to work. And do we still have *your* trust, Lieutenant Tristan?"

"Yes, Colonel," Tristan said. "For the liberation of Mars."

Colonel Nathan nodded. "And the girl?" He turned to look at Tristan's reaction.

Tristan appeared visibly taken aback for a moment. "The...girl?"

"Kira Skyler. I hear you two have... become close?"

Tristan cleared his throat. "Yes, she was an invaluable asset to our mission. That is all she is." His voice contained a sharpness that made it clear he wanted the conversation to end there.

Nathan could see right through Tristan's words. He was a master of reading others, and it was obvious Tristan cared about her more than he wanted to admit. Nathan decided not to press any further, though, not just because of how uncomfortable it made Tristan but because this development could open further advantageous possibilities.

"And what of the good captain?" Nathan asked, changing the subject.

Captain Darien, the noble beacon through all of this. In some ways, Nathan was proud of the captain, truly being a perfect and obedient soldier for the Kingdom. In other ways, he was beginning to become an inadvertent thorn in the side of the Cabal's plans.

"What of him?" Tristan said.

"Does he suspect anything?" Nathan asked again, turning to read Tristan's face.

Tristan shook his head slowly. "No, I don't think so. But sir, I'm just wondering..." He looked down at the floor. "Why are we leaving Captain Darien and Sergeant Marcus in the dark about this? Has the Cabal considered letting them in on the plan? This would be so much easier if I didn't have to—"

"Because you're special." Nathan put his hand on Tristan's shoulder. "You are the most important person in this plan. You know it. You are the most gifted Zeltan in the Kingdom. You know it, the city knows it, and the King knows it."

Tristan clenched his teeth, looking up at the Sovereign castle just down the road. The building towered over the city, seemingly to mock Tristan in its elegance and glory.

"You should be King," Nathan said, sure to deliver his lines sincerely. "You *will* be King. You deserve it more than anyone else. We can give that to you. But for now, this all stays between us. Captain Darien and Sergeant Marcus, for as wonderful soldiers as they are, are still only that. Soldiers. You are meant for greater things."

Tristan nodded.

It was easy for Nathan to discern what Tristan truly wanted. And in that way, the young prince was easily manipulated. As they stood together watching the sunrise, Nathan opened up about his vision for the future of Mars.

"As long as we keep pushing forward, we can make this vision a reality," Nathan said.

"I'm with you, Colonel," Tristan said, a sense of determination in his voice.

"Good," Nathan said with a smile, "because we have a lot of work to do. Trust is the most important thing we have, Lieutenant. But it's also the hardest to come by. Just remember that. It is all we have holding this together."

The two men stood in silence for a while longer. As the sun rose higher into the sky, Nathan's thoughts turned to the Ark. The powerful technology within could be used for great good or evil. It was imperative that they get their hands on it to carry out their manifest destiny.

CHAPTER

FIFTY-NINE

Benny Fong experienced misery like he had never imagined. For months, he was subjected to cruel experimentation by the Corsairs. At first, he begged for them to simply kill him or at least put him to sleep with hypno, something to relieve the anguish they were inflicting daily. The inhuman cyborgs barely said a word to him. After some time, Benny reached the plane of insanity.

Now, every day when the experiments began anew, his mind blocked out the agony. The pain was still there, but he learned to separate himself from it, perhaps to salvage the last amount of stability his psyche had left.

His mind escaped to another realm where he found an unusual peace while growing bloodthirsty for violence and revenge. He dreamt of lying on the golden grass of the Zeltan Plains with Kira, staring up into the sky. There, they lay in serenity for eternity. However, in almost every reverie, he would eventually imagine the multitude of the armies on Mars surrounding them, threatening to take away their tranquility. Hundreds of thousands of men and machines on the horizon in every direction, ready to wage war on his patch of peace. He fantasized about taking them all head-on himself, slaughtering his enemies in a homicidal rage that brought him blissful satisfaction.

"This one is still alive?" a familiar voice asked.

Benny opened his eyes, staring up at the ceiling. He was again on the experimentation table he had grown to know as home and hell. He learned to stop trying to move; it only made the pain worse. The cyborg researchers rarely talked to each other. Whenever they did, it brought a sense of rare excitement for him. This time, the voice happened to belong to Blackheart, the tyrant who put Benny here in the first place.

"Yeah, this kid just won't die," one of the scientists said. "He's the only one left from the group."

"Well, what does he *do*?" Blackheart asked. "When I said I wanted results after we returned, I expected something. It's been seven goddamn months! He just looks the same."

What does he mean I look the same? Benny wondered. They spent months poking and prodding him with an infinite number of needles, injecting him with an ocean full of poison that ran through his veins like burning acid. They cut into his skin and exposed muscle and bone in front of him. His own blood completely painted the table and floors. *How could I possibly look the same? What have they been doing to me this whole time?*

"Well, we were experimenting with one of those unmarked biofuel samples from the ship," the scientist said. "There was no indication of what the liquid was used for. It doesn't power any engines, is not combustible, and so far, doesn't seem to have any purpose. We used the subject to see how the liquid interacts with human cells. It does seem to drastically interact with the human nervous system."

"What do you mean?" Blackheart asked.

"When we started injecting the subject with the fuel," the scientist continued, "he began demonstrating a noticeable electromagnetic profile. He's been radiating this for weeks."

"Meaning?" Blackheart sounded bored.

"We're not quite sure yet," the scientist said. "For now, it seems like this Old Earth biotechnology was meant to create a cybernetic link between the human nervous system and electromagnetic material. Certain metals in his proximity change their magnetic profile randomly and continuously."

"So, he can move metal?"

"No," the scientist said. "The radiation he is emitting doesn't seem to have enough effect on magnetism to cause any observable kinetic movement."

"But you said he's emitting radiation?" Blackheart asked, looking at Benny with disgust. "Like, he's radioactive?"

"Unfortunately, yes," the scientist said. "We will have to look into developing this for practical use. For now, we will continue our work on the subject until he inevitably succumbs to the radioactive decay of his cells. Although, he has endured far longer than would be expected—"

"Alright then," Blackheart said, waving them off. "Whatever you need to do. I'll get cancer if I keep standing too close. Gods, I should kill him and bury the body. Deep. I don't want you making the men sick from whatever it is you're doing."

"We assure you, Blackheart," one of the scientists said, "we are making a breakthrough here. We need more time."

There was a pause. "In a worse mood, I would have shot you dead on the spot. But today, I'm feeling generous. Go on, carry on with your nonsense."

"With this technology..." one of the scientist's voices trailed off as they walked out of the room together.

Benny lay staring at the ceiling in the dark, alone. *What have they been doing to me?* He wished he was dead every second of every day, but never more than he did now. He was some kind of radioactive experiment. He would probably die of a slow, decaying death. In a sense, that gave him hope. There was an end somewhere.

SIXTY

K ira Skyler sat next to her brother Owen in a church pew, listening to the preacher Ezekiel Rayge drone on about the coming of the end times. After all she had been through, she couldn't help but admit that the prophecies had some validity. Many in the town regarded Raymond and the Zeltans as the four Angels of Deliverance. Whether the prophecies were true or not, above all, she considered them friends.

She harbored a deep sadness for the past few months, however. Her best friend Benny was still missing. He had apparently crossed paths with Darien, and they escaped the Corsairs together. During the Battle of Remnant, Benny even rode into the battlefield but was not seen again. Kira and the townspeople scoured the battleground for the dead and injured. Despite weeks of searching, Benny was never found. Perhaps he died from an explosion, was crushed beneath a large vehicle, or even worse, captured by the Corsairs or Raiders.

Kira missed him every day. She wanted him to be there when the town of Remnant rose in its darkest hour and flourished. Raymond cured Crimson Fever. Her brother Owen was alive and well, sitting next to her in the pew. The Zeltans Darien, Tristan, and Marcus had stayed around to help rebuild the town. She and

Tristan even developed an unexpected attraction toward each other over the months. Overall, the townspeople came to know the Zeltans as saviors and friends. In all their hardship, they finally found peace and prosperity. *Benny, I just wish you could have been here to see it.*

The preacher recited the Prophecy:

"In the days before the end, the blue god will break his vow of silence, having pity upon his forgotten people. He will send a sign of flames from the sky. From the East will arrive four angels of deliverance. They will bring healing, wisdom, power, and courage to the people of the Frontier. Under a mighty sword, they will deliver the people from evil. And the people should rejoice. It will be a sign of the one who is to come. The hero, the one who will save us all. Enemies will tremble, and armies will fall at his feet. He will lead our people to salvation. Eagerly, we await his coming. The silent savior from the shadows."

SIXTY-ONE

B enny summoned the strength to lift his head to look down at his body. There was a blanket draped over him with a strange hue. He lifted his arm but saw nothing. Again, his other arm showed nothing when he brought it to his face. *Oh god, they took my arms off?* he thought.

Suddenly, his arms reappeared before him, fading in like a dream. Benny deduced he must have been hallucinating because of the many medications they were pumping into him. He looked down again at the blanket. It dissolved in and out like he had a transparent cloud surrounding his body.

After a few moments, he realized this was occurring at will. He sat up on the table, ignoring the pain screaming from every cell in his body. He brought his hand to his face, seeing it there, scarred and discolored from the many experiments. Benny consciously thought to have the hand disappear, and just as he willed it, his hand dimmed to nothingness. He could see right through it.

... And the people should rejoice. It will be a sign of the one who is to come...

He proceeded to do this with every part of his body, seemingly making entire limbs disappear at will. After a few minutes, he quickly mastered the ability to make his entire body transparent. Even more shocking, any object touching his skin also seemed to disappear. The blanket and any parts of the table he touched appeared to vanish in the invisible cloud emanating from his body.

... The hero, the one who will save us all. Enemies will tremble, and armies will fall at his feet...

Benny stood up, examining himself in a mirror against the wall. His skin was lined with hundreds of scalpel marks and grafts. With his newfound abilities, he made himself disappear again. He couldn't take looking at himself any longer.

...He will lead our people to salvation. Eagerly, we await his coming...

"What is happening to me..." Benny said. "What... am I?"

...The silent savior from the shadows...

EPILOGUE

PREVIEW OF THE RED DESTINY: BOOK 2 OF THE RED TOMORROW

Ghost stood perched atop the corner of a roof overlooking the center square of Sovereign City. It was nighttime, and hundreds of Zeltans adorned in their magnificent clothing and riches bustled about the cobblestone streets under the light of the moon, stars, and streetlamps. This was a world far detached from his meager upbringing on the Frontier.

His cybernetic bodysuit was black as the night sky, but to be sure, Ghost willed himself to become invisible to the naked eye. He took care not to overestimate his invisibility. It was difficult navigating through a crowd when no one realized he was there. He had many close calls making his way into the city. More often than he would be comfortable with, unsuspecting citizens would nearly walk into him. The city streets were the worst. He dodged and dived to avoid people just to stay in one place. Ghost told himself he would need to be more careful.

Likewise, he was consciously aware of any cameras or soldiers wearing advanced visors. Ghost still had a detectable heat signature and electric profile. He was an invisible cyborg carrying a bevy of weaponry. If he were caught, they would unleash the full force of the city guard upon him. Despite the sniper rifle and sword on his back, the pistol at his hip, and his inherent ability to become invisible, Ghost still felt vulnerable and alone. He was deep into dangerous territory on his own.

He crept slowly over the rooftops until he came to his destination. The screen display on his visors fed him an overlaying map leading him to his target. Meanwhile, it noted where cameras, guards, and other threats were located. It took him quite some time before he could get used to processing all the information at once. Despite his hurried training, they sent him directly into the heart of the capital city alone.

He even had to leave behind his new advanced Wraith drone that would usually hover high above him on missions. It would have given him an even better idea of what dangers he was walking into. His cybernetic allowed him to control the Wraith using only his thoughts. With his visor display, he could instantly transplant his consciousness into the drone and use its mobility to his advantage. But for this mission, he was sent in alone with one objective: Eliminate the target.

He finally found a balcony to slip into. He found himself creeping into the bedroom of a military officer who was busy singing to himself in the shower. For his sake, this man's life would be spared. The target was one floor above. Ghost stealthily slipped into the hallway undetected. As he walked down the hall looking for another opportunity, a tall, beautiful woman wearing a tight red uniform suit and glasses walked by him. He froze in place, pressing his back against the wall. He tensed as she barely brushed against him.

Ghost watched her closely, checking whether she had noticed him. She walked down the hallway without hesitating or changing her pace, and he deduced that he remained undetected. He breathed out a slow sigh of relief. Her life would be spared. Ghost would rather not stab her with his sword and make a mess to complicate the mission.

He edged into the open door of another room. According to the arrows on his display, he was now standing directly below his target. He crept into the brightly lit room where four heavily clad guards sat talking to each other in front of a fireplace. It was some form of a recreational smoke room.

Ghost considered his fortune. They were not in the mindset to be on the lookout here. Even more fortunately, a balcony was open at the other end of the room. He made his way there slowly and with precision. He kept his eyes on the guards. They were drinking, likely too drunk to notice had not been invisible at all. The room smelled thick of burning harsh and adrenol. Ghost held his breath. He would rather not start hallucinating during an assassination mission.

At the balcony, he took in the night air, a refreshing change from the wine, smoke, and sweat of the guard quarters. Ghost looked up; the target's balcony was just overhead. He aimed his wrist at a corner and shot out his winch. After it appeared to wrap around, he gave it a tug that responded with a satisfying resistance. He climbed up the wall, acutely aware that a small wire was the only thing keeping him from falling to his death.

After an eternity of careful wall scaling that covered a much smaller distance than it seemed, he finally threw his legs over the top balcony. For a moment, he was too tired to concentrate on maintaining his invisibility. When Ghost was distracted like this, he found himself unknowingly exposed. Generating his invisible field required focus.

"Shit," he whispered, staring down at his hands.

He was visible again. Ghost looked around, but no one was there on the balcony. Earlier in the day, he had tried to get a visual on the target. After several failed attempts, he realized there were no vantage points to easily attack this position, even from a sniper distance. When he realized his original assassination plan wouldn't work, he reverted to going in directly.

When his body and clothing were sufficiently invisible again, he made his way inside. It was a grand room with a wide open space in the middle. With the ornate decorations and exquisite paintings along the walls, Ghost first assumed this was a ballroom. Gleaming chandeliers hung from the ceiling. He took note of plush mannequins propped up across the floor. Dozens of various swords were stacked on racks lining the sides. This was some kind of practice hall for fencing.

Ghost walked around the room, admiring the beautiful artistry of the swords. Suddenly, his visor blared red, a warning that someone was approaching the room behind him. He wondered why he hadn't been alerted to this sooner.

"Ah," a voice behind him said. "You came ready with your own sword; how serendipitous."

Ghost shuddered, looking down at his body, wondering if he had forgotten to cloak himself. He checked. His body, clothing, and gear were, in fact, all still invisible. *How did he know about the sword?*

Colonel Nathan stepped into the light. The target had regal blonde hair combed backward that complimented the golden half-coat draped over his left shoulder. It was near midnight, and the Colonel was still in fully decorated attire. He had a monocle over his right eye with a thin chain hanging from his ear.

"I can see you with this," Colonel Nathan tapped his monocle. "Now, please, at least do me the favor of showing yourself."

Ghost panicked. His mission was completely compromised. He reached for his pistol, but Nathan moved across the floor like lightning, grabbing the gun away and throwing it back out onto the balcony.

"Please." Nathan looked down at Ghost with a condescending smile. "In a fencing hall? I find that disrespectful."

Ghost tried to punch him in the face, but Nathan casually stepped aside. As the momentum of the punch took him forward, Ghost stumbled onto the ground. By now, he was fully visible. Nathan walked over to the rack of swords and picked up a thin, gleaming rapier with a golden-decorated hilt.

"This is a dance of finesse," Nathan said, taking his monocle off. "And mutual respect."

Ignoring Nathan's subtle invitation to a fair duel, Ghost made himself invisible again. He hoped Nathan would not be able to see him without the monocle. Ghost grabbed the katana at his side, focusing to make it disappear as well. He stepped forward slowly, approaching in a semi-circle to avoid detection.

Nathan closed his eyes, stepping forward with the blade of his sword resting in his gloved hand. He walked to the middle of the hall, breathing deeply in what appeared like meditation.

Ghost figured this would be the best time to strike. He was just behind Nathan and brought his katana sideways in a cutting motion. Nathan twirled around in a casual yet nimble motion. The katana's blade just barely missed the fabric of Nathan's half cape. In a nearly mocking fashion, he pushed Ghost's katana to the side with his rapier.

"Finesse," Nathan said.

Ghost's frustration reached a boiling point. He began to hack and slash at Nathan with the katana with anger and deliberation. Nathan simply dodged every attack with a graceful step backward, sideways, and even turning his back to Ghost and walking away.

"And mutual respect," Nathan said as he knocked the katana out of Ghost's hand with the simple flick of his rapier.

Off-balance, Ghost stumbled to the ground, trying to catch his katana in mid-air. He felt the blade of the rapier touch the front of his neck, and he froze in place. Ghost took a moment to process the situation. This was a duel, and he had lost. His mission failed. Ghost wondered if he would be killed here and now.

"Kill me," Ghost said bravely.

"Oh, no, no." Nathan stood over him with the point of the rapier on Ghost's neck. "You misunderstand. That would be far counter-productive to our goal. You may not realize it now, but you are becoming a most integral piece on the game board."

"I'm no pawn," said Ghost through gritted teeth.

Nathan gave him a devilish smile. "My friend. You are certainly no pawn. You have the power to alter the course of mankind. You can be unstoppable, a god-like force for change."

"I don't understand," Ghost said. "What am I supposed to change?"

"Quite simply, Benjamin, you will change our destiny."

Continue the adventure with **The Red Tomorrow** series

Visit **AuthorJosephCruz.com** for the full list of available and upcoming books in the series.

Join the **Red Tomorrow mailing list** for weekly updates, as well as exclusive lore content, free or discounted books, and early releases.

The Red Destiny: Book 2 of The Red Tomorrow

The second book of the main Red Tomorrow series. The fate of humanity rests upon two unlikely heroes at odds with each other. The fallen prince and the invisible assassin are on a collision course with each other as they race to discover the secret destiny of the red planet.

Dawn of the Red Tomorrow: The Timeline and Lore of Mars After the Silence

A prequel novella to The Red Frontier

The Warrior Prince: A Tale from the Red Tomorrow

A prequel novella to The Red Frontier

The Zeltan Initiative: A Tale from the Red Tomorrow

A prequel short story to the Red Frontier

The Legend of Jonathan Cable: A Tale from the Red Tomorrow

A prequel short story to The Red Frontier

The Ark of Mars: A Tale from the Red Tomorrow

A short story set before Book 2 The Red Destiny

Blade of the Ghost: A Tale from the Red Tomorrow

A short story set before Book 2 The Red Destiny

The Red Fall: Book 3 of The Red Tomorrow Series

www.ingramcontent.com/pod-product-compliance
Lightning Source LLC
Chambersburg PA
CBHW060240030726

47493CB00024B/1436